What People Are Saying
About *Understanding Ursula*

"A rare, immediately immersive experience in literature."
Scott Hayes, journalist, *St. Albert Gazette*

"Corinne Jeffery is a very fine storyteller."
Todd Babiak, *Edmonton Journal* columnist, screenwriter, and award-winning,
best-selling author of *The Garneau Block* and *Toby: A Man*

"Part of the reason for the book's success is the way it describes the immigrant
experience, whether or not the reader's experience matches the Werners.'"
Glen Cook, journalist, *St. Albert Leader*

"Jeffery paints a vivid portrait of a bygone era, deftly weaving the lives of a memorable
ensemble into an enthralling, epic narrative."
Kevin Walsh, producer of the award-winning *Marwencol* and screenplay consultant
for Dreamworks, Castle Rock, and Paramount Pictures

"Corinne Jeffery's story of a homesteading community on the Canadian prairies
in the 1920s and 1930s chronicles the joys and sorrows, tragedies and triumphs of
ordinary people grappling with the challenges of forging their identities in a new
land. Jeffery's no-nonsense representation of the gamut of human experience—birth
and death, transgression and reconciliation, love and loyalty—results in a story that
is both poignant and refreshingly unsentimental."
Arlene Young, professor and head, Department of English, Film, and Theatre,
University of Manitoba

"In book two, the great Werner family story continues and complex new characters appear. Life on the prairies continues to heat up and this book makes me want book three. Right now."
Steve Erwin, best-selling co-author of *Left to Tell: Discovering God Amidst the Rwandan Holocaust* (#1 Amazon, #4 New York Times)

"An inspirational story of the power of spirit, will, family, and friends. *Thriving* clarifies the importance of attitude in facing the challenges of a new culture, new technology, and an economic depression."
Brian Hesje, corporate director and son of a Saskatchewan homesteader

"In *Thriving*, Corinne Jeffery embraces the human desire for sovereignty without flinching. We want to be known for who we are and what we stand for. At a time horizon not far behind us, *Thriving* taps into the distinct character of very recent ancestors steeped in a familiar terroir rarely used as a backdrop for story—open, severe, beautiful, and exposing. *Thriving* is a story about the desire held by generations to surge ahead, converting shared identity into their potential, meeting the inevitable pain of intermittent belonging to difficult loves, families, and nation tribes along the way. *Thriving* is a compelling read for every Saskatchewanian and an important portrait for anyone wanting to understand the essence of a most gracious and tenacious people."
Ian Chisholm, founding partner, RoyGroup.net, Maidstone, Saskatchewan

"After thoroughly enjoying *Arriving*, I eagerly awaited this next installment... and it was well worth the wait! The continuation of this historical-fiction family saga reads like a true story. The characters are well-developed, relatable, and engaging. It's easy to become emotionally connected as we relive the relationships, dreams, dramas, sorrows, and pleasures of these immigrants and pioneers as they build their families and communities. Although set in and around Neudorf, Saskatchewan, in the 1920s and 30s, many of the issues they are forced to contend with, and which ultimately shape them, are very familiar to us today."
Heather Dolman, public services manager, St. Albert Public Library

"I can readily see this on screen!"
Leon Logothetis, reality TV show producer and author, *Amazing Adventures of a Nobody*

"*Thriving*'s people, purpose, and place on the prairie are made vibrant through the rare storytelling of Corinne Jeffery—a genuine-Canadian author."
Donna Hastings, CEO, Heart and Stroke Foundation, Alberta; chair, editorial board, International Trauma Life Support

"These intriguing and piquant characters will remain in my memory for years to come."
Ronald Russell, award-winning journalist and author of *Don Carina*, now an award-winning screenplay

"A sneak peek at the second novel *Thriving* will whet your appetite for more."
Joan Ritchie, *Moose Jaw Express*

"I was quickly engrossed by the lives of the pure and not-so-pure Werner family members. They face one unpredictable drama after another as they grapple with natural hardships and human folly. A really special book."
Sharrie Williams, author, *The Maybelline Story—and the Spirited Family Dynasty Behind It*

"Engrossing! A fun read from start to finish."
Jane Congdon, author, *It Started with Dracula: The Count, My Mother, and Me*

"I love to see other Canadian authors shine, and shine she does! Simply a wonderful book."
Charmaine Hammond, author, *On Toby's Terms*

"*Arriving* is like a raw and racy *Little House on the Prairie* that throws the reader right back in time. Can't wait to read the sequel!"
Marla Martenson, author, *Diary of a Beverly Hills Matchmaker*

"An impressive debut by an author of Canadian historical fiction."
Christine Ducommun, author, *Living with Multiple Personalities: The Christine Ducommun Story* (a 2012 TV movie)

"[*Thriving* is] a story that exudes the strength of the pioneering spirit..."
Joan Ritchie, *Moose Jaw Express*

"Everything that happens in today's, fast-paced world occurs in Corinne Jeffery's delightful debut about German Lutheran homesteaders arriving in Saskatchewan at the turn of the twentieth century. But few of the antics are ever discussed, as those sneaky pioneers maintain their proclivity for silence and secrets. I loved my front-row seat!"
Aura Imbarus, author of the Pulitzer Prize entry, *Out of the Transylvania Night*

"Corinne Jeffery's writing is full of poignant prairie stuff: The survival of body, spirit, and family under big skies that are as foreboding as they are full of promise. Jeffery is a mild annoyance to those of us who scribbled away for years—or decades—without producing a book, let alone a trilogy. I hope she keeps writing. But I reserve the right to be jealous."
Scott McKeen, 30-year Edmonton journalist and writer

"...last year at Whispering Waters Manor, we started our fireside reading of the *Understanding Ursula* trilogy every Friday.... The conversations with our residents after the readings have been incredible. They have become excited to share their own stories, and those with early stages of dementia and Alzheimer's are recalling their own early memories and feeling a great sense of accomplishment... It has added a bounce in their step, increased their social interaction, and increased their participation in other activities."
Kim Abraham-Schutz, Meridian Foundation, Stony Plain, Alberta

Choosing

1940–1989

To - Elisse,

Be surprised as all the Werier secrets unfold...

Corinne Jeffery

May 26, 2018

Choosing: 1940–1989

Book three of the *Understanding Ursula* trilogy

by Corinne Jeffery

Published 2013 by

Roadie Books
Edmonton, Alberta

Book and cover designed by Teresa Wang.
Printed and bound in Canada by Friesens.

Jeffery, Corinne.

Choosing: 1940–1989: a novel by Corinne Jeffery

ISBN 978-1-927754-02-3

Dedication

To Faith Farthing, who believed in me and my
Understanding Ursula trilogy from the beginning

Acknowledgements

After publishing the first two books of the *Understanding Ursula* trilogy, I am convinced that most of my readers take the time to peruse my acknowledgements. I certainly hope so, because it is you, my devoted followers, whom I want to recognize for the success of my novels.

During the past three years, I have met and interacted with a host of wonderful persons, who as avid fans of my Canadian historical fiction novels, have endearingly shared their insights and reviews. When I started upon my incredible journey as a published author, my motto was "Believing makes everything possible." Beyond a doubt, one by one you have confirmed for me the truth of this statement.

My incomparable team—Faith Farthing, Teresa Wang, Karleigh Stevenson, and Brittany Foster—first supported its plausibility, and it is with deepest gratitude that I thank each of you for your commitment, determination, enthusiasm, and dedication during the years since we embarked upon our exciting journey. I truly believe I could never have found four other women more inspiring, creative, and capable to share the pursuit of bringing my lifelong dream to fruition.

Lastly, but most importantly, I offer special thanks to my family: Jack for his support and accounting expertise, Ruben for his constant encouragement and guidance, Sara for her comprehension of the significance of legacy and soul, and Aidan for persisting as my number one fan.

Cast of Characters

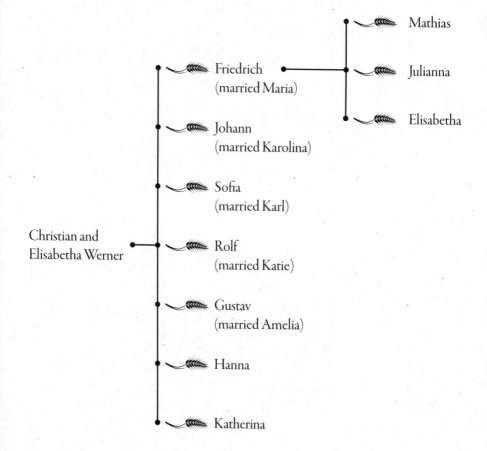

Christian and
Elisabetha Werner

Friedrich
(married Maria)

Johann
(married Karolina)

Sofia
(married Karl)

Rolf
(married Katie)

Gustav
(married Amelia)

Hanna

Katherina

Mathias

Julianna

Elisabetha

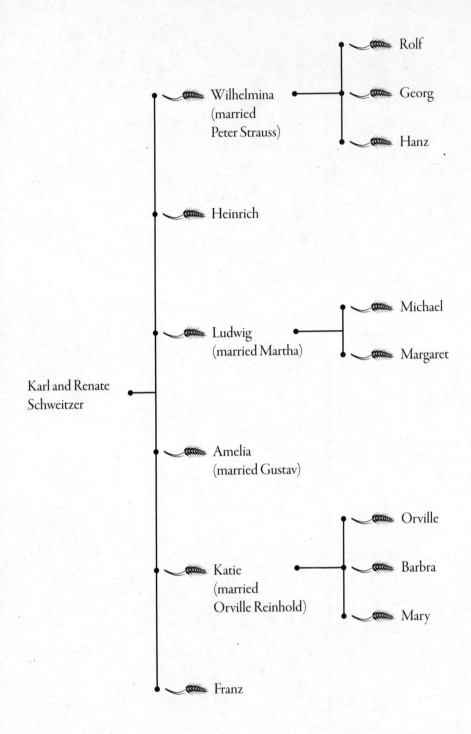

Rolf

Wilhelmina
(married
Peter Strauss)

Georg

Hanz

Heinrich

Michael

Ludwig
(married Martha)

Margaret

Karl and Renate
Schweitzer

Amelia
(married Gustav)

Orville

Katie
(married
Orville Reinhold)

Barbra

Mary

Franz

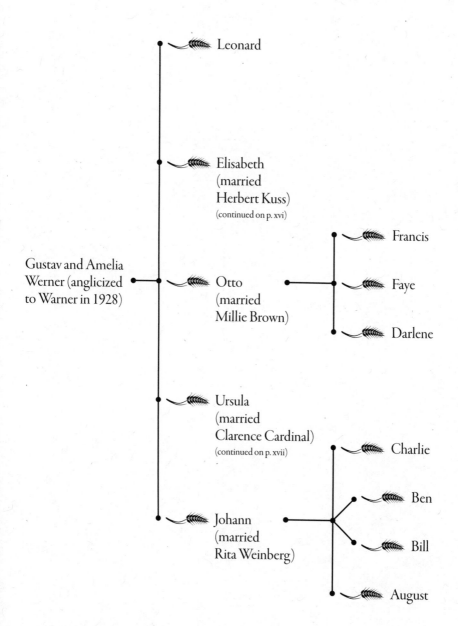

Gustav and Amelia Werner (anglicized to Warner in 1928)

Leonard

Elisabeth
(married
Herbert Kuss)
(continued on p. xvi)

Otto
(married
Millie Brown)

Francis

Faye

Darlene

Ursula
(married
Clarence Cardinal)
(continued on p. xvii)

Johann
(married
Rita Weinberg)

Charlie

Ben

Bill

August

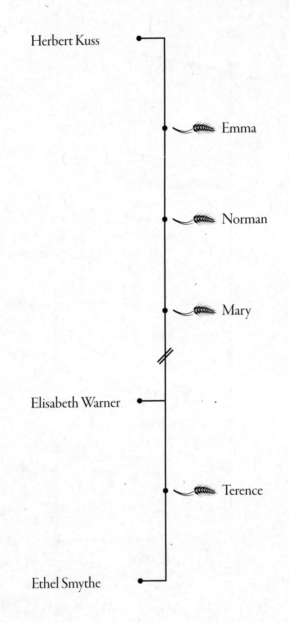

Herbert Kuss

Emma

Norman

Mary

Elisabeth Warner

Terence

Ethel Smythe

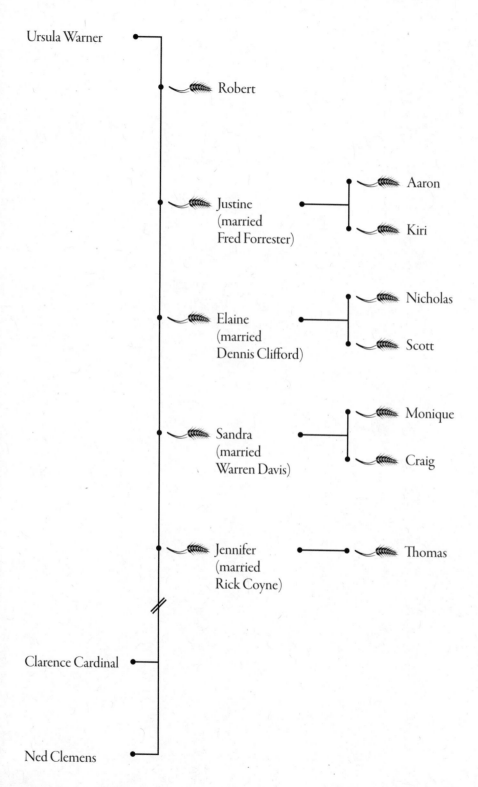

Ursula Warner

Robert

Justine
(married
Fred Forrester)

Aaron

Kiri

Elaine
(married
Dennis Clifford)

Nicholas

Scott

Sandra
(married
Warren Davis)

Monique

Craig

Jennifer
(married
Rick Coyne)

Thomas

Clarence Cardinal

Ned Clemens

Choosing
1940–1989

⟫⟫~ 1 ~⟪⟪

The past ten years snailed by as they waited interminably for rains that never came, but this new decade would soon clip along at a pace they could not have imagined.

It started with many men from the English Methodist township joining the prevailing crush of the unemployed who rushed to the militia armouries to enlist, although far fewer of their German Lutheran neighbours from the other side of the road allowance were ready to go to war.

Jurgen Kuss departed on the Monday afternoon train for Regina. Anyone speculating that he was about to begin an exodus from his townships would have quickly been proven wrong. Peter Lutz's two oldest sons would eventually go in the spring of 1941; but over the next year and a half, no other young men were ready to defy their fathers to fight amid the hostilities across the ocean.

Now that the drought was on the verge of ending, the federal government was prepared to pull the country's defunct economy out of its protracted depression and let men return to their fields to grow wheat to feed the Allied troops. The sons were—as were their grandfathers and fathers before them—farmers, not soldiers.

Soon even the prairie air began to change, and the burgeoning optimism was more than the anticipated effects of the restoring rains. The atmosphere would long be charged with hope and expectations as those individuals with historical grasp began to realize that the world at war could bring prosperity back to Canada.

By the summer of 1940, when Britain and her dominions remained the solitary force against the combined military might of Hitler and Mussolini, C.D. Howe was one of those insightful men. As the newly appointed minister of Munitions and Supply following Mackenzie King's landslide federal election, he unequivocally understood that anything Canada could produce would be required to support the Allied nations. Although Howe poured his dynamism into gaining the confidence of the leading industrialists and businessmen, this was especially salient news for the Canadian farmer.

It had always been his purpose to grow and raise the produce essential for sustaining the urban populace. It was what he lived for—to till the soil, to plant the seeds, to harvest the grain, and to rear the livestock for feeding the hungry city hordes. Now with the prevailing feeling that Canada was rediscovering its youth and vigour, every farmer still owning an acre of cultivated land joined wholeheartedly in the common purpose of contributing wheat for the war.

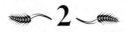

The German farmers, who had homesteaded the thirty-six sections of land surrounding Lemberg and Neudorf and designated by Sir Clifford Sifton for their townships, were no different. Although not prepared to fight for the new country in which each had thrived over the decades, they were ready to do all they could to sustain the Canadian troops.

Since Mother Nature at long last cooperated with a moderate snowfall the past winter and several earth-soaking spring rains, one by one they set to work. Across the road allowance on the Warner homestead, knowing full well that Otto had little interest in school, Gustav decided to keep his second-eldest son at home to replace his hired man.

It was the answer to Otto's prayers. All he had ever wanted was to become a farmer like his father. Within a day, he went from being bored in a tedious classroom to rejuvenated, now that he could be active and productive by working the land with his father. Before long, whenever he accompanied Gustav into town to buy the necessary supplies for the spring seeding, he felt more like a man than an errant schoolboy.

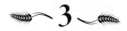

Elisabeth Warner also had a new lease on life. The postmaster's brother's youngest son was sweeping her off her feet. Herbert Kuss first came to Neudorf to assist ailing Uncle Adolph in the autumn of 1939 and was immediately mesmerized by the beautiful young woman playing the organ in church. He could hardly wait for his aunt and uncle to make formal introductions before asking her to walk with him to their home for a cup of coffee.

Since Herbert spent the entire winter helping the town's postmaster, the two young people had courted for months before he had to return to Summerberry to begin the spring planting on his father's farm. On the Sunday morning before he planned to depart, he anxiously approached Elisabeth's father to ask for her hand in marriage as soon as the year's harvesting was finished.

"Good morning, Mr. Warner, could I please speak with you in private before you leave for home?"

"Yes, of course, Herbert." Gustav knew what he wanted to talk about, but he was not certain he was ready to give his consent. From everything Amelia told him, it appeared Elisabeth was in love with Herbert, and since she would not be married until later in the fall, she could still finish her grade twelve and graduate from secondary school. Although he assiduously concealed his dream of Elisabeth becoming a pianist, he hoped she would follow in her brother's footsteps with higher education and ask to attend the University of Regina to study music. Now he realized he must relinquish his coveted expectations in pursuit of her happiness, although it gave him cause to wonder why he had bartered so much wheat for a piano.

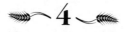

The only Warner offspring who seemed completely out of sorts was Ursula. She was full of resentment and behaving even more rebelliously than usual because everything and everyone was changing, embarking on new endeavours, and leaving for greener pastures. As far as she was concerned, she was in a rut.

She simply could not believe what was happening. First Leonard and then Jurgen had left the farm within one year, and neither of these favourite men in her life would be home in the spring to celebrate her birthday. Other girls her age in school kept going on about how they planned to celebrate their sweet-sixteenth birthday, but when she asked Mama if she could do something special, she was told there would be the customary family supper with a birthday cake.

When would her mother realize that Elisabeth was not the only one growing up? How could she let Elizabeth court that Herbert Kuss while insisting that she still wear childish pigtails and not cut her hair?

It did not help that Otto was now allowed to leave school to work with Papa on the farm. Ursula missed him dreadfully, especially those days when she could not seem to get along with the older girls or even her sister. Since the beginning of the school year, the only topic of conversation during lunch hours and recesses was boys. And then when Elisabeth met Herbert, she was immediately taken into the fold by the three others also courting, and she actively joined in excluding the younger girls.

The afternoon when Margaret, the oldest pupil in Pheasant Forks School, rudely told Ursula to go away and leave them alone, she defiantly did what she was told. Still, it was not as easy to play hide-and-seek, baseball, or the other games the boys were playing.

Only on the rare day did the boys allow Ursula to come onto their side of the schoolyard, and more often than not it was because they were a player short. Then perhaps they were just paying her back for having been forced to include her during all those years when Otto had taken charge of all the playground sports.

Now that he was starting his third year of school, Johann had made his own friends, and he felt embarrassed and annoyed when his older sister bothered him when they were playing outdoors. Subsequently, Ursula began to sit in the shade by the door or to wander about the schoolyard alone.

As the autumn months passed, Ursula began to understand the subtle difference between being alone and being lonely, and what surprised her most was how well she felt about herself when she allowed her mind to be free and to experience the energy of being in nature. Suddenly she did not have to listen to someone criticizing or comparing her to Elisabeth or to try to live up to her mother's expectations.

Nonetheless, it soon appeared that she had no satisfying classmates at school. They clearly did not want her near them; but now that she left them alone, they didn't seem to like her habit of wandering off by herself and calling to the wind.

One evening as they prepared for bed, Elizabeth said, "Ursula, I have no idea what you think you're doing during recesses and the lunch hour, but could you please stop walking around like some lost soul?"

"What does it matter to you?" Ursula snapped back while changing into her nightgown. "You and your friends told me to go away, and now you even tell me what to do when I'm not in your company. I like strolling around outside, so forget about ordering me to stop."

"You obviously can't realize how ridiculous you look," said Elizabeth, "not to mention that the whole school knows you don't have a single friend. I think even Johann is embarrassed by the way you don't try to get along with the other pupils."

"Maybe for the first time in my life, I like who I am. When you and your three precious friends rudely told me to leave, I felt sorry for myself. But then during these past weeks, I have come to understand that a person could spend her life trying to please others. If you then have a tiff with who you're trying to please, you suddenly have no one to rely on. If you can become your own best friend, you can be sure you'll always be there for yourself."

"I don't know where you get your selfish notions," countered Elizabeth. "Of course, we need to depend on our family and friends. Or what is the point of living? I will always want to make other people happy and be as pleasing as I can be. But you've spent most of your days thinking only about yourself. I'm telling you, Ursula, that one of these days you will be sorry for thinking you are better than everyone else in the school."

"And I'm telling you that there will come a time when you'll be sorry you spent your whole life pleasing other people."

The two quarrelling sisters settled into a truce, each lost in her private thoughts. Elisabeth knew that Ursula always had to have the last word and there was no point in saying more, but she continued to wonder how she'd become so self-absorbed after being born into the same family and being taught the same Christian values. When would she learn that it was wrong to be so selfish?

For her part, Ursula quietly seethed that her older sibling always suggested that she was so much more virtuous simply because she would never stand up for herself and say what was important to her.

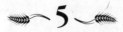

At long last it was the end of May, the university year was finally over, and Leonard was coming home. At least three times every day during the last week of the month, Ursula had asked her father if she could go to town with him for Leonard's Saturday morning arrival at the train station.

In the end Gustav became exasperated and told her that she would stay home if she said one more word about going to Neudorf with him. She was much too excited to sleep the Friday night before, and dawn had barely broken when Ursula burst into the kitchen to help her mother prepare breakfast. Although Leonard's train was not scheduled to arrive until early afternoon, she hoped Papa could be talked into going to town as soon as the chores were finished.

She then realized that time would pass more quickly if she could visit and drink tea with Grandmama in her cozy loft. There Ursula often became engrossed in one of Margareta's tales about how her family had escaped from Russia or, better yet, how she had outwitted her nemeses, the Silent Critics, who were now all dead. Once she got Grandmama into storytelling, the two could lose hours talking about the events from the past.

As luck would have it, Gustav did have business to do in Neudorf. When he came in carrying the cream from the separator room, he said to Amelia, "I need to go to town this morning because I must see if Tomas has been able to weld that broken part for the drill. The fields are probably dry enough for Otto and I to begin seeding by Monday morning. So, Ursula, if you are coming with us, you better be ready to leave the minute I have washed and eaten breakfast."

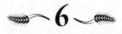

As soon as she heard the whistle, Ursula was on her feet and Grandmama yelled at her to be careful as she ran down the stairs. Of course, her words fell on deaf ears. The youth bolted towards the station, wanting to be the first person on the platform when Leonard alighted from the train.

Other passengers descended the three small steps, and then there was a lull. Where was Leonard? Why was he taking so long to get off the train? Oh, what if he had decided not to come home today, or even for the summer? Questions and then fears raced through her head when Ursula saw a handsome young man with blond hair appear at the top of the stairs, stop and glance around, and then hop down the short distance. And at last, right behind him, Leonard stuck his head out of the doorway and flashed his brightest smile at Ursula.

Within seconds she embraced him in a huge hug.

"Hello, Ursula. I was certain that you would convince Mama and Papa to let you come to greet me. It is great to see you, and I want you to be the first to meet my friend from university, Hans Gerhart, who will spend the summer with us working on the farm."

Ursula was taken aback by the idea of having to share her brother with a stranger for the entire time he was home, even as she wondered why her parents had not told her. As she held out her hand to Hans's extended hand, she looked up into the deepest brown eyes she'd ever seen and suddenly became uncharacteristically shy.

"Cat got your tongue, my favourite sister? Or have you forgotten your manners? We don't want Hans to think he is not welcome, so please speak to him in English or German. He understands both."

In the ensuing silence, Hans suddenly thought he'd made a mistake. What family would want to take in a hungry man for all of the summer months, especially when Saskatchewan farmers were just starting to recover from the Great Depression?

Although the two friends and classmates had discussed the proposal in detail, Leonard assured Hans that he would earn his keep, particularly since his father's hired man had gone to fight in the war. He was so confident that Hans would be openly welcomed into his home that he had not bothered to tell his parents. His mother would be only too happy to have his friend stay with them, and Papa could always use another pair of hands around the homestead.

Now here he was meeting the first member of Leonard's family, and the young woman could not speak to him. Hans nearly offered to take the train back to Saskatoon when Ursula graciously replied, "I'm so sorry, Mr. Gerhart. I don't know what came over me. Thank you for coming home with Leonard, and please know that the rest of the Warner family will not be as slow in welcoming you to our townships."

"Oh, please call me Hans. I can't ever recall anyone addressing me as mister. Quite frankly, I don't like the sound of it." Laughing gently as he gathered up his worn brown valise, he continued, "I've been waiting to meet you, Ursula, because Leonard talks about you most of the time. But even with everything he told me about you, he never once mentioned how pretty you are."

Leonard knew not what was more surprising: his friend resorting to flattery? Or the sudden blush that spread from Ursula's neck to her cheekbones? Over the past year, he had become accustomed to women being attracted to Hans, and he agreed that his roommate was a very handsome man.

But Hans's remark now caused Leonard to really look at his little sister, and he realized that during the months he had been away, she had indeed matured into a comely young woman. Then he remembered that she'd celebrated her sixteenth birthday in the spring, and she might soon be courting boys and thinking about becoming a wife. After all, Mama was married by the time she was Ursula's age, and he'd read in one letter that Elisabeth would wed in the autumn.

At any rate, the two were engaging in lively conversation, which ended abruptly when Gustav and Otto stepped onto the train platform.

"Good afternoon, Papa and Otto. How nice to see you," Leonard said, as he heartily shook their hands. "I would like you to meet my friend Hans Gerhart, whom I have invited to spend the summer with us. He has never been on a farm, and I thought it was about time that he learns some of the daily chores and hard work necessary to look after land and farm animals. Hans just sits down to eat without understanding what it takes to put food on a table or the hours of toil needed to produce it."

Gustav was instantly annoyed. What was his son thinking by inviting a stranger to live with them during the busy summer months? "Well, then you must be a town boy who doesn't know the true meaning of work," said Gustav, with an edge that took Leonard by surprise.

What was wrong with Papa? Why was he being rude to his friend? Usually he was open to meeting new people, but this afternoon he seemed to have taken an instant dislike to Hans. Of course, Otto picked up on it instantly and responded with a gruff hello.

Before Leonard could smooth over the troubled waters, Hans jumped in with both feet, "Why, yes Mr. Warner, I grew up in the town of North Battleford, but I would dearly have loved to have been raised on a farm. But I can assure you that I am no stranger to hard work."

"So, what kind of work does your father do in North Battleford?"

Leonard had never seen his father treat a person so obnoxiously. He was on the verge of responding in kind when Hans took command of the conversation.

"As it happens, I don't know who my father is—or my mother, for that matter— since I was abandoned on the front door steps of a Catholic church just hours after I was born. But one of the first things an orphan learns is that you work for everything you get or you not only go hungry but you're beaten within an inch of your life. I think we were rigorously disciplined to teach us that life is hard, as if being cast off by one's own mother and father had not already taught me that."

Stunned by the young man's words, it took Gustav several minutes to recover. What kind of a mother left her offspring on a doorstep? Surely her family could have helped her raise the child? No decent person gave away her child. It simply was not done.

He soon turned to Otto and asked him to take his sister and their guest to Aunt Margareta's, where they had been invited for coffee before returning home. He had another issue to deal with, and be damned if he would apologize to a stranger. Leonard should have known better than to bring a foreigner to Neudorf and to their townships.

7

As soon as the other three were out of earshot, Gustav upbraided his eldest son.

"What were you thinking when you decided to bring that man home with you? It's bad enough that the townspeople still gossip about me purchasing Andrew Thompson's homestead and moving my family to the English township. Now they can also go on about my son bringing home an outsider from the university."

"Oh, Papa, the Silent Critics are all dead, and no one could care about me bringing home a friend. And what is this business about an outsider? Hans is as German as you and me and every other person in this little corner of the world, so I fail to understand why you are making such a fuss about my decision to invite him home. He had no place to go with the residence closed. And can't you imagine how it will feel for him to live with us for the summer? The poor fellow has never known what it is like to be part of a family, or even to live in a house instead of an orphanage or a student residence."

"I sometimes wonder what you are learning at that university," said Gustav, "because you don't seem to be able to think anymore. Since nuns raised the man, he is obviously a Catholic. But then what is it you are studying? Oh yes, science not religion."

"Perhaps, it is a major mistake to separate people because of either language or religion. You know very well that I am learning to become a pharmacist, which certainly requires me to study many science subjects. But I am also taking courses in English, philosophy, and theology to give me a rounded education so your dollars do not go to waste.

"I consider it unhealthy and even dangerous to exclude one group of people at the expense of another. Furthermore, I believe that this war in Europe will prove me out. So, Papa, I have invited my Catholic friend to spend the summer on the Warner homestead. And if he is not welcome to stay, then neither shall I. I have no doubt that we shall both hear what Mama has to say should Hans and I return to Saskatoon on the next train."

"If I didn't know better, I'd think you were threatening your own father," said Gustav. "But since it is getting late, we should get on our way to Aunt Margareta's."

Leonard knew his father's deflection was the extent of resolution or apology he could expect. "Yes, Papa. Mama will be worrying about what has happened to us."

As soon as Aunt Margareta opened the door to welcome her three young guests, she had sized up the situation. Although the family matriarch had recently celebrated her eighty-seventh birthday, she knew from the scowl on Otto's face that the stranger was a bone of contention.

Margareta decided to be as charming as possible. She immediately focused her attention on the stranger and amiably extended her right hand.

"Good afternoon. Since I have not had the pleasure of making your acquaintance, I shall initiate our introduction. I am Margareta Mohr, and I most heartily invite you into my home. Furthermore, being the oldest person in our town, I also welcome you to Neudorf on behalf of all its citizens."

"Thank you, ma'am. My name is Hans Gerhart, and I don't remember having been received so graciously into a home."

Of course, Margareta had no awareness that Hans had seldom been welcomed into any house, nor would she have cared. She had always enjoyed meeting new people, and she could not understand why Gustav had developed an aversion to strangers. It had definitely heightened since Rolf Spitznagel had died two years ago.

When their long-time friend was alive, Gustav had purportedly accepted the new Dr. Roth and his family; but now he did his best to avoid them, as though he'd only respected them on the credence of the town's original doctor. She was determined to show Gustav that, at least in her home, Hans would be treated like a member of the family.

By the time Katherina served coffee and apple strudel, Hans was marvelling about how comfortable he felt in the presence of the dignified Grandmama, as Ursula called her. And when she inquired about his history, he found himself opening up to her. There was no anger or resentment in his disclosure, and indeed before long he was regaling all with some of the humorous incidents that occurred when he was a boy.

Even Otto chuckled when Hans recounted the day he had to wear a dress because, against strict orders of the nuns, he ventured onto the slightly frozen pond, promptly fell in, and got soaked to the skin. Since it was a Monday and his only other pair of trousers was in the laundry, he had to spend the balance of the day carrying out his chores and eating with the other boys in one of the frocks worn by the girls in the orphanage.

Throughout it all, Gustav sat with a stiff upper lip, impatiently waiting for the young people to finish their coffee before gruffly announcing that it was time to leave for home. But, naturally, the minute Hans said he had been raised by the Catholic sisters, Margareta acutely understood what was causing her brother to be grumpier than usual about a stranger in their midst.

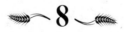

8

When climbing into the automobile, no one questioned that Otto would sit in the front seat beside his father while the other two men prepared to ride in the back seat with Ursula between them. Hans took the spot behind the driver to ensure that Gustav could not glare at him from the rear-view mirror.

He spent the short journey from town gazing out the window, fascinated by how precisely straight and even the rows of green were sprouting up in the black fields. When coming up to what he later learned was the pasture, he suddenly shouted, "Stop the car."

Perhaps because everything seemed so vividly coloured had Hans been drawn to a patch of bright red, which turned out to be the shirt of a young boy racing like the wind. Only when he looked more keenly did he realize that the child was running for his life just a few feet in front of a large, charging animal.

Hans leaped out of the car before it came to a stop, covered the distance within seconds, and bounded over the barbed wire fence as though he did it every day. He quickly reached the boy and pulled him into his strong arms without breaking his stride. Now he needed to put some ground between them and the beast that was rapidly gaining on them.

In his peripheral vision, Hans saw Leonard and Otto now in the pasture, trying to distract the ranting animal. Glancing ahead, Hans caught sight of Gustav in front of him at what appeared to be a gate, so he slowed down to gently place the boy into Gustav's arms.

Hans turned around and shouted to the other two men to get out of the pasture, while he invited the animal in his direction by flailing his arms wildly. As soon as he saw Leonard and Otto were safe on the other side of the fence, he again leaped over it, this time tearing the seat out of his trousers.

After hurrying from the garden, Amelia took Johann from Gustav's trembling arms, examined him carefully, and determined that he was not injured before she scolded him for wearing his new red shirt to do his chores.

Gustav was on the verge of spanking his youngest son for being in the pasture, but Amelia intervened. "No, Gustav. I sent him to get the cows for milking. So please let's be thankful that he was not harmed, all because of this young man."

Before Leonard could respond, Otto stepped forward to introduce Hans to his mother. "Mama, this is Mr. Hans Gerhart, Leonard's friend from the university, and he is going to spend the summer with us."

Then breaking into a smile and turning to Hans, he continued, "I will run into the house and get you a pair of my trousers. You can be certain that we will not insist that you wear one of Elisabeth's or Ursula's dresses for the rest of the day."

If ever there was a way to endear oneself to Gustav Warner, it was through the quick actions of his young guest. Had Hans not saved Johann's life, thought Gustav, he certainly spared him from serious injuries.

Once the others heard Hans's story and Otto returned with a pair of pants, the women made their way to the house with Johann in tow. Changing in the yard, Hans thanked Otto before he and Leonard returned to the pasture to find the errant cows.

Ready to accompany them, Hans was surprised to feel Gustav's hand on his shoulder. Then and there, Gustav asked, "Will you forgive me, Hans, for how I greeted you at the train station? Because of your quick thinking, I owe my son's life to you, and you can stay in my home for as long as you want, whenever you choose to visit us."

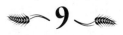

During his first summer on the Warner homestead, Hans came to know how it felt to have been born and raised in a loving family with parents who not only wanted children but also cherished their presence. Amelia, in particular, after hearing how Hans had saved Johann from the raging bull, soon treated him as a long-lost son. There was no limit to what she would do for Hans, from repairing his torn trousers to frequently preparing his favourite supper of chicken and dumplings.

She was not the only member of the Warner family to soon become favourably impressed by Leonard's friend from the city. From the initial day of his arrival, Hans was invariably the first person to be awake and up out of bed. Throughout the summer when Gustav made his way into the kitchen to stoke the stove for Amelia to begin breakfast, he discovered the fire already burning brightly.

On that first Sunday morning when Gustav heard Betsy's bell, he looked at the dawning light and was surprised to see Hans herding their three cows into the barn to be milked. Hurrying into the bedroom to wake his two elder sons, Gustav admonished them for still sleeping while their guest was about to embark upon a task he could not expect to accomplish alone since he had never before been on a farm.

But all of the Warner men soon saw how quickly Hans could grasp the rudiments of any chore required on a farm—from milking the cows to driving the tractor and to mending fences—until they had to admit that he was a natural farmer.

Although initially assuming that the young man was only trying to prove that he did know the meaning of work, Gustav soon revised his thinking.

The exhilaration Hans experienced—from learning new tasks and then readily carrying them out—was apparent on his face and in his voice. And he never seemed to tire, even at the end of a day of constant activity. Likely because hard physical labour had, throughout Hans's life, provided him with a sense of accomplishment and emotional equanimity.

Nonetheless, Gustav reached the point of wondering how, once the seeding was finished, there would be sufficient work to keep four adult men busy for the summer months, when it occurred to him that now was the ideal time to break the sod at the east end of the pasture for cultivation next spring.

Although the task was much easier now that he had the tractor to pull the plow, there was still the back-breaking job of picking the stones before he could get on the land to uproot the prairie sod.

Whereas Otto fully expected to outlast both men since they had sat idly on their bottoms at the university for the past nine months, he was amazed by the fact that Hans kept pace with him from dawn to dusk, unlike Leonard who begged off in the early afternoon of the second day, complaining that every muscle in his body ached.

As it happened, it took the better part of the summer for the Warner family to appreciate that the wellspring of Hans's enthusiasm and dynamism came from his delight at living in a home where he was accepted. It was not long before everyone thoroughly enjoyed his lively presence, and none more so than Ursula.

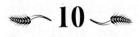

10

The summer passed all too quickly, particularly for Hans and Ursula. Once she started joining Hans and Leonard on their established evening strolls, she forgot about her unusual physical responses to Hans. Whether this happened because they were always with Leonard or because she had just chosen to view Hans as one of the boys, would not become apparent until the autumn when the two men returned to Saskatoon.

Not until they were separated by distance would she realize how close they had become, and then an unfamiliar ache in her heart would permeate her whole being, night and day. Of course, she had missed first Leonard and later Jurgen when they had left the farm, but this was different. She could not seem to get Hans out of her mind. She found it increasingly difficult to concentrate in school, and she felt sad a good deal of the time. Not even Johann could cheer her, until at last Ursula decided to seek the advice of her aging and beloved Grandmama one Sunday as they enjoyed a cup of tea in Margareta's loft.

"I don't understand what has happened to me since Hans came to spend the summer with us, Grandmama. When he first arrived, I was completely tongue-tied in his presence, and I behaved just like the older girls at school when they would talk endlessly about boys—what I vowed never to do in my life. I was going to ask you about it during the summer; but once Leonard, Hans, and I started walking most evenings, I became my normal self. But now that they've gone back to the university, all I can think about is Hans, and I miss him so much that I have a constant pain right here," Ursula lamented, as she touched the left side of her chest.

"Oh, my dear child, from what you have just described, you surely have been smitten by Cupid's arrow. I wondered whenever I saw the two of you together. Well, my darling, I am very happy for you because Leonard's friend is a fine young man; if all goes according to God's plan for the two of you, we may have another wedding in the Warner family as soon as next autumn."

Gently caressing Ursula's forearm and gazing off into the distance, it was some time before Margareta continued.

"I firmly believe that each of us has only one authentic love, and those of us fortunate enough to find our rightful mate with whom to go through life are truly blessed. From the first time I saw your great-uncle Phillip, I knew we were meant for each other, and now I think the same will be the case for you and Hans. Let us not forget that we must write to Leonard and make sure he brings Hans home to the farm again next summer so you two can follow your destiny."

11

Against adamant protestations, Amelia insisted that Elisabeth make Ursula her maid of honour. Fortunately, to the surprise of both of them, her younger sister had become less of a tomboy and more like a lady during the past summer. Elisabeth wondered if perhaps it had something to do with Hans Gerhart, but she had quite simply been too busy planning her own nuptials to spend much time contemplating the reason for

Ursula's changed behaviour. In fact, Elisabeth had little patience with Ursula ever since their quarrel.

What did her little sister know about getting along with people? For several days after the evening of their more than unusually intense bout of bickering, Elisabeth was extremely upset by Ursula's prediction that she would find herself alone when she expected people to help her. All of her life, Elisabeth had been taught to serve others, first at home by her mother and father, and then certainly from Reverend Ulmer's teachings about Jesus Christ.

On the other hand, from all accounts, what she had yelled at Ursula about her thinking she was better than everyone in school was already proving accurate. Papa had twice been called to Mrs. Anderson's classroom to discuss Ursula's behaviour.

It was only the first month of the new school year and Ursula was already causing trouble by not paying attention in class and by refusing to participate with the other pupils during recess and lunch hour. It was little wonder that Elisabeth did not want Ursula in the wedding party. But she was consoled by the fact that she would never more need to share her bed and room with her pesky younger sister.

From the moment Elisabeth glided down the aisle of the Neudorf church, tenderly ushered in on her father's arm, and gazed lovingly into Herbert's deep brown eyes, she was determined to perform her spousal and maternal responsibilities with the utmost assiduity for the duration of their marriage. She listened intently to every phrase of her marriage vows, never once taking her adoring eyes from her soon-to-be husband's face, and she was particularly attentive when Reverend Ulmer said those three all-important words: Love, honour, and obey. A brief smile flittered across Elisabeth's serene face as she thought about the unlikelihood of Ursula ever being able to make such a profound commitment to another human being.

From her wedding day onward, Mrs. Herbert Kuss did become a model wife and mother, more and more frowning upon many of Ursula's antics in the ensuing years.

12

Although Hans vividly remembered Mr. Warner graciously saying he was welcome to stay in his house on any occasion, he was still averse to taking Leonard's father for granted. So he wrote an endearing letter requesting that he accompany his friend home for the Christmas season.

As much as Hans eagerly looked forward to seeing everyone and being embraced again by the warmth of the Warner family, he could not believe how much he wanted to rest his eyes upon Ursula's beautiful face. When he had first returned to the university, he thought he was just missing the novel experience of being part of a family; but as the weeks passed, he began to realize how much he longed for Ursula's company.

Initially, Hans was alarmed by the possibility that his intense feelings towards Ursula were romantic in nature, given that she was almost six years younger than him. What would her family, and particularly her father, think of him when they came to know his intentions?

After fretting for days after realizing he was in love with Ursula, Hans finally mustered up the courage to share his dilemma with Leonard. "I'm not sure how to tell you this, especially after you have been the best friend I have ever had. But the longer I am away from her, the more I am aware of my true feelings."

"My good fellow," answered Leonard, "my feelings toward you are mutual, but I don't have the slightest idea who you're talking about or why it is any business of mine."

"It has plenty to do with you, since it involves Ursula. I believe I am in love with her, but I realize she is only sixteen years old. I am almost six years older, and I wouldn't blame your father for opposing my courtship."

"Well, congratulations, Hans! That is exciting news, and I can assure you right now that you can stop worrying about how old she is and about your age difference. Papa is more than five years older than my mother, and they had an arranged marriage when Mama was only sixteen. Surely you would wait until Ursula has completed her grade twelve and you have graduated from university. And yes, I would be most willing to be your best man on that happy occasion." Leonard gave Hans a brotherly hug.

Delighted and relieved by Leonard's endorsement, Hans could hardly contain himself until he saw her again. In his excitement Hans counted the number of remaining sleeps, as he had done as a small boy, before he and Leonard wrote their final examinations and could board the train that would transport him to the young woman he loved.

Of course, he was unaware of whether Ursula felt the same way about him; but he was quick to console himself by remembering when they had initially met last summer, which to him now felt like love at first sight. The more Hans thought about Ursula, the more he longed to be with her, until he had to force himself to concentrate on studying so he could graduate as a pharmacist. He knew only then would Mr. Warner consider him an acceptable suitor and spouse for Ursula.

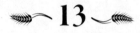

13

The two-week sojourn at Leonard's home was everything and more than Hans could have imagined. He knew from the moment he crossed the threshold of the Warner hearth that Ursula did in fact care for him—as much as he did for her. Her eyes shone whenever she gazed into his face, and his heart raced as she focused on him.

The days passed quickly as Hans and Leonard sat with Gustav in the parlour, listening to music when the chores were done, while Johann and Otto sprawled on the rug in front of the fire reading or playing board games. Herbert and Elisabeth were soon expected to arrive home for the holiday season, and although Amelia missed her capable assistance with all the cooking, she was pleasantly surprised by how helpful Ursula had become since her older sister's departure.

Aunt Margareta and Katherina were also coming for the Christmas feast, which would now include eleven people. But as much as Amelia needed Ursula's help, she did not want her to miss out on all the fun, so often in the late afternoon she sent her to join the men. When Ursula entered the parlour, Hans would quietly motion for her to sit with him on the comfortable davenport while Leonard obsequiously slipped down onto the floor. Other than Leonard, no one seemed to notice the developing intimacy between Hans and Ursula. With the passage of each day, their love was being confirmed as they peered into each other's eyes, as if to carve each other's image in memory for the long months ahead.

As soon as Aunt Margareta arrived and saw how Ursula looked at Hans, she became fully aware of what was happening between the two young people. But Grandmama would not say a word, never mind discourage a young man of whom she had become particularly fond over the past summer. In her heart, Margareta Mohr would remain a romantic until the end of her days, and she was thoroughly convinced that Hans Gerhart was Ursula's one true love.

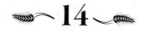

14

There were those in the family who were quick to think and to say that the fault began in the spring of 1941, when Albert Schultz most unexpectedly returned to Neudorf. His mother was so shocked to see him that she very nearly suffered apoplexy, and then it was his turn to be stupefied when she explained that he had been legally declared dead for a number of years..

Of course, Albert came home expecting to take over the Schultz's hotel from his father, but he soon learned that Rudolph had met his demise... not before, however, transferring the title of all his property to his daughter, Frieda, and her friend Katie Reinhold.

Presumed dead, Albert was left without a penny. In his fury, he marched across Main Street, eventually coming to the dead spinster-sisters' vacant house. With little foresight, he promptly removed the restraining boards that had been placed over the door and windows years before, and strode into the abandoned two-storey hovel.

Within weeks, Albert opened a beer parlour on the main floor and installed three ladies of the night, one in each of the diminutive bedrooms on the second floor. It soon became apparent that the harvest of the previous fall had been productive enough to put money into the pockets of the local farmers and that plenty of them were happy again to pay cash for their pints of ale rather than having to bring produce for barter in the basement of the Traders' Dining Room.

Although everyone would have vehemently denied it, there were sufficient patrons to keep the three women adequately busy. It was quite by accident that Otto Warner stumbled upon the brothel, not aware that places of such repute even existed.

He had also become something of a man about town, more so in the spring when Gustav had given him the old family car and a sizeable portion of the profits from the previous harvest; but he was still very naïve. His father, favourably impressed by how hard Otto had worked alongside him on the farm, considered it fair to reward his son for his labour.

Furthermore, when the price of wheat soared in the spring of 1941 and Gustav decided to empty out several of his granaries, he ordered a new automobile to transport the family, enabling Otto's own independence. Otto had driven into town to purchase a new blade for the cultivator. Suddenly feeling thirsty, he decided to stop for a beer at the new public house Albert Schultz had recently opened.

A few short weeks ago Otto would not have thought about making such an impetuous decision; but with the obvious vote of confidence from his father, he felt intoxicated with a surge of personal power. Imagine walking into a beer parlour by his own volition, and in the middle of the day.

As his eyes adjusted to the dimmed light of the dingy room, Otto noticed the Lutz brothers sitting at a table in the corner. Once they recovered from their surprise, they motioned for him to join them.

"Good afternoon, Otto. What brings you into this little hole in the wall, and what would your Papa have to say about it?" Adolph inquired congenially.

"I imagine I have come here for exactly the same reason that you two have," Otto answered, and even he was a little surprised by the irritability in his voice. He had always liked Adolph and Fred Lutz, and he wondered if he was feeling somewhat ashamed of being caught in a tavern, as Adolph had implied.

Glancing quickly at his brother as both Lutz men started to chuckle, Fred replied, "You are likely not here for the same purpose as are we, but why don't you get a beer and come sit down with us?"

Following several minutes of small talk, Adolph asked, "Did you know that Fred and I are leaving on the morning train tomorrow for Regina? We have both decided to enlist in the Canadian Army?"

"No, I didn't know you were thinking of joining the forces," said Otto. "Why in God's name would you go to fight in Europe?"

Looking sheepishly at his younger brother, Adolph explained.

"As complicated as that is, this is the first time we have come into Albert's establishment, and I assure you it is not to discuss our purposes for going overseas. Several of the more experienced men in town have finally convinced us, since neither of us has ever been with a woman, to avail ourselves of the services of one of the ladies on the second floor before we go off and get killed in the war."

15

It took a great deal of time and talking for Otto to understand what they were contemplating, and after each man had consumed two pints of beer, they convinced him that the third woman on the upper level of the house might feel very left out. So why not come along up the stairs?

Otto knocked gently on the door. Although he did not know what to expect, he was surprised by the pleasant voice inviting him to come into the room. He was more astounded when he beheld a young attractive woman with raven black hair sitting on the single bed situated by the wall, reading a book by the soft light of the small bedside lamp.

"Come in and make yourself comfortable. My name is Millie, and what shall I call you?"

"Thank you. I am Otto Warner, and I am pleased to meet you."

Feeling more than a little foolish, he quickly sat down on the only chair in the sparsely furnished bedroom. In the silence, Otto studied his feet while Millie stared at the young farmer through a smirk on her pretty face.

"Ah, it is your first time, Otto. Well, you can't get your money's worth by staying over there on that wobbly chair. So why don't you come closer, and make sure that you bring your cash with you?"

"Actually, if you don't mind," answered a subdued Otto, "I would rather just sit here and visit with you."

"Suit yourself, Otto Warner, but when your time is up, I still expect to get paid."

Thus it was that Otto met Millie Brown. And throughout the many initial months of their acquaintance, not once did they do more than sit and talk. She gave him no indication of her true identity; perhaps if Otto knew her real Christian name, he might not have returned to the second floor of the spinsters' old house.

But return he did, time after time. And even though he only conversed with Millie, he could imagine what she was paid to do with other men, until he began to hate the nature of her livelihood.

Another man who would have been upset, had he known, was her father. For a number of years, the gentleman had been at his wit's end with his eldest child, having long ago realized his mistake when he had given into her persistent tantrums and allowed her to come with him to Canada. But at the time he had been so infatuated with his young secretary that he would have done practically anything to facilitate his escape from England.

When he had finally come to his senses, he had been appalled by the rumours circulating on campus about his daughter. Then during an urgent meeting when the Board of Directors presented him with an ultimatum of either dealing with his daughter's promiscuous behaviour or forfeiting his position as the president of the University of Regina, he was compelled to take immediate action.

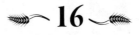

16

It was soon after he and Gustav finished the spring seeding that the plan began to form in Otto's mind. What if he were to marry Millie and bring her back with him to the Warner homestead to live? Then she would not need to support herself by selling her body to any man willing to pay.

Not once did Otto think she had chosen her particular calling, just as her father could not comprehend her predilection. Nonetheless, Otto realized that if he were to convince Millie to marry him, he would need to provide sufficient enticement, knowing only too well that she tended to view him as little more than an inexperienced youth, who consistently paid for services he never collected.

Then one morning while mending the pasture fence, he remembered one of their chats when Millie complained about being cooped up in her tiny bedroom—especially on Sundays when the establishment was closed—because Albert was afraid of how idle tongues would wag. Staring out the unwashed window, she said that one day she would buy her own house, which would be surrounded by a white picket fence, and she would come and go as she pleased.

Almost hitting his thumb with the hammer as the answer popped into his head, Otto quickly finished his task and decided to ask his father about building a house in one of his favourite spots. Nestled in the grove of conifer trees at the end of the narrow road leading to his parents' house was an open area just large enough for the home and fence.

There was very little Otto would not do for Millie, such was the extent of his love for her. But his parents had not even met Millie, much less come to accept her as a suitable wife for him. Given that he'd only recently turned eighteen, he'd also have to convince them. But love is perhaps the greatest motivator, and buoyed with his new sense of confidence, Otto knew he would find a way.

As he walked toward the yard, he decided that rather than start with his father, he should first speak to Mama. Once his mother chose to support him in his venture, regardless of how much Papa might be opposed, he would eventually listen.

So Otto went in search of her in the garden, and after finding her weeding the potato plants, he excitedly exclaimed, "Guess what, Mama. I have met a very nice young woman in Neudorf, and I would like to invite her home for supper tomorrow afternoon following church."

"Of course, Otto. That would be just fine. What is her name? And will we meet her at the service?" his mother said, as she continued gardening.

Bending down to help her pick the persistent thistles and quack grass, Otto, as he would continue to do over the next few days, chose his words carefully. "I don't know if Millie will be able to come to church tomorrow, but I will be sure to ask her this evening when I go into town. Thank you, Mama. I know that you will like her."

"Well, my son, if you are fond of her then I shall expect to like her too. It's hard to believe that you are so grown up already, just like Leonard and Elisabeth, but I guess that's what happens. Before we know it, all four of our older children will be married, and only Johann will be at home with Papa and me," Amelia responded pensively, thinking affectionately about her youngest son, while having a sense of foreboding. To the best of her recall, Amelia had not had one of her premonitions for years.

"Actually, now that I am farming with Papa, I will not be going far. In fact, I have been thinking about asking you and Papa if I could build a small house where that grove of trees ends at the turn of the road into the yard. Then if everything works out between Millie and me, we would have our own place to live when we are married."

"It sounds like you have been thinking a lot about what you want to do, Otto. I always thought you would grow up to be a farmer like your papa. Then if you are living at the end of the road, when you have children I will be able to see my grandchildren every day."

"Oh, Mama, thank you. I am so glad I decided to talk to you about Millie and about building our house. If Papa needs any convincing because I am still young, you will be sure to help me."

~ 17 ~

Careful preparation can go a long way to bringing about expected results. None other over the next several months was as assiduous as Otto Warner in implementing his grand plan. Even Margareta, the grand matron of intrigue, would have been proud of her great-nephew if she knew how he had attended to every detail.

Millie Brown did come to supper, Gustav did heartily object to building another house on his land, Amelia did manage to change Gustav's mind, and then, in time, all family members became fond of Otto's young lady. Gustav asked her questions about her upbringing, but Millie deflected his inquiries so capably that she was well on her way back to Neudorf before he realized he had not gotten a straight answer from the woman.

Within a few weeks, as Millie endeared herself to them, it didn't seem to matter that they knew very little about her. Even though surprised by how readily Otto's family accepted her, Millie was more astonished by her own reaction to them. She had only agreed to go for supper with Otto because she hated spending an entire Sunday in the house with only Albert and the two other women. Otto's parents didn't seem to care that she was at least five years older than their son, or they simply were not aware of the fact, and they treated her as though she was one of their own.

Of course, at twenty-three, Millie no longer needed motherly solicitude, but still she found herself enjoying the feeling of being so accepted. So much so, that when Otto suggested she meet his Aunt Margareta about taking a job in the General Store, she agreed. And before any of his family discovered her previous employment, Millie was behind the counter selling dry goods very successfully and living under Margareta's roof.

Soon Millie was partaking of a delicious supper every Sunday at Amelia's table, and one afternoon when Otto walked her to the site where he had begun the construction of their home to propose to her, she agreed to become his wife.

Not for one minute did Millie Brown delude herself into thinking that she loved Otto; but she could appreciate the advantages of being a Warner, which had escalated when his older brother and that handsome Hans Gerhart arrived home from university. She would have been only too happy to take him to her bed; but for some strange reason Hans seemed totally infatuated with Ursula. Only time would tell which of the women would satisfy the hunger in Hans's eyes; but her chances were considerably better if she too lived on the homestead.

At any rate, with all the strong men around the farm, the building of the house and picket fence Otto had promised her were readily becoming a reality. Although they had originally planned to marry in late autumn once the harvesting was completed, Millie wondered why they should wait. She was becoming bored with working in the store.

Because Millie Brown was all about Millie Brown, she convinced Otto to move their wedding up to early July.

18

Some in the family were quick to place the blame on Margareta Mohr, which seemed terribly unfair given that in her eighty-ninth year her health was steadily failing. It all started on the last day of May of 1941, when Leonard and his friend Hans arrived in Neudorf on an earlier train than expected, and as soon as they alighted, Leonard dashed off to see his beloved Great-Aunt Margareta, leaving Hans to visit with Katherina in the store.

He knew his great-aunt now spent most of her days basking in the sunshine, which radiated through the sunroof in her loft. So without stopping in the kitchen, he bounded up the stairs two at a time, almost knocking over the young woman in the open doorway.

As Leonard was about to speak, he felt like a gangly schoolboy when his mind suddenly went blank. "Ah, I am so sorry. I didn't expect anyone to be at the door, and I very nearly ran you down. Please pardon me for my rude behaviour. I am Leonard Warner, and I thought I would have a quick visit with Aunt Margareta, but I should have been more careful."

"Hello, Leonard. Fortunately, I saw you making your hasty hurtle up the stairway, so no harm has been done; an apology is hardly necessary. I am called Fraya Roth, and I shall continue on my way."

On sudden impulse Leonard almost asked her to stay, but then realized that he had come to check on Aunt Margareta who, according to everyone's letters, was not doing well. Walking at a considerably slower pace, he entered the loft and was met with a bright smile and open arms by one of the people he held most dear.

"Leonard, how nice of you to come and see an old lady like me. I knew you were returning today, but I must be the first person to welcome you home. And where is that good-looking friend of yours? Surely Hans came with you for the summer, or Ursula will be so upset with you that you will need to go back to Saskatoon to fetch him."

As Aunt Margareta chatted gaily with him, Leonard began to hope and pray that his family had been wrong about her state of health. She still seemed as vibrant and alert as he had always known her to be, and perhaps the new doctor had misdiagnosed her.

"Aunt Margareta, you seem perfectly sound to me, contrary to what everyone has been writing to me. How are you feeling?"

"Oh, they will not get rid of me as easily as they might think, but I always feel better when spring arrives and brings delightful young people to my loft."

"Well, you do seem to have your share of youthful visitors. Was that attractive lady I nearly barrelled over in my haste to see you Dr. Roth's daughter?"

"Fraya is Max and Rebecca's older daughter, and she has been accepted into the nursing school in Saskatoon for September. She is always going on house calls with her father. I daresay she could finish her training in record time with all she must already know."

"In that case, perhaps she should consider becoming a doctor like her father. Does she come to visit you often? Does she ever accompany her parents? Because I would like you to formally introduce me to her family. Preferably sooner than later."

Margareta pondered the propensity of Amelia's children to love at first sight, when suddenly her amusement gave way to alarm. Of course, she must do nothing to encourage Leonard to pursue even a passing interest in Fraya. For some time now, she had tried to forget that the Roth family was Jewish in case she inadvertently let the truth slip.

Her dear friend and physician Dr. Rolf Spitznagel had died, and she knew that when she too was gone, not a single soul in the townships would know of Dr. Max Roth and family's religious beliefs.

Over the years, there had never been a favourable time to disclose their faith to the German Lutherans of their community, and given the current speculation about Austria and Germany, now was certainly not it.

Realizing that she could not facilitate any kind of relationship between Fraya Roth and her great-nephew, Margareta struggled to think of a rationale. Knowing he was not easily discouraged once he made up his mind, she was at a loss. She sat in complete silence for so long that Leonard feared she was having a heart attack.

"Auntie, are you alright? Can you hear me?"

"My dear nephew, I will ask you to humour an old lady by just forgetting about the young woman you met at my door—because of a promise I made years ago to Rolf Spitznagel."

"I'm sorry, Auntie, but you have lost me. All I want to do is meet Fraya and invite her for a cup of coffee or perhaps ask her to go for supper."

"That is precisely what I am asking that you not do. Leonard, I am asking you to stay away from Fraya Roth."

"Good heavens, Aunt Margareta. You make it sound as though she is dreadfully contagious. Or does she come from a family of thieves and murderers?" Leonard chided his aunt.

"No, Leonard. Nevertheless, I must insist that you put aside any notion of courting Fraya."

"Why would you ask such a thing of me? It makes no sense at all, and if you persist with your ridiculous request, I will simply call around at the Roth residence to meet her by myself."

Thinking that desperate times call for desperate measures, Margareta accepted she must break her promise to Rolf Spitznagel, but not before extracting a new one from her nephew.

After all, intermarriage would never be an option. The two townships in Canada were still as insular as their small village in Austria had been, with people of different races, cultures, and religions not coexisting. For decades, the absolute belief was that every person living on the other side of the road allowance across from the English Methodists was German and Lutheran, certainly not Hebrew.

Margareta Mohr simply could not take the chance of unintentionally betraying the Roth family because every member had become her cherished friend.

"My dear boy, you leave me very little choice. But before I disclose the truth, I am compelled to have you take an oath—on the Bible, if necessary—that you will never breathe a word of this to another living soul."

"Oh, Auntie, now who's being dramatic?"

"Hush, and listen carefully, Leonard. In these times, what I am about to tell you is no laughing matter. Firstly, do you give me your word that you will never repeat it to anyone?"

Standing up from the chair with his left hand placed over his heart and his right resting on an imaginary Bible, Leonard said, "I solemnly swear, in the name of God, our Father, his son Jesus Christ, and the Holy Ghost, to take this information to my grave without revealing it to another human being."

"I trust you implicitly, Leonard, and I thank you for your sombre commitment. As you know, Dr. Spitznagel was our devoted physician long past the time he wanted to work. It was very difficult to convince any doctor to come to Neudorf and Lemberg during the Depression.

"For a number of consecutive years, he faithfully wrote letters to his alma mater in Austria, offering his practice to any interested graduate from the medical school. He had given up hope when Dr. Roth responded that he was eager to come to Canada. His only request was that he could also bring his parents and his sister, his nurse. They were extremely anxious to leave Austria because with the rise of the Third Reich, Maximilian Roth and his Jewish family were afraid their days would be numbered."

"Ah, and so you and the considerate doctor decided to keep the good citizens of our village in the dark, since they were at least the right colour and spoke the local language fluently?"

"It's easy to understand why you are at the top of your class, Leonard. That is precisely what we did. And if you were not so insistent, our innocent contrivance would have died with me."

"Now that is an oxymoron if I ever heard one. What a pair of rascals the two of you were. But I have met students who are of different colours, cultures, languages, religions, and nationality, and I have come to learn that we are the same, regardless of those superficial distinctions.

"In fact, now that I have become more aware, it boggles my mind that in more than fifty years these townships have only seen German Lutherans. What a drastic decision it must have been when Papa chose to purchase the Thompson's farm in the English township, because he is not a modern thinker. However, it is of no importance to me that Fraya Roth is Jewish."

"You may have hit the nail on the head regarding your father. But I am certain that he will be unrelenting about you having a relationship with a Jew."

Standing up and hugging the elderly family matriarch as he prepared to leave, Leonard jested, "But he will never know because neither of us will ever tell him."

20

Amelia was very much aware of Ursula's obstinacy and, sadly, that she was becoming more stubborn with each passing year; but it would not have occurred to her that she considered Hans Gerhart in any other light than as one of her brothers. Even when she refused to allow Ursula to accompany Leonard, Otto, and Hans to Neudorf that first Saturday evening, it was because Amelia was more worried about what the folks in town would say than of any concern for her daughter.

But when Ursula threw a tantrum that would've put the most obstreperous two-year-old to shame, Amelia's resolve weakened by the subsequent Saturday and she consented to let her go as long as her sons promised to bring her home at an acceptable hour.

Soon the four young people were rushing through their chores and bounding into Otto's car to drive to town every Saturday evening without waiting to have their supper. When Amelia asked them where they ate, they said they were always welcome at Aunt Margareta's table, or sometimes they treated themselves to a meal at Traders' Dining Room.

Neither Gustav nor Amelia thought to question whether Ursula remained in their company and thus always under their watchful eyes. Naturally, they expected Otto to spend some of his time with Millie, since they were to be married within the next two months; but they did not know that Leonard was stepping out with Dr. Roth's elder daughter. Hans and Ursula were only too happy to find themselves alone in each other's arms, very often in the dimly lit parlour of Margareta's home after eating supper with Grandmama and Aunt Katherina.

Several weeks later, on one such occasion when Katherina had gone into the sitting room to retrieve the book she'd been reading, she was surprised to find her niece on the sofa with Leonard's university friend, Hans, in what she considered a compromising position.

The two young people instantly sprung apart when they became aware of her presence, but not before a tremor of alarm flashed through Katherina's mind. She nearly spoke, when a vivid memory of David Hardy assailed her. Suddenly in the throes of profound longing, the urge was so haunting and overwhelmingly powerful that she stopped dead in her tracks. Oh, how she still yearned for the one true love of her life.

Although she tended to agree with Aunt Margareta, she felt that she had to express her displeasure to her niece, who had only recently turned seventeen. If indeed they were lovers, would either of them even listen to her, and should she bring it to Amelia's attention?

Standing still as she tried to make up her mind, Katherina was startled when Ursula leaped off the couch, kissed her cheek, and cheerfully exclaimed, "Oh Auntie, we had decided to sit for a minute after your delicious supper before we went outside for a stroll around town, and we must have dozed off. Thank you again for feeding us so well. Now we will leave you to enjoy your evening. Are you awake, Hans? Shall we go find Leonard and Otto and ask them to come for a walk with us?"

Taken aback by Ursula's quick recovery, Katherina bade them goodnight and wondered if she'd read too much into what could've been a perfectly innocent situation. After all, as far as Aunt Margareta was concerned, Ursula could do very little wrong.

For some time, Katherina wondered if she had done the right thing by keeping her mouth shut instead of following her intuition. On the one hand, she didn't want to be thought of as an interfering spinster aunt; on the other, she was still fiercely loyal to Amelia, never once forgetting how she had saved her life when David had been killed in the war.

Then when Hans and Ursula never frequented Margareta's parlour again, she began to think her imagination had run away with her as she became lost in her own long-cherished memories.

Nonetheless, for several Saturday evenings Katherina watched them leave after supper to check that they were strolling about town with either Leonard or Otto. She was well aware that Ursula was clever, but she underestimated just how devious her niece could be when she decided to be.

➤~ 21 ~➤

Sitting in the church beside Ursula as they waited for Millie to be walked down the aisle on Gustav's arm, Hans found it overwhelmingly sad that the bride had not one family member in attendance. He wondered if Millie was an orphan too, and if so, in which institution she had been raised, since she was far more confident and outgoing than he could imagine himself ever being.

Fortunately, Otto came from a large family with many aunts, uncle, and cousins who had come to the service, along with most of the townsfolk and, to everyone's surprise, Albert Schultz. Then realizing that most would also come to his wedding, his melancholy lifted.

Later, only the immediate family gathered around Margareta's table that had been generously filled by Amelia and her sister Katie. Hans hoped that after they had eaten, Ursula and he could slip away for a few moments while the rest of the family visited with the groom and his bride. Perhaps they could even rush away to their little hideaway in the grove of trees on the knoll at the outskirts of town.

When Ursula began to help her mother and aunt clear the table, Hans also stood up and started to carry dishes to the kitchen. As soon as they had a moment alone, Hans whispered that he would quietly go out the back door and wait for her to join him when she could escape without attracting anyone's attention.

He had not been outside for long when he noticed someone lurking around the corner of the spinsters' house across the street, watching the goings on at Margareta Mohr's home through the back window. Standing motionless until his eyes adjusted to the lonely street light, Hans decided it was Albert Schultz, again where he was least expected.

What did the man want, and why was he so piqued by Otto and Millie's wedding? It was perfectly clear that no one counted on him being anywhere near the festivities; yet there he was, both at the church and now, for all intents and purposes, acting like a peeping Tom.

Although Hans had not been introduced to Albert, he was told that he was Frieda Mohr's brother and that he had only recently returned to Neudorf from parts unknown after years of being gone. There was a rash of rumours about the man, not the least of which was that he had skipped town with Peter, Frieda's husband, who had abandoned his wife and young daughter in order to run away with her brother. The question now bantered about by the townsfolk was what had happened to Peter, and why had he not returned?

Not prepared to give Albert Schultz the slightest reason to snoop around and witness his liaison with Ursula, Hans promptly decided to return inside and stop her, while making a mental note to be wary of the man.

Growing up in an orphanage, if nothing else, had taught him to be vigilant about what others might be saying. Hans had never understood how any of the boys could inform on his fellow orphans when they were all in the same potentially punitive boat.

From the earliest age, Hans vowed that he would never tell tales about the other boys, even though, and perhaps because of his decision, he very often was the recipient of tittle-tattle and its consequence. Subsequently, over the years, Hans had developed the habit of being cautious when in the presence of someone he did not trust.

Quickly opening the door, he intercepted Ursula as she was making her discreet exit. Taking her gently by the arm and speaking quietly, Hans explained, "I think we must forget about our rendezvous and stay at the wedding supper. It is not a good idea to go out together right now because I spotted Albert Schultz across the street watching your family's festivities through the back window."

Without giving Ursula a chance to interrupt him, Hans continued, "What I don't understand is, if he has just returned to Neudorf, how could he even know Otto or Millie? I do not trust that man. I love you very much, Ursula, and I will not allow anyone or anything to taint our courtship."

"But I was really looking forward to having you all to myself, even for a short time," Ursula protested, as she tried to urge Hans to follow her out the door.

"No, Ursula, we must be careful about when we go to our hideaway. You know that as soon as I graduate as a pharmacist, I plan to ask your father for your hand in marriage, but we don't want anyone to know that we sometimes slip off by ourselves without your brothers chaperoning. If your parents ever found out, they would not let you come into town on Saturday evenings, and then we will never have time for just the two of us. Tonight let's enjoy the wedding party, and if all goes according to plan, we might be able to be together next week."

22

When they finally escaped to their secluded shelter among the conifer trees, things quickly got out of hand. Until then Hans had exerted rigorous control over his emotions and had always stopped their embraces from going too far, but on this Saturday evening he seemed wholly devoid of will power. He ardently yearned to make Ursula his own, and it didn't take him long before his advances were fervently reciprocated. In the back of his mind, Hans knew it was his responsibility to rein in his urges, but perhaps just this once they could be as one.

Later, as Ursula lay contented in his loving arms, Hans was abject with shame and guilt. "Oh, my darling Ursula, I am so terribly sorry. I never meant to let this happen, and I promise you that it will not occur again. Did I hurt you, and can you ever forgive me?"

"Shush, my dearest. There is nothing to forgive, Hans, because I have longed to be with you as much as I could see that you wanted to be with me."

"No, not here, not now, not sneaking around as though we are a pair of thieves, stealing what is not ours. We do belong to one another; but we must wait until we are married, and I still have two more years before I graduate from the School of Pharmacy."

Hans confided, "As it happens, Leonard and I invariably vie for the highest grades, so I will let nothing prevent me from completing my five years. And as much as I would like to marry you now, I must finish university and you must finish the last two years of high school. Then we shall have a lovely big wedding with all of your family to wish us well."

With his bright clear vision of the future, Hans abruptly stood up, bringing Ursula with him. "We must stop coming here because it is far too tempting. And, Ursula, I give you my word of honour that we will not allow ourselves to get carried away again, regardless of how much either of us longs to be with the other."

Against her protestations, Hans gently pointed Ursula in the direction of town, totally believing in the firmness of his convictions.

 **23**

"Hello, Frieda," said the man she had glimpsed stepping down onto the train platform, although she had paid him little heed. She was much more interested in determining if the new chairs she had ordered from the catalogue had finally arrived, and when he had spoken to her she nearly jumped out of her skin. Now turning to give him a thorough look, she was surprised to be staring into the face of her long-lost husband, Peter, dressed in a Canadian army uniform.

"Well, well. Look what the cat has dragged into town on a Thursday afternoon."

"You are looking very well, Frieda. I am being shipped overseas in a matter of days and was given leave to say goodbye to my mother, if she will still talk to me; but I never intended to see either Christine or you."

"I must say that I wondered when you would show up after my brother returned to Neudorf expecting everything to be the same and that he could still freeload off our hard-working parents. As it turns out, he was very much surprised to learn that since he had disappeared for so long, he had been declared dead, as were you, and you can anticipate a similar reaction from all of us. Anything you thought you owned has been liquidated to either Christine or myself. You don't have a cent to your name, unless perhaps your mother feels more kindly disposed towards you. Moreover, as far as your daughter knows, you died when she was a baby, and I will not have you suddenly turning up like a bad penny to upset her."

"I can completely understand your rancour, and I'm glad that we bumped into each other because now I can go away knowing you are better off without me. I was not the kind of husband any decent woman should have been saddled with, and it is obvious that you have landed on your feet. Please, Frieda, always remember that I did love you in my limited way, and not a day passes that I am not filled with remorse for abandoning my wife and child to run away with your selfish, mean-spirited brother. All I can do is wish Christine and you a happy life."

As Peter turned and began to walk slowly toward his mother's house, he was surprised to feel Frieda tug at his sleeve. "Good luck in the war, Peter, and thank you for telling me that you did care for me. I blamed myself for years."

"No, Frieda, it was never because of you that I left. As much as I did love Christine and you, because of some bizarre quirk of nature I just loved your brother more, and I will not make any excuses for my shabby treatment of either of you. All I dare hope is that one day you might find it in your heart to forgive me; but for now I will gratefully accept your well-wishes. If I do survive this horrific war, I would like to come back to Neudorf and see you again."

Watching him go before climbing the stairs into the station to check on her delivery, Frieda wished things could have been different. From the time Peter Mohr had been a boy, he had always been under Albert's thumb. She still did not understand what Peter meant about loving Albert more, and she did not want to know; but he had been right about her brother's character.

Now walking back to get ready for their lunch trade, Frieda hoped that Peter's mother would welcome him, because when all was said and done, he had always been a kind and loving son who simply had the misfortune of growing up with Albert Schultz.

~ 24 ~

If Otto had been averse to availing himself of her services while she was employed at Albert's place of business, he definitely had no such compunction now that she was his wife. At first Millie took pleasure in teaching her virginal husband the delights of the marriage bed; but being a quick study, Otto soon required no instruction or enticement. He was ready to exercise his husbandly prerogative at a moment's notice, and when Millie tried to warn him about the danger during the ovulatory phase of her cycle, he refused to listen.

After all, was that not the reason for their coupling, and since he wanted a large family, why would they not get started right away? Millie, on the other hand, had not the slightest inclination to have a child, and before long the newlyweds were having more than their share of quarrels.

Otto did not believe for one minute that his obstreperous wife would have curtailed her outbursts, regardless of who was in the next room, and it was not long before the eighteen-year-old began to wonder what he'd got himself into when he chose to rescue Millie from the likes of Albert Schultz.

Fortunately, Otto's mother had a calming effect on Millie, and she was on her best behaviour during meals, all of which they ate with the rest of the family. Amelia spent hours patiently trying to teach her daughter-in-law about the extensive workings of a farm kitchen and the necessity of growing a bountiful garden.

Within the short time Millie had been on the farm, it was patently clear that the only person to whom she intended to give respect was Amelia, somewhat to Otto's surprise. He had been certain she would be cowed by his father, but Millie paid Gustav little heed.

On the whole, she was also indifferent to Ursula until one evening she observed the hungry glances exchanged between Hans and her youthful sister-in-law; in an instant she knew what was likely transpiring during their evening dalliances in Neudorf. Knowing full well that the day would come when she could put her discerned information to good use, Millie decided to befriend the besotted Ursula.

So on the Thursday morning that Gustav had carried two small valises to the car, followed by Amelia and Johann, who was delighted to be the first to see his newborn cousin, Millie sprang into action. Although her list of chores was not nearly as long as Ursula's, Amelia had asked Millie to lend her daughter a hand in running the household.

However, if she played her cards right, she would not have to do much, other than maybe drying the dishes, because she knew she could give Ursula exactly what she wanted while meting out some retaliatory justice to her overbearing young husband.

Before the dust had settled from the automobile tires on the dirt road leading away from the farmhouse, Millie had asked her sister-in-law to walk with her to the garden, on the pretense of picking some lettuce for their dinner.

Millie said, "It feels like it will be another scorching day, and if we get some vegetables now, then we could relax inside the house this afternoon out of the heat of the sun."

Then as soon as they were out of earshot of the three men who would spend the morning haying, she continued, "Ah good. I think we are far enough away from the men so they can't hear us. I wanted to have a heart-to-heart with you. Ursula, I know that Hans and you are very much in love and are desperate to have just a little time to be alone together, so here is my proposal. If you agree to take care of all the household chores, which I am confident you can manage with help from Hans, I will make certain that Otto, Leonard, and I are out of your way for a few hours every afternoon or evening while your parents are visiting your sister."

"How will you do that?" Ursula asked, surprised by Millie's candour since she hardly ever took any notice of her.

"You can take care of yourself, as well as the meals, the garden, and the chickens. You don't need me, so at dinner I will ask Otto to drive me into town to visit with Albert and my friends at his tavern because I am getting bored with sitting around on this farm. I know Leonard will want to come along since it will give him a chance to see Fraya Roth. If Otto argues with me, I will simply tell him it is too hot to be out in the afternoon sun, and we will be back home in time for them to milk the cows. In the meantime, you think of an excuse for staying at home, perhaps you are not feeling well or you want to read a book, but make certain you have coaxed Hans ahead of time to volunteer to remain behind and keep you company. So, what do you say? Is it a deal?"

"Sure," said Ursula, "if you think we can get away with it, I will have no trouble doing all the chores. In fact, I will get started right now."

"Good, I will leave you to it. I am going back to bed because, for some strange reason, I feel really tired. Now remember, not a word to the men about our little arrangement. If you keep your end of the bargain, I promise that you and Hans will have time for just the two of you; although you better be busy preparing supper when we drive into the yard."

25

At first Leonard was hesitant about leaving Ursula at home alone with Hans.

It would be a blistering hot day, and Millie did have a valid point about taking advantage of driving into Neudorf in the afternoon to enjoy some refreshments at Albert's tavern. Otto did briefly wonder if Leonard's friend could be trusted around his younger sister; but if she wanted to remain at home, why not let Hans stay behind to make sure she did not get lonely.

He immediately expressed his consent, saying that he could go for a beer to quench his thirst, a habit he had become quite accustomed to since Papa had given him his old car. When it was decided and Hans agreed to dry the dishes for Ursula, they were quickly on their way.

26

Opening the door to Dr. Roth's office, Leonard was warmly greeted by Trudi, his nurse and sister, who promptly offered to go in search of Fraya. Before long, the singular object of his unexpected visit came running down the stairs.

"How nice of you to call, Leonard. I don't think you have ever come into town during the day, except on Sundays for church. I was getting ready to visit Aunt Margareta, and she will be delighted to have you join us for tea."

As the handsome young couple was about to leave, Trudi inquired, "Will we see you later, Leonard? And shall I ask Rebecca to set a plate for you at the supper table?"

"Thank you, but no. Otto and I will need to be on our way home in time to milk the cows before Hans tries to have a go at it again. The animals must realize that he is a city boy, because whenever he sits down on the milking stool, they become very frisky. Please say hello to Dr. and Mrs. Roth, and I hope to see them on Sunday."

Watching Leonard and her niece cross the street to Margareta's home, Trudi was very happy for Fraya, if not a little concerned. The Roth family was all becoming fond of the intelligent, broad-minded, and polite gentile who admitted that he had literally forced his aunt to share the secret of their true religion with him.

However, as Trudi returned to the task at hand, she apprehensively thought about Leonard's father. She was certain that she was not alone in her fear that Gustav Warner would be quite a different matter when he came to know that Fraya Roth was Jewish. The only positive outcome might be that, given Gustav's tendency to reticence, he hopefully would not spread it around the townships.

27

Without stopping to see Katherina in the General Store, Leonard and Fraya went straight to the kitchen to prepare a pot of tea and to search out what was available to munch on while they relaxed with Aunt Margareta. They found half a coffee cake, and as soon as the kettle boiled they headed to the staircase leading to the loft, where to their surprise they interrupted a man in a uniform sitting on the lower step deep in thought.

After a few moments, Leonard recognized him. "Why Peter, what are you doing here? Do you even know who I am? You've been away from Neudorf for so many years."

Lifting his head and gazing intently at his cousin, Peter replied, "Yes, hello. You are Leonard, Uncle Gustav's eldest son, and I appear to be blocking your way."

"May I introduce my friend, Miss Fraya Roth? This is Peter Mohr, Aunt Margareta's son. We will join her for afternoon tea, but why have you not gone up to see her?"

"Hello, Fraya. It's nice to make your acquaintance. Quite frankly, Leonard, I have been perched on this step for some time now, trying to muster up the courage to go see my mother. I am not sure she will speak to me after all these years, but as you no doubt noticed, I have joined the army. In three days, I will be shipped overseas. Right now I am on leave, and I had to at least try to visit her before I go to war."

"Peter, she will be delighted that you've come home, even though it's to say goodbye. Fraya, would you mind going back to the kitchen for another cup and saucer while Peter and I go up to the loft to see her?" Leonard just about commented about

Margareta's long-lost son, but he bit his tongue just in time. Leading the way, he called out, "Auntie, look who I've brought to visit you."

It was a lucky coincidence that her great-nephew had happened upon Peter and ushered him into the room, because the moment Margareta saw her son, she bristled. However, it was impossible not to feel Leonard's enthusiasm at seeing Peter. Then when Fraya arrived with a fourth cup and saucer and began eagerly conversing with him, her resistance began to subside.

When Margareta finally spoke to her wayward son, she was overcome with emotion. Realizing how much she had longed to see him at least once more, she opened up her arms for a salutatory hug. Astonished by his mother's response, Peter rushed over. Kneeling in front of her, he went into her welcoming embrace with the delight of a young boy.

It was obvious to Leonard and Fraya that mother and son were anxious to catch up, so after a rather hurried cup of tea, they excused themselves. Before long, Margareta had Peter engrossed in stories about Julia and Robert's adventures with their two highly active and bright sons, about Leonard going to university and bringing his friend Hans home to the Warner farm, and about how Fraya's father, Dr. Roth, had brought his whole family from Austria.

Indeed, Margareta was enjoying the opportunity to regale her son again, and she was not certain she wanted to know what he had been up to since he'd run away with Albert. From the accounts, Albert Schultz had not reformed. If anything, he was even more of a rascal since he'd returned to Neudorf.

At his mother's invitation Peter spent the first and second nights of his leave curled up on the sofa in the loft, not departing until the morning of the third day when he raced to catch the early train to Regina. Recognizing he would likely never see his mother again, Peter was reluctant to say goodbye, until Margareta enveloped him in an enormous hug, thanked him for coming home, and hurried him out the door, saying she did not want the army to come searching for him in the privacy of her loft.

With each passing day, she knew her life was ebbing away, and she was ready to join her beloved Phillip in God's kingdom. But for now she was blessed by being reconciled to her only son.

28

As far as her brothers knew, their sister had finished all of her household tasks while enjoying the company of a thoughtful friend who had remained behind so she would not be lonely.

Millie, on the other hand, surmised immediately what had happened between the young man and woman, and inwardly she smiled with glee for her part in bringing about their liaison. Biding her time until the next day, after dinner Millie again suggested that they spend the summer afternoon in Neudorf. Since all except Millie had rushed about completing their necessary chores, they readily agreed that no harm could come from enjoying a couple more hours of relaxation in town.

When Ursula begged off, saying that she needed to do more, Hans volunteered to stay behind and work with her. Since they assumed nothing untoward had occurred the previous day, neither Leonard nor Otto had any reason to protest. Besides, they were much too busy thinking about their own agendas.

Leonard would surprise Fraya again, and Otto was looking forward to having a couple of cold ales with Albert who, although previously standoffish, had now unexpectedly befriended him. For her part, before she had left the previous day Millie surreptitiously asked Albert to invite one or two of her favourite former patrons to her old room at the top of the stairs, on the obvious understanding that he must keep her husband duly occupied in the beer parlour.

29

Leonard had burst at the seams with joy since Fraya Roth announced that she'd been accepted into the School of Nursing and would be leaving on the same train as the two men. In fact, Hans was envious, particularly because upon Gustav and Amelia's return from Summerberry, he'd had not one minute alone with Ursula.

To make matters worse, the young people had not even gone into Neudorf for the last two Saturday evenings because Millie had felt like vomiting at any hour of the day and especially in the mornings. Otto did not think it was right to go out and leave his ailing wife, and since Leonard would see Fraya every day at the university, he did not accept Otto's offer to drive his vehicle into town.

Then. as if fortune was at last to shine upon Hans, on their final Saturday evening before taking the Sunday afternoon train to Saskatoon, Millie announced it must be time for the young people to have a night out on the town. Amelia first thought about keeping Ursula home; but on second consideration, because she'd taken such good care of everything, and particularly the garden, she relented and allowed her to accompany the rest of them.

As soon as they arrived in Neudorf, Ursula and Hans headed to the knoll on the outskirts of town, and because everyone was dispersing in different directions, no questions were asked. By now Leonard firmly believed his friend was completely trustworthy.

It was with stirrings of trepidation, however, that at the end of the evening when it came time for them to go home, Leonard had to go searching for Ursula and Hans, only to find them hastily coming out of the bushes on the periphery of town, both dishevelled.

30

How could she go back to Pheasant Forks with all those immature girls and a teacher who had clearly disliked her since her first year of schooling? Then her mother insisted that she would fix her hair in those childish pigtails.

Of course, Mama would never allow her to decide what to do with her own hair, just as she would not permit her to choose what clothing to wear. She would not even let her walk across the field to the school alone; instead Johann had to tag along. Although she loved her little brother, she hardly wanted to arrive at Pheasant Forks with him always in tow.

31

Before Mrs. Anderson could decide the correct approach to dealing with Ursula's haughty attitude, the three other girls in grade eleven took matters into their own hands.

The incident started on a Friday afternoon, just as she was about to ring the bell for dismissal. The girls, led by Rachel Doyle, grabbed hold of Ursula's pigtails and dipped them into the inkwell of the desk behind her. Before Mrs. Anderson could stop them, they reached for several others from the surrounding desks and emptied every one over Ursula's braids.

Ursula rose from her seat, and with ink spattering from her now-soaked hair, she made a hasty retreat out the door. She ran to Johann, who was waiting by the gate of the schoolyard, took hold of his hand, and quickly reached the boundary of their father's land. Then without even a backward glance, the two sauntered across the field as though they had not a care in the world.

By the time they arrived home, the ink was dry and her pigtails were irrevocably stained; Amelia had little choice but to cut off the damaged locks of hair. As Ursula finally saw the end of the dreaded braids, she smiled to herself, thinking that she might thank her classmates, until she saw the distress on her mother's face.

"Oh, Mama, I know it's upsetting you to have cut off my hair, but it will grow back, and you can still brush it for me before I leave for school in the mornings."

"Thank you, Ursula. I guess I still think of you as my little girl, and you are growing up so fast. I don't know where the time has gone, but soon you will be leaving home just like Leonard and Elisabeth, and we will only have Johann to keep us company in our big house."

32

Through diligent observation, Mrs. Anderson prevented further actions against Ursula within the classroom, but neither her husband nor she could circumvent what soon began to occur in the schoolyard, particularly by the older boys.

They would wait at the school door for when Ursula would come out for recess or after lunch. Without advancing far, she would suddenly trip over an extended leg or lose the book she was carrying. Ursula would stumble or fall almost every time she left the relative safety of the classroom; but on the day that one of the boys threw a cow pie at her, that was the last straw.

Mr. Anderson hauled the four culprits one by one into the basement and soundly strapped each of them, thinking all the while that it was good he was a sturdy man. Regardless, the pushing and shoving continued, and Ursula frequently ended up with holes in her stockings until finally her father arrived at the school one morning, wanting to know what was happening to his daughter.

When Gustav discovered that the older boys were ganging up on Ursula, he made it abundantly clear to both Mr. and Mrs. Anderson that he would tolerate no further nonsense from any student in the school. He announced that the slightest additional incident would instantly be brought to the attention of the school board, and that the perpetrator would face immediate expulsion.

Nonetheless, within days the clever offenders were back on the attack, now shrewdly limiting their actions to verbal assaults. Interestingly though, they were always beyond earshot of Johann.

The chant soon to follow Ursula around the school ground was "Go home, you dirty German. Go back with the rest of the Krauts." Mrs. Anderson, upon coming around the side of the schoolhouse one afternoon, surprised the boys and could barely believe her ears.

Without a word she turned and hurried back into the school in search of her husband to tell him what she had heard. And it was only when she found him in the basement that she realized she was trembling. Mr. and Mrs. Anderson quickly rang the school bell to start class, choosing to wait until the evening to try and come up with an answer.

They certainly could not go to Gustav Warner and apprise him of how the pupils were slandering his daughter. On the other hand, if they went to the school board, as many as half of their senior students could be expelled.

Certain that the racial slurs would not be repeated within the confines of the school, in the end, husband and wife prayed for an earlier than usual onset of winter.

Although Ursula seemed to be doing a remarkable job ignoring the taunts, they agreed that it was critical, at all costs, that Johann Warner be protected from ever being a recipient of the overt discrimination; but they could hardly keep most of the pupils indoors on the beautiful Indian summer days.

In the meantime, instead of acknowledging their awareness of the bigotry being directed at one of their students, Mrs. Anderson decided to favour Ursula by asking her to assist her with the younger boys and girls, including Johann, during all of the scheduled breaks.

Beverly Anderson thought it'd be preferable for Ursula to be called "teacher's pet" than the current names. Then Clarence would assiduously shadow the older students in the schoolyard, and together they could effectively limit the offenders' access to either Warner child.

34

Ironically, the sting from that horrible-sounding word, Kraut, cut far deeper than any bumps and bruises from being physically pushed around, and when Mrs. Anderson suddenly began to treat her with kindness, Ursula became uncharacteristically weepy.

She had always preferred to be with the younger children. Would it last, or would Mrs. Anderson just as quickly revert to treating her with the same disregard that Ursula had felt for most of her school years?

When one day became two and then three, until a full week had passed and then continued the following Monday, Ursula started to believe that Mrs. Anderson really did want her to assist with the lower-grade pupils. As Mrs. Anderson observed her most difficult student relate with tender, loving care to the little boys and girls, she began to wonder if she had seriously misjudged her.

Why, then, did Ursula feel like crying every time she was out in the school ground with a teacher she was just beginning to like? She had managed to be stoic, as Papa would have wanted her to be when the other students mistreated her; but now that Mrs. Anderson was being considerate and the little girls and boys all ran to her the minute they were outside, she seemed unable to handle their favourable attention.

Perhaps she simply was not well. When she started to run after the children in their games of follow-the-leader or hide-and-seek, she would soon tire out. Still, Ursula did not want to bother Mama with what might be wrong with her, and since she dared not ask Papa what a Kraut was, she hoped Grandmama was feeling strong enough on Sunday after church so they could have a chat.

On Sunday morning, Margareta awoke with more energy than she'd had in weeks. And when Ursula arrived at her door in the early afternoon with a tray of tea and coffee cake, she was ready to receive her granddaughter.

When they were settled comfortably in their easy chairs after Ursula poured their tea, Ursula blurted her question: "Grandmama, what is a Kraut?"

"Good heavens, child. Wherever did you hear that word, and why do you want to know what it means?"

"Please don't tell Papa, but some of the older boys in school were calling me a dirty German and telling me to go back home with the rest of the Krauts. At recess and lunchtime, Mrs. Anderson now lets me help with the younger pupils, and then Mr. Anderson walks Johann and me across the road to Papa's field, so they can't say it anymore."

"Kraut is a rather nasty nickname for a German, because we are well known for making and eating sauerkraut. I know it can be very upsetting to be called names, but the best thing you can do is simply walk away as though you have not heard them."

"It really hurt, Grandmama, even more than when they were tripping and pushing me down every time I went outside. But when Mama told Papa about all of my ripped stockings, he went to the school, and Mr. Anderson strapped every one of the four boys. It was after that that they started calling me a dirty German and a Kraut."

"Oh, my darling, you are having a bad time, and the school year has only begun.

"One evening before Elisabeth left home to marry Herbert, she and I had a big fight, and she predicted that one day I would have all this trouble at school. Oh, and the reason Mama cut my pigtails off was because my classmates had been dipping them into the inkwells."

"I wondered how you convinced your mother to let you cut your hair," said Grandmama. "Elizabeth might have said you'd have trouble because she was angry with you.

"At any rate, my dear Ursula, I want you to always remember that you are a very special person. And regardless of what anyone says or does to you, I love you like my own child. There are other names that thoughtless and cruel people might call you, such as Square Head, which is equally uncomplimentary, but if anyone ever calls you a Nazi, you must tell your Papa right away."

"Thank you, Grandmama. You have more than answered my question, and I think that we should finish our tea so I can help you back to your bed for a rest." Ursula had realized that she should wait for another day to talk to her grandmother about her fatigue and weepiness.

36

When Dr. Roth confirmed her suspicions, Millie was furious. For years her careful approach had been effective, and there were even times when she wondered if she was one of the lucky women who had been born unable to conceive.

Now, less than four months into this sham of a marriage, Millie knew she was trapped. To be certain, Otto would be delighted to be a father, Amelia would be thrilled to have another grandchild and one within throwing distance, and even Gustav and Johann would be pleased with the arrival of a baby.

All of her life Millie Brown had vowed to not be dependent on a man. Not like her mother, who had been saddled with six children. And then when her husband had taken a fancy to his young, attractive secretary, all she could do was weep in despair at being left behind while they sailed for Canada.

Fortuitously, Millie had been old enough to insist that she accompany her father who, in the end, gave her little resistance; he was so besotted with his new love that he scarcely knew she was around. Millie quickly discovered that she was as welcome as a mother-in-law on a honeymoon; but before long she had found her own friends on the university campus where her father was the newly appointed president.

She was a beautiful young woman, though, so within a short time she had a lengthy list of personal conquests, which grew steadily until she realized that with the slightest ingenuity she could turn her popularity into a tidy profit. Then and perhaps for the first time since they had arrived, her father noticed her—particularly when the board of directors of the university took him aside and told him of his daughter's disreputable activities with a host of the young male students on campus.

Since she was enrolled in no programs at the university, why was she frequenting its hallowed halls of learning? It was immediately after Millie's confrontation with her father that she left Regina, and when her money ran out, she eventually found herself at Albert Schultz's house of ill repute in the town of Neudorf.

Perhaps what had attracted Millie to Otto Warner was that he was the only man who never took advantage of the service she rendered, although he had always placed his cash on her bedside table.

But now he would pay dearly for impregnating her. She would insist that he pamper her whenever he was in her presence, and finally she could control his expectation to couple the minute they lay down in their bed. After all, he would hardly want to harm his unborn child.

Then it occurred to Millie that she must stop her return trips to her old room in Albert's tavern. If she was now found out, her husband would go on a rampage. Saddened by her decision, she realized she had come to enjoy the two or three older men who still visited her while Albert plied Otto with beer.

As far as caring for the child, Millie knew Amelia would look after the baby just as she prepared all of their meals, did their laundry, and even did the cleaning since she had moved into her house.

Several days later when Otto discovered that his mother had been cleaning their home, he demanded to know what Millie did with her time. He was promptly set straight when she angrily explained that when growing up in England there were servants to handle the domestic chores.

⟫~ 37 ~⟪

It took Amelia weeks to believe what was happening. The next morning after Ursula and Johann left for school, she asked Gustav to drive her into Neudorf, and before Katherina could open the General Store and dress shop, Amelia asked to place a telephone call to her brother Ludwig in Saskatoon.

Amelia was well aware from his brief and infrequent letters that his wife Martha constantly needed someone to assist with running his household and caring for their two children. Once she confirmed that Ludwig would take Ursula in as his hired help, Amelia walked over to the train station to inquire about the schedule to Saskatoon, before stopping to visit with Margareta for a cup of coffee.

It was not until they were driving home that Amelia explained to her husband the plan, for their younger daughter to stay with Ludwig in Saskatoon.

"Good heavens, woman, have you taken leave of your senses? What makes you think I would allow you to take Ursula out of school before she has finished grade twelve?" Gustav answered.

"Yes, yes. Ursula will finish her schooling. But Gustav, as you well know she is being mistreated in that school by both the older boys and girls, and she is making herself sick every morning over it. There is no way to change how the other pupils treat her, so the best thing we can do is tell the teachers we are taking her out of class and sending her away to another school."

"I knew they were picking on her, but I thought it had stopped after I spoke with Mr. Anderson who said he had strapped the four boys involved."

"Yes, they no longer knock her down or hit her with anything, but now they call her names, and she would be very angry if she knew I was telling you about it. Since they do not bother Johann yet, who has many more years before he finishes school, the best we can do is take Ursula away from those terrible young people. Perhaps then they'll forget about their nasty names and Johann will not suffer the same treatment." Amelia knew Gustav would not want his youngest son to be called a dirty German or a Kraut.

From years of experience, Amelia knew when she'd said enough, and she knew it would only be a matter of time before Gustav would agree with her about sending Ursula away to Saskatoon. As she waited, Amelia Warner solemnly vowed that this would be the last lie she would tell her guileless husband.

Still, she understood that they must keep this secret for rest of their lives, and before leaving home that fateful day, she entreated Ursula to take a sombre oath, which Amelia said her erring daughter must take to her grave.

The only other comment Amelia ever made when Ursula was leaving Ludwig's home in Saskatoon a week later to return to the farm was this: "You stupid, stupid girl. Whatever happens to you, always remember that you brought this entirely upon yourself."

News that first Fred, the oldest of Peter Lutz's four sons, and then, just days later, Adolph had been killed in the fighting overseas came the same week, and it hit the German communities hard. In particular, Otto Warner could not believe both young men had come to their demise in a battlefield at Dieppe. He still remembered the afternoon that the three had congenially shared a pitcher of beer.

Had he not happened upon the men in Albert's tavern, Otto would not have even said goodbye. He became so upset that he left his half-finished beer and drove home. He had grown up with the Lutz boys, and now two of them were dead, their bodies blown to bits in some faraway country.

Whatever had possessed them to leave their small farming community in the first place to fight in a war against their own countrymen? Could they have battled against and even been killed by a member of their own family, maybe an uncle or cousin? Otto wondered if his father could shed light upon why they had felt compelled to enlist or could at least comfort him about the distressing news.

When he arrived home, Otto found Gustav in the parlour listening to music from his homeland. The sound of the lyrics must have set him off, because soon he was so angry that he began shouting at his father.

"So what are we then? Germans living in an English township, or are we now Canadians? If we're Canadians, why do you only listen to German music? And shouldn't I join the army to fight for my country? Just now in Albert's tavern I heard that Fred and Adolph Lutz were both killed. And then some older men from town started to talk about whether they had been fighting for Germany or Canada."

"Please, calm down, Otto. Of course, not every young man is expected to leave his home and family to join the army. If they did, who would do the farming to raise the grain? Since the federal government has not yet brought in conscription, every man and woman in Canada still can choose whether or not to join.

"At any rate, if you recall, we are pacifists. Your grandparents left Austria and then later fled from Russia to come to Canada because they did not believe in fighting. I can assure you that no child of mine will ever go to war, although we will all work very hard."

39

Sitting on the train, staring out the window, and smiling to herself, Ursula could hardly believe her good fortune. When Mama told her that she was going to her Uncle Ludwig's, she thought she must have been hearing things, and as soon as Mama left Saskatoon, she would go to the university to find Hans. They would be together again, and then everything would be worked out. Once Hans and she found a place to live, Ursula would thank Uncle Ludwig and write Papa a letter with her new address.

Imagining how wonderful her life would soon be after two months of constant harassment in school with her horrible classmates, she drifted off to sleep. Soon she was happily dreaming that Hans was waiting at the station to take them to their little home near the university; after treating her mother to a relaxing supper in a restaurant and then delivering her to Uncle Ludwig's, they would return to their love nest arm in arm.

40

Certainly for the week that Mama stayed to visit, there was not the slightest indication of what it would really mean for Ursula to live in Martha Schweitzer's home. Her aunt was every bit as gracious to her as she was toward her mother. Her son Michael and his sister Margaret were equally polite, and although Uncle Ludwig was often away from home for his work on the railway, he remained for those days to spend time with his sister and niece.

The nightmare began the minute Amelia walked out the door with Uncle Ludwig. A few moments later, Michael and Margaret left for school and Ursula had her first introduction to the real Martha.

She was sitting on the bed in the spare room she had shared with her mother for the past week, when the door flung open and her aunt stood glowering, "Get up off that bed, gather whatever you have brought with you, and come with me to the room you will occupy now that your mother has gone."

Ursula, dumbfounded by the abrupt change in her aunt, hurriedly did as she was told. Once she had hastily thrown her few belongings into her mother's worn valise, she was ushered down to a small, dark bedroom in the basement. As soon as the door was opened, Ursula noticed bars on the window.

Hesitant to enter the damp, musty room, she was cruelly pushed into it by Martha, who handed her what looked like a maid's dress and told her to change into it before coming upstairs to start cleaning the house.

From that moment on, until Ursula finally escaped more than seven months later, she became a servant in her Uncle Ludwig's home; although, on the rare days he was home, he never seemed to notice her being treated little better than a slave.

When his wife demanded that Ursula accomplish six different things at once, he simply walked out of the room. Even when his children ordered her about or yelled because she had failed to do something to their specifications, it was as though he was blind and deaf to his offspring's complete lack of manners.

Ursula could have handled all the drudgery, and even their contempt, if she had not been locked in her dingy bedroom every night as though she was a criminal. She was permitted no time for herself other than when within her ghastly cell, and she was not allowed out of the house except to weed the big garden in the backyard while Martha sat and watched as though Ursula might make her getaway.

Suddenly the torment Ursula had experienced at Pheasant Forks School paled beside the horrid treatment she received from every person in her uncle's godforsaken home.

41

If Fraya Roth had the slightest notion of what stirred within Leonard's heart and head, she would never have confided her fears about the possible fate of her mother's family in Austria.

Now that the two young people studied in adjacent buildings on the campus, they saw each other every day, and they realized that they wanted to share the future as man and wife. What Fraya did not know was that whenever she mentioned her parents and their families, Leonard was overwhelmed with guilt and anguish.

Would she still love him if Hitler and his Nazis had persecuted and killed all of her relatives because they were Jewish? After all, he was a German, and could she always accept that he did not share the fanatical hatred of Jews, which the news broadcasts increasingly attributed to the Führer and his henchmen?

The more Leonard thought about it, the more he believed there was but one way to prove to his beloved Fraya that he was not a Nazi. As if in answer to his prayers, he came across an article in the newspaper about the Royal Canadian Air Force Elementary Flying Training School, which had been under construction during the late months of the past year in Caron, Saskatchewan, with flying training to begin on January 11, 1942.

As the idea began to ferment in his head, Leonard decided to ask Hans if he would be interested in going to the Caronport air base with him. During the past semester at the university, the two friends had begun to drift apart for a number of very sound reasons.

Firstly, Leonard now spent every spare minute with Fraya, as had been his custom with Hans during their first three years of studying. Secondly, Hans was invariably irritable when Leonard tried to engage him for a walk or a coffee; but when he asked what was eating him, Leonard was usually rebuffed.

Leonard might have been avoiding his friend ever since that terse letter had come from his father, saying that under no circumstances should he bring Hans Gerhart back to the Warner homestead; although, in typical fashion, he had provided no explanation.

Once Leonard recovered from his shock, he wrote an equally curt note to his father asking what became of his open invitation for Hans to visit "whenever he chose." Leonard still hadn't received a response from Gustav, nor had he found the courage to tell Hans that he would no longer have plans for the Christmas holiday.

When the skies opened with freezing rain the next evening just as the roommates were returning from the meal hall, they found themselves alone for the first time in weeks. It had been a surreal Indian summer day, and every student on campus had sat on the browning grass to enjoy the waning rays of autumn sunshine as soon as their classes had ended.

Cognizant of Saskatchewan weather patterns, the men decided to remain indoors.

Eager to speak with Hans before he became engrossed in his books, Leonard said, "Actually, I'm glad the weather is so miserable, because it seems we have no time to talk anymore. Aside from missing our conversations, there are some things I would really like to discuss with you."

About to respond that Leonard was to blame for that, Hans bit his tongue and decided to be more affable than he'd been of late.

"I would enjoy having one of our chats. You are quite right; we've been going in different directions this semester. I must admit that I have been more than a little envious that you are able to see Fraya every day—especially since I miss Ursula terribly. To make matters worse, although I have written to her every single week and sometimes twice, Ursula has not answered one of my letters. I can't imagine why, unless I said something that upset her before we parted. What does your father say about her, or does she write to you?"

"Hans, I'm sorry. What an insensitive boor I have been. Here I see the woman I love every day, and you have not even heard from Ursula. And to think I kept asking what was bothering you! But it's funny, now that you mention it; I have not heard from Ursula either. I don't expect her to write to me, with her schoolwork and chores, but it does seem strange that Papa has written nothing about her this year. In my next letter, if you would like, I can certainly ask Ursula to make time to respond to your letters; although it is not like her to ignore your love notes, given how she cried when you boarded the train for Saskatoon."

"What are you thinking, Leonard? You have a strange look on your face."

Wanting to think it through, but knowing he could hardly sit in front of his friend staring into space, Leonard changed the subject. "You are quite right. I have several perplexing things on my mind lately, but definitely the most important one is that I am considering leaving university and joining the Royal Canadian Air Force. An air base with a pilot training school has been established in Caron, and I wanted to ask if you might be interested in enlisting with me at the beginning of January."

"Good God, man. One minute we're talking about Ursula, and the next you're going on about becoming a pilot before finishing your studies. How can you spring such a request on me? Besides, whatever would motivate you to quit with less than two years before you graduate as a pharmacist to go fight in that bloody war?"

"You are quite right, I am distracted these days. I seem to have trouble concentrating, I think, because I'm trying to make up my mind about becoming a pilot. The truth, Hans, is that I can't tell you the real reason I feel compelled to fight against

Hitler and the Nazis except that they must be stopped, and it is as if the training school was opened just so I could join the Royal Canadian Air Force. I suppose I hoped that you'd enlist with me and thus confirm that it's the right decision."

"Stop a minute, Leonard, and think about what you are asking of me. And you won't even tell me why? Unlike you, I do not have a rich father with bushels of wheat to pay my tuition, and how would I ever reimburse the orphanage if I quit before I graduate?"

Only stopping long enough to catch his breath, Hans continued.

"All of that aside, I have no interest in giving up my life for people who have never done a thing for me. For as long as I can remember, I have spent my days fending for myself, until I met you. You and your family are the only people who have ever treated me with any respect and kindness.

"Now you have brought up the other thing that is weighing heavily on my mind. Some time ago I received a letter from Papa telling me not to bring you home to the farm this year for Christmas; although, as is characteristic for him, he gave no reason. I hadn't told you yet because I wrote back to him demanding to know why, knowing how much you would want to see Ursula."

"Aren't you the fount of good news today, my loyal friend," said Hans. "You have no idea how I yearn to be with Ursula. I love her with my heart and soul, and you drop a bombshell like that? If I can't go home with you, where in God's name will I see her, and when? Come to think of it, I remember your father telling me I was welcome in his home at any time, so what caused him to do such an about-face?"

Hans stood up and grabbed Leonard by his shoulders.

"This is precisely why I was waiting for Papa's answer before telling you. I don't understand it either; but don't forget that I am on your side, Hans."

"Sure you are," said Hans. "With my luck, I'll probably never see either Ursula or you again. As it happens, I don't have an illustrious history of people staying in contact with me. Now all I can do is hope that Ursula will wait until I graduate, and then I will go to the farm to ask your father for her hand in marriage."

"Actually, the solution is obvious, Hans," said Leonard, in his most convincing voice. "Join me in the first class for the pilot training, and we will be in the same squadron where we can look out for each other. I'm certain this interminable war will soon be over, and then we can return to university to finish our degree."

Experiencing an overwhelming sensation of dread, Hans fervently appealed to his only friend. "I don't have a good feeling about you becoming a pilot and going to war, Leonard. Seriously, please reconsider and stay here at the university with me."

For several weeks Hans had been restless and anxious, which he attributed to a sensation that all was not well with Ursula, but he had consistently chosen to ignore his emotions. Once or twice he considered talking to Leonard and asking him to telephone his Aunt Katherina in the store to check that nothing had happened to Ursula, but each time he chided himself for being foolish.

If anything had been seriously wrong with his sister, Leonard would have told his friend and roommate, because he knew Ursula was his one true love. Still, he continued to have a nagging feeling that something had befallen Ursula, until one night Hans awakened in a cold sweat, having dreamt that she was trapped in a cavern deep under the ground. Try as he might, he had been unable to reach her and bring her to safety, and even when the disturbing dream returned night after night, he did not consider that perhaps his subconscious mind was trying to spur him into action.

42

In the loft of her home in Neudorf, Margareta Mohr was asking for Ursula. Since autumn, she had been confined to her bed, and when her "granddaughter" had abruptly stopped her weekly Sunday visit, she wanted to know why. For the first time in all the years she had known her, Margareta suspected Amelia was not being entirely honest with her.

During their next visit Margareta would get to the bottom of what was transpiring with Ursula by talking to her nephew. So the minute she sent Amelia down to the kitchen to make a fresh pot of tea, she came right to the point. "I want to know why you have sent Ursula to stay with her Uncle Ludwig in Saskatoon, Gustav, when you could have straightened out the situation with the teachers or with the school board."

"Oh, Aunt Margareta, I'm sure Amelia has told you how unhappy Ursula was and that we had to find somewhere else for her to finish her schooling. Between you and me, I have my reservations about how Ursula will make out in Saskatoon. And as you might be aware, Amelia wears the pants in our family, although I would appreciate you keeping that bit of information to yourself."

Bursting into laughter, Margareta replied, "I could have told you that years ago, and I am surprised at myself for bothering you about it. Nonetheless, I want you to promise me that you'll bring Ursula to see me at Christmas when she comes home. I have something I want to give to her. I have been saving it for a long time, and it is meant to help her to become a nurse."

43

Christmas 1941 came and went with Margareta impatiently awaiting the arrival of her cherished Ursula. Certainly she did not lack for visitors, and she fortunately felt well enough to enjoy Julia, Robert, and her two robust grandsons when they came for an extended three-week holiday because Dr. Cameron desperately needed a rest from his busy practice.

Then Margareta considered herself truly blessed when Katherina came running up the stairs to say she had received a telegram saying that Peter had been wounded in the war so he would be coming home in time for the Christmas festivities.

Still, she waited. And three days before Christmas when Leonard arrived to greet her with neither Ursula nor Hans in tow, Margareta was distressed and more than a little surprised.

"My dear boy, how nice it is to see you. I must tell you how I appreciate that I'm always the first person to welcome you home on your return from the university. And where did you leave Ursula and Hans? Have they stopped at the store to visit with Katherina, or have they already gone for their customary stroll on this mild winter day?"

"Hello, Aunt Margareta. You are looking very well, and I am happy that you are awake to receive a visitor.

"Unfortunately, Hans could not come to the farm this Christmas, so just Fraya and I rode the train home. As for Ursula, I'm sure Johann and she are on their way into town with Papa. You thought Ursula would be with us?"

"Yes, Leonard. Ursula is not at home. She was having so much trouble at Pheasant Forks School that in mid-November your mother decided to take her to Saskatoon on the train. I am astonished that she has been at your Uncle Ludwig's home—within ten blocks of the university—for the past six weeks, and you didn't even know about it."

"I'm sorry, Auntie, but you must be mistaken. Neither Hans nor I have heard anything about Ursula being in Saskatoon, and you can bet that if he knew she was, Hans would have gone at once to see her. As a matter of fact, just a few weeks ago he was lamenting that Ursula had not answered a single one of his weekly letters, which now makes sense since he always addressed them to the farm."

Now it was Margareta's turn to question her great-nephew's state of mind. "Leonard, surely you are chiding me. Enough! If she is hiding outside the door, you can please ask her to come in and finally give her grandmama a big hug and kiss."

44

It was obvious that Aunt Margareta knew what she was talking about, so what was going on at the Warner homestead? If Mama had decided to take Ursula to Saskatoon as Auntie said, why in heaven's name had Papa not written him about it so he could help to make her feel at home in the city? She had to have been lonely living with an aunt and uncle she barely knew, having probably met them only once or twice in her life.

Why had Ursula not come to the university to see Hans and him? Or at least called them on the student telephone in the residence? She must have wanted to visit with them. And even if Mama and Papa forbade her, it was not like her to submit, especially from so far a distance. And why had she not come home for Christmas with him? With many more questions than answers, Leonard realized he must immediately tell Hans about Ursula's whereabouts. He was on the verge of dashing down the stairs to telephone him from the General Store when Julia pushed open the door carrying a tray filled with delectable-smelling food.

"Hello, Leonard. I happened to see you go flying up the stairs, so I made sure we'd have enough dinner for you. Sorry, Mother, that it took me longer, but I am only too familiar with the appetites of hungry young men."

As he greeted his cousin, Leonard realized he should ascertain what was transpiring at home before getting in touch with Hans.

After all, he was about to be the bearer of very distressing news. Perhaps he should not upset his parents before he had a chance to talk with them. From the day he'd received his letter of acceptance from the Royal Canadian Air Force Flying Training School, he'd decided to wait until after Christmas Day before telling them he was leaving the university to become a pilot.

Once Fraya accepted that he was determined to go to war, they discussed the possibility of Leonard staying with her parents in the event that his father was so angry that he threw him off the farm before it was time to leave for Caronport. The Elementary Flying Training was scheduled to commence January 11, 1942, and Leonard would need to inform his parents before the end of the year. Otherwise he would not be able to explain why he was not returning to Saskatoon for the start of the next semester.

Margareta asked Julia to return to the kitchen for more coffee cake before continuing.

"Alright, Leonard. What is this all about? I might be too old to get out of this bed, but I can still smell a red herring as quickly as the next person. I want to know why Ursula would have been sent to Saskatoon without our knowledge and now has not come home for Christmas."

"Please, Aunt Margareta. I am as anxious as you are to get to the bottom of this mystery. As soon as I find out, be assured that you will be the first person I report to."

Over the next two weeks he would return to visit her time after time, but he could only shake his head when pressed about their common concern for Ursula. He shared his frustration about not getting a straight answer from his parents; he said they were like talking to a stone.

Their silence prevailed in relation to Ursula and was then overshadowed by the conveyance of Leonard's drastic decision, which brought forth the opposite response. During his entire stay in the home of his childhood and youth, not another word was spoken about Ursula.

45

The ride to the farm had been a dreary affair. It actually started the minute Papa and Johann had bustled into Margareta's loft without Ursula. Although Leonard was now prepared for her absence, it was still a shock.

Then his father was in a hurry, certain a storm was coming. He did not want to wait for coffee. After a quick embrace, Johann had little to say, like usual.

Leonard gathered his suitcases and followed them to the vehicle, which was parked in front of the General Store. When Leonard told his father he wanted to stop and say hello to Aunt Katherina, his only rejoinder was, "Be quick about it."

Once they were all in the car, Leonard did try to make conversation, alternately with Johann and Papa, but when he received only monosyllable responses from both, he too fell silent. He could not remember such a dismal homecoming, but then he realized that it had always been Ursula's excitability that set the tone for merriment.

When he was at home and his parents maintained their reticence about Ursula, except for the unsettling disclosure that she would not be home until the end of the school year, Leonard realized he would likely not see Ursula again before being sent overseas.

If not nerve-wracking enough that he had to tell his parents about the unusual path he would take, he now had to come to terms with how he could explain it all to Ursula in a letter. At least if she'd been at home, they could have talked. He would have hugged her as she wailed out her sorrow before walking arm in arm around the farm as they had when she was younger and upset about one thing or another.

Leonard thought of going to Saskatoon before going on to the training school; but last month when he purchased his ticket home with the money Papa had sent to him, he used the balance to buy a one-way train ticket to Caronport.

Knowing he would not receive another cent from his father after telling him about becoming a pilot, Leonard went for a long walk across the fields, trying to think of the words to write to Ursula. If Fraya had not been so distressed about his departure, he would have asked her to help, but she vacillated between being furious and then pleading with him to change his mind. Chances were that she would ask Ursula to assist in knocking some sense into her brother's thick head rather than attempting to help her to accept his sudden and unnecessary choice.

Then because he did not want to put it off, on his second day at home he chose to write her the truth as gently but succinctly as possible, hoping she could eventually accept his decision and still love him as her favourite older brother.

After reading and rereading the letter several times, he painstakingly wrote out the final copy and sealed it in an envelope, which he placed in the inside pocket of his suitcase. Leonard planned to ask Aunt Katherina to mail the epistle the day he departed by train for Caronport.

~ 46 ~

As the week before Christmas unfolded, Leonard was glad he had written Ursula's letter and tucked it safely away. Whatever had befallen the Warner homestead, it had created an atmosphere that was incredibly tense. Mama had been delighted to see Leonard; but then she became very quiet, speaking in hushed tones as though afraid of waking a sleeping baby.

After two or three meals with Otto and Millie, Leonard began to understand why. The two of them could hardly be civil to each other, and practically everything would set Millie to complaining.

True, the woman was heavy with child, but he remembered when Mama was carrying Johann. She certainly had not behaved so atrociously or Papa would surely have had something to say about it. For his part, Otto only seemed intent upon wolfing down his supper and getting to the parlour as quickly as he could to listen to the radio.

Still, it did not explain the heavy sadness that seemed to permeate the walls of the house. Fortunately, as soon as Millie had eaten her fill, she would yell for Otto and wearily trudge home supported on his arm. If it was possible, Papa was even more silent and more engrossed in his phonograph than before. And now Johann always had his nose buried in a book, never saying boo unless he was spoken to, and sometimes not until the second or third time.

But the person most noticeably changed was Mama. Naturally she had to miss having neither of her daughters at home, especially when Millie was such an unpleasant substitute. Although she assiduously went about her preparations, baking and cooking, it was clear her heart was not in it. Initially, Leonard had considered inviting Fraya to join them for dinner; but he soon thought better of it, deciding to wait until he had returned from the war and they were married instead of letting her believe that Christmas was the cheerless event it was shaping up to be this year.

The longer Leonard was at home, the more he dreaded what lay ahead of him. He had moments when he actually thought he had told his parents. Then at the last minute Elisabeth and Herbert decided that with the unusually mild winter weather, it would be reasonably safe to bundle the baby onto the train and arrive at the homestead the day before Christmas.

Their unexpected homecoming saved Christmas Day. Again there were sounds of talking, laughter, and an infant's cries arising in the kitchen, even if the men sat in their sullenness transfixed to the sounds of the radio. Soon Leonard decided to remain at the table, chatting with his mother and sister and holding Emma while Elisabeth helped Mama prepare the meals and wash the dishes.

It was comforting to cuddle a child as he had when Johann had first come along. But the serenity that again appeared on Mama's face delighted Leonard more than anything. Gazing upon her loving countenance, her eldest son suddenly realized that the only human being to definitively restore the joy in his mother's eyes was a baby.

It had been three days since Christmas, and Gustav had just arrived home after returning Elisabeth and her family to the train station. Leonard knew the time had come; he could not postpone his news any longer. After dinner, before his father could drift off to sleep while listening to the gramophone, he asked him to accompany him on a stroll about the farm.

At first Gustav was ready to protest, but something about his son's demeanour made him change his mind.

"What is the matter, Leonard? You have been as fidgety as a penned-up animal ever since you have come home."

"As it happens, Papa, I have an important decision I must speak to you about, and my time is running out. I prefer to talk it over with you first, before I tell Mama. And since the weather is cooperating, I would find it easier if I could tell you outside." He knew that he'd only have the courage to say what he had to say when outdoors, surrounded by the peace and energy of nature.

Stifling a yawn, Gustav gathered up his coat and hat before telling Amelia that he was joining Leonard on another stroll about the pasture and the frozen creek bed. With any luck, he planned to be back within the hour, and he would need warm coffee when they did so.

Waiting until they were beyond the view of the kitchen window and well out of earshot of the house, Leonard came straight to the point.

"Papa, I will not be returning to Saskatoon and the university. Rather, in early January I shall go to Caron, Saskatchewan. I have recently joined the Royal Canadian Air Force, and I start pilot training on the eleventh of the month."

"I know where Caron is, and there is no air force training school in that little town. I have paid for your university up until the end of this year, and then you have another year of studies before you become a pharmacist; so it will be awhile before you can think about being a pilot. By that time, you better hope the war is over, because you will not go to fight against your homeland."

"In case you have forgotten, Papa, Canada is my native country," said Leonard. He was surprised by his father's comment, and was not sure he still considered Germany his homeland. At least Gustav had not said "the Fatherland," which would have really alarmed him. But what did he know about how his father felt about Hitler and the Nazis and what they were doing to the Jewish people in Europe?

"When I have qualified as a pilot, no doubt I shall be sent overseas to fight with the Allied Forces."

"Young man, you better think about what you are saying. As long as I am paying your way, you will do what I tell you, and don't you ever take that tone with me again. Your grandfather fled with the clothes on his back to bring his family to Canada so that none of us would have to go to war. So as a matter of fact, in a few days you will take the train back to Saskatoon to finish your studies. You will not get one cent from me to go to Caron."

"Don't worry, Papa. I already figured that out, and I will not be asking you for any more money."

"You stupid, stupid boy. What do you know? If you want to give up your life so quickly, then leave. Just go. Get out of my sight. Get off my land...."

Gustav stopped dead in his tracks with déjà vu. It could not be happening again. First Mathias, who must be dead since no one ever heard from him, then Jurgen Kuss, who was apparently killed his first day of battle, and now Leonard. No, no, no. He would not doom his first-born to the same fate.

Shuddering, Gustav forced himself to recover, knowing he could not allow history to repeat itself again. With as much composure as he could muster, Gustav tempered his words.

"Look, son. It has nothing to do with money and everything with risking your life by going to fight for something that does not concern you. You have your whole future ahead of you, and you won't have to work nearly as hard as I do to make a living once you have finished your education."

48

Leonard's common sense prevailed. He decided that since he had absolutely no knowledge about Papa's feelings toward Jews, he should present his case in general terms.

"I remember as a little boy how you always told us you felt compelled to be a farmer, that you knew from the time you could talk you would follow in your grandfather's and father's footsteps and work the land. As much as I enjoy my studies at the university, I have never desired to be a pharmacist. Papa, I agreed to study at the university to please you; although I can certainly appreciate that higher education could be the means to a successful life. However, when I heard the call to join the Royal Canadian Air Force, I was seized by the notion of becoming a pilot, in a way that I have never been before about anything."

"That would be all good and well, if you were just learning to fly an airplane; but once the Air Force has trained you, you will be sent overseas as a fighter pilot, and then you can rest assured that you will not be the only one dropping bombs and attacking from the sky. Do you even listen to the radio or read the newspapers about what this war is like?"

"Good Heavens, Leonard. You could be blown to bits and never know what hit you, and this is what has gripped you for your future? Where in God's name did you ever learn about wanting to fight and kill other human beings, and what are you planning to tell your mother?"

"I don't expect you to understand, Papa, but it is my destiny. Do you think I have come to my decision lightly? Without regard for the consequences and how it will affect all of my family?"

With a derisive laugh, Gustav answered, "I can hardly wait to hear what you will tell her, since, if anything, you will likely put her in her grave with your foolhardy decision."

In the days to follow, during his or her innumerable attempts to convince Leonard to change his mind, Gustav would yell until anyone within a mile from the farm could hear him, and Amelia would sob with abject sorrow, until her eyes were perpetually red. His father could not stop his shouting any more than his mother could cease her crying.

In the end the only place where Leonard could find any peace was with Aunt Margareta who, knowing the truth about his compelling need to rid the world of Hitler and the Nazi Party, could accept that he must join the Allied Forces.

Of course, she feared the ultimate consequence of her great-nephew being a fighter pilot to an equal extent as Gustav and Amelia; but because of her heart-rending conversations with Dr. Roth and his family, she was beginning to grasp the malevolence of the Nazi regime against the Jewish people.

49

She quickly learned the truth when she accidentally dropped a porcelain vase while dusting it. Ursula had been told countless times, actually screamed at because of it, that she was like a bull in a china shop and she needed to be careful when cleaning Martha's treasures.

Before she knew it, her aunt slapped her across the face, knocked her to the floor, and began kicking her arms and legs until she was finally able to struggle back to her feet.

With more contempt than usual, Martha shouted, "Clean up this mess right now, you stupid, clumsy girl. And don't you dare touch any of my precious ornaments again. Then get into the kitchen to make supper."

It was not until she was safely in her room much later in the evening that Ursula saw the dried blood on her left foot. She must have stepped on a piece of the broken china, but she had been so shocked by her jailer's physical outburst that she'd not noticed or even felt the injury.

After pouring water into the basin, she carefully washed the wound and checked to make sure that no glass was left in her foot. Before crawling into the comfort of her bed, Ursula went to the only other piece of furniture in the room, an old beat-up dresser that housed her few belongings, and found a small cloth to wrap around the cut.

Since she was only allowed to wash her linen once a month, she did not want the sore to bleed on the sheets during the night. After she had washed her body and taken note of the many areas that were already showing purplish bruising, she lay down on her bed, curled into a ball, and cried herself to sleep.

Although the next time Martha struck her Ursula was not as surprised, she was still unable to stay on her feet. Strangely, though, whenever her aunt was striking her, she became silent. Ursula could never predict when a beating was imminent because violent verbal outbursts bookended the physical abuse.

Before long her face and her extremities were discoloured by various stages of bruising. It seemed that once Martha Schweitzer had crossed the boundary into physical abuse, she relaxed into the idea of knocking her niece about, almost revelling in her viciousness.

To make matters worse, Margaret sometimes joined her mother in the beatings. The two men in the household seemed oblivious to Ursula and her plight, unless of course their meal was not on the table on time.

Soon Ursula longed to be locked in her bedroom at night; at least there she would not be kicked around, given that she had completed every bit of drudgery expected of her that day. But there soon arrived many nights when Martha would unlock the door, haul her out of bed, and make her rewash a floor or polish the silver again because it was not up to her standards.

Every night before succumbing to an uneasy sleep, Ursula ranted at Mama for abandoning her to such a wicked and ill-tempered woman.

50

Leonard kept putting off writing the letter to Hans to tell him about Ursula being in Saskatoon. In the ensuing turmoil at home, he would begin a note to his friend, but then he would wonder what had occurred to turn his father against the man who had saved his youngest son's life.

If only he'd been thinking straight, he'd have dredged up the truth before disclosing anything about his situation to his parents. Now he had neither the presence of mind nor a desk upon which to jot down the essential details in a letter.

It was no better when he went to visit Fraya because she wanted to spend every available minute with him before she left for Saskatoon. She had little understanding about him wanting to do something without her now that he'd have plenty of time to do so once she was gone. Fraya made an excellent point when she said that Leonard had another week at home before going to Caron, and he could just as easily post the letter then as have her deliver it to Hans.

So Leonard waited and wrote the epistle two days after Fraya tearfully climbed aboard the train for Saskatoon after clinging to him until the last minute, vowing to see him again.

He planned then to ask Aunt Katherina to mail his letter to Ursula on the morning of his own departure. From the instant Katherina saw the two letters together, she predicted their contents, and as much as she loved all three of the young people, she could never bring herself to betray her sister-in-law and her most trusted friend.

Katherina Werner eventually chose to place both letters in the bottom of her bedside table, where she would completely forget about them and they would remain until her death.

⇒~ 51 ~⇐

It became clear that Leonard could not learn more about nor change his younger sister's situation, and Margareta lost all hope of seeing Ursula again. The day Leonard boarded the train to Caron spelled the beginning of the end for Margareta Mohr.

Through the sheer force of her indomitable will, she had lived for Ursula's homecoming at Christmas, but now there was no purpose in prolonging the inevitable. She was tired, she was worn out, and she wanted at last to be with her beloved Phillip; she could not possibly hold on until the late spring when Amelia finally announced that Ursula was expected to return.

When her time drew near, Margareta asked her niece to drive to the Warner homestead and to bring Amelia to her. Realizing the urgency behind her aunt's appeal, Katherina hurriedly left Christine in charge of the store and returned within the hour with Amelia at her side.

Although the tone of her voice revealed little of her frail condition, Margareta feebly motioned with her right hand, first to Katherina, and said; "Come sit beside me one last time, my dearest."

As her niece hastily complied, the elderly woman said, "My darling Katherina, I have loved you as though you were my own flesh and blood, and you are as precious to me as my only daughter. I cannot begin to thank you for taking care of me all these years; but please do not grieve for me when I have at last passed, because I want to go. I am eighty-nine years old, I have had a good long life, and I yearn to be with your Uncle Phillip. Promise me that you will always look after yourself. I'm sure that you will follow in my footsteps, no doubt living to a ripe old age. I do have one final request, Katherina, before I kiss you goodbye. Could you reach under the foot of my bed and please hand me the small black box. And could you ask Amelia to please come over to my bedside?"

When Katherina was slowly released from the elderly woman's embrace, she fought back the tears. She knew her aunt had endured agonizing arthritic pain for several years. Not trusting herself to speak, Katherina found the black box, gave it to her aunt, and waved Amelia toward Margareta before making a swift retreat from the loft to sob her heart out in private.

When Amelia leaned over to hug Margareta, she too had difficulty restraining the flow of her tears. But her beloved aunt quickly stopped them when she grasped her arm and pleaded, "Amelia, how could you not let Ursula come home for Christmas? You surely realize that I am dying. The reason I have hung on this long was to visit with her one last time. I never thought you could be so unkind—you know that Ursula is like a granddaughter to me."

Taken aback by the accusation, Amelia was momentarily speechless, not that she could provide an acceptable answer. Realizing that her best recourse was to not respond, she waited until her aunt spoke again.

"No, I didn't expect that you would tell me, but now I will hold you to a promise that you will keep if you don't want me to haunt you for the rest of your days. In this strongbox, there is a considerable amount of cash that I have saved over the years for Ursula. It is not to be opened or touched by anyone other than her, and on my deathbed, I want you to vow that you will respect my wishes. Now can you give your word that you will do precisely as I ask?"

"Oh, Auntie," said Amelia, "please don't be cross with me. I can't say why Ursula did not come home for Christmas, but I can promise you that I will take your gift to her. I shall hide it until I can go to see her, and I won't tell another soul, even Gustav, about the box. And please believe me that it was not my doing that she stayed in Saskatoon."

Brightening briefly, Margareta said, "Ah, now I see. There was someone more important for her to visit than her old grandmama." She paused for a moment.

"Well, if that's true, then I have done you an injustice by blaming you for Ursula's decision. I'm sorry, Amelia. Come and hug me before you fluff up my pillows. I feel very tired, and I just want to sleep while you sit by my bedside."

For a woman who had been so verbose and, on a good many occasions, remarkably outspoken, Margareta Mohr went to her grave quietly and with little fanfare. She drifted into a comatose state, with Amelia stroking her hand and humming softly to her as she had years ago when she put one of her babies down for the night.

It must have been in the wee hours of the morning when Margareta stirred. Tenuously touching Amelia's hand, her last words were barely audible.

"Oh, Ursula, my darling girl, I knew you would come to me before I departed. I love you and I will be with you always."

Amelia took quite some time to realize that Margareta was gone; but once she did, she decided to remain respectfully by her bed until the dawn heralded the beginning of a new day. There was little point in waking Katherina and disturbing her sleep when the only thing she could do was alert Dr. Roth.

Amelia was surprised and perhaps even a little displeased that she had been mistaken for Ursula. It was her granddaughter for whom Aunt Margareta called with her dying breath.

 52

Would it never end? How had women throughout the history of mankind endured such pain, and why would any female give birth to a second child?

Millie had laboured for only a few hours, Amelia by her side all the while, before she asked Otto to drive to Neudorf and return with Dr. Roth and his nurse. Amelia vividly remembered the delivery of her firstborn, and she wondered if Millie was experiencing the same problem, the baby's bottom coming out before his head, as when she was birthing Leonard.

However, when they arrived and Dr. Roth had completed his examination, he assured them that everything was as it should be, and with due passage of time, Millie would deliver. Suggesting that Otto take the doctor and his sister down the lane to her house, Amelia said she had left a freshly brewed pot of coffee on the back of the stove and a poppy-seed cake in the pantry.

She knew that Dr. Roth and Trudi would wait until her daughter-in-law was ready; but Amelia was highly embarrassed not only by Millie's screaming but also by her choice of words, neither of which had been heard before on the Warner homestead. Even amid Millie's barrage, Amelia could only wonder where she could have learned such language.

Fortunately for the entire family, Millie birthed a baby girl—Amelia's second granddaughter within a relatively short period of time. When Dr. Roth noted that she'd actually been blessed with a relatively easy labour and smooth delivery, Millie retorted that she'd decided to put an end to her agony by simply pushing the baby out of her body.

Then Millie was equally abrupt with Trudi who tried to put her newborn to her breast, saying she would have none of that and that she had better find another way to feed it, before she promptly fell into a deep sleep. Amelia could not begin to fathom how this poor infant would receive her sustenance, when the compassionate Dr. Roth brought forth a small, glass bottle with a nipple attached to it.

"I always carry one of these in my medical bag just in case a mother is unable to feed her baby, although I must admit that Millie is the first who would not even give her babe a chance to suckle at her breast."

"Thank you, Dr. Roth. I have some milk in the cold storage room in the basement, and if you or Trudi will please tell me what to do, I will make sure that this child is fed."

Carrying Millie's baby securely in her arms did feel strange after all these years of not holding an infant so small. Amelia, with babe, quietly closed the bedroom door and she and Trudi walked back to her house.

Trudi told Amelia that the nipple, bottle, and milk must all be boiled and the milk poured into the sterilized container. Then she assured her that on the morrow, when her brother returned to check Millie and her baby, she would send another five or six bottles with him. Once she had supervised Amelia's efforts and determined that the baby would suckle the bottle, Trudi left to join Dr. Roth by his automobile where he waited for her.

While Millie was still sound asleep, he had taken Otto aside and encouraged him to bring their baby to his wife as soon as she awoke to ensure that they would begin to form a bond. But for the balance of the day, Max pondered Millie's total lack of interest in her baby.

53

As he entered the kitchen, he found Rebecca busily preparing supper.

"I'm so glad that you are alone. I have to get something off my chest, and I don't want to talk about it in front of the rest of the family. Millie did not even look at her beautiful baby girl before she turned over and went to sleep. Had it not been for Amelia, I may have been forced to bring the infant home."

Rebecca took a moment before responding.

"I'll admit that my first thought was about how nice that would have been; but I can see you are clearly distressed, so I shall be serious. If Millie had a prolonged labour and a difficult delivery that wore her out, I can certainly understand her overwhelming need for sleep. I'm not sure that any man, even you, my dear husband, really knows how taxing birthing a baby is for the new mother."

"That's just it," said Max. "Millie had the easiest and shortest delivery that I have attended in my entire medical career. It was as though she said 'enough' and then, as she expressed it, she pushed it out as if the baby was an intruder. I tell you, my dearest, I honestly don't think Millie would care if her healthy baby girl starved to death."

"Oh, Max, that is disturbing. Thank God then for Amelia. And hopefully by tomorrow Millie will feel differently and want to look after her baby. I'm sure Otto is excited to have a daughter, since every time I've seen him lately, all he could speak of was becoming a parent."

Then, as though thinking out loud, Rebecca said, "What do we really know about this young woman, other than that she used to work for Albert Schultz?"

Mentally he agreed with his wife, but he dared to hope she was wrong. "I do think you might be right," he said, "and by the time I return to the Warner homestead tomorrow, I will find Millie happily cuddling and nursing her baby girl."

54

The next morning before Dr. Roth started off to see his new patients, he stopped at the General Store to purchase several of the glass baby bottles that Katherina had begun to stock on the shelves. When he arrived at Otto and Millie's house at the top of the lane, he could hear shouting the minute he turned off the motor of his vehicle.

Instead of getting out he drove down the treed road to confer with Amelia and obtain an update on what was happening. He hoped, for the baby's sake, that the infant was still with her grandmother. He was astonished when Amelia told him that both Otto and his newborn had spent the night with them and that Millie had just awakened now. The rest of the family had been up every two or three hours during the night, and Millie had slept almost fifteen hours. In fact, Otto had just gone to his own home to take his wife breakfast and to speak to her about caring for their child.

During the days and weeks to come, every member of the Warner family, including Johann who was enthralled with his niece, tried to persuade Millie to take an interest in her infant, to no avail. Dr. Roth, thinking that she might be depressed, arranged for Trudi to accompany him on a consultation, although he came to agree with his sister that the new mother seemed perfectly happy so long as she was not required to be near her baby.

When Millie even refused to select a name for her daughter, it became sadly obvious to all that she had no inclination to be a mother. So it was Otto and his mother, with generous input from Johann, who decided to call the contented baby girl Francis, in time for her baptism.

During this ceremony, perhaps under one threat or another, Otto coaxed Millie to hold her baby while the Reverend sprinkled water on the infant's head. Still, even the many compliments about her beautiful blond-haired and bright-blue-eyed child did not keep Millie in the church until the end of the service.

But with Amelia's early gentle and loving care, Francis would fare so much better than either of her two younger sisters. For when Millie gave birth to Faye within fourteen months and then to Darlene just seventeen months later, Otto finally ordered his wife to mother their daughters... perhaps to their detriment.

Every night as he was falling into an exhausted sleep after hours of intensive training from dawn to dusk, Leonard vaguely wondered why neither Ursula nor Hans had answered his letter. Since they had not parted on the best of terms with Hans continuing to dissuade him from going to Caronport, he could understand why his friend had not yet corresponded, but what would be stopping Ursula from dropping him a line.

As the days became weeks and he still did not receive a letter from his sister, he found himself becoming irritated. Leonard knew he could write to her again, since he did have Uncle Ludwig's address in Saskatoon. But perhaps because of fatigue, he stubbornly refused to do so until hearing back from her.

When he'd first arrived at Caronport and been directed to the major's office, he was pleased when informed that because of his university education he would be conferred with the commission of captain.

However, the requirements for officer training were much more demanding than for the rank and file. There was so much to master, from learning the primary skills of flying a 56 DeHavilland Tiger Moth biplane training aircraft, to being in charge of the crew of his airplane and dropping bombs on people who shared his heritage, a detail he kept carefully concealed within his heart and mind.

Perhaps his father had been right after all. But whenever this thought crossed his mind, it only heightened his resolve. Soon he became so focused that he no longer worried about either his father or his sister, and with perseverance and dedication, by the end of April 1942, Leonard Warner became a member of the first class to graduate as pilots from the Elementary Flying Training School at Caronport, Saskatchewan.

At the beginning of May, Gustav drove Amelia to Neudorf to board the late afternoon train to Saskatoon. Amelia had hoped to sleep for most of her journey, but a profound sense of foreboding allowed her no peace of mind.

How would she ever tell Ursula that her grandmama was dead, much less explain why she had not permitted her to come home for her funeral? Anticipating that her daughter would take a long time to forgive her, Amelia felt in her valise for the small black box that she had promised to deliver. She was certain that its contents would help, but Ursula would still be furious that she'd not been able to see her grandmama at Christmas.

Amelia had actually expected her daughter to write to her father and plead with him to come home with Leonard during his break from school, when it occurred to her that Ursula had not written to any of them since leaving home. This thought heightened Amelia's impending dread.

What was happening with her children? Except for Elisabeth, and Johann who was too young to make his own decisions, they had all chosen distressing paths, possibly even deadly in Leonard's case.

Otto had impetuously married a woman about whom they'd known nothing, and their grave misgivings were confirmed when she wanted nothing to do with her own baby. It was fortunate that Katherina had agreed to come to the farm to help Otto and his little brother take care of Francis while Amelia was gone; otherwise she might have had to travel with the baby.

Leonard's decision to leave university and fight in the war as a pilot was beyond her grasp. Then of course there was all the heartache caused by Ursula's clandestine actions.

As the hours passed Amelia became more and more fretful until, by the time she arrived in Saskatoon, she was quite agitated. When Ludwig met her at the train station and said they were going straight to City Hospital, her overwrought nerves nearly snapped. Was something wrong with Ursula? Why was she in hospital when she should have been at her uncle's home?

Ursula would neither call her Mama nor look at her when speaking to her, but she continued to berate and accuse her until the day she walked out of the hospital without waiting to be discharged.

"How could you? Don't I mean anything to you? That wicked woman locked me in the basement as soon as you went home and soon after started to kick me around. For months I've been a slave in that godforsaken home, and now you show up here as though everything is fine."

When it became apparent that Amelia could do little to placate Ursula, she asked Ludwig to take her to his home. To her surprise, Martha greeted her as if she was her long-lost friend and was completely amicable for the three days of her stay. Her nephew and niece were equally pleasant until Amelia wondered if Ursula had made up the whole story of her maltreatment while living at her uncle's house.

Still, the nurse who had greeted her when she arrived on Ursula's ward would hardly have told her untruths. Before she showed Amelia to her daughter's room, she said there were various stages of bruises on Ursula's arms and legs. The next morning when she returned to the hospital and tried to determine the truth, Ursula again became furious, vacillating between sobbing and shouting at the top of her lungs until a nurse came to sedate her.

Amelia took the bus, as Ludwig had directed her. She arrived at her brother's house, let herself in, and found it to be silent. The children were in school, and Martha must've been napping, leaving Amelia with a perfect opportunity to check out the basement.

She opened the door and saw the light switch, but she waited until she'd gone through before turning it on and walking quietly down the stairs. Amelia then proceeded to do a very thorough inspection of the cellar. Although she did find a small room, which to her surprise had metal bars on the window, there was no sign of a bed, mattress, linens, or any of Ursula's belongings that might indicate that she had lived within the tiny space. In fact, other than two wooden boxes in one corner, the room was empty. Could this be the bedroom where Ursula claimed to have been locked up every night after Amelia had returned to the farm? She acknowledged to herself that she knew very little about Martha, but she had been congenial on the two visits she had made to her brother's house.

Could she really have been so cruel to Ursula who, for her faults, was a hard worker and would have helped her aunt with the household chores and the limited care her children required?

At that moment, Amelia was startled by Martha who had silently crept down the stairs.

"Are you looking for something?" she asked.

Thinking quickly, Amelia answered, "Yes, Ursula told me that she had left one of her blouses down here and she asked me to bring it to her."

"I have no idea why Ursula would ask you to look in this storage room. She knows perfectly well that the laundry area is on the other side of the basement. Let's have a look, but it does not appear to be here either. You are also welcome to search for it in the guest bedroom where you are sleeping, since that's where she stayed."

After returning upstairs to the spare room, Amelia saw Ursula's schoolbooks on the small writing desk in the alcove by the window, but of course no sign of the alleged blouse. Then she thanked Martha and said she was tired so planned to lie down for a nap.

Who was she to believe? It certainly seemed that no one had been living in that dark little room in the cellar, so why would Ursula have occupied it when this spare bedroom would have been empty? Amelia seldom thought ill of any person, and she could not bring herself to accept that her brother could be married to such an unkind woman.

On the other hand, Ursula was extremely upset. Why would she make up such an unlikely story? Throughout her childhood and youth, she had been very difficult and tended to rebel against her mother, but she was rarely faulted for telling falsehoods.

Unable to decide the truth, Amelia, on her way to see Ursula in the evening, chose to say nothing further about the strange situation. Instead, she retrieved Aunt Margareta's small black box, put it into her large purse, and carried it to the hospital.

Rather than upset Ursula again, she planned to give it to her without saying her grandmama had died; there would be plenty of time to tell her daughter when she was released from the hospital.

Fortunately, when Amelia arrived Ursula had just finished eating her supper and appeared to be more welcoming toward her mother. Not daring to wait, Amelia immediately took the box from her purse.

"I have a gift for you from your grandmamma, which I promised I would bring to you. I have no idea what it is, nor does anyone else, and if you don't want me to know, you can wait until I leave before you open it."

As it happened, Ursula chose to tuck the box under her bedcovers and leave it concealed until her mother departed. It did seem to have the makings of a peace offering, and although she still would not let Amelia hug her, she exhibited far less animosity toward her. Soon after, they even progressed to talking about the more ordinary aspects of life on the farm.

Amelia very carefully refrained from saying a word about Leonard going to Caron to become a pilot, again believing that she could mention it at a more opportune time.

58

On the third morning of her stay in Saskatoon when she arrived at City Hospital, she was informed that Ursula had left in the early hours of the morning and asked if she knew of her whereabouts.

Amelia was so upset that she could barely answer their questions, even when one nurse kindly offered to converse with her in German. When they started to suggest that as her mother she should know why Ursula had discharged herself without the doctor's permission, Amelia decided to make her own escape. She arrived at Ludwig's house soon after and rushed in the door, expecting to see Ursula waiting for her.

Amelia stayed with Martha for the balance of that day, and when there was still no sign of Ursula the next morning, she concluded that her daughter had taken the train back to Neudorf without her. Annoyed that Ursula was being so surly with her, she asked Ludwig to drive her to the station for the evening train. She knew she could stay in town with Katherina until she could get a ride home to the farm. She fully expected she would find Ursula with her aunt, and Amelia did not look forward to seeing Ursula's reaction to discovering that her grandmama was dead.

It was with total surprise then when Amelia discovered that Ursula was neither at Katherina's house nor had anyone seen her get off the train from Saskatoon the previous day.

Where could she be? And what would she tell Gustav and Johann when she came home without her? How could she explain that Ursula had simply walked away from the hospital and that no one had seen her since, either in Saskatoon or in Neudorf?

After Katherina calmed Amelia down and gave her breakfast, she decided to drive her home before opening the store, but not before making her sister-in-law promise to not blame herself nor allow Gustav to fault her for Ursula's behaviour.

However, it was not her husband but Johann who was very angry, claiming that his mother was the reason Ursula did not come home with her. His nine-year-old mind decided that since Mama was responsible for taking his sister away months ago, it had to be her fault that she did not want to return to the farm.

When Amelia tried to comfort him, he pulled away from her arms, sobbing as he ran out the door, no doubt to seek solace in his tree house. By his bedtime Johann still didn't allow his mother to cuddle him. When he asked where Ursula was and when she was coming back, Amelia was forced to make up a little white lie, although the reality was closer to the truth than she would have imagined. "She is spending some time with her new friend in the city before she comes back to us."

For his part, Gustav said very little when Amelia explained what took place at the hospital and how she subsequently could not find Ursula. If anything, he became even more sullen than since Leonard's departure and worked even harder to get ready for the spring planting. Long before spring arrived Gustav realized that he would be required to do most of the farm work himself since Otto was busy looking after his wife and child.

But then the older he became, the less he comprehended what was happening with his family. It seemed that he was losing control of all of his children, except for his youngest son, and thank God for him. Gustav remembered when Amelia told him she was with child again more than seven years after the birth of Ursula, how upset he had been; but now Johann was the only offspring with whom he seemed able to converse.

Within the confines of the hospital, quiet was strictly enforced. Even then it was only with the greatest restraint that Ursula did not shout out a cheer of joy when she opened Grandmama's gift. She could scarcely believe her eyes, and then when she counted the five- and ten-dollar bills in the fading light from the hallway, she repeated her enumeration three times because she could not accept that it was the correct amount.

Five hundred dollars. It was more money than she'd ever seen, it was all for her, and if she could believe her mother, no one knew what she'd just received. Trust her beloved grandmama to know precisely what she would need at this time in her life.

Sleep was out of the question that night as Ursula began to plan her escape. The minute she walked out the front door of her jailor's home she knew she would never again set foot in it, so she'd brought her precious few belongings with her. She'd considered that she had little choice but to return to the farm with Mama when she came to Saskatoon; but now if everything went according to plan, Ursula could be gone by the time her mother came to visit her the next morning.

The trickiest detail of her flight would be slipping out of the hospital without anyone noticing. To that end Ursula waited until the night nurse came into her room with her early-morning medication before going to the bathroom to change from her hospital garb into her own clothes, making sure to cloak herself in the bath robe as she returned to her bed.

Her roommates were sound asleep when she crawled back under the covers to wait until the nurses were occupied with the morning shift change. Then tossing the dressing gown aside, Ursula tucked her small valise under her arm and walked down the hallway at a normal gait before exiting the double doors at the end. As soon as she was in the stairwell, she quickened her pace until she reached the main floor. After coming out a side door of the hospital, she saw a city bus. Remembering her mother say that bus drivers were very polite about giving directions, she asked the man how she would get to the university.

Within minutes Ursula was aboard the bus that went directly from the hospital to the university campus, and the kind driver let her off in front of the pharmacology building. She stood still in the quiet corridor for some time before an older man came around the corner with a mop in hand.

"Hello, miss. May I help you?"

"Yes, please. I am looking for a student who is studying to become a pharmacist. His name is Hans Gerhart, and he has been at the university for four years now along with my older brother."

"My dear young lady, most of the classes finished for the year at the end of April. Only a few students are still on campus to take summer courses. Is your Mr. Gerhart likely to be studying during the summer months?"

"I don't think so. At least he has not stayed at the university for the last two summers. Do you know if there is anyone else here that I might ask?"

"Yes. I saw the dean of the department come into his office this morning. Let me just finish washing the floor of the main entrance, and I will take you to see him."

60

An elderly gentleman with a balding head and bushy beard opened the office door at the janitor's knock.

"Good morning, John. My floor has already been washed and polished." Then seeing Ursula, he continued, "Oh, I see that you have brought one of the summer students."

Welcoming Ursula into his office, Dr. Thompson closed the door before motioning her to a chair off to the side of the room, away from the large mahogany desk. Sitting opposite her, he said, "I'm Ben Thompson. I had a fresh pot of coffee brought up from the cafeteria a few minutes ago. Would you like a cup, miss…?"

"My name is Ursula Warner. And yes, please, I would enjoy some coffee."

"Ah, I thought you looked vaguely familiar. Are you related to Leonard Warner? He was one of my top students before he left the university at the end of December."

"I'm his younger sister, but what do you mean he left in December? He still has another year of study before he becomes a pharmacist," Ursula asked anxiously. Leonard would hardly leave unless something had happened to Papa, she thought, but Mama had said nothing.

"I'm sorry, sir, but you must be mistaken. It had to have been another student."

"Ursula, I wish I was wrong, but Leonard started pilot training in Caronport at the beginning of January. In fact, he has likely finished by now and has been sent overseas to be a fighter pilot. Did you not know? Have you been away from home?"

A plethora of questions were indeed running through her mind, yet Ursula could not seem to find her voice to ask any of them. Why would Leonard go to war? How could Papa let his eldest son go across the ocean and fight in the old country? Why did Mama not tell her when she had been to visit her three times in the hospital? Did Hans go with Leonard to become a pilot, and had he also been sent overseas? As she thought about Hans, she became cold with fear. She drank the entire cup of coffee before asking, "Did Leonard's best friend, Hans Gerhart, go with him to learn to be a pilot?"

"No, as hard as Leonard tried to get Hans to enlist, he was determined to finish his studies and become a pharmacist before he could consider fighting for his country. How well do you know Mr. Gerhart, may I ask, Miss Warner?"

"I first met him two years ago when Leonard brought him home to my father's farm for the summer, and then again last year."

"Hans has always been a driven student, and he would not even consider leaving until he graduated from the pharmacy program. Since Hans would probably not go to your home without Leonard, you're no doubt wondering where he went for the summer. But I'm afraid I do not have the slightest idea. All I know is that he has left the campus."

"Would he have gone back to the orphanage in North Battleford?" Ursula inquired hopefully, already planning to buy a train ticket.

"No, I think that would be even more unlikely. As you seem to know, he is a very proud man, and I think the last place in the world he would go is back to the orphanage. To be perfectly honest with you, Ursula, I know very little about Hans's background."

Lost in reflection, it was some time before Dr. Thompson continued.

"There was one thing. He always wore a large lapel pin on his cardigan. So finally one day after class I asked him about it. He said he'd been a foundling, left on the doorstep of the Good Hope Home in North Battleford. The pin he wore had held the tattered blanket around his tiny body. It had a sheaf of wheat with the inscription of Brandon, Manitoba. The only other detail he shared with me was that it was the single link to his past and one day he intended to travel to Brandon in search of his true identity.

"I hardly think he would venture to Manitoba until after he has graduated though," he continued. "That's about it, my dear young lady, and I'm sorry but I cannot help you to locate Hans."

61

She did not remember arriving at the train station, although she did recall that for the first time in her life she had money of her own to purchase her ticket, and lunch. As soon as she devoured her meal, she curled up on the seat and was fast asleep. She did not move a muscle until the train stopped in Virden, and a pretty woman not much older than Ursula sat down in the opposite seat.

Sitting up, Ursula noticed that her counterpart was wearing a tailored brown uniform. But before she could ask about it, the woman spoke, "Oh, I'm so sorry. I have disturbed your sleep."

"No, I was just waking up. Where are we? I think I may have been asleep for a long time."

Sally Jones was returning from her parents' farm outside of Virden to her base in Rivers, where she was Aircraftwoman First Class in the Royal Canadian Air Force.

"What a coincidence," said Ursula, while straightening up in her seat and smoothing her skirt. "I just found out that my oldest brother, Leonard, joined the air force in January and has probably been sent overseas as a fighter pilot."

"How exciting for him! I wish women were allowed to become pilots because I would take the training right away. Are you on your way to Rivers so you can enlist?"

"I am going to Brandon to find the man I love, although I don't know where to begin looking for him."

After hearing the story, Sally looked skeptically at Ursula, dishevelled from her long journey, and replied, "It may be more difficult than you think to find your young man when you don't have an address. I have a better idea. Why don't you come to Rivers with me, join the air force, and then on our days off we can go together to Brandon to find Hans? I really don't like the notion of you wandering around a strange city alone looking for a man."

At least they regularly received letters from Captain Leonard Warner, first postmarked from Caronport, and later from London, England, but months passed before Gustav and Amelia heard a word from their wayward younger daughter. Her mother worried herself sick, of course, not understanding why Ursula would leave without telling them where she was going and what she was doing.

Then to make matters far worse, Gustav was still so angry with Leonard that he would neither respond to his letters nor allow them to be opened, thus ensuring that Amelia could not ask Johann to read them to her so she could at least send a short note. She was certain that her eldest son had long ago forgotten how to read German, and since she could not write English and was hesitant to ask Otto—who was having more than his share of problems with his recalcitrant wife—to reply, Leonard's letters continually went unanswered.

In fact, the only way Amelia learned that Leonard had been sent abroad was because Johann noticed the unusual stamp on their most recent correspondence. Shortly after Johann explained to his mother that now Leonard was probably flying an airplane across the ocean against the enemy, for the first time in her life Amelia Warner became seriously ill. She could not eat or sleep, and as she became exceedingly pale, developed dark circles under her eyes, and dropped weight off her body, Gustav took her to see Dr. Roth.

The gentle doctor diligently performed all tests in his repertoire, but he was unable to diagnose a specific physical ailment responsible for Amelia's symptoms. Then he suggested that they sit in the parlour. Over a cup of tea, he soothingly inquired about what was happening in her life.

Whereas Amelia was filled with worry about Ursula, she was overwhelmed with an ominous feeling of dread regarding Leonard. Eventually she shared that she did not want to go to bed; whenever she drifted off into a restless sleep, she had a recurring nightmare that Leonard was drowning, sinking deeper and deeper, and she would awaken abruptly just as he started calling to her to pull him from his watery grave. Max Roth became apprehensive for his daughter, suspecting that Amelia could not be aware of the love between Fraya and her son. Had she known, she would never have spoken so candidly with him.

Max remembered the several occasions when Margareta Mohr had mentioned Amelia's unusual gift of foresight, and given that Leonard was regularly flying across the English Channel, her dream was certainly not beyond the realm of possibility. The more they conversed, the more Dr. Roth appreciated that her fears were very plausible, and he could only conclude that Amelia's malady was caused by her premonition that she would never see her eldest son again.

What could he prescribe to alleviate the foreboding of a loving mother who would be broken-hearted by the untimely and unnecessary death of her child? What possible treatment was available to stop the pain and suffering caused by this godforsaken war? In the end, all Max Roth could do was to arrange with Katherina for Amelia to stay in Neudorf under her care until she was able to rest.

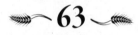 **63**

Perhaps the person most surprised by his aptitude for learning to fly the heavy Lancaster bombers was Captain Leonard Warner himself. Within six months of beginning his basic training, he was routinely piloting the long-range aircraft across the English Channel during night raids on Germany. Because the Luftwaffe had quickly improved their fighter airplanes, the Allies were forced to switch to nocturnal flights of "area bombing" the major industrial regions rather than doing daylight precision attacks. Leonard seemed to have exceptional night vision, and his accuracy steadily rose until he became known for the most strategic strikes.

Subsequently, in 1943 when the British Air Command decided to mount a major assault against Germany's Ruhr industrial regions, Captain Warner was selected to be the lead pilot for No. 617 Squadron, which was created specifically for the air offensive. On May 17, 1943, the unit flew nineteen converted Lancaster bombers in one of the most celebrated bombing raids of World War II. And even though they did not achieve the results they'd anticipated, it was a significant morale-booster to the Royal Air Force.

Leonard was sombre on the day following the foray into western Germany; three of the dams had been breached but the squadron had lost eight aircraft. He heard his name for mail call.

It must be a letter from Fraya, the only person who corresponded with him. He had long given up hope of receiving letters from any member of his family, and even from Hans. This letter, however, was full of important news about Fraya's future plans.

At last she recognized that she did have the capability to study medicine and she had received confirmation that she was accepted into the medical faculty for the fall semester. As excited as Leonard was by her communication, he was even more fascinated by what she had discovered one day when perusing the photographs of past graduates of the University of Saskatchewan Medical School.

Much to her surprise, she had noticed the name Mathias Werner. Later she went back to study the picture of his particular graduating class, and she was convinced that there was a marked resemblance between him and Leonard's father.

Did he have a relative who was a doctor, and if so why had he never told her? Was it possible that the university had spelled his name wrong, or had Leonard's family changed their surname to reflect a more English version?

With a start, Leonard remembered the punishment meted out when he'd started at Pheasant Forks School because he'd persisted in spelling his name incorrectly. In fact, it had taken a visit from his father to the schoolteacher before he learned that Papa had decided to anglicize their family name so his children would fit in with the other students in the English township.

Suddenly he recalled Mama talking about Mathias, her nephew who had lived with them along with his mother and two sisters in the old stone house. Could this be the same person? How old was Mathias when his mother, along with Aunt Hanna, moved her family to Melville? Beginning to calculate that Mathias must have been a young man by the time he was born, Leonard realized with a jolt that Dr. Werner might well be his cousin.

How strange that neither Mama nor Papa had ever said a word about having a doctor in the family. Come to think about it, his father had always remarked how proud he was that Leonard would attend university because he would be the first member of the entire family to graduate from a school of higher education. Taking his letter, pen, and paper, Leonard went to the small comfortable library in the officers' quarters and immediately began to reply.

True to her word, Sally Jones took Ursula to Brandon on three different occasions over the next several months to attempt to locate Hans Gerhart. From the moment the two women alighted from the train in Rivers, Sally took her younger protégé under her wing and became her "big sister." She introduced Ursula to the commander of the Royal Canadian Air Force Base, saying she'd travelled to Rivers because she wanted to join the same branch of the armed services as her brother.

Ursula was of age, so after passing the physical examination she decided to enlist; whereupon at Sally's request, Ursula was assigned to her barracks. That way she could help Ursula to adjust to becoming a member of the air force. But what she really wanted was to watch over her. She liked her well enough, but there was something sad in her gaze when she thought that no one was looking, which concerned Sally. As time passed, the desolate look in her eyes began to fade, and Ursula soon became one of the most enthusiastic recruits at the base. By the middle of September they stopped their forays into Brandon to find Hans because Ursula was certain that he would have returned to the University in Saskatoon, and she could not go back to Saskatchewan until she was eligible for a leave of absence.

It was usually only at night as she was dropping off to sleep that Ursula would ardently miss Hans, but the rest of the time her days were so busy with her duties that she would often forget about him. Perhaps all would have gone well had Sally not included Ursula in the group of women invited to a dance at the army base in Shilo. They no sooner stepped off the bus than a private, whom she later learned was Clarence Cardinal, arrived and attached himself to Ursula as though she was a magnet. He spent the entire evening by her side, chatting and dancing with her to the exclusion of all others, and by the time the bus was ready to take them back to Rivers, he extracted her promise that she would return the following Saturday.

Ursula was captivated by his attention, and even before she could consider whether she was attracted to him, she found herself agreeing to see him the next week. On the way home Sally sat beside her and inquired, "Did you have a good time at the dance, Ursula, even though that one fellow seemed to monopolize you for the entire evening?"

"Yes, Sally, that was fun, and I rather liked being the centre of attention with Clarence. At least I didn't have to sit in the corner waiting for a man to ask me to dance."

"Well, Ursula, since there were twice as many men as women, I don't think that anyone was a wallflower. I wonder, though, if I could give you a word of advice. Should you come again, and please let me finish explaining before you become upset, we are expected to mingle with all the men on the base during these functions."

"I don't understand what you are getting at, Sally. I did not encourage Clarence to dance with me all evening. He just seemed to always be by my side. What am I supposed to do?"

"Of course not, Ursula. You don't need to be rude; you can simply express that you would like to meet some of the other men in his unit."

"But what if I don't want to be with anyone else? I thought that Clarence was very nice, and I felt comfortable with him, so I promised him I would see him again next Saturday evening."

Over the next several months, Sally began to suspect that Ursula Warner was not as naïve as she originally thought. When she was certain that Clarence was suitably smitten with her, she began to flirt with his friends, as if deliberately trying to make him jealous.

Then one unusually balmy spring evening in May 1943 when Sally realized that Ursula must have slipped out of the dance hall with Clarence, she decided that she needed to warn the girl about the possible consequences.

Waiting impatiently, shifting from one foot to the other outside the mess hall the following morning, Sally gave serious thought to what she would say. She did not want to put ideas into Ursula's head, but it was imperative to convince her that if she played with fire, she could get burnt.

"Good morning, Ursula. Shall we walk together to chapel? I was wondering if you are no longer enjoying the dances in Shilo. I hardly saw you on the dance floor last night, so you must have been sitting in the back corner of the hall."

"What does it matter to you where I was? You are not my keeper."

"Actually, I do feel responsible for you, Ursula, since I am the one who encouraged you to come to Rivers and then invited you to go to the dances at the army base."

"Well, I would have gone without your invitation, and I am perfectly capable of looking after myself, so I certainly am not going to answer to you," said Ursula, as she stormed away from the woman she once held in high regard.

Sally watched her go. She could almost predict what would happen to her protégé; she'd seen it happen several times before on the air force base.

As far as Sally Jones was concerned, each occurrence of a young woman going astray only heightened her resolve to pursue her own career and to make her own choices about the direction of her life. From that day onward, Ursula Warner became just another AC. And even when she was promoted from second to first class, Sally did not join in her gay celebrations because she knew it was just a matter of time before her world would come crashing down.

66

How could Hans Gerhart graduate summa cum laude on a beautiful day in the spring of 1943 and yet feel like convocation was the saddest day of his life? Two of his benevolent benefactors from the Good Hope Home in North Battleford were proudly present, of course, claiming that they knew all along how gifted their young orphan was. That's why they'd given him the opportunity to go to the university.

The department head presented their top student with the Faculty of Pharmacy class ring, and all of his professors openly honoured him with their heartfelt congratulations; but none had genuine love for him. When Leonard was still in the program, Hans often envisioned celebrating their graduation together with all of his family—and most especially Ursula—cheering them on for their achievements. Instead, when he walked across the stage to receive his degree, he felt more alone than he'd felt in all those years in the orphanage. At his gloomiest moment, as he was cursing fate for the day he'd ever met Leonard Warner, Fraya Roth touched him gently on the shoulder.

"Congratulations, Hans, on your prodigious accomplishment. How wonderful for you to graduate with the highest honours, although I suspect that if Leonard had not left he would have challenged you for the top spot," Fraya teased.

"Thank you, Fraya. I was just feeling like I had no one in the audience who cares about me."

"Well, now you know that is simply not true, Hans. And to prove it, I shall treat you to dinner at The Bessborough this evening."

⇒~ 67 ~⇐

There were advantages to graduating at the top of the class, as Hans was quick to learn, because he instantly had several job opportunities. He wrote letters expressing his gratitude to all of them; but following careful consideration, he met with the chief pharmacist at the University Hospital to determine if he could have leave to fight for his country before accepting the position.

Several days later, after saying farewell to Fraya, Hans purchased a train ticket to Neudorf. Now that he'd graduated as a pharmacist, he fully intended to ask Gustav Warner for Ursula's hand in marriage. Once they were betrothed, Hans thought, he could depart for Caron to enlist in pilot training, as he had always planned to do after graduation.

⇒~ 68 ~⇐

On that fateful morning, he stepped off the train, onto the platform, and into Gustav Warner.

Taking a few seconds, as if confirming that the man really was his son's university friend, Gustav stated, "Well, you have your nerve! What are you doing in Neudorf, and what have you done with my daughter?"

"And a good afternoon to you too, Mr. Warner. As it happens, Ursula is the very reason that I have returned to your fair town, since I have not seen her now for nearly two years. I was about to ask Katherina if she could drive me to your homestead so I could speak with you to ask for Ursula's hand in marriage. But since you have accosted me, I shall immediately make my request, after assuring you that I am a graduate pharmacist and I now have a job waiting for me at the University Hospital. Therefore, Mr. Warner, may I have the honour of marrying your lovely daughter?"

"Did you not hear me, man? I just asked you where you took Ursula, and you stand there expecting me to agree that she can be your wife. Good God, are you deaf?" Gustav bellowed at Hans as several people on the street turned to listen.

Aware that passers-by were starting to stop and stare, Hans tried to keep his voice down.

"I don't know what you are yelling about. As I said, I have not seen Ursula since I left Neudorf almost two years ago. Are you telling me you don't know where your own daughter is? Yet you expect someone you ordered to never return to your farm to know? Where did she go, when did you last see her, and what have you done to try and find her?"

"What do you take me for, a dumb old farmer? The last time Amelia saw Ursula was in Saskatoon, the exact city where you have lived since my son had the misfortune of meeting you. Now where is she?"

Now Hans was angry and had to resist grabbing Gustav by the collar.

"What part of the city was Ursula staying in? Give me the address and tell me why she was there."

"What does it matter? Ursula has not been living at her uncle's home for over a year," replied Gustav, as he turned and walked away.

Striding back into the station, without a further word to Gustav, Hans asked the stationmaster when the next train to Saskatoon was departing and immediately bought a one-way ticket. Perhaps Leonard had mentioned his uncle's name to Fraya. Maybe they'd even gone together to visit with him. What if Ursula had come to the university looking for him? His mind was assailed with questions, as his fears about Ursula continued to mount.

69

Hans eventually learned that Ursula had met the dean of the department either at the end of May or the beginning of June the previous year. Yes, she was a delightful young woman who was very eager to find him, but as to where she had gone, Dr. Ben Thompson simply could not say. Fraya did remember having dinner on one occasion at Leonard's Uncle Ludwig's home, which interestingly was within walking distance of the university.

One late afternoon as soon as Fraya had finished her summer class, they walked the same path that Leonard and she had taken more than two years ago, and within thirty minutes they saw a large bungalow the colour of a fire engine with an emerald green front door. Before they reached it, even in his distress Hans chuckled, "Now, I understand why you would not forget the house. It looks like Christmas. I only hope Ursula's uncle will be able to tell us where she went."

The woman who answered the door did not recognize Fraya, which was understandable given the time lapse; although she remembered her as Ludwig's wife. When she explained that she'd accompanied Leonard Warner for dinner, she finally acknowledged that he was her nephew, but she said she'd not seen him for years. And no, she did not really know his sister Ursula, and she certainly could not tell them of her whereabouts. It was obvious that she was anxious to get rid of them. Before they could ask any more questions, she quite literally closed the door on their eager young faces.

As each road came to a dead end, Hans realized that he would soon find himself without money. As much as he wanted to continue searching for Ursula, he had to pursue his own future, and the subsequent morning he arrived at the recruiting office for the Royal Canadian Air Force. When he told the man at the front desk that he was specifically interested in enrolling for the pilot training at Caronport, he was ushered into the lieutenant's office.

Given his university education, he'd receive the commission of captain. As soon as he completed his medical examination, he could depart on the evening train for Caronport. Hans Gerhart would, however, be thwarted in carrying out the plan when the doctor said he was not eligible to become a pilot because he was colour-blind.

⟫⟩~ 70 ⟨~⟪

As Sally pulled herself back to the sound of Ursula Warner dry-heaving in the lavatory, she had no recourse but to take her to the doctor to have the appropriate tests completed. And when the answer came back in the affirmative, as she predicted, she would be required to report it to their superior officer.

Within a matter of days Ursula was given a medical discharge with the perfunctory well wishes, and her whole world tumbled down around her ears. And, again, as Sally had witnessed already with three other young recruits, the man responsible for her plight would carry on as though he were perfectly innocent.

Oh, what could she do to hold Clarence Cardinal accountable for his actions and ensure that he provided for Ursula and their baby?

Sally realized that there could be a resolution in relation to Clarence Cardinal and on a much broader scale if she threatened to prohibit the aircraftwomen from participating in the dances at the army base. After all, Sally had been placed in charge of the social activities for the Rivers Air Force Base. If she approached Major Burns in Shilo to disclose that Clarence was the father of Ursula's baby, she might be able to encourage him to compel the private to take responsibility for his paternity.

Should she not find a sympathetic ear, she would not be above cancelling all social interaction with the women. As she was only too aware, William Burns was sweet on her. She was certain that if she could play her cards adroitly, she could persuade Major Burns to force Private Cardinal to do the right thing—that is, to marry Ursula and give her baby a proper surname. If she was victorious, then she intended to ride the wave of her success and propose that the aircraftwomen continue to be permitted to socialize with the men at the army base, on the condition that everyone remained in the dance hall during the evening.

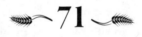 **71**

When she arrived in Shilo, she had scarcely announced herself to the major's receptionist when she was ushered into his office. "Good afternoon, AC Jones."

"Thank you for agreeing to see me so quickly, Major Burns, but I must say that I have come on some rather delicate matters. I've just discovered that one of my aircraftwomen, who was recently promoted to AC First Class, is with child. I know with certainty that the father is Private Cardinal because I have frequently observed the two of them slipping out of the dance hall on Saturday evenings and not returning until the bus is ready to depart. That is another concern that I plan to discuss with you, but first we need to determine if we can find a quick solution for Ursula Warner."

"I am genuinely distressed that Private Cardinal has taken advantage of your AC. You can rest assured, AC Jones—may I call you Sally?—that I shall hold Private Cardinal accountable. As a matter of fact, I have never liked the man, and my first action will be to give him a dishonourable discharge. But first, what do you propose to rectify the situation with AC Warner."

Having watched her coquettish behaviour during the past several months, Sally was not convinced that Ursula was as naïve as Major Burns was suggesting, but she was not about to reveal her suspicions.

"I agree that since Ursula will be discharged, in all fairness, so must Clarence be discharged. Furthermore, I think he should be required to marry her before he leaves this base. Then in regard to my other concern with the Saturday evening dances, I believe that we must thoroughly monitor that the men and women remain in the hall at all times."

Within the week Ursula Warner and Clarence Cardinal had a quiet ceremony in the chapel at the air force base before they were both discharged from their respective military services. Where they would go and how they would survive away from the air force and army bases were of little concern to either AC Jones or Major Burns. The newlyweds had quite literally made their bed, and if they had nowhere to lie in it, at least they were together to make the best of it.

From her perspective, Sally Jones had genuinely tried to teach Ursula about the consequences of her errant behaviour before being told that she was not her keeper. However, once Clarence Cardinal placed the thin gold band on the third finger of Ursula's left hand, Sally experienced a smug sense of exoneration that she had spared the nineteen-year-old soon-to-be mother from having a baby out of wedlock.

 72

On the morning following the ceremony, the commanding officer from the Rivers Air Base put Ursula and Clarence on the military bus to wherever they wanted to go in Brandon.

If only that busybody of a Sally Jones had minded her own affairs, Ursula would not be sitting on the bus with a man about whom she knew very little and had even less interest in learning than she did in becoming a mother. Prior to the involvement by AC Jones and her aspiring suitor, Major William Burns, Ursula had not the slightest intention of keeping this baby, expecting to give it up as soon as it was born.

"So where are these people that we'll live with in Brandon?" Clarence demanded, as he tried to bring Ursula out of her reverie.

"What are you talking about? I don't know anyone in Brandon. I thought they were sending us here because you knew someone we could live with until you found work and we could get our own home."

"Find work? I had a perfectly good job before you got me discharged and roped into an unwanted wedding. Why didn't you just leave and have the kid instead of getting both of us in this pickle? That's what the other girls did if they messed up!"

"It took two of us to make this pickle, as you so rudely call it. Why should the woman be ruined and the man just walk away free? At any rate, if you don't know anyone either, we better start thinking about what we will do when they toss us off this bus. How much money do you have?"

"Not enough for us to live on in this city. I never paid much attention to saving money, so all I have is from the last cheque. How much do you have?"

During the past year and a half, she had grown quite accustomed to living in a comfortable environment with other women her age and being able to walk over to the mess hall for all of her meals.

Without warning, Ursula burst into tears, overwhelmed with homesickness. She missed her mother more than she could have imagined. She longed to see Papa and Johann, and even Otto and Millie. And how could she have gone so long without hearing from either Leonard or Hans?

Then she began to sob inconsolably. When Clarence could not comfort her, he eventually came up with the idea that they could stay with his folks in Amaranth, and he subsequently asked the corporal to take them to the bus depot.

73

As soon as they boarded the Greyhound, Ursula curled up on an empty seat and fell sound asleep. She was exhausted from the events of the day. Not having eaten since the light lunch they were served after the wedding, she simply did not have the energy or the will to care where they were going.

"Hey, wake up. We are in Neepawa, which is the end of the line for the bus." Clarence shook Ursula by her shoulders.

Not in the best of humour after her rude awakening, Ursula sat up and rubbed her eyes. "What do you mean the end of the line? I thought you said we were going to some place called Amaranth. If we are not there yet, why did you disturb my sleep?"

"The bus does not go to Amaranth. We will just go into the hotel to get something to eat and drink and then wait for one of the trappers or fishermen from there to give us a ride. Unless you want to try your luck at hitchhiking?"

It was another day before Clarence and Ursula finally climbed into a rusty old truck owned by Walter Clegg, a jovial heavy-bearded trapper, who was returning home with his supplies for the winter months. He was quite happy to give them a ride, although they would be required to share the dilapidated front seat with his sheep dog, Browser, an animal that looked more ancient than either his owner or the truck.

Walter had come into the hotel for his dinner, and by the time he was ready to leave, Clarence was slumped over in his chair from alcohol and lack of sleep. Rousing him, the bartender demanded payment; but when Clarence turned out his trouser pockets and came up short, Ursula grudgingly handed over her last remaining cash from her paycheque.

Now she was anxious to depart as soon as possible because she did not want her husband to have yet another drink. Oh, she still had money in her small strongbox from her grandmama, but the last thing she intended to do was tell Clarence about her stash. The money had been left to her, and not a penny would be spent on any other person.

By late afternoon, Walter safely arrived with his two bedraggled passengers. If Walter had wanted company during the ride home, he was disappointed. Even when he stopped the truck in front of Clarence's parents' bungalow with its picket fence, they slept.

Closing his door quietly, Walter went to call on his old friend Henry Cardinal to prepare him for the return of his long-lost son.

After knocking, Walter was greeted by Henry's wife, Alma, and immediately asked to come in out of the evening's gathering gale off the lake, but he explained that he had driven two passengers home with him.

Turning around in his chair, Henry said, "In that case, you better ask them to come in as well."

"I'm not so sure that you want to see one of them. When I stopped in the hotel for my dinner, I could hardly believe my eyes. Although he was slouched over the table from too much drink, there was no mistaking that it was Clarence. Wilbur, the bartender, said they'd been waiting for a ride to Amaranth, and when this nice girl named Ursula said they'd just gotten married, I took pity on her and drove them here."

Henry and Alma were speechless and could only stare at each other. It had been so long. Vivid memories of all the pain and grief from Clarence's disturbing departure, which had been charged with his rage and accusations—followed by the uncertainty and worry of more than seven years—suddenly whirled around the tiny kitchen as if the blustery squall off the lake had permeated the house's walls.

But as it always would, their love for their prodigal son won out, and soon they were all seated around the table drinking coffee and eating bannock with gooseberry jam. Clarence's ill grandmother, Marie, propped up in her bed in the little adjacent parlour, was perhaps the most pleased to see her grandson. She had forgotten about his wrath when the boy had stormed out of his parents' house, calling his mother and her 'dirty Indians.'

"I can't stand to spend another day in this dingy little house," Ursula snapped, as she put her feet on the hand-woven mat at the side of the bed. It was mid-morning, but it was still as dark outside as if it were night, with the incessant rain pelting down on the thatched roof for the third consecutive day.

Not that either Ursula or Clarence could really count their first day in his parents' home, because following their light meal, they had fallen into the three-quarter-sized bed and slept around the clock. They occupied the bedroom Clarence had shared with his brother James since the day Henry had brought them home, and it had always seemed large enough for the two growing boys. But already it felt cramped with his new wife.

"At least we have a roof over our heads. And let me tell you, when we get one of these storms off Lake Manitoba, it can go on for a week. So stop your complaining, and be thankful that we got here when we did. I don't know about you, but I sure didn't have the money to get a room at the hotel in Neepawa."

"You don't need to tell me that. I had to spend the last of my hard-earned cash to pay for all the beer you drank."

"Well, if you don't have any money either, maybe you should just be a little nicer to my folks, because the way I see it we are pretty much going to need to rely on them. We might have to spend the winter here with them, but then I could earn some money by helping my father with his ice fishing."

"There is no damn way that I will live in this piddly little hovel with two Indians any longer than I have to. As soon as this storm is over, we are leaving."

It was strange, but suddenly Clarence resented Ursula bad-mouthing his grandmother and mother, although he'd thought nothing about calling them dirty Indians and worse when he had flung his racial slurs at both of them before slamming the door seven years ago.

"Just where do you think you will go, and how do you plan to get there when we are both broke, Miss Know-It-All? And at least as long as we are staying here and eating at their table, I don't want to hear you talk about them as Indians again."

"I sure as hell wouldn't have agreed to this marriage if I had known you were a half-breed," Ursula barked at Clarence.

"Keep your voice down. You can hear everything through these walls," Clarence hissed. "Henry and Alma are not my real parents, although they apparently gave James and me their surname and raised us since I was about five and a half and my brother was seven. Neither James nor I ever remembered what the kids at school taunted me about when I was sixteen, and then when I discovered we weren't even adopted, I accused them of making me think that I was a half-breed before I ran away. And I never returned until now. The only thing I remember is being very hungry and cold, although it was still fall when Henry found us crying in a ditch on his way home from setting his traps."

"What a likely yarn. Do you really think I believe you?" Ursula said with disdain.

"It doesn't matter to me whether you do or not, but who would make up such a story? Henry brought us here to his home, and since Alma and he could never have their own children, they decided to keep us. They always told James and me that we were their blessing from God, and they loved us from the moment we stepped through the door."

"Oh, don't start playing like you would be the decent daddy with me. If it hadn't been for Sally Jones and then William Burns, you would have dumped me like a hot potato to have this kid on my own."

"Since you think you are so clever, maybe you can tell me where we are going, and just how the hell we might get there."

Feeling overwhelmed, Ursula again burst into tears. Waves of homesickness washed over her like the icy cold water that splashed relentlessly against the rocky shore of the lake across the road. When Clarence told her to stop blubbering, she cried even more.

He reluctantly embraced her in the hope that she would calm down before his parents began to wonder what was going on. In the three days since their arrival, Ursula had only emerged from the small bedroom to gingerly pick at the food placed in front of her, and whenever the two were within the confines of its paper-thin walls, they were invariably quarrelling.

Even at the height of their bickering, Alma and Henry would never have dreamt of intervening, but the ailing matriarch was not so diffident. Finally she told her daughter that she would ask them to leave as soon as the rain stopped—especially since Clarence's wife clearly did not think highly of either their home or their meals.

~ 75 ~

On the dawn of the morning the rain stopped, Henry was out in the yard making sure his truck would start. When Clarence arrived alone at the breakfast table, he spoke frankly to his son.

"As relieved as your mother and I are that you decided to come home, you cannot stay here. This house is too small, and your sick grandmother will no longer put up with your endless fighting. We overheard; it is impossible not to listen since you both spent most of your time shouting that you are a little short of cash right now. When your wife is awake, I want you to ask her where she wants to go. Then you can gather your things, and I will drive you to Neepawa and loan you the money for the train or bus fare."

Thus it was that by late morning Clarence and Ursula sat beside an unusually silent Henry Cardinal while being transported back to Neepawa.

76

As soon as he saw her, he was overcome with delight and ran straight into her open arms. Johann had never accepted that Ursula would have left them because she'd wanted to, without even saying goodbye to him, and now he held onto her for dear life as though she might disappear again. He did not care that he was a grown boy of eleven years; he could not stop his tears of happiness at seeing his favourite sister, who had played with and watched over him throughout his childhood.

As it was, Johann need not have felt sheepish about his unusual display of emotion, because when he glanced around, Mama was weeping with unabashed joy and even Papa had to look away to hide the tears in his eyes. In the more than two years that Ursula had been gone, Johann had asked repeatedly where she was and why she had not come home.

77

Clarence was amazed to find out that he had married into a German family, but even more amazed by Amelia's openly warm affection for her children and granddaughter. Her father was reserved, speaking only when necessary but also quietly, so where had Ursula learned to yell about everything?

Gustav, on the other hand, was not nearly as quick to approve of Clarence, and as soon as they had eaten dinner he told him to come help with the fencing Otto had started that morning. When they were out of earshot of the house, Gustav said, "Thank you for bringing my daughter back, but since winter is coming, I want to know if you are planning to stay, and what you know about farming?"

"Since I was raised in a fishing and trapping village, I have never really been on a farm, but we don't have any place to live. With a baby coming, we are hoping that we can spend the winter with you."

"Well, she will be plenty busy helping her mother with her household tasks and you will soon find out about the chores on a farm; although now that the harvesting is finished, there is not nearly as much to do. But I warn you, if you choose to live under my roof, both of you will earn your keep, and most of the time when you are being told what to do, you will have to listen to Otto who, I think, is younger than you."

Then, almost as an afterthought, Gustav added, "I will not put up with any squabbling with my son or with anyone else, for that matter, because Otto will eventually take over working all of my land. Do you understand?"

78

Otto and Clarence similarly got off on the wrong foot. From the first time that they met, the sparks began to fly and were always substantially increased the moment Millie came on the scene.

She was obviously with child, and it was equally evident that she was not happy about giving birth to another baby. Even Clarence could see that Amelia was more of a mother to Francis than Millie wanted to be. Otto, on the other hand, would sit with his daughter on his lap at the kitchen table and let her eat bite-sized pieces of food from his dinner plate.

Soon Clarence would care little about Millie's caustic tongue, because he had never been so sore and tired in his life. Every bone in his body ached by the end of three days of Otto's tutelage to farm chores, from sitting on the small three-legged stool to milk cows to bending over all day digging holes for fence posts. Still, Clarence had never eaten such delicious food, and Ursula and he had more than adequate space in the upstairs of the house. In addition to the large bedroom, up another short spiralling staircase were three small rooms, one of which could be used for the baby.

Since he fell into bed exhausted very early most nights and Ursula remained in the kitchen talking to her mother while she crocheted or knitted for her two expected grandchildren, they had little time to resume their quarrelling. When the snow began to fly and they were settling into winter, Clarence was becoming accustomed to the daily chores and was starting to think that maybe things could work out for them on the farm.

79

On the spring morning after Otto hurried to Neudorf to fetch Dr. Roth for Millie's confinement, Amelia was surprised to look through the small ice-free spot on the frosty kitchen window and see Katherina drive into her yard.

Millie had been screaming with labour pains since the middle of the night, and after waking Francis to take her to his mother's house, Otto brought Amelia to his home to stay with Millie until he could bring the doctor. Amelia had rubbed her lower back and, in between contractions, was getting her a drink of water.

Opening the door, Amelia said, "Good morning, Katherina. What brings you out to the farm so early when you should be in your store looking after your customers?"

Fortunately, Katherina waited before answering Amelia's question. She waited until Dr. Roth had arrived. She waited until Millie had delivered her second daughter, and then she waited until Amelia had taken Dr. Roth and her into her kitchen while Otto remained with his wife and their new baby.

When she asked Ursula to put on a coat and go to the barn to bring her father to the house, she waited until Gustav had come in and taken his place at the table.

Although she'd always had very little regard for the woman, for the rest of her life Katherina would secretly thank Millie for her fortuitous timing. It had facilitated the presence of Dr. Roth at the homestead on this crucial day, the one and only time when Amelia Warner would require a drug to be administered.

The telegram read: "Mr. and Mrs. Gustav Warner, we regret to inform you that your son, Captain Leonard E. Warner, J/86329, Pilot Officer with the Royal Canadian Air Force, was killed in action. Captain Warner's aircraft, a United Kingdom Royal Air Force Avro Lancaster Mk I, was shot down over the English Channel on 19 April 1944. Captain Warner had flown 59 night bombing raids and has posthumously been awarded the Distinguished Flying Cross."

Amelia started to wail and did not stop until Dr. Roth took her into her bedroom and injected her with the strongest sedative he carried in his medical bag, while Gustav walked out the front door and was not seen again until the next morning.

Even later, when the Distinguished Flying Cross medal arrived—along with a marble monument presumably to mark Leonard's grave in the family cemetery as if to provide a measure of solace—Amelia and Gustav responded with total apathy. Similarly, when they received an official notice from the Canadian government that Warner Lake in northern Saskatchewan, 59L and 109 longitude, was named for their son, they were equally indifferent. It was all meaningless. There was no honour in having their son recognized as a war hero when they did not believe in war.

A memorial service was held in the Neudorf Lutheran Church. Supported on Otto and Elisabeth's arms, Amelia was present, at least in body, but anyone who dared to glance into her unresponsive eyes knew that her heart and soul were far away.

Then there was Gustav, flanked by his older brothers, Johann and Rolf, looking as though he had neither eaten nor slept since the morning Katherina had arrived. He'd always been thin, but now he was gaunt as a walking skeleton, and his vacant stare looked as if he was the one who'd passed into the next world.

During those first few days, he walked for hours and miles around his farm, haunted by his morbid thoughts that yet another of the men in his life was dead. First, he had lost his nephew Mathias, followed by his best friend Andrew Thompson, and then Jurgen Kuss, a man who over the years had become like a brother to him. Only this time it was his son, his eldest son, his own flesh and blood.

80

When he began to recover from the shock of Leonard's death, anger took hold of Gustav and eventually propelled him to work like a man possessed. As the days passed, he became filled with fury and self-loathing about having allowed his son to leave university and enlist in the air force. If only he'd been as strict and unbending as his own father had been with his offspring, Leonard would still be alive. He wondered if Amelia would ever stop blaming him for not putting his foot down and forbidding their son to go off to war.

She cried in the house, she cried as she took solace in her garden, she cried when she was alone, and she cried when the house was full of people. Since Gustav was a man, though, he could not express his profound feelings of sorrow, and the only way he could mourn the death of his son was to work his fingers to the bone.

The days passed, and a steady stream of family members and friends visited to carry on the daily tasks in the Warner household. Katherina came early every afternoon and stayed late into the evening, leaving her cousin Peter to run the General Store, and his daughter, Christine, in charge of the dress shop.

Of the five men from the German townships who had enlisted in the Canadian Armed Forces, Peter Mohr was the only one to return, albeit missing the better part of his left arm. More and more he helped operate Katherina's two businesses, and was willingly joined by Christine, of whom he was becoming fonder with every hour they spent together. At the end of the workday, they would walk arm in arm to Trader's Dining Room, and more often than not Frieda, the woman he had married in what seemed like another life, would sit down with them. At Katherina's suggestion, Peter had moved back into his childhood room in his parents' home. Making a concerted effort to avoid Albert Schultz at all costs, he was happily picking up the threads of his life.

Nonetheless, only Katherina would truly understand that Amelia was inconsolable—that her heart would never heal. Having lost first her unborn child and then her husband, David Hardy, in the First World War, Katherina knew that all any of them could do was be present with Amelia, as if to affirm her continued existence in the world of the living.

As soon as she arrived every afternoon, Katherina would gently guide Amelia to her soothing garden, where together they would till the soil and prepare it for the coming season. Seldom would the two women converse. Rather they would work or sit side by side, and when Amelia cried, her sister-in-law and friend would never try to stop her tears. Instead, Katherina would lower her hoe to the ground and take Amelia into her arms until she was ready to be released.

81

Vaguely remembering that Elisabeth had long since taken Emma and her infant son back to her own home in Summerberry, Amelia realized that there were still two babies in her home most of the time.

As she thought about it, she began to recall that Millie had delivered another infant girl on the morning that Katherina had brought the ghastly news about Leonard, but could Ursula have already been confined? Her baby was not due until the beginning or middle of July. Could three months have passed? Did she have such little awareness of what was happening around her that her own daughter had had a baby without her knowing? Still, when she saw Ursula trying to nurse an infant, it dawned on Amelia that indeed she must have another grandchild.

Fortunately, as he visited his patients in the farming community, Dr. Roth had made it a practice to stop by the Warner homestead, sometimes twice a day, after being present when Katherina had read the fateful telegram. At first he was extremely worried that Amelia would not survive.

Then he fretted that he was giving her too much medication, because whenever he arrived during the afternoon or evening, she would walk around in a stupor and, if not cry, be as silent as a stone.

Amelia seemed to notice no one but Katherina. She was oblivious to every other member of her family, including her beloved grandchildren. But what Max Roth found most disturbing was the seeming total lack of communication between Amelia and Gustav. Husband and wife seemed as alienated as strangers.

 **82**

When Fraya came back to Neudorf for Leonard's memorial service, the entire family sat around the kitchen table. Together they wailed, they prayed, they hugged, they held hands, they talked, they chanted, and they even laughed at some of their humorous memories of Leonard as they expressed their overwhelming sorrow for the loss of Fraya's betrothed.

When the doctor and his wife returned home after the ceremony, Rebecca set a cup of tea on the table for Max.

"That had to be the saddest celebration of a person's life I have ever attended. Poor Amelia. In the eyes of his country Captain Warner is a war hero, but in his own community, and possibly his own family, there seems to be no recognition for his ultimate sacrifice."

"You could not be more accurate, my dear," Max said, "and I feel for Fraya because Katherina was the only member of the Warner family to offer her condolences. At one point when we were having coffee, Ursula kept staring at Fraya as if she wanted to come and talk to her. But she obviously decided against it, and she also turned away. They are the most taciturn people I have ever met, but what I find most distressing is that no one in the family seems capable of comforting another. In addition to being worried about Amelia, I fear for Ursula."

The next morning, recalling that Ursula had spent considerable time with Trudi when she was interested in going into nursing school, Dr. Roth decided to take Trudi with him. As they drove into the yard, they saw Ursula sitting dejectedly in the grass by the garden.

"While I go into the house to check on Amelia, maybe you can go to Ursula and see if she will talk to you," said the doctor.

Walking slowly toward the despondent young woman, Trudi quietly said, "Hello, Ursula. I wonder if you remember who I am. May I sit down here beside you? It will be a warm day again, and soon all the buds on the trees will open. Before you know it, the mother robin will have laid her pretty blue eggs, and then there will be three or four baby birds. My brother, Dr. Roth, was telling me that your baby is coming at the beginning of summer. Have you thought of any names yet?"

A full minute passed before Ursula spoke in a barely audible voice.

"I wish I was like that bird and could fly far away from here. The only reason I joined the air force was to be sent overseas to find Leonard. Now he is dead, and all I have left from him are my three letters that he answered after I came home. Did you know that my mother gave me a box of unopened letters that Leonard had written from the time he enlisted, and no one ever replied to them?"

"I'm sure you were upset to discover that none of your family had written to him."

"Poor Leonard would have wondered why none of us could take the time to drop him a note. I was away from home for almost two years and came back only a few months ago; but as soon as Mama showed me all of his letters, I immediately read them to her and then wrote to him. He was so happy to hear from me that he replied right away, but I am angry with Papa that he would not let Otto or Johann read Leonard's letters to Mama. How could he be so mean with his own son and wife?"

"My dear girl, I have no idea why your father would not allow either of your brothers to correspond with Leonard."

Raising her head for the first time, Ursula replied, "Now I remember you. I talked to you about becoming a nurse before I decided to enlist."

In her tranquil and trustworthy way, Trudi was able to assist Ursula to come to grips with her grief and to begin her preparations for the birth of her baby. His nurse would be present with Dr. Roth during the delivery of Ursula's only son, and on the spur of the moment, recalling the morning when Trudi had gained her confidence by sitting beside her and quietly watching the robins, Ursula decided to name him Robert.

Seventeen months later when Ursula gave birth to her daughter, Dr. Roth delivered a baby on another farm in the German townships. And after Trudi brought her into the world, she was delighted that Ursula honoured her by giving her infant girl Trudi's middle name, Justine.

Similarly, it would be Trudi in attendance when a second daughter, Elaine, arrived fifty-one weeks to the day after the birth of Justine. By the time a third girl, Sandra, was born another seventeen months later, Trudi was relieved that Dr. Roth had accompanied her because she found herself increasingly irritated by the always-truant Clarence.

Although Clarence shirked all responsibility to be by his wife's side during the labour and delivery of any of his offspring, he was clearly ready to climb back into Ursula's bed to resume his husbandly duties at the earliest opportunity, even during the recommended period of abstinence following her confinement.

84

"You must feel even more than I do that we are becoming like rabbits. It makes me think someone told both of our husbands that Amelia needs to be surrounded by babies to make her happy," Millie said, when she went to visit Ursula after the delivery of her fourth child.

Millie herself had three daughters, and after the birth of her last, Darlene, months before the arrival of Justine, she barred Otto from the bedroom. It didn't seem to distress him in any way, because once he came in from the fields or the barn, Otto only paid attention to his three "precious" daughters.

And Millie certainly did not miss his advances—not now since Clarence had willingly snuck away from Otto's control almost every afternoon to join her for an illicit romp in her bedroom while her mother-in-law cared for her three children; although soon she started to have other concerns about Clarence's proclivity for procreation.

Good God, what would happen if she became pregnant when she'd not slept with her husband for nearly three years?

As chance would have it, Millie's fate would shortly be determined by Gustav, who was just about at the end of his tether with the child-raising demands being placed upon Amelia. She was not getting any younger and, yes, she loved her grandchildren with all her heart and soul, but it was far too much.

During the day, Amelia would usually have seven children underfoot. Even though Ursula was following through with her father's expectation that she work earnestly alongside her mother with the household chores and, under Amelia's supervision, care for her own family, Otto's wife was becoming increasingly neglectful of her growing daughters.

Millie had never been very interested in her children, and when Amelia was grieving for Leonard, had it not been for Otto and Johann, Gustav was certain that Francis and Faye would not have fared well in their mother's negligent care. Now that Darlene had come along, Amelia was either feeding her or carrying Sandra until Johann came home from school. And then, fortunately, during the evenings Otto spent every waking moment with his two older girls and rose during the night to feed the baby.

It came to a head one evening when Amelia, who was not feeling well, asked Millie if she could help Ursula wash the supper dishes.

"No," said Millie. "I am also a little under the weather, and I want Otto to walk me back home now."

Enough was enough. Gustav rose and bellowed before Otto could stand up from the table to do his wife's bidding.

"Sit down, Otto, and finish your tea. Millie, you get over to the sink this minute and start drying those plates before you cause me to do something that I have never done before."

Even the children were so startled that the subsequent silence was profound enough to hear a pin drop. No one could determine what Gustav Warner was threatening, but for once Millie held her tongue and did as her father-in-law ordered her to do. Of course, that only lasted while she was under his roof, and the minute they were within the confines of their own home, she tore into Otto.

"That is the one and only time that domineering old man will decide what I will do, and when you go back there you can tell him exactly what I've said."

85

Later, rather than take his three children to their own beds, Otto asked his mother for a pillow and some blankets and proceeded to put them to sleep on the parlour floor. He spent a restless night on the short sofa until the early hours of the morning when he decided to join Francis and Faye on the floor beside Darlene's cradle. As one or another of the small children or babies cried out for attention at practically every hour of the night, Otto paused to wonder how his mother managed to stay upright on her feet all day.

When he awoke at the light of dawn, he was not surprised that Amelia was already in the kitchen with the coffee brewing and breakfast nearly on the table. Once Otto was up and washed, it occurred to him that he vaguely recalled hearing an automobile start up sometime during the night. But turning over on the hard floor, he was certain he'd been dreaming. It was not until he went outdoors to milk the cows that he realized his car was gone from its usual parking spot in front of his home.

"Clarence, you go ahead and start the chores. I will be along in a few minutes," Otto uttered, before running up the short lane to his house. He threw open the door, yelling at his wife as he ran straight into the bedroom. His shirts and trousers had been tossed about the room, the bed was rumpled, the dresser drawers hung open, and his undergarments and socks were on the floor.

When he realized that the valise and Millie's clothing were gone, he strode over to the night table to check his billfold. Sure enough, all of his money had disappeared. He knew exactly where she would have gone, so dashing back to his parent's home, he asked his father if he could borrow his car to drive to Neudorf.

"Why do you need to go to town before breakfast, and what's wrong with your own car?"

"Papa, I don't have time to explain right now. Can I please use your vehicle?" asked Otto, as he turned and headed back out the door. He pushed his father's new Ford car as fast as it would go, and within minutes he arrived in Neudorf, screeching to a stop in front of Albert Schultz's place of business.

Looking around, Otto was surprised that he did not see his car, but he bolted up the three stairs in one leap and pushed open the door of the tiny room at the back of the beer parlour.

"Alright, you heathen, where is she? Have you set her up in her old room?" Otto shouted.

"Good God, what time is it? And, whoever you are, what makes you think you can bust in here barking out orders?" demanded Albert, as he sleepily emerged from his bedroom, pulling on a pair of trousers. "Oh, it's you, Otto. Well, I guess you are searching for your lovely wife, but you should know that she wouldn't be out of bed at this ungodly hour, and I am not too pleased to be disturbed this early either."

"How would you know what time she got up, since she spent the entire day in bed when she was working for you?"

"Well, you were the dim-wit who married her. Millie Brown came to me almost as soon as I opened my pub, proposing her preferred employment, and she became my meal ticket before you rushed in headlong to save her. So now I take it she has flown the coop, but I have news for you. As much as many of her old customers and I would gladly welcome her return, I have not seen her in months. But then I guess her lot in life improved when your sister brought that husband of hers to live with your folks."

"What the hell do you mean by that? You can't be suggesting that Clarence was bedding my wife under my nose. You really are a despicable old bastard, just as Peter Mohr always claimed. Now where is she?"

"I told you, I have not seen her. Are you deaf as well as dumb? Nobody talks to me like that in my own establishment. Now get out, and don't show your face in here again."

"You don't need to worry about me spending another cent in this hellhole!"

Otto strode to the front door, slamming it so hard that it shook the frame as he left. He leapt down the stairs and walked all around the dilapidated old house. Then he walked up and down Main Street, searching for any sign of his vehicle before returning to his father's automobile and, on the spur, deciding to drive to Melville.

Otto spent the entire day driving around the city looking for his car. He didn't care if he ever saw Millie Brown again, but be damned if she would get away with stealing from him. Fortunately, at the end of a fruitless day of searching, he remembered the address of Aunt Hanna's bakery, and she kindly took him home for his first meal of the day and offered him a place to sleep.

The next morning following a hearty breakfast, Otto fuelled up the car and drove to Regina. But after driving up and down empty streets, he returned to the farm in the waning hours of the day.

87

It was beyond Amelia's nature to utter a single word of complaint; although it was becoming abundantly clear to Gustav that her grandchildren were wearing her out. Seven children under the age of six would have required the energy of a youth and the patience of a saint, never mind the care of an aging grandmother.

Even at fifteen, the minute his school day was over Johann would dash across his father's field to come home to help his mother. And once the spring seeding was finished, Otto would take his three daughters home as much as possible during the afternoons and in the evenings as soon as they had eaten supper.

Other than the months when Amelia was grieving for Leonard, Millie had rarely looked after her daughters. And then her mothering had consisted primarily of tossing all three of them into bed, as Otto discovered when he invariably came home to a chorus of crying children.

In fact, the three girls now spent less time with their grandmother than before Millie had abandoned them. Otto had stopped expecting his mother to care for his daughters during his frequent afternoon or evening forays into the beer parlour in Neudorf, and he now devoted his every spare minute to the needs of his children.

It was with Ursula that Gustav became increasingly disappointed and irritated when it came to mothering her children. She had nursed Robert, and initially when he was born, she seemed interested in learning about her new maternal responsibilities from Amelia. But when Justine had arrived a year and a half later, she refused to breastfeed her and, worse, to have much to do with her. Ursula's response to her first daughter was unusual to the point of detachment, and had Amelia not fed her with a bottle and provided her care, Gustav feared, she might not have survived.

By the time Sandra was born, Ursula, perhaps from sheer necessity, did become more attentive; although she decided that it was much easier to simply use a bottle than to nurse. And as soon as each baby could hold the bottle, Ursula would prop her child in a wooden infant seat rather than hold her in her arms.

He was thoroughly bewildered by his younger daughter, wondering if she had spent too much time around Otto's wife and picked up her unnatural indifference to her own offspring. And then there was Clarence. Even when Gustav's own family was young, he had been so busy that he'd not spent enough time with them. But now, counting Johann, there were four men to share the chores. Still, Clarence's only interest in his children appeared to be limited to his siring them in rapid succession.

Why did Amelia not insist that Ursula become more responsible for her own children? If he could notice how disinterested she was, what in heaven's name did Amelia think about Ursula's lackadaisical care?

It was in the midst of his fretting about Amelia's health that an idea began to form in his mind, and one morning at breakfast he casually announced, "I am going to Melville today, Amelia, and I wondered if you would like to come with me."

"You know I can't leave Ursula with all the children, especially when Otto has gone to the pasture with Clarence to fix the fence. Another time."

In truth, to put his plan into motion Gustav realized that it would be better not to have Amelia along with him, because she would never agree with his proposal. If he could find a suitable house with a large yard for a garden, he would purchase it and then bring her to Melville, explaining that they'd move to town in the autumn when the harvesting was finished.

With a combination of fate and his sister Hanna's friend who wanted to buy a bigger house, by mid-afternoon Gustav had found the perfect home. It was a two-bedroom bungalow with running water, a flushing toilet, and a full-sized sloping porcelain bathtub. Although the kitchen was a little smaller than her existing one in the farmhouse, there was a large open room adjacent to it, which could serve as a dining room when Amelia wanted to feed her entire family.

There was a clean cemented basement with a gas furnace, and a root cellar where she could store the ample produce, which she could grow in the tilled backyard. Once Amelia accepted that she deserved an easier life afforded by the amenities of living in town, Gustav knew she would readily turn the small house into a home.

Unbeknownst to his father, Otto was busy formulating his own departure from the family homestead. Of course, he realized what he would be giving up if he decided to purchase the farm on the outskirts of Wolseley that his brother-in-law Herbert had told him about; but ever since Albert had tossed out the innuendo about Clarence and Millie, Otto could not put it out of his mind.

And the more he thought about it, the more he remembered all of Clarence's lengthy and unexplained absences from whatever chore the men had started for the day.

Whereas Otto had tolerated Clarence because he was married to his sister, he had always been suspicious of him. Although his brother-in-law could turn on the charm at will, he reminded Otto of a garter snake slithering through the prairie grass.

Over the past nine years since the Great Depression, Otto had saved his share of the steadily increasing crop yields in a strongbox in the seldom-used potato cellar. The one and only time he had taken money from his nest egg was when he'd purchased a new vehicle to replace the old one Millie had stolen.

During Otto's visits to Elisabeth and Herbert, he came to realize that he had more than adequate funds to purchase the property on the western edge of Wolseley. Furthermore, there was no doubt in Otto's mind that his three daughters could benefit by living closer to his sister and her three children.

As much as he knew that his mother loved his three girls, Otto wanted his children to spend more time with their properly brought-up cousins, raised by loving parents in a good home—not like the environment from which their mother must have come.

The next evening when his father asked him to stay in from the fields the following day and for Johann to remain home from school, Otto agreed at once. He had no idea why Gustav wanted to take Amelia to Melville, but this was the opportunity he'd waited for, so he decided that Clarence could handle the morning chores.

As soon as his parents left for their outing, he hurried his girls into his own vehicle and drove to Wolseley. Otto expected that he could finalize the sale of the land with the elderly owner by the end of the day and still be back to the farm to help with the evening milking.

89

With a start, Ursula sat straight up in bed. In the early dawn light streaming through the window, it took a few minutes to realize where she was, until she heard Clarence's snoring. Slowly lowering herself back onto the bed, she reflected fondly upon her dream in which she was back in the assembly hall in Rivers. She was being presented with the certificate signifying her satisfactory completion of the training requirements and that she was now Aircraftwoman First Class. Her whole life was ahead of her, and if she'd taken Sally Jones' advice, she would've progressed up the ranks and perhaps been sent to England.

Instead, here she was, five years later, saddled with a man she still knew little about and cared even less for, and four small children. It seemed the only time she and Clarence had anything to do with each other was in this bed, so the babies just kept coming.

If Otto did not have Clarence doing the barnyard chores, he kept him out in the fields from dawn to dusk, and he was never around to help her with their multiple offspring. Suddenly Ursula resented her husband's freedom. Even though she suspected that Otto could be an exacting taskmaster, Clarence was at least outdoors, away from the incessant demands of four crying kids.

How could she be so trapped by the young age of twenty-four? Ursula had readily come to realize that she did not even like children very much. When Robert was born, she honestly tried to learn from her mother about caring for him, but when Justine arrived, in her mind she had very good reason to have not the slightest interest in her daughter.

It occurred to Ursula that being a mother was the most thankless job in the world. Most of the time, Ursula felt like sobbing right along with them, since she'd still not accepted that her beloved brother Leonard was dead. Every spare minute she found, she would collapse in a heap by the kitchen stove to reread his letters.

When Millie had stolen away in the middle of the night, Ursula secretly wished that she had known what she was planning because she would have gone with her. Right from the beginning, the two women had been kindred spirits, and now it was not fair that Millie was free and she was stuck on this boring farm.

Had she escaped, Ursula would have used the last of her money from Grandmama and begun looking again for her darling Hans. She would have searched to the ends of the earth until she found him, and then she would never have let him go. Hans Gerhart was her heart and soul and the only man she would ever love. Had Ursula given birth to *his* children, she would have cherished them.

90

Why was she always so tired? Since this baby girl that she christened Mary, Elisabeth could not get her energy back. She had been to see the new doctor, but rather than take her seriously, he had gently chastened her to allow time for her body to heal and to remember that she was getting older.

Although it was not possible for Amelia to come to help, her mother-in-law came every day and Elisabeth followed Dr. Sterling's advice of napping whenever she put Mary down during the afternoon.

Instead of invigorating her, her rest often fatigued her more. Herbert knew that Elisabeth was eager to resume her usual activities with their family, and especially to tend to her garden, but after a half hour outdoors, she would need to sit down on the grass. Finally, during a visit to her parents, Elisabeth decided to go see Dr. Roth.

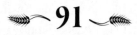

91

As luck would have it, Fraya was home for a brief vacation with her folks in Neudorf. And since she was in her final year of medical school, she offered to examine Elisabeth.

For the briefest moment during the checkup, Fraya had a niggling thought beyond the reaches of her consciousness. She'd felt an irregularity in Elisabeth's right breast until she remembered her saying she was lactating. Milk was probably secreting and filling the ducts in preparation for the baby's next feeding.

Much more obvious were the indications that Elisabeth was suffering from anemia. The dark circles under her eyes, combined with the pallor of her skin, her fingernail beds, and the mucous membranes of her mouth, could account for her fatigue and general malaise. Fraya was convinced that a regime of iron and vitamin replacement would soon restore Elisabeth's state of health and the energy she needed to care for her family.

As soon as her father finished with his patient, she would recommend that he write Elisabeth a prescription for iron and vitamins, which she could readily fill at Wirth's Drugstore.

Later, Dr. Max Roth would confirm his daughter's diagnosis by ordering an appropriate blood test and would concur with Fraya's treatment.

 **92**

While the family still sat around the table that evening after their return from Melville and before Otto left to take his daughters home to bed, Gustav cleared his throat, glanced at Amelia, and expressed that they had an announcement to make.

"I took your mother to Melville today to show her the house I purchased for the two of us. It is a comfortable two-bedroom home right beside St. Paul Lutheran Church and across from the CNR rail yard."

Taking advantage of the unusual stillness in the normally boisterous kitchen, Gustav continued.

"It is time that your mother had an easier life with things like electricity, running water, and a central gas furnace, which heats the whole house. But mostly, your mother deserves a rest."

They all sat in stunned silence, including Amelia. She was still in a state of shock, and it did not help that every member of her family was now looking at her. All the while in Melville and on the long ride back to the farm, all she said to Gustav was that she liked the big garden in the backyard, but her mind was otherwise in turmoil.

What had he been thinking? Who would care for her grandchildren, her garden, and her house here? Surely Gustav could not believe that Ursula could step into her shoes and look after the chores she'd managed for nearly forty years. Did he not realize that some days his daughter sat by the kitchen stove, reading until her mother finally prodded her to help?

Within minutes, Otto broke the hushed tension with a declaration of his own.

"As it happens, Papa, I have made a purchase of my own today, and as soon as this year's crop is harvested, my girls and I are moving to our farm on the outskirts of Wolseley. Mama will no longer be responsible for raising my daughters, and I absolutely agree that it is high time Ursula and Clarence took care of their own family."

"What are you saying? Why would you buy another farm when I have always said that you will get this one?" asked Gustav.

"I am a grown man now, and I don't need you to dole out money to me when I am perfectly capable of earning my own living. I want the freedom to make the decisions for my family instead of having you control when I get paid and what we do," Otto said, with a surly glance at his father.

"I don't tell you what to do! Where did you get that idea? If you wanted money before the fall, why didn't you just say so, and I would have gone to the bank?"

"That's exactly what I'm talking about! I don't need you to get money for me. In case you have forgotten, I am twenty-five years old. As I recall, you had your own homestead by the time you were eighteen, and I'm sure your father didn't dare decide what you were supposed to do every day," Otto snarled before draining his coffee cup and pushing away from the table.

"Well, since that's how you feel, you don't have to wait for the crop to be taken off. If you think that I am controlling you, you can leave right now," bellowed Gustav, as he also rose from his chair.

"By this time tomorrow, my daughters and I will be gone," Otto snapped, as he gathered his girls to his side.

Amelia found her voice.

"Your children. Who will look after your daughters if you leave the farm? Has their mother come home?"

"Mama, please. I know how to take care of Francis, Faye, and Darlene. I love my girls, and even if that woman came back, I would not let her step foot in the door. Good night, Mama. Come along now, girls, give your grandma a hug and kiss before we go home to bed."

The next morning, when Otto and his daughters did not arrive for breakfast, Amelia put bread, milk, and a jar of coffee into a wooden basket and walked up the lane to her son's home. The door was open and each of them, including three-year-old Darlene, was busy carrying small parcels to be packed into the car.

"Oh, Otto, you really meant what you told Papa last night?" Amelia asked, as her grandchildren came running to hug her.

"Thank you, Mama, for bringing us breakfast, and especially the coffee. Yes, I did mean every single word I said," Otto replied, as he gratefully sipped the hot coffee.

It was not until the car was overflowing and Otto was getting ready to put his girls into the back seat that the finality of her son's departure struck Amelia, and she burst into tears.

"Please don't cry, Mama. I know you have practically raised my daughters and you love them, but you will still get to see them. Once Papa has cooled off, we will visit often. In fact, when I return to get the rest of my belongings, why don't you come and stay with us for a week or two? Now, Mama, could you please kiss the girls goodbye so we can be on our way?"

Amelia stood and watched another one of her sons leave home, until the car was nothing more than a speck in the distance. Then gathering up the empty basket, she started back to the house before deciding to find solace again in her garden.

94

"Why would you not give one third of your land to Clarence and me right now? We heard you tell Otto that you would make him that offer if he stayed here on your farm," Ursula demanded of her father.

Gustav took a prolonged and stern look at his daughter, wondering what had happened to her since she'd left his home.

"There are many reasons why I would not just hand over my land to you and your husband, but the main one is because Otto has been running this farm for nearly ten years now. Both of you need to prove to me that you can look after my homestead without running it into the ground. You have been away for a long time, Ursula, and you seem to have forgotten how to work hard."

"What do you mean, Papa? I work right beside Mama all the time, helping her with the chores in the house and outside. And what makes you think that I can't look after my own children?" Ursula snapped, as she glared rebelliously at first her father and then her mother.

"If you're such a good mother, why don't you attend to your children when they are crying? And when they need something, tell me why they all go to their grandmother? I often think that if their grandma was not always hugging and kissing them, the poor little souls would not know the meaning of love."

Sitting on the other side of the table, Clarence cringed. Whereas he realized that what his father-in-law was saying was absolutely true, his words still hit below the belt, and this kitchen was just too small for them to be spoken here.

The two sat in sullen silence as they glared across the table at each other. The impasse finally came to an end when Ursula lowered her eyes and uttered, "Well, Papa, can you please tell us what you have in mind?"

"Your mother and I have decided that we would give Clarence and you three years to show us that you can handle everything that is needed to make a success of farming. And let me tell you, it will be a lot easier for the two of you than it was when I was proving my land. There was nothing here but thick green grasses blowing in the wind, and the prairie sod was so tough and matted with roots that your grandfather's oxen could hardly pull my new steel plow through the ground. There was no house with furniture, no big tilled garden to grow vegetables, and no farm animals to feed you during the winter months. To my reasoning, if a country could expect a man to break and seed up to fifty acres of land, build a home, and live in it for at least six months of each of the three years, your mother and I should be justified in asking Clarence and you to prove that you can take over our farm in three years' time."

"Papa, you've never said anything about being a homesteader. I had no idea that you didn't just buy this land."

Gazing out the window, Gustav quietly answered, "As a matter of fact, I did buy this land from my friend's wife, Sarah, when her husband Andrew Thompson was accidentally killed by falling out of the hayloft. In 1909 your Uncle Rolf and I became homesteaders at the same time, and we claimed two quarter-sections of land adjacent to each other. However, before I bought this farm, I sold my homestead and your grandfather's, which I had purchased years earlier, to Rolf."

Suddenly turning to Ursula, Gustav exclaimed, "So, that is my offer. Take it or leave it. The choice is yours. But you should be grateful for having this chance."

How fortunate that Herbert Kuss's family had lived their entire lives in Summerberry. They knew everybody in the community, and as it happened, Herbert's eldest sister, Marjorie, had a spinster friend, Ethel Smythe, who was interested in becoming Otto's housekeeper.

In short order, many of the neighbouring farm wives began to spread the rumour that Ethel was searching for a husband, and because she had reached the advanced age of twenty-seven, she was hoping to find a man with a ready-made family. Almost as soon as Otto moved into the house on his recently purchased farm, the volume of the gossip started to swell.

Unknown even to her closest friend, Ethel had always loved her brother Herbert, and she'd been devastated when he courted and married a woman from another township.

Not above listening to rumours herself, Ethel had clung to the recent hearsay circulating in the farming community that Elisabeth Kuss was seriously ill. She had spent her youth dreaming of becoming Herbert's wife, and after his unthinkable wedding to a total stranger, he had stayed at home with her aging parents rather than consider any other suitor.

Now she felt that she was biding her time until the inevitable occurred, and what better way to wait and prepare than by practising caring for a man and his young family? In addition, she'd be in the position of being able to invite Herbert and his family to her employer's home for supper and thus prove her housekeeping prowess to her future husband. Furthermore, Ethel could observe firsthand Elisabeth's state of health and determine for herself whether there was any truth to the rapidly spreading notion that she was dying.

Most importantly, though, while working in the household of another family, there could be no suspicion that she was scheming after a married man.

There was no deterring Gustav from his plan. He staunchly refused to hear Amelia's pleas that Ursula was not capable of caring for her four young children.

She was in her garden every day, as though she could will the vegetables to grow faster so she could preserve more for the winter months. Over the summer, Amelia picked fruit to make jam and jelly: strawberries, raspberries, saskatoons, chokecherries, and gooseberries. And every time she went into town, she bought baskets of peaches, pears, and grapes to can and store in the cool cellar.

It was a beautiful autumn with Indian summer lasting well into October. Gustav and Amelia waited until the weather started to turn inclement before leaving the homestead where they had lived for over twenty years. Rather than haul their outdated furniture to Melville, Gustav decided to surprise his wife with a new kitchen and living room and bedroom suites. His last effort to smooth the transition for Amelia was to purchase a new automobile and to give Ursula and Clarence the car he had bought only a few years ago. Gustav's sole purpose in offering the generous gift to his younger daughter was to make sure they would not be stranded on the farm.

By bleak mid-winter, with its fierce cold and squally winds, Elisabeth had to acknowledge that she was not getting any better. The vitamin and iron medications no longer helped as she thought they'd done during the summer months, and most mornings she had neither the will nor the energy to get out of bed.

By January, when the roads became almost impassable, Herbert arranged for his two older children, Emma and Norman, to bunk together, and insisted that his aging parents move into his daughter's vacated bedroom until spring. Elisabeth desperately wanted to return to Dr. Fraya Roth, who for the past year was practising medicine with her father in Neudorf, but Herbert repeatedly placated her by saying it was too far to travel. After all, it was better for her to rest than to risk going outdoors. Taking her into his arms, he promised his cherished wife that the first day the snow began to melt, they would be in the truck on the way to Neudorf.

It was one of those years when it seemed that spring would never come. However, on the morning when Elisabeth was washing and found a sizeable lump under her armpit near her right breast, Herbert was spurred into action. Regardless of the foul weather and road conditions, he knew he must get Elisabeth to the doctor.

Dusk was rapidly descending, and like so many evenings of this never-ending winter, Clarence was nowhere to be found. Ursula knew she needed to milk the two cows, but again she worried about leaving her children on their own. She always left Sandra in her crib—she was sure she could not get out—but Robert was far too young to be expected to look after the other two girls for even the thirty minutes it took to tend to the cows.

Although he was not quite five years of age, Ursula was pleasantly surprised by how capable and serious her only son was about helping with his sisters, and she knew that Justine would be responsible enough to listen to him. It was Elaine who could not understand that her mother needed to leave them while she hurried out to the barn to do the chores.

Previously, Ursula had placed Elaine in with Sandra; but the evening she'd fallen out and split her head open, she realized that was not the solution. Ursula sat her three older children at the table and, as she always admonished, told them to look at their picture books until she returned.

For whatever reason, that particular evening Elaine was not content to sit with her older brother and sister in the kitchen. Try as hard as they could, neither Robert nor Justine could stop her from running outside into the night soon after their mother had left. So they stood hopelessly at the open door and watched in the shadowy light of the kerosene lamp as their younger sister flailed about in the snow banks just beyond the fence.

Soon they were frightened by first one set of headlights and then another entering the yard. It was purely by the grace of God that Elaine was still standing on her feet and that Herbert saw the little girl in time to stop. On the other hand, the driver of the vehicle, which had turned into the lane shortly after he had, was coming with much more speed and was forced to slam on the brakes to avoid rear-ending them. Herbert was out of the truck and dashing through the drifting snow toward his niece without even realizing just how close the car had come to hitting them. He gathered her into his arms and called back to Elisabeth, telling her to wait in the truck until he returned, as he carried Elaine into the warmth of the house.

Elisabeth hurried out of the truck and followed her husband into the house. Minutes later, when a drunken Clarence stumbled into the kitchen, he demanded, "What the hell is going on here? Why did you stop that old jalopy in the middle of the yard? I damn near ran into the back of it."

Ignoring their brother-in-law completely, Herbert heated the kettle while Elisabeth wrapped Elaine from head to toe in one of her grandmother's comforters. When the water was warm, Herbert poured it into a basin and, motioning for Elisabeth to sit down at the table with Elaine on her lap, slowly immersed her tiny hands into it.

Herbert would never forget how his mother had saved his father's feet the winter he'd frozen them after being lost in a snowstorm. She repeatedly immersed them in a tub of tepid water until their normal temperature was restored.

Clarence continued to rant and rave by the stove, with Robert and Justine looking on as though they were frozen in position, until again the door burst open, this time with Ursula echoing her husband. "What the hell is going on in my house?"

"That's exactly what I want to find out. Your know-it-all sister and her husband came to such a sudden stop in the yard that I just about hit the rear end of their god-forsaken truck," Clarence bellowed.

"Well, none of it would have happened if you could ever get your ass home in time to do your chores," Ursula yelled back, without taking notice of her three anxious children.

"They're hardly my chores, since nobody bothered to ask me if I wanted to be stuck on this bloody farm to milk cows the whole winter."

"Don't talk to me about being left in this hellhole. At least you go into town practically every day and sometimes the entire night. What I want to know is where you sleep and with whom?"

"Stop it right now, both of you," said Herbert. "In case either of you has the slightest interest, Elisabeth and I are trying to save Elaine's hands from frostbite. Because neither of you takes any responsibility for your own children, she ran outside looking for you. If we'd not come along, Clarence might well have run over her before she froze to death in the snowdrift. Not to mention that you sound like two old drunkards verbally brawling in a beer parlour."

Before they finally laid their sleeping niece down into her bed, Herbert and Elisabeth felt confident that she would suffer no permanent damage to her hands.

When Elaine's fingers became warm, Elisabeth carefully wrapped each one in flannel and tied them loosely with torn strips of the soft cloth.

Once the children were all asleep, Elisabeth asked her sister, "Is Clarence's drinking a regular occurrence? And do you usually leave your family alone while you tend to the chores?"

Ursula first bristled at her sister's question, but then she realized that Elisabeth might actually want to help.

"It certainly is happening more and more often. The worst thing Papa could have done was give Clarence that car. You can't honestly think I like leaving my kids by themselves in the house, but what else can I do when I have to milk the cows?"

Even as she tried to console Ursula, her mind raced. Tomorrow when they left the farm, Elisabeth would ask Herbert to drive to Melville and stop at her parents before they went to Regina to visit the specialist Dr. Roth had recommended. She would apprise Mama and Papa of the problems Ursula was having. Perhaps together Herbert and Papa could put the fear of God into her worthless husband.

Following a restless night, Elisabeth broached the subject with her husband, but Herbert would not hear of it.

"We do not have time to visit your parents before your appointment with Dr. Hancock. Once the specialist has given you a clean bill of health, then of course we will go talk to your parents about Ursula's sad situation."

"It is more than sad, Herbert. What's happening there is dangerous."

"My darling, I couldn't agree with you more, but for once you need to take care of yourself before others."

99

In his many years of practice as an oncologist, Dr. Charles Hancock could not remember palpitating such a large and obvious lump. How could neither this young woman nor her husband have felt the unshapely mass? Surely she had noticed it and even felt uncomfortable when she clasped her arm to her chest. Why did most of his patients wait too long before seeking medical attention?

As he examined Elisabeth, he knew he'd be scheduling her for major surgery and performing a radical mastectomy to excise all adjacent lymph nodes from her right axilla and from the underlying pectoral muscle. But would the extensive disfiguring surgery and aggressive radiation be enough? He augmented his distress when he checked Elisabeth's nipple and observed the secretion of milk, which proved she was a recently lactating mother.

"Could you please get dressed, Mrs. Kuss? If you need assistance, my nurse will be happy to assist you before bringing you to my office."

Dr. Hancock asked his receptionist to bring a fresh pot of coffee and then asked Herbert to join him in his comfortable office.

"Please help yourself to a cup of coffee, Mr. Kuss, and then have a seat," he began. "I'm afraid that the news I must give you is very grave, and I want to speak with you before Mrs. Kuss joins us. I have just finished examining your wife, and I intend to admit her to the hospital immediately for surgery first thing tomorrow morning. Once she's been given a general anaesthetic, I will take a biopsy of the lump on her breast, but I strongly suspect it's malignant. If I'm correct, I shall have to remove Elisabeth's right breast and considerable surrounding tissue. It is called a radical mastectomy. It's major surgery, which means she will be in the hospital for some time."

He knew he was nervous and thus speaking in medical terms, so Charles consciously changed his approach.

"I am very sorry to bear such distressing news, Mr. Kuss, and I realize you need time to digest what I'm telling you. However, I have asked my nurse to bring your wife to my office, and before she arrives, I want to ask you how much I should tell her. As I've told you, I think that she has breast cancer, but do you want her to know?"

"No, no! Please do not tell her the truth," said Herbert, "at least not right now. Oh, this is entirely my fault. Elisabeth wanted to visit her family doctor in Neudorf during the winter, but she was feeling so poorly that I didn't want to take the chance with the bitter weather and terrible road conditions."

"Please, Mr. Kuss. We cannot accomplish anything if you blame yourself. Your wife will need your love and support to help her through this ordeal. With your permission then, I will tell your wife that I'm admitting her to complete some tests. But I shall not give her my unconfirmed diagnosis. However, in all honesty, I must prepare her that she will awake from surgery with considerable pain and be covered in bandages and drainage tubes."

The warm rays of the sun were imparting their energy to the awakening earth on the bright spring morning in early April when Gustav, Amelia, and Johann drove into the Warner homestead.

They had not been home since Christmas, and although they'd planned to come for Easter in mid-March, they spent the last three Sundays in Regina visiting Elisabeth as she began her arduous recovery from surgery.

They had barely opened the doors of the car when their four ecstatic grandchildren came running through the gate to greet them. On their way into the house, Gustav thought it strange that Clarence was gone with the automobile so early in the morning. But in the excitement of their arrival, he chose to not ask Ursula about her husband's whereabouts.

Later, after Amelia served the coffee and cinnamon buns she had baked yesterday, as though she'd never been away from the farmhouse kitchen, Gustav turned to his grandson.

"Come with me, Robert. Let's check how things are on the farm now that spring is returning to the land."

Robert liked nothing more than walking around the farm with his grandpa, and soon man and boy were out in the yard appraising how his treasured homestead had weathered the winter. As they strolled toward the barn, Gustav noticed that the animal trough on the eastern wall still had all the dirt and mouldy remnants of winter.

"One of the first things we will do this morning is to clean out this trough and fill it with water so the cows and horses can come here for a drink. Soon the puddles will dry up and the animals will get thirsty."

Looking at his grandfather as if a light had just gone on, Robert replied, "So, that's why my dad goes into Neudorf. Mommy says he has gone back to his watering trough again."

"Tell me, Robert, how often does your father go into town?"

"Oh, whenever it stops snowing and the roads are open, he leaves us here. And then he stays away for a long time, except after the day Elaine froze her hands. He didn't go for quite a while because they had a big fight about it, even louder than usual. But yesterday he put a hook at the top of the door so Mommy can lock us in the house while she milks the cows, and he has been gone ever since."

How dare Clarence Cardinal, a man whom he'd trusted, taken into his home, and offered one-third ownership of his land, abandon his family in the middle of winter? And what was this about Elaine freezing her hands? The child was only two years old. What in God's name was she doing outside? It took Gustav several minutes to speak, before gently asking, "Is that where your father is now? In Neudorf? Did he not come home last night to do the chores?"

"Yes, Grandpa. He left yesterday and he has not come home yet," said Robert, suddenly frightened by the look on his grandfather's face.

"Let's go back to the house, Robert. We will clean the water trough this afternoon. Right now there is something else I must do, but you can help me later."

Gustav flung open the door and quickly motioned for Amelia to come to his side. He explained that he and Johann were driving into Neudorf and then he told his youngest son to grab his coat and come with him.

Gustav would get the car key away from Clarence and have Johann return with the vehicle, first to the farm, and tomorrow he would drive it to Melville where Gustav would lock it in his garage. He had no qualms about Johann driving the automobile, but he did not want his sixteen-year-old son going into Albert's disreputable beer parlour, where he knew he would find Clarence.

Then it occurred to Gustav that he would ask his close friend, Max Roth, to come with him to fend off Clarence and Albert Schultz. Dr. Maximilian Roth, the reluctant Jew. And who could blame him?

Driving to Neudorf, Gustav felt his composure returning as he reminisced about the strong friendship he had with Maximilian. Gustav had actually initiated it a few months after Leonard's death when he found himself on the doorstep of Dr. Rolf Spitznagel's home and medical office. Oh, how he missed his friend and confidant, especially with the tragic end of his eldest son, one of the numerous babies that the kindly doctor had brought into the world.

Rolf had always spoken very highly of the farmer who had purchased his dead friend's homestead in the English township to save his wife and children from a life of backbreaking drudgery or, worse yet, abject poverty. Gently touching Gustav on the shoulder, Max had invited him in for a cup of coffee, and it had been several hours later before they emerged from the comfortable parlour.

From that day onward, whenever both men were in Neudorf, they could be found in Max's home. As the weeks and months passed, Gustav realized that he was coming to terms with Leonard's tragic death, because of Dr. Max Roth.

Nonetheless, Gustav had been surprised by their appreciative behaviour as, one by one, Max, his parents, Rebecca, Trudi, Fraya, and Vera Roth had expressed their profound gratitude, during the celebrations in Neudorf on Victory in Europe Day on May 8, 1945, for his eldest son's ultimate sacrifice.

Nothing could have prepared him for the truth. He knew that at the end of the war Max expected to hear from his two brothers, and Rebecca was beside herself anticipating news from her parents and her three sisters and their families. They waited and waited, until almost two years had passed, but they still had not received a single word from one of them.

In the spring of 1947, Max and Rebecca booked their passage across the Atlantic for the long journey to Salzburg. When the heinous findings of the Nuremberg trials of Nazi war criminals during 1945 and 1946 began being released all over the world, in the face of the cumulative atrocities against Jews, they realized they could no longer wait and hope.

Dr. Fraya Roth had taken over the lion's share of his medical practice, and Max decided that Rebecca and he must return to the old country. They both recognized that they could not return to the beautiful countryside they'd fled in 1932, but it was with their families that they most sought to be reunited.

⟫⟫~ 101 ~⟪⟪

The scorching heat of the prairie summer was at its peak that Thursday afternoon when Gustav drove into Neudorf to welcome his friends home.

When he parked his car in front of the doctor's house, he noticed that the parlour curtains were still drawn, and even the office looked vacant.

Gustav knocked on the door and then waited a long time before it was opened by a gaunt, much older version of Max Roth. The man had always been robust, but now he was skin and bones, his hair was totally white, and his dark eyes were lifeless. What in God's name had happened to his friend?

"Max, it's me, Gustav. Have you been ill? Or was your journey that strenuous?"

Max broke down in his doorway.

"They are gone. They are all gone. Rebecca's parents, Aaron and Anna Sheps, her three sisters and all of their families, and all of my family. There is no one left."

"I don't understand, Max. Where did they all go? Please let's go sit in your parlour."

At last, through agonized sobs, Dr. Maximilian Roth uttered his horrifying soliloquy.

"God only knows when, but sometime between 1933 and 1945, they all must have been cremated in the ovens or machine-gunned down by the SS. We searched and searched the whole time we were there, but we located none of them. Every man, woman, and child of Rebecca's family and of mine along with all our friends and colleagues have disappeared without a trace. We can only conclude that the Nazis annihilated every single Jew we ever knew in Salzburg. If not for one of my old university professors, we would've been on the street. He found us a room in the residence and gave us food to eat, not that we had an appetite. We only wanted to escape from the unspeakable horrors of the Holocaust and come back home. I'll bet you did not suspect that I am a Jew, did you Gustav, my good German friend."

"I was never a Nazi," answered Gustav.

Max and Rebecca became frequent visitors to the Warner homestead; the men walked about Gustav's land, and the women communed in the garden. Friendship and nature slowly revived their spirits and Amelia's cooking helped to put some meat back on their skeletal frames. But the pain and sadness in their eyes would never again be replaced with joy.

～ 102 ～

Coming out of his reverie as he reached the outskirts of Neudorf, Gustav drove straight to Max's home. With the automobile still running, he told Johann to come around to the driver's side and to return immediately to the farm. As the men walked across Main Street to Albert Schultz's business, the blight of the village, Gustav told

Max that they would likely find his son-in-law inebriated. It simply was not within Gustav's frame of reference, however, what they would encounter.

Gingerly opening the door to the beer parlour and seeing the owner behind the bar, Gustav tersely asked the whereabouts of Clarence Cardinal. Perhaps without thinking, Albert responded, "He is in the first room on the right at the top of the stairs."

Then realizing who was inquiring, he added, "But he is busy at the moment, and you will have to wait before you can see him."

Neither man heeded the advice as they charged up the short stairway. Without bothering to knock, they pushed open the flimsy door. In the dingy room, in front of their startled eyes, they saw Clarence in bed with a strange woman, vigorously engaged in the act of fornication. Dumbstruck, they watched until a female voice rose from beneath her debaucher, "Who the hell are you and what are you doing in here?"

Spinning his head around, Clarence, in his nakedness, was now the one stunned by the two interlopers. Leaping from the bed, he grabbed his pants and turned to face his father-in-law.

Gustav, however, had recovered sufficiently.

"Hand over the key to my automobile. I don't care how you spend your days and nights, but this is the last time you will use my vehicle to get you to the place of your sins."

By this time Max had found Clarence's coat hanging on the back of the door and deftly lifted the key from the inside pocket.

"I have found what we have come for, Gustav, so let's leave right now—before I lose my temper."

➤ 103 ⟵

Even as he performed the surgery, Dr. Hancock was alarmed by the size and thus possible spread of Elisabeth's tumour. As soon as the pathologist confirmed that the biopsy specimen was malignant, he rescrubbed, changed the surgical drapes, and proceeded with the radical mastectomy.

During the operation, he excised the right breast, all adjacent lymph nodes, and the pectoral muscle. The skilled surgeon went right down to the chest wall, and yet he worried that he'd not been able to cut away enough to prevent the cancer from metastasizing to her lungs and possibly to elsewhere within the blood and lymphatic systems.

When Mrs. Kuss recovered from the surgery, Dr. Hancock would arrange for her to receive radiotherapy and some drug therapies, which had recently been introduced to treat the metastases of hormone-dependent cancers. He'd done the operation on women for a number of years now, and again it occurred to him that his patients were getting younger and younger. This fact made it even more difficult for them to accept the radical treatment for often such a small lump in their breast.

Perhaps he was becoming too old for his surgical practice, especially when he lost what seemed to him a disproportionate number of young women to this dreadful killer. What bothered Dr. Hancock the most was meeting with his patients on the morning after the surgery and explaining the indignities he'd had to perform on their bodies while entrusted to his care. Then there was the dilemma of how much to tell each woman about her condition and the truth about her prognosis. Most of his colleagues believed the patient should be the last to be told she would likely succumb to the cancer, but Dr. Hancock felt an inherent repulsion about lying, particularly when she likely already knew. Still, as her hospitalization lengthened, Dr. Hancock would be surprised that Herbert would be the one adamantly insisting that his wife be told nothing about her illness.

When she awoke from the anaesthetic, Elisabeth was in unbearable pain, and Dr. Hancock could not understand why she did not respond to the analgesics he had prescribed. The drugs were effective for most women as they began their long road to recovery. When the nurses gently changed her position in bed, she cried out in anguish, until Herbert finally told Dr. Hancock that she'd not suffered such agony even in childbirth.

After three days without the slightest improvement, the surgeon decided that something must be wrong and that he must take Elisabeth back to the operating room. She was barely cognizant of her situation, and when Dr. Hancock sought Herbert's permission, he took considerable convincing.

No one in either Herbert's or Elisabeth's family had been hospitalized, much less operated on. And given her condition after the first operation, it was hardly surprising that he hesitated to consent again. Herbert Kuss's confidence would definitely not be heightened when Dr. Hancock explained that her pain was due to him having left a Halsted's forceps in the surgical site during her original operation.

If not for the love from her ten precious grandchildren, Amelia would have found little joy throughout the past decade. It had been a long, lonely winter in Melville. She had so much time to crochet that after she made her first tablecloth, she began working on a set of curtains for her living room. Essentially cut off from her grandchildren, she now appreciated their outpourings of affection even more than when she'd been living in the same house surrounded by seven of them.

During the past ten years since the end of the Depression, Amelia had struggled with all the upheavals within her family. And for a long time after Leonard had been killed overseas, she felt that she could not carry on with life. It had been the little ones constantly needing her love and attention that brought Amelia back from the abyss, and now with Elisabeth's illness and the unrelenting disruptions in her remaining children's lives, her cherished grandchildren remained her reason for being.

How had Gustav thought she would stop worrying about them by being away from all of the turmoil? In all these years, her husband still had not accepted that it was her nature to fret and that she far preferred to roll up her sleeves and work through the disorder in her family. During the spring and summer of 1949, Amelia would be so busy caring for Elisabeth's three children during her protracted stay in the hospital and trying to help Ursula that she would not have time to plant her large garden plot in Melville.

From the day he sent Johann back to the farm alone from Neudorf and then asked him to drive his mother home to Melville in their old automobile, Gustav remained on the homestead. Amelia would never learn what Gustav had discovered in town with regard to Clarence. When he arrived home that day, Gustav had only said that Clarence was not yet ready to return to the farm, but that when he did, he would do so like a "dog with his tail between his legs."

~ 105 ~

Until the end of his school year, Johann drove his mother back and forth between Regina and the farm and then returned with her to Melville while she sat transfixed in the passenger seat and worried. Amelia's apprehension was not lessened when Gustav spent the entire spring on the homestead rather than return to the house in town that she thought he'd too hastily purchased.

At breakfast the morning after his last day of school, she asked Johann to pack sufficient clothes for the summer because they were locking up the house and moving back to the homestead. Enough was enough. If Gustav could abandon the house to stay on the farm, so could she.

After spending the long winter in Melville, Johann was equally happy about returning to the homestead and working alongside his father on the land. Although he had every intention of going to university and following in Leonard's footsteps by studying pharmacology, like Gustav, Johann enjoyed the hard work demanded by tilling the soil in the peace and serenity of the outdoors.

Their arrival prompted the usual squeals of delight from Ursula's children as Robert led the way, closely followed by Justine and Elaine, with Sandra weighted at the rear by a sodden diaper. Dropping to her knees to hug each child in turn, Amelia felt her spirits lift.

When Amelia gathered Sandra in her arms, she was appalled by the smell emanating from the tattered rag that served as her diaper. How could a mother leave a child in such a state? Walking briskly into the house with only a terse salutation to her daughter, Amelia carried Sandra straight into the bedroom, cleansed her, and found a decent piece of cloth to wrap around the baby's bottom.

There was little point in talking to Ursula again about her obvious neglect, and right after she made lunch, Amelia asked Johann to drive her to Neudorf. She planned to invite Rebecca and Max to come for supper and to visit with Katherina. While she was in the General Store, she would buy several bolts of fabric to sew new diapers for her grandchild.

As spring gave way to the days of summer, the homestead regained its feeling of warmth and wholesomeness. Even Clarence settled down with Amelia back in charge, preparing the meals, nurturing the children, tending to the garden, and re-establishing the sense of family.

The never-ending tasks of farming, gardening, and raising a family kept them all busy. When Johann was not using the older car to drive Amelia to Summerberry to visit Elisabeth who was finally home from the hospital, Clarence tried to convince his young brother-in-law to hand over the key.

Clarence had sufficient sense to realize that if he wanted to imbibe, he could ill afford to be caught again staying overnight at Albert's. A second occurrence would no doubt result in Gustav throwing him off his precious farm. Clarence thought he could persuade the seventeen-year-old boy to let him use the car, but he'd seriously underestimated Johann.

During his first attempt, he turned on his charm as they walked back from the fields.

"Johann, if you are not going anywhere this evening, I was wondering if I could borrow your car for a couple of hours to drive to Neudorf tonight."

"Although I am not planning to use my car tonight, there is no way that I would loan it to you," Johann answered.

"Since you like to stay at home and play with your nieces and nephew, I can't think of why you wouldn't let me drive that old jalopy to town."

"If I had to give you a reason, I could think of plenty, but since Papa gave me his car, I am not going to bother," said Johann.

"Well, as a matter of fact, your father gave that car to me and then one day, without explanation, he took back the key before you got your hands on it."

"Which is precisely why you don't deserve to have it."

"Now listen here, you young punk," said a riled Clarence. "It's bad enough that I've put up with your father's rudeness to me, but I will certainly not take it from you. Hand over the key before I get angry and relieve you of it, you dirty Kraut."

Johann Warner was perhaps half an inch shy of six feet tall. and although he was not big, he was strong and muscular like his father. Before the barely five-foot-six-inch Clarence could bat an eyelash, Johann collared him around the neck and lifted him into the air.

Glaring into his brother-in-law's frightened eyes, he roared, "If I ever hear you say that name again, I will throw you off this farm and make sure you never set foot on it for the rest of your life."

Then tossing him on the ground as if he was a stick, Johann strode away without a backward glance.

～ 107 ～

Clarence forgot about going to Neudorf for a time, but then he became restless again. God, what did these people do for fun and excitement? Sure, the whole family went to town each Sunday to go to church and visit with relatives or friends. They also went to the fowl suppers and other silly activities in the township, including funerals for everyone who'd finally packed it in to escape the boredom.

And what had happened to Ursula? Where was that flirting, dancing, gay young girl he married? Now all she did was sit around with her mother, eat like a pig, and go to bed as soon as their brood was asleep. With the birth of every baby, she'd put on more weight, until now she was practically rotund.

Not only was she no longer pleasing to look at, but on the rare occasion she was amorous, she was awkward to couple with in their small bed. He was still a young man, and who could fault him for needing to meet his physical needs? And could he help it that even though he was already bald, women found him very attractive? He had to find a way to get back and forth to that two-bit town.

Clarence Cardinal had always been able to find a man or, in his later years, woman after his own heart. His good friend, Albert Schultz, was the only German that Clarence would ever meet who was not morose, boring, a slave to work and responsibility, and annoyingly god-fearing.

So on one Sunday morning as they all stood around chattering outside the church, he slipped away undetected to have a quick pint or two of beer. Albert had given him a key to the backdoor, and when he went in, he was greeted with a cheery good morning.

"I've missed you. Where have you been? Don't tell me that old man Warner has tied you to the bedpost and forbidden you to come in for a drink."

"He might just as well have," grumbled Clarence, "since he took my car away from me and gave it to that smug, big-mouth son of his. Now the only way I can get here is to walk, and I don't dare stay overnight because they would come looking for me."

"I've been thinking about that, because I was the one who told those two Nosy Parkers where you were that morning," confessed Albert. "And I do believe I have the solution for you.

"I happen to own a bicycle with a small motor on it. It doesn't go fast, and it's noisy as hell, but it would be easier than having to walk back and forth. I bet we could attach a small light and you could see in the dead of night with it, or you could wait until the grey of dawn. Then you could hide it somewhere until you wanted to use it again."

"Good God, Albert, I don't know how to ride a bike. I'd probably fall off and break my neck."

"I can teach you, and then the rest would be up to you."

In short order Clarence became very competent on the bicycle, the only skill he would ever teach his son when he became a youth. One evening he walked to Neudorf and, a bit wary at first, limited his consumption of alcohol before riding the bike home in the wee hours of the morning. He decided to hide it in the east corner of the pasture to avoid being heard or seen, and noticing the cows, he herded them to the barn for milking just as Johann was heading out to attend to the task.

Quite by accident, Clarence had stumbled upon a way to possibly redeem himself with Gustav. If he returned home at dawn, it might seem that he was rising early to begin the chores. Then in the afternoon he could sneak away to a quiet spot to sleep while Gustav had his usual after-dinner nap. Clarence knew he could readily give Johann the slip if he was at all bothered about what he was doing.

 **108**

Anything that could go wrong did go wrong in relation to Elisabeth Kuss's treatment for breast cancer. After Dr. Hancock had taken her back to the operating room to find the surgical instrument he'd left in the site, she developed a blood clot from the intravenous, which nearly cost the function of her left arm.

It was small wonder that Herbert would not allow the doctor to discuss the disease with Elisabeth, when day by day it got progressively worse. He wanted to wait until she was stronger and had a chance to go home to see their three children before Dr. Hancock outlined the balance of her therapy and her prognosis.

Herbert was scared to death about what might happen to Elisabeth, and he just could not subject her to the same level of fear. Once she returned home where both his and her mother would provide their loving attention, surely she would begin to recover. She was a young woman. She would only turn twenty-eight in September, so she could surely expect to live for many more years.

Finally by late summer Dr. Hancock decided that Elisabeth was well enough to return home for several weeks before returning to begin the radiotherapy. He had no doubts that by being in the presence of her children and caring family members she would improve. Her pathology report had been far from encouraging, but he was determined to attempt every known treatment to save her life.

From the moment Elisabeth opened the door of the car when they arrived home, she could barely contain her excitement. She had not seen her children for thirteen weeks and three days, but she was not prepared for their reaction to her. The two older ones, Emma and Norman, were clearly angry that their mother had been gone for so long, and it was not until the next day that they came near her.

And Mary, her baby, was making strange. The minute her mother-in-law placed her in Elisabeth's arms, she began to wail without a hint of recognition. The sad ramifications of her protracted absence started to dawn on Elisabeth, and for the rest of the day it would take all of Herbert and his parents' solace to bring her out of her silence and despair.

 **109**

Not until Amelia arrived three days later did Elisabeth's well of tears run dry. At last when she was able to speak, she asked, "What will happen to me, Mama? Did Herbert tell you that Emma and Norman didn't want to come to me and Mary still does not know who I am? Then before I was discharged Dr. Hancock told me that in four or five weeks I would have to return to the hospital for more treatment. How can I possibly leave my children a second time?"

It took every last ounce of Amelia's energy not to join Elisabeth in her anguished weeping, but now her poignant questions cut her to the quick. To make matters worse, she kept remembering her recurrent nightmare in which Elisabeth died from her illness. If that happened, her children would be without their mother forever. How could she provide any answers to her daughter when her own desolation threatened to engulf her?

Amelia had barely recovered from losing her firstborn. Surely a merciful God would not take her second child before her time?

110

During her third week with Elisabeth, Amelia, while helping her to bathe, noticed her right arm had become visibly swollen. Perhaps it had been puffy before? Amelia knew she should mention it to Herbert in case it was serious. Could anything else possibly befall Elisabeth? At least during the time Amelia had been in her daughter's home, she'd had no more disturbing dreams about her.

After breakfast when she took Herbert aside and told him about the swelling, he seemed almost to expect it. Dr. Hancock and the nurses had in fact warned him to watch for symptoms of infection, he recalled, which might include fever, pain, or red streaks on her arm. He said that even a slight infection could lead to a disabling complication called lymphedema, either right after her surgery or months or even years later. But after Dr. Hancock had explained why Elisabeth needed a second operation, Herbert could bear to hear no more and began to tune the doctor out.

111

Wouldn't you know it. Elisabeth could always find one way or another to get most of Mama's attention," Ursula complained to her hung-over husband at breakfast several days after Amelia left for Summerberry. Clarence had remained there, nursing a third cup of coffee long after Gustav and Johann had left for the fields.

"And why do you come to the table most mornings looking like you've been pulled through the wringer? What time did you come to bed last night, and since when have you started to get up before dawn?"

"What is this, thirty questions?" he asked. "Can't a man have a cup of coffee in peace? Besides, didn't I hear your father say that your lovely sister was deathly ill? Surely not even you are selfish enough to resent your mother spending time with her dying daughter?"

"Don't talk to me about being selfish. I've never met anyone who looks after himself better than you do. All I do is sit here in this house with all your kids and cook meals for three thankless men."

Ursula raised her hand to strike Clarence. The first two or three times Ursula smacked him on his head in frustration, he had been totally surprised. But now he had the good sense to move out of her way when she was in one of her moods.

"Don't pull that Hitler act with me again, you dirty German. Now let me finish my coffee before I have to go out to work in the heat all day."

"Oh, that's a load of manure. I always hear my father say that you hardly do a thing to help my brother and him on this farm, you lazy half-breed. So when I have dressed Robert and Justine, you can take them outside with you this morning. Elaine and Sandra were sick sometime during the night. They smell awful, so I have to bathe them and wash all their bed sheets."

"I have shovelled enough cow shit and hauled it out on that old stone boat to last me the rest of life. So don't talk to me about doing nothing around here. Besides, what am I supposed to do with two little kids?"

"Of course, you wouldn't know what to do with your own children. Take them to the grove of trees and play hide-and-seek or some other game with them." Ursula hurriedly dressed the two older children to ensure Clarence didn't escape without them in tow.

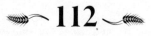

112

Gustav wondered what prompted Johann to be so insistent that they return to the farmhouse in the midmorning. At any rate, he would not be deterred, and finally Gustav unhitched the tractor from the stone boat where they were picking rocks from the hilly field near the pasture.

Gustav stopped the tractor in front of the smokehouse, and Johann jumped to the ground, listening to the eerie silence. "Papa, something is not right. I don't hear the kids playing in the yard, and Ursula always sends them outside in the morning. I will check the barn while you go to the house."

Without another word, Johann dashed to the barn, leaving Gustav looking around the yard. Now he too noticed how quiet the homestead was. Strange, especially since Ursula was usually yelling at either Clarence or one of her children.

Glancing in the kitchen, he saw that the table had not been cleared from breakfast and there was no indication that dinner was underway. Rushing to the back door, Gustav stepped outside and strained to hear his grandchildren playing in the grove of trees behind the house. Again, not a sound. Becoming alarmed, he returned to the house and went first to the bedroom.

Still no sign of anyone. What was going on? He climbed the two steps to Robert's small room and found Ursula sound asleep with Elaine and Sandra curled up on either side of her. Before waking her, he ran up the next step to the two tiny rooms where the older children often played house.

Seeing neither Robert nor Justine in the alcove of either room, he returned to Ursula and shook her awake. Placing his finger to his mouth to ask her to remain quiet, he motioned for her to get up before placing a pillow on the outer side of each sleeping child.

Once they were in the big bedroom, Gustav demanded to know where Robert and Justine were. Rubbing her eyes, Ursula said, "They are out in the yard with their father. What are you so fussed about, Papa? It's not as if I was doing anything wrong. I just put the two young ones down for a nap and fell asleep."

Dragging her down the stairs into the kitchen, Gustav was about to demand how she could be so neglectful as to entrust her children to their father, when Johann burst through the door. "I found Clarence dead to the world on a mattress he'd made for himself in the hayloft. He has no idea where Robert and Justine are or even that he was to be responsible for them. His only response was that looking after the kids is their mother's job."

"Birds of a feather, those two. I found Ursula up in Robert's bedroom sleeping like a baby, but at least she had the two little ones beside her."

"With Clarence, it was more like he was sleeping one off."

Making a mental note to follow up on Johann's comment once his grandchildren were found, Gustav took control. There were so many places that two active children could wander around the farm, and God only knew how long they'd been on their own.

Glancing at the clock on the parlour mantle, Gustav saw that Johann and he had been out in the field for over two hours. Even as he spoke, he was silently praying. "Dear God, please let my grandchildren be safe."

"Johann, I want you to go and check every building in the yard inside and out. If you don't find them, start down the lane to Otto's house. You, Ursula, go back upstairs and stay with your two children whose whereabouts you do know, and listen for when Clarence comes in the house. If he's been unsuccessful, send him back out to help Johann. The minute Robert and Justine are found, shout as loud as you can. I am going down to the slough."

Moving faster than he had in a very long time, Gustav was thankful that the summer had been long and dry and that little water remained in the marshy area. The ground was still wet and miry; but as he knelt down in the soft mud, he thanked God there were no little footprints to be seen. Standing back up and rapidly walking several feet to the right and then to the left, Gustav was satisfied that wherever Robert and Justine had disappeared to, it was not into the swamp.

Heading back to the yard, Gustav saw Clarence coming out the door with a coffee cup in his hands. "Did you find your children in the back of the house?"

"No, I've seen neither hide nor hare of them, although I told them in no uncertain terms that they were to stay right there until I came back for them," Clarence whined, as he took a drink.

"Put that cup down this minute and come with me. I've sent Johann up the lane to Otto's house, and we will help him. We will search every square inch of this farm until we find Robert and Justine, if its takes us all day and night. And you can forget about drinking or eating until they are safe and sound. What kind of father are you?" Gustav had to stop himself from striking his son-in-law.

When they caught up with Johann, he was standing very still near Otto's vacant house. Waiting until Gustav was beside him, he asked, "Papa, do you hear that? I think I can hear crying, but it seems like it's coming from deep in the ground. How could that be? I have been in the house and the root cellar, but I could not find them."

Listening intently for several seconds, Gustav thought that he too could hear a muffled sound coming from a hollowed depth.

"What are you two going on about? I don't hear a thing," Clarence snapped, as he looked disdainfully at father and son. He just wanted those damn kids to be found so he could get something to eat. And he desperately needed coffee.

"Shut up!" Gustav snarled, no longer concealing his disgust for Clarence.

"There it is again. It is crying. But where is it coming from? Wait! When Otto built this house, he did dig a well. Let me think. Where was it? My God, you don't suppose they could have fallen down the well, do you? Come on, Johann. Yes, I think I can hear it stronger."

Striding toward the rear of the house, Johann was the first to see the circular rim of stones protruding above the ground. "Could this be it, Papa, although it does not seem to have a pump?"

"Yes. Otto did not bother to put in a pump. He just covered the well with a board and used a bucket and a rope to bring up water when he needed it. As I recall, the well was quite shallow."

Rushing through the overgrown vegetation and reaching the edge of the well, Gustav immediately noticed that the board had been partially moved from the round hole in the ground. Leaning over the stones, he called out.

"Robert! Justine! It's your grandpa. Can you hear me?" Without waiting for a response, Gustav turned to Johann and said, "Son, run back to the house and bring a kerosene lamp, blankets, and as much rope as you can quickly find."

While waiting for Johann's return, Gustav told Clarence to search the vicinity for the pail and the rope, before he turned his attention back to the well. He then continued to talk to his grandchildren, saying that he'd soon have them out of there and back home.

In record time Johann was back, and Gustav's first action was to tie a rope onto the handle of the lamp. Motioning for Clarence to come near, he said, "With a rope tied around your waist, we will lower you down into the well, and then we will send the lamp down so you can see what you are doing."

"No damn way. I am not going down that bloody hole in the ground if my life depends on it," Clarence argued, but Johann was far too quick. While Gustav was talking, he had already slipped the rope over Clarence's head.

"Robert's and Justine's lives depend on being brought out of the well," Gustav retorted, "and I could care less if we manage to get you back up out of the ground once they are safe and sound."

The shadowy light cast by the kerosene lamp revealed his two eldest children standing knee deep in a cold puddle of water. "Yes, they are here. Now how am I supposed to get them up to you?"

Tying another rope to a blanket, Gustav shouted down to Clarence, "First, wrap the blanket completely around Justine and then secure the rope under her arms so we can pull her to safety. Once she is up, repeat the same thing with Robert."

With his feet in the frigid water, Clarence moved faster than any Warner would've thought possible, and within fifteen minutes both children were out of the well. If Clarence Cardinal expected in turn to be pulled to the surface immediately, he was sadly mistaken. Calling down to him, Gustav announced that he and Johann were carrying Robert and Justine to the comfort and warmth of the house and would be back shortly to get him out.

It seemed like a very long time before Gustav and Johann returned, and Clarence would never be convinced that their delay had not been deliberate. When Clarence complained, Gustav answered, "Just think about how it must have felt for Robert and Justine, since only God knows how long they were trapped in that dark, cold well. You should consider yourself very lucky that the water was deep enough to break their fall but shallow enough not to drown both of them, because I would have negligence charges against you faster than you would blink an eye."

⋙⟶ 113 ⟵⋘

By the time Elisabeth Kuss returned to the hospital in Regina, her right arm was at least double its normal size. Dr. Hancock could scarcely believe his eyes, particularly since he'd told Herbert to telephone as soon as he noticed any swelling. He was well aware that the radiotherapy would likely aggravate the lymphedema, but he dared not wait any longer. This second phase of Elisabeth's treatment was critical to prevent further metastases to other parts of her body.

It seemed to Charles Hancock that every time he took one step forward in managing his agreeable young patient's breast cancer, he would encounter another complication. He had become aware of a new piece of equipment called a circulator, which was being used with a modicum of success in treating lymphedema, but patients spent as long as four hours a day using the cumbersome machine. Dr. Hancock decided to combine the two therapies, even though he realized that Elisabeth's stay in the hospital would again be lengthened as a result.

But Charles was quite glad to have Elisabeth back in the hospital where he could see her every day. He was vaguely aware that his feelings were not what a doctor ought to experience for a patient; yet whenever he saw her, his spirits were lifted within the otherwise dismal cancer ward.

From the beginning, he'd been moved by Elisabeth, how she maintained her affability in the face of life-threatening circumstances, how her serenity had not been altered with each setback, and how she continued to show her love for her family. Still, Charles realized that Herbert Kuss was devoted to his wife, as profoundly as he knew that the only way he could express his fondness for Elisabeth was to do everything he could to save her life.

～ 114 ～

For the better part of a week after Robert and Justine fell down the well, Clarence spent his nights at home. He had overheard that snot of a young man telling his father that he'd smelled of liquor when he'd awakened him in the barn. Interesting how he should know the scent of alcohol. Then there was the dilemma of where to sleep during the day since his cozy hideaway in the loft had been discovered and removed.

But the lures of nightlife, even in a godforsaken little dump like Neudorf, were strong, and by the following Saturday evening, Clarence returned to the pasture where he had stashed his bicycle. He'd stomped away in anger that day after eavesdropping, although he would have been well advised to stay. He'd missed the most critical part of the discussion, their follow-up strategy.

As it happened, ever since Gustav's discovery of Clarence's illicit dealings at Albert's beer parlour, he intensely abhorred his son-in-law's activities, and when Johann offered to follow him on his next escapade, his father readily concurred.

The gleaming light cast by the full moon across the clear open skies of the Saskatchewan prairie illuminated the countryside, as though precocious rays of the sun were eager to creep over the horizon. Following from a considerable distance, Johann had little difficulty keeping Clarence in his sights, although he had to pace himself to not overtake the older man.

Clarence had headed down to the slough and then followed the trees until they came to an end before turning toward the east corner of the pasture. Stopping in time to conceal himself behind the last stand of willows, Johann watched as Clarence uncovered a bicycle, started a small motor attached over the rear wheel, and went riding off in the direction of Neudorf.

Expecting his brother-in-law to not come back for several hours, Johann decided to go home and get some sleep. He was not concerned about missing Clarence's return, because from the age when he understood the notion of time, Johann could will himself awake at a specific hour by saying it over and over in his head before falling asleep.

The bedroom was still cloaked in darkness when Johann sat straight up. Checking his watch, he jumped over the edge of his bed with the energy of a young man about to embark upon an adventure. Quietly dressing and then letting himself out of the house, he walked back to the same stand of trees and waited in the pre-dawn for Clarence to return from his night of drinking and carousing.

He could still remember Leonard's university friend, Hans Gerhart, spending two summers on the Warner farm. He had always hoped his favourite sister would marry him when she came of age. Many of his fondest childhood memories were of Ursula playing with him as they ran around in the outdoors. Johann had loved being with Ursula, perhaps because she had been so lively and eager to teach him games and the delights of nature.

Now she seemed like an old woman with little interest in anyone or anything, and he was certain it was the fault of her useless husband. But that was about to change. Johann Warner intended to put an end to Clarence's wanderings once and for all.

115

Soon enough, Johann heard a noise in the distance and then saw a wobbly light coming across the fields toward him. Moving deeper into the grove of willows to maintain his cover, he waited until Clarence stopped the bike before throwing it under a bush. His obviously tired and inebriated brother-in-law gathered the blanket to him rather than using it to conceal his bicycle and started up toward the yard, skulking behind the granaries as he went.

When he reached the yard, instead of turning toward the house he headed down the lane in the direction of Otto's abandoned home. Whatever he might think of Clarence, Johann had to credit him with ingenuity. No one ever went inside Otto's house, and since Robert and Justine's dangerous mishap with the well, the whole family gave the entire vicinity a very wide berth.

Waiting a few minutes after Clarence's entrance through the front door, Johann crept up to the single living room window and confirmed the drunken stupor. Then returning to the hidden bicycle after a brief stop in the barn to gather an old rope, Johann prepared to implement the next step in his plan.

Dawn was fast approaching as Johann quietly wheeled the bicycle behind the buildings of the yard and up the lane before bringing it to a stop in front of the well. He securely tied the rope around the bicycle and lowered Clarence's latest vehicle of transport to the bottom of the very well into which his two oldest children had fallen. With a flourish he tossed the rope down the well before covering it with the board and even more stones. He knew beyond a doubt that Clarence Cardinal would never return to the well beside Otto's house.

Over the next several weeks, Clarence was beside himself with his apparent misplacement of Albert's bicycle. He knew he drank excessively the last night he'd used it, but he was almost certain he returned it to the usual hiding spot. So where the hell was it? He searched and searched until he'd covered every square foot of the willow grove, without finding a trace of it. It simply could not have up and disappeared, but then he could hardly ask Gustav or Johann if they happened to come across a bicycle while they were in the pasture.

And what about having to tell Albert he'd lost his motorbike. As it was, the two were not on the best of terms lately; Clarence's tab at the beer parlour was so high that Albert refused to let him go up the stairs for his usual tryst.

Come to think of it, it was Albert's fault that he'd spent the entire evening drinking and then lost the bicycle. It had not been, nor would it ever be, a problem for Clarence Cardinal to persuade one of the many patrons to ply him with liquor during the evening. The more he drank, the more charming he became.

Never once had it occurred to her that she could lose any of her children, and especially not her only son. Until then Ursula had taken her offspring for granted, with her mother primarily responsible for their upbringing and care.

How would Amelia have reacted if she had returned home from Summerberry to learn that two of her grandchildren had drowned? For days following their near-disastrous accident, Ursula would not let any of her children out of her sight.

Slowly it began to dawn on Ursula that she had been lost to the world and those around her for nearly the past decade. As she reflected back, the last eight years were a blur, with her only vaguely aware of what had been happening to her. How could she not have cared about her own children? Ursula could remember when Johann was born—how thrilled she was to have a baby in the house. And when she had fallen in love with Hans Gerhart, she had longed for the day when she could give birth to her own child.

But then in rapid succession she had four babies within four years and never seemed to have a minute to catch up with herself. To make matters worse, Clarence had only been around when he wanted to have his way with her, which invariably resulted in her becoming pregnant again. Clarence Cardinal was certainly not the man she had loved and wanted, but now he was her husband and the father of her children, and maybe she should try to make the best of her life. The three oldest ones were becoming more self-sufficient. Soon Sandra would be out of diapers, and if Ursula was careful about when she coupled with Clarence, she might be able to avoid more pregnancies.

Furthermore, there was her father's offer for Ursula to receive the title to one third of his land, which was clearly turning a profit with bumper crops of wheat year after year. After all, Gustav had purchased the house in Melville, a new vehicle, and several new farm implements, and he always had money in his billfold if Amelia wanted a new dress or something for her many grandchildren. Could Clarence and she make a go of farming her father's land?

If Ethel Smythe understood anything about life, it was that everything had its time. She had worked diligently as Otto Warner's housekeeper now for years, and subsequently she'd been invited regularly to Herbert Kuss's home along with Otto and his daughters.

But to her surprise, Ethel realized that she could hardly look at Elisabeth without feeling jealous. How many times had she sorrowed that Herbert had met and chosen Elisabeth as his bride, when it had been obvious for years that Ethel had had her heart set upon him?

Now whenever she glanced into her rival's eyes she saw the spectre of death. She would never forget that lifeless, faraway look of impending death in the eyes of those soon to meet their Maker. Ethel first saw it in the gaze of her maternal grandmother, but as a child of eleven, she had no idea why beloved Oma would stare at her so dreamily, so absently.

Now when Ethel looked into Elisabeth's soft blue eyes, she shuddered with the recognition of what she beheld. No, she had never longed for Elisabeth's death, but Ethel was enough of a realist to appreciate that Herbert's young wife's time was soon coming.

At the beginning of September when Elisabeth returned to the hospital and Amelia went home, Herbert's mother Esther was again completely responsible for looking after his three active children. Within weeks Ethel began to notice how exhausted and feeble the elder Mrs. Kuss was becoming. To her mind, the last thing those poor children could withstand was to lose both their grandmother and their mother within a short period.

It was high time for Ethel to make her move. As much as she realized that Otto depended upon her to raise his daughters, Herbert's need was far greater.

~~~ 118 ~~~

Seldom did Gustav Warner repeat the same mistake twice, and he fully intended to ensure that Clarence had neither the means of transportation nor the money to abandon his wife and children for days at a time once he and Amelia returned to

Melville. When Ursula and Clarence asked for their share, as no doubt they would, he would have his response ready.

Given that the price for wheat had fallen so low over the summer, he would simply say that he had chosen to purchase another granary to store this year's crop; thus they would all benefit from a much higher rate of remuneration at a later date.

On the other hand, since the children had all grown by leaps and bounds, the little cash that he received from the sale of the three truckloads of grain would be put to good use by purchasing the bare necessities for their offspring.

Since Clarence had yet to discover the location of Albert's bike, he was less than eager to encounter its owner.

Nonetheless, when Gustav had answered Ursula over supper one evening, about their third of the profit, Clarence saw through his father-in-law's ruse immediately. Still, it meant he was in for a long boring winter, because Clarence had long ago learned that it was pointless to argue with Gustav.

However, the following Sunday as he snuck out of the church service to have a cigarette, who should be waiting for him but Albert Schultz?

"Well, if it isn't my long-lost friend. If I didn't know better, I would think that you've been avoiding me, Clarence. Since the harvest is in and winter is just around the corner, what better time than now for you to return my bike and to clear your tab."

"Hello, Albert. You startled me, sneaking around like one of your ladies of the night. As it happens, I returned your bicycle to the back of your fair establishment some time ago. Reiner was sitting at the bar, and he told me that you were busy dealing with some matter upstairs. He offered to buy me a beer, but Ursula and the children were waiting with Gustav in the car, and so I just asked him to let you know I was bringing your bike back."

"Like hell, you did. Reiner Lutz has not been in my beer parlour for weeks, because he is cast from the same mould as you. He too has a big tab, and until he clears it, I will not let him darken my doorway either. Now where the hell is my bike, you bold-faced liar?"

"If you didn't take your bike in after I had returned it to you, don't blame me. You always were sloppy about how you ran your business. Now if you will excuse me, I am going back to the service; you might benefit from attending church once in a while yourself." Already Clarence had the reputation of being a smooth talker, but be damned if the saloonkeeper would let him off the hook.

Storming back to his beer parlour, Albert wrote up Clarence's bill in the bar, along with the cost of his motorized bike, before returning to the church just as the service was over. Ignoring Clarence, Albert marched straight up to Gustav and handed him the piece of paper.

"I have calculated what your son-in-law owes me, and because he is not honest enough to pay it himself, I would appreciate if you deducted it from his wages. Thank you, Mr. Warner. I have always known you to be a man of integrity, and I expect to receive payment as soon as you sell your grain."

119

Within the week, Albert Schultz had his money. Clarence was furious with Albert and embarrassed in front of Gustav, but pleasantly surprised by Ursula's unexpected response. For once, she did not chastise him in front of the entire family, and even later when they were alone in their bedroom, she commiserated with him.

It finally began to dawn on Clarence that Ursula was trying to be kinder toward him, especially since he had stopped his night-time roaming and was now at home with her and their children. Perhaps it was good that he had misplaced that infernal bicycle.

Besides, there was no way on God's Earth that Clarence would spend another penny in Albert's beer parlour. He was the worst fair-weather friend any man could have, and Clarence fervently hoped that his business went bankrupt. Certainly his head was clearer, and if he made up his mind to meet Ursula halfway, they could likely still succeed in proving Gustav's farm. If his wife was more energetic and still willing to be with him, maybe they could be happier together.

As they prepared to go home to Melville for the winter, Gustav insisted that Ursula accompany him to Regina to visit her only sister before they left. Amelia was quite happy to remain on the homestead with her grandchildren.

The new treatment was worse for Elizabeth than when she'd had her surgery, and she was now so thin that her bones stuck out through her skin at all her joints. It was something called radiotherapy, and Amelia was beginning to fear that it would kill her elder daughter before the cancer got her. She had lost all of her hair, she could not keep food in her stomach because she was retching all the time, and her eyes glazed over from the effort of talking to her family.

Ursula had not seen Elisabeth since the summer, and when she arrived in her hospital room, she was shocked. For the first time, it occurred to her that her sister might be dying, and all the while Ursula had selfishly complained about the care and attention she'd received from their mother.

Upon her return to the homestead, Ursula became even more determined to count her blessings and to strive harder to become a better wife and mother. At least she would have the time and opportunity to mother her children, unlike Elisabeth whose family would grow up barely knowing her.

The day before Amelia and Gustav left to return to Melville, they had decided to take their three eldest grandchildren with them to visit several of their cousins who had been staying with Rolf and Maria Werner.

Once all of the children had eaten, they were excused to go play in the yard. And although warned to stay away from the poultry, the older ones thought it would be great sport to chase the geese. They had no idea that an angry gaggle of geese could be provoked to attack until the tide had turned and the boys and girls were fleeing. That is, everyone except Elaine who had stayed behind to pick flowers for her grandma. Not until they all burst into the house and had been there for several minutes did they realize that Elaine was missing.

Gustav listened intently until he heard a commotion behind one of the granaries. He raced around it and, to his horror, saw Elaine lying on the ground while being assailed by an irate gander. Gathering her up into his arms, he shooed the furious goose away by kicking at it until it retreated. As he carried his sobbing granddaughter to the house, Amelia greeted them and took her into her arms.

Fortunately, Elaine had been found before the gander did her any real harm, although she had marks on her arms and legs from his strong beak. Naturally she was terrified by the experience, but it could have been far more damaging; it was not uncommon for an angry adult male to peck out the eyes of its prey.

After ministering to her wounds, they returned home. Upon their arrival, they told Ursula and Clarence what had befallen Elaine. As her parents listened to Gustav, they glanced covertly at each other, remembering the day he had berated them when Elaine had frozen her hands. Whereas Ursula and Clarence felt somewhat exonerated by the fact that even Elaine's loving grandparents could not prevent untoward circumstances from occurring, their daughter would likely be terrified for life around barnyard birds and animals.

⟫⟩~ 120 ~⟨⟨

As Christmas rapidly approached, Herbert had reached the end of his tether with the treatment that Dr. Hancock had determined was critical for Elisabeth. The children were asking when their mother was coming home, and he was finding it more and more difficult to believe that anything being done in the hospital could cure his wife's disease. Finally, one morning as the doctor was making his rounds, the usually malleable Herbert demanded to speak with him.

"Dr. Hancock, I must know how much longer you will give Elisabeth the radiotherapy before you allow her to leave the hospital. I am convinced that it is only making her worse. In the spring when I brought her here to be treated, my wife was a reasonably healthy woman, and look at her now. After being subjected to radically disfiguring surgery, her arm has swollen to more than twice its original size, she has lost every hair on her body, she can't eat a morsel of food, she is skin and bones, and to top it off, she has the worst burns I have ever seen. Not once have you said whether you can actually cure her disease and save her life. To my mind, what you call 'treatment' has made her sicker than her disease ever did."

The longer Herbert expounded, the angrier he became, and before Dr. Charles Hancock could speak, he'd reached his decision.

"I have had enough. I am taking Elisabeth home this minute, and we will care for her where she is surrounded by her family and friends who love her. If I leave her here, she will die in this miserable hospital and never see her children again."

Gazing at Herbert for several minutes before replying, Charles Hancock could not help thinking that the man was correct. If Elisabeth were *his* cherished wife, he would take the same action. Why not cease the devastating therapy and let her live out the balance of her days with the love and serenity of her family and home.

With every test he ordered, the results clearly indicated that Elisabeth's cancer was spreading to her lungs and liver and, in only a matter of time, it would metastasize to her bones and blood. There was no known medical treatment. He knew that as the end drew near Elisabeth would suffer tremendous pain, but he could send oral analgesics home with her husband. The morning before they departed, he would also ask the nurse in charge of narcotics to teach Herbert how to give Elisabeth injections of morphine during her final stages of the cancer.

"Thank you, Mr. Kuss, for being so clear in your decision. Do you have family to help you care for your wife at home?"

"My parents live on a farm three miles from ours. I realize that both sets of parents are getting elderly, but a family friend recently offered to become my housekeeper and to look after the children."

"Well, Mr. Kuss, you have certainly thought about what you need to do, but I will request that you wait until tomorrow morning. I plan to ask the nurses to provide some instructions for her care and the treatment of pain as her disease progresses."

A week before Christmas of 1949, all medical treatment was stopped and Elisabeth Kuss was discharged from the Regina General Hospital, never to return. Even though she had readily submitted to every therapy Dr. Hancock had ordered, she could not have been happier to leave the hospital. Elisabeth had known from the beginning that she was dying. The word "cancer" was enough to fill a person with dread, but Elisabeth had always recognized Amelia's proclivity to prognosticate the future, and her beloved mother had been unable to conceal the foreboding in her eyes.

Since she did not have long left to live, Elisabeth wanted to be in the comfort of her home, surrounded by her loving husband, children, family, and friends.

⇒⇒ 121 ⇐

One day in early spring when Amelia was again with Elisabeth, Gustav and Johann were attacking the weeds to prevent them from taking over, when the elder man spoke.

"Son, this week before I drive to Summerberry to bring your mother home, I intend to go to Manitoba to look at a farm. It's a little more than a two-hour trip from here, and even though I plan to leave very early tomorrow morning, your mother and I shall not get back for several days. Will you be alright getting up for school and fixing yourself enough to eat?"

"Of course, Papa, but why are you driving all the way to Manitoba to see a farm?"

"That is something I've been meaning to talk over with you, Johann. I know you have your heart set on going to the University of Saskatoon to study pharmacy this fall, but I have a serious problem with my farm. As you know, I have given Ursula and Clarence three years to prove that they can properly look after my land. I shall honour my word, of course, but it has been clear to me from the beginning that I cannot trust those two to do anything correctly."

"I am glad to hear you say that, Papa. I agree. But I can't believe that you had to pay off his bills to Albert Schultz, of all people. The worse thing is that Clarence thinks of himself as a charmer who can get whatever he wants. Although I feel badly for Ursula, I couldn't be happier that you will not let them stay on your farm."

"But then, who will work the land when I become too old?" asked Gustav. "Is it right for me to ask you to change your plans and to become a farmer rather than a pharmacist? And if you said yes, will you resent me in the years to come?"

"Ever since I followed Clarence that night and learned that he was a drunk, I have thought about what would happen if you left him to run the farm. As it happens, Papa, I like farming too, and if you were to offer me the same deal, I would forget about going to university."

Putting his hoe aside, Gustav motioned to his youngest son.

"Come into the house, and I shall tell you the deal I will offer to you. Unlike Ursula and Clarence, there will be no proving time before I put your name on the title of one third of the farm, but we will have to wait until their three years are up. Then we will go to the Dominion Lands Office, and I shall legally sign 214 acres over to you. I shall also have the lawyer draw up the balance of the agreement, which says that when I die you will receive another third of the land. The last third will belong to your mother until she passes on. After her death, the entire section of land will become yours. What do you think, Johann?"

"Thank you, Papa. Your offer far exceeds my expectations. But, you still have not told me why you are going to Manitoba."

"As you can well imagine, neither Ursula nor Clarence will be very happy when I tell them that they have not proven to me they are capable of running my farm. Over the past years, your mother and I have bought all of the clothing and shoes for our grandchildren, so when I turn them off the farm, where would they go? And what will they do?

"I have given it a lot of thought, and I recently read about a half-section of farmland that was for sale not far across the Manitoba border. I began looking for a farm some time ago, and since Clarence's parents live in Manitoba, I considered that they could finally get to meet their grandchildren. In all these years, I can't recall Clarence ever talking about taking his children to see his family. So I intend to buy this farm outright and move them to live on it after the harvest in the fall of 1951. However, Johann, I will ask you not to breathe a word of this to anyone."

⋙～ 122 ～⋘

Knowing that Gustav still wanted him to graduate from secondary school, Johann wrote his grade twelve examinations. But by spring he was anxious to spend his days on the farm. If he experienced any sense of loss about not going to university, it was short-lived.

Even at the tender age of seventeen, Johann could recognize the potential of owning farmland in the breadbasket of the world. He was determined to learn everything that he could from his father. It was easy enough to keep his word to his father about their secret, because the closer he worked with Gustav, the less Clarence ventured out into the fields.

As the warm days of spring returned, instead of proving to his father-in-law that he was eager to become a skilled farmer, Clarence moped around the house or gave the appearance of helping Ursula in the garden. With Amelia spending so much of her time caring for Elisabeth, it was not uncommon for Gustav and Johann to return from seeding to find all four children playing in the yard. On those occasions, as soon as the two men entered the house, Ursula would come hurriedly down the stairs from their bedroom, followed later by her desultory husband. It was one thing for them to be getting along better, but quite another to leave their children unattended.

Four energetic, bright children could naturally be expected to be involved in any amount of mischief, particularly when left to their own adventures on a farm, and Ursula's offspring were no exception. Was it Robert—or was it Justine—who had decided late one afternoon when they were pushing Sandra in the oversized and dilapidated baby carriage that they would explore their Grandpa's smokehouse?

When they went around to the front of the rickety granary, the door was loosely fastened with a small piece of wood. The makeshift lock was no more than a small rectangular board hammered in the centre with a long nail and rotated in order to open the door, but still it was too high for even Robert to reach. Eventually, Justine realized that if the three of them held the carriage and stood Sandra up in it, when they showed her what they wanted her to do, she could stretch her hand close enough to turn the wooden latch.

The plan worked, the door was opened, and soon Robert, Justine, and Elaine were in the smokehouse, leaving Sandra standing in the carriage when the door swung closed. Crying after being left alone when her older siblings disappeared, she decided to move the latch again. As she locked the door, her movement in the pram got the rear wheels turning and then rolling backwards down the decline, building speed as it descended the slope toward the slough.

Johann, who was herding the cows in from the pasture for milking, could not believe his eyes. It looked like the baby carriage was flying through the air and that one of the children, likely Sandra, was in it. Where had it come from? Leaving the cattle to graze by the fence, Johann dashed after the runaway carriage, catching up to it in time to grab it before it overturned in the willows and sent his niece tumbling into the bushes.

Gathering Sandra out of the carriage, he held her snugly until she stopped crying and glanced around to determine how she'd ended up in her predicament. Still baffled that she appeared to be alone, he started up the incline toward the house, carrying her in his arms.

"Sandra, can you tell Uncle Johann where you were playing with Robert and your sisters?"

"They won't... let... me come in with them," Sandra blubbered.

"Sh, sweetie. Listen. I hear something. It sounds like someone is banging on a door. Wait now. I hear yelling. Where are they, Sandra?"

"In there," Sandra said, pointing to the smokehouse.

Johann quickly opened the door to find his nephew and his two other nieces struggling to get out.

Setting Sandra down on the ground, he first lifted Elaine and then Justine over the board in front of the door as Robert scrambled to free himself.

"Sandra," said Robert, "why did you lock us in there? How were we going to get out?"

Johann ordered the four of them to the house while he locked up the smokehouse. Now strolling behind the children, it occurred to him that his mother did have good sound reasons to worry about the plight of these four grandchildren. Amelia Warner had often told her youngest son that each of Ursula's offspring must have a vigilant guardian angel, and from their past experiences, he solemnly hoped it was true. Once they moved to the farm in Manitoba, their guardian spirits would need to be very assiduous indeed.

➤➤➤~ 123 ~◀◀

Perhaps Ethel Smythe would be as surprised as anyone in the family that she soon came to care deeply for Elisabeth Kuss. She had expected that, given time, she would become fond of the children of the man she'd been enamoured with since her youth, but it would not have seemed possible that she could ever love the woman who had so abruptly taken Herbert from her.

Ethel had always heard about Elisabeth's sweet and gentle nature, but she'd been hard pressed to accept it while grieving the loss of the man that she wanted.

In her own innocence, it would not have occurred to Elisabeth that Ethel had ulterior motives. She believed in Ethel's sincere concern for her family, which she was constantly demonstrating through her demeanour and diligence.

The long-time friend of the Kuss family had so completely earned Elisabeth's trust and respect that one morning Elisabeth finally made the request that had weighed on her mind since she'd come to terms with her impending death.

"Ethel, since my older children are in school and the baby is sleeping, would you have a few moments to sit with me so we can talk? I have something very unusual to ask of you."

"I was planning to tackle the weeds in the garden, but they can wait. Would you like me to take you to the veranda and make us a fresh pot of tea? It is such a pleasant morning, and the fresh air would do you good."

"What a thoughtful idea," Elisabeth responded eagerly, even more convinced about the appropriateness of her decision.

When the two women were seated comfortably on the veranda, a shawl snugly wrapped around Elisabeth's frail shoulders, she initiated her remarkable request.

"Ethel, I want you to make me a promise when I die. Please don't look so alarmed. I have surprised all my doctors by living longer than they expected, and I feel better every day with the heat of summer.

"First of all, I want to thank you for your excellent care of my family and, of course, of me. Please understand that as much as I appreciate all of the love and attention both my mother and Herbert's give us, I know we tire them out. At the best of times, my children are a handful, even though right now I am needier than they are.

"Yet, you look after all of us, without a complaint, as if we were your flesh and blood. So my request, although it may seem strange to you, feels perfectly right to me. After an acceptable period of mourning, I want you to promise that you will marry Herbert and become my children's mother. I honestly cannot think of anyone who would love them and care for all of my family more than you."

Ethel had to secure her scalding cup of tea to prevent it from spilling over her lap. Words escaped her. How could this young woman, dying long before her rightful time, ask her, Ethel Smythe, to marry the man she had coveted throughout their wedded life?

When Ethel failed to answer her, Elisabeth considered that her appeal was too bizarre and began to qualify it.

"I had always thought, when you became my brother's housekeeper, that you were intent upon him. And then when I had heard that Millie had come with her father to take Otto's children back to Regina with them, I was surprised you left his employ. However, I soon realized that the neighbours would talk if a single woman stayed on in the house of a man without children, but I could scarcely believe it when Herbert told me that you were coming to us. What a kind and loving woman you are to have offered to take on all of the responsibilities of my household with three active children and an invalid mother."

Unable to listen one moment more, Ethel started to cry. Finally realizing that Elisabeth was every bit as sweet and gentle as her reputation, Ethel managed to pull herself together.

"If you are certain that is what you want, my dearest Elisabeth, I shall promise to marry Herbert after he has had time to grieve and to always care for and love your children."

Never before in Summerberry, perhaps in all of Saskatchewan, had a terminally ill person received such unconditional love and devoted attention. From early morning until late at night, Ethel worked her fingers to the bone, assiduously caring for Elisabeth to her dying day.

In the bleak mid-winter of 1953, when Elisabeth Kuss was sorrowfully laid to rest, there was not a dry eye in the church. And to the community's surprise, Ethel Smythe ironically sobbed the hardest and the longest. Whereas no one in the township was surprised when Herbert Kuss eventually married Ethel, most would ponder her broken-hearted weeping at Elisabeth's funeral.

124

The solution that Johann proposed in the autumn of 1950 was perfectly reasonable. Without making reference to the deal he'd made with his father, he suggested that he stay on the farm during the winter months. He knew his mother was fretting about how Robert would get to school when the weather was inclement, which on the Saskatchewan prairie could be the better part of the season.

Amelia had been worrying about the problem for most of the summer when Johann suggested that Robert live in town with his grandparents during the week and begin his education in Melville.

Robert could hardly contain himself with the prospect of spending so much time with Grandma and Grandpa. And he was the envy of his sisters, most especially Justine. Since she was so close in age to Robert, she thought it was not fair that she had to wait another year before she could start school. But the idea that her brother would be staying with their grandparents five days of the week was almost more than she could bear.

Because of her grandfather's assistance, Justine already knew the entire alphabet and was beginning to read words. In fact, she was much more interested in book learning than Robert was, and why should she have to stay at home? She begged her mother to let her start school with Robert in Melville, and she did not understand when told that she was too young.

In her mind, she could do anything, even more than her brother could. In addition, she promised to help Grandma look after both of them. But all of her pleading and protesting was for naught, and the Sunday evening when Robert left the farm to move into Melville, Justine sobbed and sobbed until she finally succumbed to sleep. Her only consolation was that by next fall she too would be sitting in the backseat of Grandpa's automobile, waving goodbye to her parents.

When Justine found Robert's first-grade reader, she began to pour over the pages until she was piecing the words together and starting to read the short sentences out loud. Since her brother far preferred to be outdoors with Johann, he was quite willing to let Justine study his schoolbooks. Had his mother permitted it, he would have cheerfully let her do his homework.

She began to ask Robert if there were other little books he could bring home for her, but he said he had only to learn to read the one his teacher had sent with him.

Overhearing Justine on a Sunday afternoon, Great-Aunt Katherina sat down beside her at the kitchen table. By the following day before the end of classes, Katherina was at Pheasant Forks School to ask the teacher if she could provide her with a list of other beginning storybooks. Throughout that winter, much to Justine's delight, her great-aunt supplied her with a steady collection of readers that she'd ordered either from the small school library or others.

~~~~ 125 ~~~~

The house was so empty. Otto was still reeling from losing his three daughters. Who could have suspected that the lady of the night whom he'd rescued from Albert's brothel in Neudorf and made an honest woman of was actually named Amelia Browning and was the daughter of the president of Regina University?

It had taken him considerable time to understand what she was telling him when she'd abruptly arrived at his breakfast table one autumn morning, but it would take him much longer to come to terms with her unexpected actions. As soon as Otto began to read the legal papers, though, it occurred to him that Dr. Browning knew the law and that Otto would have little to say about keeping his daughters with him. It seemed to matter little that Millie had abandoned her children in the dead of night. Suddenly she wanted them with her, and the custody order left no doubt about her potential success.

Within the hour their meagre personal belongings were gathered together, and Francis, Faye, and Darlene stared accusingly at him with tearful eyes and bewildered faces through the small rear window of their grandfather's fancy automobile. The remnants of their meal remained on the table until the following afternoon when hunger pangs finally forced Otto back into the kitchen.

It had not taken Millie Warner long to come to her senses once she saw her father drive by and turn into University Drive from behind the steering wheel of a flashy yellow sports car. With his position including accommodation at the aging but impressive President House and the services of a full-time housekeeper, he surely would have considerable income at his disposal.

Why had she foolishly left it all behind to seek her own path, especially when she was his only heir in Canada? Naturally, upon his retirement they would not continue living on the campus, but once he stopped working, he would likely purchase a home that she would inherit upon his demise. They could live comfortably on his pension—that is, if he would allow her back into his life. They had neither seen nor spoken since the day she stormed out of his home because of his ridiculous condition.

She desperately needed a trump card. Fortuitously, one evening when reminiscing about how fond her father had been of her when she was a little girl, she sat upright in her chair as though struck by lightning. Of course, she had three daughters of her own whom she could use to gain her way back into her father's good graces. Once Dr. Browning found out he had three grandchildren, he would surely come to love them and dote upon them as he'd always done with her.

It had to have been more than two years now since she was in Emergency at the Regina General Hospital receiving treatment for the deep knife gash on her neck, when she had noticed Gustav and Amelia Warner getting on the elevator. After being stitched up from the attack from the nasty patron, she took the stairs to the next level and walked up and down the corridor until she observed that her former in-laws were indeed visiting someone in the second ward.

Eventually she found out that it was her sister-in-law, Elisabeth Kuss, who occupied the bed in room 202. She returned the following day with the sole purpose of waiting to catch Herbert visiting his wife so that she could ask about her daughters. Millie hoped he would be more charitable than judgmental about her escape from her mundane existence on the farm and that she could find out if her girls still lived on the Warner homestead.

As it happened, Herbert had been pleased to see her, and over a cup of coffee in the hospital cafeteria, she heard about Otto purchasing a farm adjacent to the Kuss farmland in Summerberry.

As she formulated her plan, Millie Warner, nee Brown, recognized the obvious advantages of resuming her true identity as Amelia Browning. She could even use the scar from the wound on her neck as evidence that Otto had beaten her in order to convince Dr. Browning of the importance of rescuing his granddaughters from such a father. Furthermore, on those occasions when her urges got the better of her, Amelia was confident that she would experience no scarcity of discreet tryst opportunities on campus.

⟫⟫⟩ 126 ⟨⟪⟪

All three girls eagerly helped to clean the house. It was always easy when Grandma and Grandpa were coming for supper. Their mother was making fried chicken, hot German potato salad, and a medley of fresh vegetables from their large garden. She had saved some of the rich, thick cream from the morning separating since Grandma had promised to bring plum perogies for dessert and orange cordial to drink.

It was nearing the end of August 1951, and within days Justine would be old enough to go live with her grandparents and to start school in Melville. In her excitement, she'd been falling asleep later and later every night as the month passed. Nonetheless, she would be the first awake and ready to begin the day. But at least from the time she had learned to read, she would remain quiet and not disturb the rest of them. Even though Robert had not brought extra books home, Justine knew from Great-Aunt Katherina that every school had a library, and she could hardly wait to search for more stories to read. Soon she would also learn arithmetic, because if there was anything Justine liked better than words it was numbers.

As the family was finishing the last of the delectable perogies, Ursula asked her children to listen carefully.

"We will live in a different house, on our own farm in Manitoba. We will be moving there this fall as soon as the harvesting is done."

Justine burst into tears, and without asking to be excused, jumped up from the table and ran outside. She could not believe what her mother was saying. How could she stay with Grandma and Grandpa in September if she would be living in some place called Manitoba? And then where would she start school? She wept so hard that she felt a pain in her chest, as though her heart was breaking in two.

The sight of her grandfather coming towards her favourite spot among the grove of evergreens only increased her disappointment and rejection. Gustav tried to calm her, but she was inconsolable. As she tried to wipe away her tears, Justine sobbed, "How can you send us away, Grandpa? I love you and Grandma more than anyone else. I love your house. I love this farm, and I have waited for a whole year to come live with Grandma and you in town to start school."

Although Gustav was not a demonstrative man, he could appreciate how devastated his granddaughter was by the unexpected news, so he knelt down on the grass to take her into his arms.

"I chose to buy a farm for you in Manitoba because I too love this homestead. I bought it years ago from my only friend after he died by falling out of the barn, and I had promised him that I would look after his wife and children. I gave your mother and father three years to prove to me that they could run my farm, but your dad is not a farmer. If I leave him to care for my land, he will eventually destroy it. Your grandma and I will come often to see you in Manitoba and make sure that your parents are doing alright on your new farm. Now dry your tears, Justine, and come into the house. Grandma bought orange cordial, your favourite, and you have not had any yet."

As they slowly walked back to the house with Grandpa holding her hand, Justine resolved deep within her soul to not allow herself—for a very long time—to cry such tears of anguish and desolation. Even the pain of falling off her chair and severely cutting her left knee on the broken glass after spilling her orange cordial would pale beside the searing memory of when she had to leave her cherished grandparents behind in Saskatchewan.

127

As the hot days of autumn passed after her mother's announcement, Justine spent most of the time when not required to do chores, sulking about in the evergreens, trying to understand what her grandfather had told her. She was not yet six years of age, but already she realized that Grandma and Grandpa would always be two of the most important people in her life. But if they really loved her, why could her family not stay on their farm?

However, because the harvest was late, the decision was reached that Robert and Justine would begin the school year at Pheasant Forks. Each morning she was awake before dawn, getting ready to walk between the rows of her grandfather's wheat field, holding Robert's hand to reach the two-room schoolhouse just beyond the fence on the other side of the gravel road. School was everything—more than Justine had expected and dreamed about for over a year. She had a beautiful teacher with brunette hair and lovely soft brown eyes like a fawn. Her name was Miss Downing. She was tall and willowy, and she wore a different pretty print dress every day.

Justine had her very own little desk to sit at every morning when she arrived, and she could leave her pencil and notebook inside if she wanted to at the end of class. There were all kinds of books everywhere, and because there were eight grades of girls within the one large classroom, Justine continually listened from the moment she entered the door until she regretfully had to leave at the end of the school day.

After the school bell rang to end class for the fourth week, Miss Downing asked her to fetch her brother and to return to the classroom. As they stood politely in front of the revered teacher, Miss Downing told Robert and Justine that they were not to come back to Pheasant Forks School.

The rumour that the Cardinal family was moving to Manitoba had been circulating since the beginning of September. During the school board meeting the previous Thursday evening, the board had unanimously voted that there was little purpose in having the two extra students in the overcrowded classrooms. The school was bursting at the seams, and it was challenging enough for the two teachers to educate the children from the community without wasting their time and energy on those who were leaving anyway.

Discussion quickly turned to who would be responsible to break the news. Since haste was of utmost importance, it would be expedient for Miss Downing, the more senior teacher on staff, to tell the Cardinal children at the end of the school day on Friday.

After a sleepless night, Miss Downing arose with a sense of dread. How would sweet little Justine respond to the news that she could not return to school?

Had any of the curt school trustees asked, Miss Downing would've cheerfully provided a list of other girls she would've sooner dismissed than Justine Cardinal. She spent the day on pins and needles, apprehending the outcome of her sad tidings. Miss Downing stood at the door of the schoolhouse, watching as the Cardinal children walked home hand in hand across their grandfather's field, Justine sobbing until she was out of sight.

➤➤~ 128 ~⬩⬩

At last they were ready to leave. The only occurrence in an otherwise dreary autumn for Justine and her siblings was being invited to spend three days with Grandma and Grandpa in Melville, unaccompanied by their parents. It had been more than two weeks since they'd visited the farm, but when Gustav heard about Robert and Justine being thrown out of Pheasant Forks School, he was furious.

Had it not been a Saturday morning, he would have marched across his field and demanded that the teachers readmit his grandchildren the very next day. Later, during the afternoon once he had calmed down he asked Justine to accompany him on a walk through the stubble of his once-golden wheat field.

Eventually they came strolling across the land by the school. Gustav tossed down a stalk of ripe wheat he'd been chewing on and clasped Justine's hand into his.

"I was just thinking about how upset you must have been when you were told you had to leave the school. All in all, this has not been a happy time for you; but regardless of what happens to you throughout your life, there is one thing I always want you to remember: You have the right to be you and to go wherever you want, Justine, with confidence."

Wondering what Grandpa was really saying to her, she would not give his declaration another thought until she was much older. For the moment, she was much more interested in his next comments.

"When Grandma and I leave on Sunday evening to return to Melville, we will bring all four of you back to stay with us for a few days. Grandma plans to buy new dresses for you and your sisters and a new shirt and trousers for Robert because she has arranged for a photographer to come to the house in town to take pictures of you. She is as unhappy about her grandchildren moving to Manitoba as you are about leaving, and she's determined to have a nice photograph to remind her what you all look like. Could you imagine your grandmother not remembering any of you? Now come to the house so we can tell Robert and your sisters to pack their pyjamas in the valise."

~ 129 ~

On Sunday evening following supper, the four Cardinal children squashed side by side into the backseat of the automobile, giving their parents a wave as they embarked upon the first of many trips to stay in Melville with their beloved grandparents. Robert slept on the sofa in the living room, and his three sisters squeezed into the three-quarter bed in the room that he had occupied the previous year.

What a thrill to awaken every morning to the scent of Grandma preparing bacon and eggs as they began each day in Grandma and Grandpa's cozy home in town. They had from necessity always played together, and under the affectionate eyes of their grandparents, even gardening and helping in the house were appealing, particularly when rewarded by going out for an ice cream cone in the afternoon with their grandfather.

Matching light-blue dresses, four pairs of shiny black shoes, and a navy sailor suit for Robert were diligently fitted and purchased in preparation for the photographer's arrival. Robert stood beside Justine, and Sandra sat between Elaine and her oldest sister to ensure that the baby did not fall off the piano stool.

~ 130 ~

Once Ursula and Clarence recovered from the shock of being thrown off the homestead, they became furious. They spent a great deal of time complaining that Gustav was making all of their decisions, until the day when Gustav picked Clarence up and took him to Melville to sign the documents.

Glancing at the paper, Clarence soon realized that his was the sole name on title for the farm in Manitoba, so he quickly changed his tune. Clarence could not believe that it was not Ursula's name on the deed, but far be it from him to question Gustav's choice. When the older man explained that he'd purchased the land in

Manitoba because it was high time his parents were introduced to their grandchildren, it made perfect sense to Clarence.

In mid-November Amelia and Gustav left to return to Melville when a sudden blizzard struck the prairies. The temperature dropped, the wind began to howl, and big fluffy flakes of snow descended from the sky, turning the world white.

The storm raged for days, and snowdrifts piled up to the height of the front door, which was reached by climbing four steps. The back entrance of the house, totally blocked, would need to be shovelled clear before anyone could enter or exit. Fortunately, the family was well provisioned with water and food and was not required to venture outside until the morning of the third day.

When Clarence went to the small room in the basement—an indoor bathroom with a large pail to collect human wastes—he realized that the time had arrived for the family to dig themselves out. It had to be emptied, and even he recognized that Robert or Justine were still too small to have it delegated to either one of them. As far as Clarence was concerned, the lack of a proper toilet was the only thing missing from their new house.

It had electricity and a telephone, which were certainly improvements over the homestead on the bald Saskatchewan prairie where they had to use kerosene lamps and the only telephones were in town. There was even a central furnace to heat the home, and when his offspring were older he would make one of them get up in the morning to stroke the coal and bring it back to life before he had to leave the warmth of his bed.

The house itself was reasonably new and well constructed, except for the basement floor. Although concrete had been properly poured for the walls, for whatever reason it had not hardened on the floor of the cellar. There were patches that were not level, and in many places there was little more than a dirt covering.

Then there was the well, which they had neglected to secure with a pump, rather covering it with a flat piece of plywood that would rise and float when the basement flooded, as it did the following spring. The water was not drinkable because of the soil content, but it certainly saved hauling water yards away from the outside well for bathing and laundry. With three bedrooms, another good-sized room the length of the house, a spacious kitchen, and a back porch for coats and shoes, it was quite a comfortable home.

As the winter storm buffeted outdoors for days on end, Clarence Cardinal and his family were safe within the walls of the house. Not bad for a man who less than ten years ago had depended upon the Canadian Army to provide a roof over his head, to fill his stomach, and to supply the clothes on his back.

～ 131 ～

A sense of complacency had engulfed the family, including Justine, as they unpacked the boxes, became familiar with the house and its workings, and adjusted to being stranded, just the six of them in the midst of a whiteout.

Being new to the farm, neither Clarence nor Ursula had any earmarking of what lay beyond the yard and the big red barn; when the storm abated, their visibility was limited to a landscape of drifted snow banks. Even if they could remember where their lane was, there was no way that their old car would get through to the gravel road that connected to the highway to travel to Two Creeks. But when the sun finally broke through the dull grey clouds of winter, Justine began to pester her mother about going to school.

At first Ursula told her to read her many books from Aunt Katherina. But when her daughter persisted, her mother snapped.

"Look out the top of that frosted window, and tell me how we can go anywhere. I don't know what your grandfather was thinking when he decided to move us way out here in the middle of nowhere. You can just forget about going to school until a snow-plow comes along to dig us out, and if one does not come, we could be stuck here for the winter."

"But, Mom, Robert and I have to go our new school. That's why Grandpa gave Dad his other car—so he could drive us there."

The swift movement of Ursula's right hand as it lashed out to slap Justine across the face came as a surprise to both of them. Justine made not a sound as she stared at her mother, but she could not conceal the hurt in her eyes.

Without a word Ursula turned back to the stove and resumed stirring the chicken soup. Justine ran into the bedroom and sat on the bed, wondering why her mother had hit her. Was it her fault? It was not fair. She had been waiting so long to go to school, and something always seemed to keep her away. The pain from the stinging of her face was nothing compared to knowing that other boys and girls were sitting at their desks learning to write and to add numbers. Her mother could beat her, but she would persevere until her parents found a way to get her and Robert to Ross School.

The snow-plow did eventually come, the roads were cleared, and Clarence drove his two oldest children to Two Creeks only to discover that Ross School was locked up as tight as a drum. After turning the car around and driving the short distance to the General Store, he was greeted at the door by Frank Doyle, the owner and postmaster.

"Hello. You must be that new fellow in the district. I guess they forgot to phone you and tell you that the school is closed for the Christmas break and will not open again until the first week of January. With the severe winter storm, Mrs. Stone, the principal decided to extend the winter holiday since only a few students could make it in because of the blocked roads. Although I must say that I am surprised you are bringing your children when they should be picked up by George Bailey, your neighbour. I know he still has room in the big sleigh that he outfitted for the winter."

"Are you saying that someone will come and take my kids to school every morning?" Clarence asked with disbelief. "And does he bring them home at night?"

"Well, yes, it comes out of your taxes, and you can bet they won't reduce them one cent even if you drive your family every day. You need to telephone George and let him know you have kids to take to school. Here, I'll give you his number. By the way, I'm Frank Doyle. Welcome to Two Creeks."

"My name is Clarence Cardinal, and those are two of my kids." He pointed to Robert and Justine, who were huddled together at the entrance of the store. Possibly for the first time, Clarence appreciated that their grandparents had purchased new coats and boots for all of his children, and they did not look like waifs.

"So you are the family that bought the Richards' farm. We were expecting you to come in September. Dreadful time to move, isn't it?"

"Well, that's my father-in-law for you! As it was, we just got here ahead of the storm, and thank God my in-laws were on their way home, so we weren't shut in with them."

Frank decided to change the subject. "Lucky thing that you were settled before the first snowstorm hit. It was quite an introduction to a Manitoba winter, and there will be plenty more; but we make up for our winters during the summer months. One thing all of us in the district are dying to know is whether you will keep the dances that the Richards started several years ago in your barn."

"Are you telling me that they held dances in my barn?"

"Oh, yes! You have the biggest, newest, and cleanest barn in the entire community. Peter and Barbara Richards turned the huge hayloft into a dance hall, and everyone from miles around came every Saturday night throughout the summer. Best times of the whole year!"

132

Returning home, Clarence meant to telephone George right away, but he was met at the door by Ursula with the shovel. "You better start clearing the path to the well, because soon we will be out of drinking water."

When at last he came in the house, Clarence was too tired to talk to anyone and decided to wait until the following day. Then for one reason or another he neglected to telephone his neighbour, until he forgot entirely as they began to get ready to drive to Melville to spend Christmas with Ursula's parents.

Not until they'd been back home for a couple of days did he remember to call the fellow with the sleigh. And, of course, he had not the slightest idea where the paper with his number was now, two weeks later. Oh, God, he better find it; he did not want Justine pestering her mother and getting smacked upside the head again.

Think what he might about the two people who had taken in him and his brother when they found the boys abandoned, Henry and Alma Cardinal would never have lifted a finger to hurt them. There were times when they'd given them the food off their plates and the clothes off their backs. And there was no way on God's Earth that Amelia Warner would have slapped her children, especially across the face, so where had Ursula learned such harsh, humiliating behaviour?

Fortunately, Frank Doyle must have enlightened George Bailey. Because in the midst of Clarence's frantic search, the telephone rang and Ursula was asked to have her children ready before eight o'clock on Monday morning. Finally, Justine would get her wish, although neither Robert nor she was prepared for the sleigh. From the moment that Mr. Bailey drove into the Cardinal's yard, his two strong horses pulling the covered sled, Justine felt afraid of it.

In fact, had she not been so ardent about attending school, there was no way she would've been pushed through the small door at the back into the dark wooden contraption. There was only a tiny window at the front through which the driver could see his way, and there was another small rectangular opening for the horses' reins. On each side of what looked like the large wagon was a long plank on which the children sat during their ride. Finally, with Mr. Bailey telling them to hurry up, both Robert and Justine climbed in on either side and huddled as close to the door as possible.

Although Justine was very anxious about being in such a confined space, the glowing red tin stove in the middle of the sleigh frightened her the most. As soon as she looked at it, she could imagine flames leaping out its loosely attached door and burning them all to a cinder. From that first morning, she insisted upon being the last person on the wooden plank seated next to the door, but days later when the sleigh hit a hard snowdrift and flipped over on its side, it was all she could do to climb back into it.

Once the sleigh had been tossed over by a high snow bank, and Betty Bagley, who always insisted on sitting right beside the fiery heater, was badly burned before they could get her out and roll her in the snow. In time, although Betty did make a full recovery, her face and hands were scarred for life. Over the weekend, Mr. Bailey built and positioned an insulated cage around the heater, but never again was Justine Cardinal questioned about her decision to sit as far away from the stove as possible.

⇢ 133 ⇠

The snow had barely melted before neighbours began to arrive in droves to welcome the Cardinals to the district and, more specifically, to inquire if they were likely to continue with the barn dances. By this time Ursula and Clarence had climbed up into their loft to determine what Frank and George had repeatedly raved about, and both were quite amazed by the size and immaculate condition of the space under the roof.

For very different reasons, which neither of them confided to the other, both were eager to start the dances as soon as possible. Clarence quickly recognized that with liquor served every Saturday evening, he would have a constant supply of alcohol without having to leave his farm.

And Ursula realized that for the first time in her life she could be popular. She did have her qualms about what her father would think, but then he deserved that for forcing them to leave his farm. She could argue that having people pay to enjoy themselves in a barn seemed like an easy way to make extra money to buy all the clothes and books her children would require for school.

Before her parents arrived at the end of April, along with the livestock Gustav was giving to them Clarence and Ursula had agreed to not mention that they planned to host dances. They were expected to become more independent, and both were confident that they would do so, although Clarence and Ursula readily became more proficient with organizing the dances than they'd ever been with farming.

Neither would give the slightest consideration where they would store the hay to feed their animals. And, indeed, had it not been for George Bailey's offer to provide them with space in his loft, their livestock may have starved during the winter. On the other hand, had George not suggested that perhaps it was time to start mowing the grass and alfalfa, they may have had no hay for their animals. Then again if Charles Norton, their neighbour across the road, had not arrived with his tractor and seed drill to sow their crops, they would have had precious little to harvest come the fall.

During their first years on the farm in Manitoba, even with her parents spending as much time as they could to help them, it was questionable whether Clarence and Ursula would have survived if not for the generous assistance of their neighbours.

Clarence worked the bar exuberantly and progressively as the evening wore on. But Ursula would never have predicted how sought—after she would become as a dancing partner for the men. Of course, in short order the wives began to fret about the attention their respective husbands paid to the new lady of the Richards' farm. So Ursula decided to pre-empt the women's wrath by befriending them. She was the hostess, and before long she remembered how charming she could be when she put her mind to it.

In fact, as the summer passed, Ursula began to rediscover the alluring and spirited person she'd been before her father had sent her away to Saskatoon to be imprisoned by her Aunt Martha.

As she regained her youthful vigour, Ursula began to lose the weight she'd piled on during four pregnancies within four years, and to take the time to focus on her personal appearance. Even Clarence and her children began to notice that she had more energy and was far more interested in how she looked. And now, at twenty-eight years, Ursula Cardinal began to feel as attractive and vibrant as when she was young.

It had been years since Ursula thought about Hans, but suddenly when dancing with yet another partner, she was reminded.

"Oh, Hans, my darling, where did you go? I miss you still and look for you in every man I meet."

She wondered why she had blocked all memory of him, until it occurred to her that it was the only way she could have survived when she had foolishly trapped herself in a marriage with a man she did not much like, never mind love. Then when she promptly had four of Clarence's children, she had buried herself as surely as if she had been laid in the ground.

Ursula knew that if Hans were to come back to her now, she would not hesitate to leave her children and to follow him to the end of the earth.

134

It was not right. Your children should not die before you. But however hard Amelia tried to deny it, she knew that Elisabeth could not last much longer, even with Ethel putting her heart and soul into caring for her dying daughter. For the first time in her life, Amelia Warner began to question what kind of God could call first her eldest son and now her older daughter home before her. She went to the St. Paul Lutheran Church two houses down the street every Sunday, as she had since moving to Melville; but she could not listen to a word of what Pastor Lutz preached.

Instead, Amelia sat in the pew with her heart in turmoil, railing against an unloving Father. Her darkness grew until she could hardly find purpose again in her life, but now Katherina was too far away to save her.

In her bitterness she wondered why the two children who had never given her reason to worry were the ones that God took. Was it true that the good die young?

Then overwhelmed with guilt for wishing that it were Otto and Ursula instead, Amelia sinked deeper into her pit of despair. One morning because she had to get out of the house and away, she started walking down the street toward the stores. She had just turned the corner on Third Street when she heard, "My, oh my. Is that you, Amelia Werner?"

Surprised to be called Werner, a name she'd not been referred to for years, Amelia studied the tall, slim woman with graying hair who suddenly opened her arms and moved closer to embrace her. As recognition dawned on her, Amelia exclaimed, "Oh, Sarah. Is it really you, my friend Sarah Thompson?"

In the middle of the sidewalk, not caring whether they were observed, the two women ensconced each other in an enormous hug as tears of joy flowed down their cheeks. They had not seen each other for nearly twenty-five years, and neither had ever expected to again. When they finally stopped hugging, they simply stood and gazed into each other's eyes, as if trying to recapture all that had transpired during the time they were apart.

There was so much to say that neither could find a beginning. Sarah finally recovered. Placing an arm around Amelia's shoulder, she guided her into the Corner Café to locate a seat. They barely heard the waitress asking them if they wanted menus, and Sarah had to make a deliberate effort to ask for two cups of coffee.

Once they began to speak, their conversation flowed from one topic to another until the waitress eventually left them alone, just filling their cups as she passed by their table. For a slender woman, Sarah was always hungry, and her growling stomach at last alerted them to the passage of time.

"Come, Sarah, you must return with me for dinner and visit with Gustav also. He would never forgive me if I said I'd run into you without bringing you home for something to eat. We have a house about three blocks down the street."

Remembering the meals she had savoured at Amelia's table propelled Sarah to her feet. Placing too much money for what they had consumed on the counter, she wrapped her arm around Amelia's waist and they disappeared out the door.

"I'm glad you are taking me home, Amelia, because now that I have found you again I shall never let you go. I don't live more than twelve blocks from you, and when we walk as the crow flies, we can shorten it to less than a mile and a half. Since we have twenty-five years to make up, I intend to visit you until either Gustav or you become sick of seeing me."

"Neither of us would ever become sick of you, Sarah. You are like my long-lost sister, and you could not have come back into our lives at a better time. I don't want to spoil our visit today, but soon I shall tell you all that is happening to us. For right now, I hope you have kept your appetite because I just made chicken dumpling soup, and we have some of Gustav's smoked sausage from the farm."

"I don't know what I look forward to the most—seeing Gustav again or eating his homemade sausage."

～ᗡ 135 ᐊ～

She was becoming accustomed to the feeling of power bestowed upon her as the lady in charge of the convivial barn dances. Perhaps because when making announcements on Saturday evenings she had to shout, Ursula soon developed the tendency to yell as her usual method of speaking. It seemed that she could no longer talk to Clarence or her children in a normal tone of voice, and when her parents came to visit, her mother would mention that there was no need to be so loud.

It was remarkable how quickly Ursula made the transition from the downtrodden to the intimidator. Clarence and her four children quickly saw how she now intended to exercise control in one way or another.

It had been an exciting Saturday with Grandpa and Grandma arriving unexpectedly in time for dinner. They had come laden with food, all-day lollipops for each of the grandchildren, and special gifts: a toy car for Robert and two story books for Justine to celebrate their receiving excellent report cards at the end of the school year.

Clarence and Ursula exchanged worried looks when Justine suddenly stated, "Grandma and Grandpa, I am so glad you came today. Now you can stay with us tonight when Mom and Dad are in the barn having a good time at the dance."

"What are you talking about, child? Are you telling us that your parents go to a dance and leave you here on your own?"

"They don't go away, Grandpa. The dances are in our barn—in the hayloft every Saturday night—and they put us to bed early. But now that you are here, maybe we can stay up longer and watch all the people come in their cars and fancy clothes."

Leaping up from her chair, Ursula walked around the table to where Justine was seated and viciously smacked her across the face. "Has anyone ever told you that you have a big mouth? You just can't keep it shut, can you?"

Heavy silence instantly fell upon the room, and no one dared speak. However, this time Justine stayed sitting in the chair rather than escaping to the bedroom. In her mind, she had done nothing wrong. It was the truth. As she glared at her mother, she remembered Grandpa always telling her to be confident. And to her that meant saying what was right. It was only fair.

There was no fear on Gustav's face, only wrath. And before Ursula could hit his granddaughter again, he flew out of his chair and grabbed her wrist.

"That's enough. You will not strike my grandchildren. Where could you possibly have learned such behaviour? Your mother and I never touched any of you near the head. Yes, you were spanked on your bottom when you would not listen or you misbehaved, and certainly not for telling the truth. So just what is the meaning of what she said?"

Was that smugness on Justine's face as well as defiance? Ursula wondered, as she stared her daughter down. For once in her life, she stopped to think before opening her mouth to shout at either Gustav or Justine. She would show that snippy little brat for embarrassing her in front of her father.

If it was a contest of wills that this show-off kid not yet seven years of age was seeking, then that is exactly what she would get. There and then Ursula Cardinal decided she would find the way to break Justine's spirit.

For the moment, however, Ursula openly defied her father.

"As it happens, Clarence and I no longer have to explain to Mother or you what we do. This is our farm, and if we choose to hold dances in our barn, there is nothing you can do about it."

Scarcely able to believe the impertinence of his younger daughter for whom he had purchased this farm less than a year ago and paid all expenses for her family's move to Manitoba, Gustav angrily responded.

"Do what you want with the farm, Ursula, but I warn you about striking your children. Justine, when your grandma and I return home in a day or two, you are coming with us until your parents are ready to drive to Melville and bring you back."

Did Gustav Warner unwittingly give his granddaughter strong incentive to resist her mother? Justine did go to Melville with him and Amelia, and she remained for over two weeks before her parents came to take her home. However, during the month of August, Gustav and Amelia did return to Manitoba and then took Robert home with them for a summer holiday. The next year they brought Elaine to visit, and later that summer it was Sandra's turn to stay with them.

Over the subsequent decade, all of the Cardinal children delighted in vacationing with their grandparents in Melville, two each year on a rotating basis. Still, only Justine was physically beaten repeatedly throughout her childhood, and particularly during her adolescence. She was exceedingly careful never to strike her eldest daughter in the presence of her parents again; although the pattern of her mother's lashing out became well established immediately following Justine's return from her initial stay with her grandparents.

⁓ 136 ⁓

"This is the last time that I am driving to Melville until we go to Amaranth so my folks can finally meet my kids," Clarence announced on the way home from picking up Robert after he had spent two weeks with Ursula's parents.

"Like hell we are. It is too far a drive to go there and back in one day," Ursula shot back.

"Who said anything about doing it in one day? Before school starts, we can leave on a Monday or Tuesday morning and stay for a few days. As long as we are home in time to get ready for the dance. Alma and Henry will want some time to get to know their grandchildren."

"There is no damn way that my kids and I will stay in that dirty, dingy house and eat strange meals of beaver, bear, or moose meat. If we do go, we will drive back home the same day. After all, who would milk the cows and feed the pigs?"

"Who does it when we go to Melville? We will ask Cecil Clegg to do the chores for us. And for your information, my parents' home may be little, but in all the years I lived there, it was never dirty."

"Well, what would a half-breed know about clean?" Ursula was beginning to realize that Clarence meant business about going to Amaranth.

"As if a dirty Kraut had the corner on cleanliness! Gustav told me that the reason he bought this farm for us in Manitoba was because it was high time that my kids got to know their other grandparents. So like it or lump it, we are going next week."

Now that Ursula had enjoyed being in control, she liked being told what to do less and less. She had often wondered why her father had purchased a farm so far away in Manitoba, and she was annoyed that he had never told her. Yet here was Clarence boasting that he was privy to her father's reasoning, which was not only surprising but also irritating. When had he told him about it, and was there more that he had kept from her?

Then Ursula remembered the day Gustav drove to the homestead to take Clarence to Melville. The more she thought about it, the more suspicious she became.

"I don't believe you. Why would Papa give you an explanation for buying the farm in Manitoba, and when did he do that?"

"What difference does it make now? What's done is done."

The last thing Clarence wanted to talk about was the day Gustav and he were in Melville. If Ursula was irritable about going to Amaranth, she would be livid if she ever found out that the title deed was in only his name.

Wanting to mollify her, Clarence quickly returned to the subject of his parents. "Surely even you can understand that I want our children to meet their other grandparents, and we can decide later how long we will stay. I know you really enjoy the barn dances, and we will make sure we are back in plenty of time to get everything ready, okay?"

The four Cardinal children were surprised that their other set of grandparents was still alive, because up until this time, there had been no mention of them. They looked forward to going to the village their father later told them about, particularly since he'd said it was near a big lake. When he suggested that maybe they could go to the beach and go swimming in Lake Manitoba, they could hardly contain themselves.

During their entire lives, they had only met and seen white German Lutherans, and how could they handle being around an Indian and half-breeds? If Ursula had only taken the time to ask her children, Robert would have told her that he thought it might be interesting to eat a bear, a beaver, or a moose. Her three daughters were curious to meet a half-breed—whatever that was—and during the entire three days of their visit, Justine was disappointed to find not a speck of dirt anywhere throughout the house, even though she had searched everywhere.

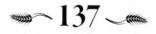

~ 137 ~

A year of companionship and love from Sarah Thompson was more than sufficient to restore Amelia's faith in her Maker, and it came just in time. The day the two women met on the street in town had gone on and on, with Sarah finally convinced to spend the night when they were still visiting late into the evening.

Amelia learned that Sarah's father had passed away several years ago. And even though her mother was still alive, she'd totally lost her memory and eventually had to be placed in St. Paul's Lutheran Old Folks Home. It surprised Amelia that Sarah had chosen a Lutheran home, until she was told it was the only facility of its kind in Melville. Then when they welcomed her mother so warmly, Sarah joined the Lutheran Women's Auxiliary, which was held in the basement of the church; although she had yet to attend the Sunday services.

Thus ironically the women were like ships passing in the night, never previously being in the church at the same time, which fortunately was on the verge of changing. Sarah quickly convinced Amelia to come with her the following Wednesday evening, and soon Amelia encouraged her friend to come along with her and Gustav for the Sunday morning service.

⋙〜 138 〜⋘

When Amelia relayed to Sarah that her elder daughter Elisabeth, at the youthful age of thirty-two, was dying from breast cancer, she understood that she could do little but listen and give Amelia a shoulder to cry on when she needed it.

As the women grew closer and closer, Amelia shared feelings and thoughts that she thought she could never reveal to anyone. She disclosed how terrible it had been to lose Leonard, but it had been a godsend that his death was sudden. Whereas with her disease Elisabeth had lingered on for nearly three years; it was exacting a tremendous toll on all of her family, and especially on her children.

Amelia finally realized the extent of the devastation when they were bringing Justine back to Melville with them and they'd made their customary stop in Summerberry to check on Elisabeth. The girl took one look at her aunt and blurted out that she was so thin and sickly that she appeared like the skeleton she'd seen in one of her school's library books.

The moment the words were expressed Justine was sorry, but it was too late. Emma and Norman, Elisabeth's two oldest children, burst into uncontrollable sobs.

It took what seemed like hours to console them, and by that time only Amelia could comfort them to sleep, cuddled with her on the guest bed.

The following morning neither Emma nor Norman wanted anything to do with Justine, and they experienced a temporary reprieve when Uncle Otto arrived with Francis, Faye, and Darlene. Since Justine had not seen her other cousins since they left Grandpa's homestead, they were quick to participate in Emma's exclusion of her.

Regardless of how many times Justine tried to say she was sorry, it was a long time before the five cousins acknowledged her. Even then she felt that she'd never again fit in with them. Perhaps her mother had been right to call her a big mouth. So Justine resolved there and then to learn to stop and think before she spoke.

139

"Help me."

The unexpected strength of Elisabeth's raspy voice startled her as much as the force of her grip. Ethel was casually sitting on the edge of the bed, preparing the needle for Elisabeth's injection of morphine, when she demonstrated more energy than she'd shown in days.

"Yes, my dear. I am just going to give you your medicine before I wash you. Herbert is making the porridge, and soon he will bring you a cup of tea. I am so pleased that you are wide awake this morning, and you sound like you are feeling a bit better."

"No, Ethel. Give it all to me now, Ethel, and let me go," Elisabeth urged, while she still had the energy to talk.

"I am hurrying, Elisabeth. I know you are in pain, but soon the needle will relieve it enough for you to see Herbert and the children and hopefully have some food to eat."

"Do you remember the promise you made to me, Ethel? You said you would look after Herbert and my children, but you are destroying them. Just take a good look at Herbert. He is becoming gaunt, and soon he will be so skinny that my niece will call him a skeleton too. My precious children are growing up surrounded by death, with no chance to know the joys of childhood. If you love them, if you love me, inject me with all of the morphine that you have," Elisabeth beseeched, collapsing back onto the pillow.

Ethel looked at Elisabeth, stunned.

"You want me to finish you?!"

~ 140 ~

It might not be too bad living in Manitoba, away from under her parents' thumb. That first autumn when they'd harvested their crop with considerable assistance from their neighbours, they actually made a fair amount of money, which Clarence immediately spent to update their vehicle. The old car was on its last legs, and Clarence wanted something reliable enough to drive during the winter.

Ursula and Clarence also cleared a modest profit from the barn dances, although in their duplicity neither would disclose to the other how they'd done it nor the amount they had secretly scammed. For his part, Clarence quickly learned that by pouring the one-ounce shot glass only three-quarters full, he could get another three or four drinks out of a twenty-six-ounce bottle of alcohol and still have enough whiskey to make him happy by the end of the evening.

Ursula might have been even more devious in her approach, deliberately initiating an animated conversation with a patron waiting in line while the paying customer expected change from his five-dollar bill. Growing impatient to join the party, most men would let it go, and Ursula would pocket his extra dollar.

In short order Ursula was putting away a tidy sum to augment the small amount she had remaining from her inheritance from Aunt Margareta. Throughout the years, she had carefully concealed her nest egg from everyone, and she'd only used it when there was something she really wanted for herself.

Furthermore, Ursula always maintained that the money had to be made by her own resourcefulness; her hoard could only be amassed by her own hands. It could not include the cash she made from the sale of eggs, always gathered by her children; the butter they would eventually churn when they were old enough to shake the jar of cream until it turned; or the berries they picked during the summer. When the winter snow began to melt, signalling that spring was on its way the subsequent year, Ursula anticipated the start-up of the barn dances, knowing that she could again supplement her hidden treasure.

Soon, back in the full swing of the summer entertainment, Ursula began to experience overwhelming fatigue. She tried going to bed earlier, especially on Friday evenings to ensure she was energetic for the Saturday night dance. Her weariness increased, but it was not until the end of June when they made their once-a-year trip to Amaranth that Clarence's grandmother brought her face to face with the reality of her condition.

"I am happy you are having another child, Ursula. When is this baby expected to come?"

"Just what makes you think that I am with child?"

Then she realized that she could not remember her last period. Oh God, how could she lose track of that? Surely she could not be pregnant again, not now that the other kids were growing up and she finally had some freedom. Four children were, to all intents and purposes, four more than enough for her.

Days later, after the long ride home when she could no longer blame Alma's cooking for her queasy stomach, Ursula acknowledged the bitter truth. She would have another child, regardless of how much she was loath to admit it, and she could not even estimate when the baby would arrive.

If she had to be pregnant again, she hoped she would not deliver before the end of the summer so they could keep the barn dances going.

141

They came from far and wide—from Regina, Saskatoon, Melville, Lemberg, Neudorf, and Duff—and from the Summerberry community, until the pastor decided that since the church was overflowing he would shorten Elisabeth's service and give the eulogy outside in nature.

It was a beautiful warm spring afternoon. Elisabeth would have been pleased that so many people had come for her funeral and even more delighted that she would be sent into the hereafter from the fresh open air of the countryside. The women of the congregation made no effort to conceal their grief, and a good number of the younger children wailed in chorus with their mothers and grandmothers, whether or not they understood. Many men could also not stop the tears welling up in their eyes from rolling down their cheeks when Pastor Hollinger extolled the virtues of Elisabeth Warner Kuss.

If Elisabeth were present, looking down upon the celebration of her life, she would have been surprised first and then full of gratitude for how much she was loved by all those she had touched throughout her short life.

First and foremost, though, she would have blessed Ethel Smythe, who would be left to wonder for the rest of her days if her overwhelming sorrow was because of her love and devotion for Elisabeth or from what she'd been persuaded to do.

~ 142 ~

When Ursula told her mother that she was with child again, Amelia was careful to keep her enthusiasm to herself, but was secretly thrilled with the prospect of an eleventh grandchild. She needed the joys of a newborn infant to bring her back from her despair from losing another one of her own offspring, and Ursula's timing could not have been better.

From the moment Amelia received the news of Elisabeth's death, Sarah and Katherina were her Rock of Gibraltar, anchoring her on either side at her funeral and in the sombre days that followed. Amelia was grateful that Max and Rebecca Roth and, surprisingly, Dr. Fraya Roth had come and buoyed Gustav up since he would never allow himself to show emotion, much less to weep over the death of his firstborn daughter.

Years before, it was almost more than Gustav could bear when Leonard was killed in World War II; but at least then he was able to grieve as he always had, by wandering aimlessly for hours on end through his wheat fields, searching for communion with God and Mother Nature.

Now they both longed for confirmation of the recurring cycle of life; for Amelia and Gustav, the birth of a child affirmed creation like no other circumstance than perhaps the arrival of spring.

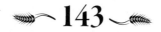

Ursula was determined to not gain back all the weight she struggled to get off during the past two years. She had recently overheard some of her female neighbours saying that smoking cigarettes effectively curtails the appetite, so she decided to take up the practice. She also found that if she joined Clarence for a drink or two during the Saturday evening dances, she had more energy and generally felt more buoyant about her unwelcome condition. Soon she was tippling on a regular basis, as long as Clarence had liquor left over from week to week. Ursula did not have much of an appetite, and indeed over the summer months she gained hardly any unwanted pounds.

Perhaps the human fetus can sense a hostile environment, which could account for this infant's premature arrival. But Ursula's rash refusal to take care of her health most certainly was the decisive factor. Nevertheless, she was thoroughly dismayed and equally annoyed when she ended up in the Virden District Hospital long before the last barn dance of the year.

From the beginning, not surprisingly given that Ursula had refused to seek any prenatal medical care, neither mother nor the three-pound baby girl fared very well. Ursula hemorrhaged until the doctors elected to perform a total hysterectomy, which included removing her ovaries. Baby Jennifer Cardinal was immediately placed in an incubator with little hope for her survival, primarily because of the undeveloped state of her vital organs.

144

This infant proved to be a fighter. For months, long after her mother was discharged from hospital, Baby Jennifer was loved, cared for, and cheered on by nurses and doctors intent upon her survival. It was as if this newborn wanted to be the first baby delivered in the Virden General Hospital to overcome such a tiny beginning and survive to tell the tale. And survive she did.

Very gradually, ounce by ounce Jennifer Cardinal began to gain weight. Her vital organs began to function without any support, and by Christmas she was discharged home to her parents, grandparents, and by now totally unbelieving siblings. She was like a doll, still only six pounds with a bundle of dark brunette hair and brown eyes, but when Jennifer was placed in Amelia's loving arms, her grandmother fervently hoped that this child would herald the beginning of better days to come.

Perhaps Jennifer began her struggle to exist from the moment of her premature birth. For once she was at home, she was ready to thrive. The same, however, could not be said of her mother.

At first she thought she'd be ecstatic following her hysterectomy, because she would be free from the burden of having any more children. But now she felt as though an overwhelming weight had been placed squarely on her shoulders. It had little to do with caring for Jennifer, because her mother, her other children, and her neighbours were always willing to attend to her the minute she made the slightest sound.

No, this feeling was much more profound than the blue days she so often experienced after the birth of her other offspring. It was as though she could not lift herself up from under an oppressive force that was with her from morning until night. Amelia finally convinced Gustav to take her back to one of the doctors in Virden. The medication, which he prescribed for depression, helped until Ursula decided to stop taking the pills because she had gained more weight in a month than she had during her pregnancy.

During the entire winter Gustav returned only once to Melville without Amelia, to visit with Johann and determine if he was faring all right on his own. By the time Gustav returned to Manitoba, preparations were under way for the first barn dance of the year, and Ursula seemed to perk up substantially with the return of the weekly entertainment. Jennifer had thrived with all of the attention she was receiving, and the older children were on their best behaviour, going about their chores in a timely fashion so they could take turns holding their precious baby sister.

For the first time in months, life seemed to be settling down for the Cardinal family, although Amelia insisted that, before they leave to go home, Gustav take Ursula to see a different doctor in Virden. She did not want Ursula to revert to feeling poorly, and the second physician prescribed another antidepressant, which she also tossed away.

It was at Ethel's insistence that they wait for at least a full year after Elisabeth's passing before they would marry. Herbert was not pressuring for their impending marriage because of a conjugal need as much as because of the reality of his children's care. Ethel was prepared to continue looking after the three young ones, but she flatly refused to live under the same roof with a widower. What would the neighbours say? And if they were to wed before an acceptable time frame had passed for Herbert to grieve his beautiful wife, their tongues would wag even more.

No, Ethel was fully prepared to honour her promise to Elisabeth, but it would all be within the appropriate passage of time. The children found it strange that after their mother died Auntie Ethel would no longer sleep in their home; but as long as she was there every morning to give them breakfast and to get them ready for school, they readily adjusted. The resiliency of Elisabeth's children both surprised and pleased Ethel who in all modesty took little credit for their steady recovery from the loss of their mother.

But if any Kuss child had been queried, each would have expressed their fondness for Ethel Smythe and professed a love nearly equal to that for their birth mother. Their bond was immutable, and three years later, after Ethel and Herbert produced their son Terence, Ethel never wavered in her affection for Emma, Norman, and Mary, loving them with the same intensity that she felt for her own child.

146

The barn dances during the spring and summer of 1954 quickly took on a different tone from those of the previous two years. The discussion began during one winter evening when a group of neighbours descended upon Charles and Mona Norton for their weekly game of canasta.

"Have you noticed that it costs more to attend the barn dances since Ursula and Clarence took them over?" asked Mona, as she prepared to serve coffee.

"Funny that you should say that. Will would always take a couple of five-dollar bills for the evening and come home with change. But last year especially, I noticed that we usually ended up spending most of it, and we only have soft drinks," Shirley replied.

"Now what are you women talking about? Surely you are not being petty about a few dollars?" Frank Doyle retorted, coming into the kitchen to check what was keeping his host. He wanted to drink his coffee and leave for home since he opened the store at seven o'clock in the morning.

"A couple of dollars might not matter to you, Frank, because you don't have to rely on earning your money farming," Mona countered, as she carried the tray of coffee and chocolate cake into the living room and set it in the middle of the card table. The other men's ears perked up, and they became interested in the conversation.

"I would agree with you," said George. "I usually ended up buying two or three more drinks each evening in order to get the same buzz that I used to get, and I have been drinking whiskey for longer than I care to admit. In fact, I started watching Clarence, who would always be lit up long before the end of the dance. I began to wonder if he wasn't skimming our drinks, since I never saw him reach into his pockets to pay."

"You make a good point, George," said Charles. "I make it a rule not to have more than two drinks in an evening, but last year I realized that I was coming home as sober as a judge. Not that that was a bad thing, as I am sure you will agree, Mona."

Will Beaver, who seldom spoke in a group unless asked a direct question, jumped in.

"Although I don't drink alcohol, as you all know, I found it strange that when I gave Ursula a five-dollar bill at the door, she never gave back any change. I just concluded that they'd raised the price."

"Well, if they did, they sure as hell never bothered to tell the rest of us," said Charles.

Drinking his coffee and eating a second piece of cake, Frank sat at the table and listened to a discussion he was finding strangely distasteful. He got along fine with Clarence, and he had liked Ursula from the moment they'd met.

"Oh, come on, you people are determined to find fault with the Cardinals simply because they are the only new folks to move into your precious farming community. Myrna, finish your cake and grab your coat. We better get out of here before I say something I regret."

When Charles and Mona returned from seeing Frank and Myrna to the door, George resumed the conversation.

"I wonder if we shouldn't all pay a little closer attention to the dealings of our dance hosts. I know that I intend to arrive with the correct amount for our admission, and then I plan to watch Clarence as he measures out my drinks. Be damned if I will be short-changed, particularly by someone we have bent over backwards to welcome into the district. By God, Charles, if you and I had not done most of their harvesting the past two falls, they would have been hard-pressed to get their crops off. Not that we received any thanks for it, but what does Clarence do but go out and buy himself that new car."

Not wanting her husband to get on his bandwagon about their new neighbours, Norma Bailey, after saying precious little all evening, said, "Come on, George. It's time we went home as well. Your mother will be tired, but she won't go to bed until we return."

In truth she rather sided with Frank Doyle. Norma immediately liked Ursula, and she'd actually felt sorry for her. Whereas she and George had only the one child, a son, Mort, she could not imagine how she would have coped with four and now a premature baby. Norma silently agreed with George about Clarence buying a new car when it was obvious that his children could do with new winter coats and boots.

It was small wonder that Ursula was not giving the men their correct change, if indeed it was the case. Perhaps that was the only way the poor woman could come up with the money to keep all her children fed and dressed, if she had a husband who thought only of himself.

～ 147 ～

Within the first month of the barn dances, both Ursula and Clarence realized they were being buffeted by the chilling winds of change. Practically every man arrived with exactly four dollars for the admission charge, and had it not been for sweet, tiny Norma Bailey who had started to press a dollar or two into the palm of her hand during the dance as a tip, Ursula would have had nothing to stash away in her nest egg.

For his part, Clarence was at first surprised and then irritated when most of the men coming to the bar watched as he measured their whiskey.

"Make sure that you pour me the full ounce now, Clarence," they'd say.

Their close neighbours also went straight home after the band finished for the evening, instead of staying behind to help them tidy up as they had over the past two years. With the sudden exodus from the hayloft, Ursula and Clarence could gather the paper cups and plates, clean the tables, and put away the chairs by themselves after a late night, or they could face the mess in the morning.

After the fourth Saturday when it was now painfully obvious that the tide had turned, Clarence spoke up.

"Just what the hell has happened to our so-called friends and neighbours? One year they are as friendly as can be, and then without warning they suddenly won't lift a finger to help. You didn't say anything to them, did you?"

"No, of course not. What would I have said?" Ursula snapped. She was certainly not going to say that she'd been short-changing them at the door.

"What did you say or do? Why do you always think I cause the trouble?"

Clarence was not about to acknowledge his short measuring, so he agreed with his wife for a change.

"You're right, Ursula. I don't know why they are treating us as if we did something wrong. All I can say is that they better watch it, or before they know it we will stop putting on these dances.

What Clarence had verbalized as an empty threat soon began to emerge as a reality. By the summer the attendance at the barn dances had dropped off substantially, particularly with people from the surrounding districts. The original core of immediate farmers continued to arrive every Saturday evening, but they soon learned that a sober Clarence was not nearly as charming a host.

Charles Norton was taken aback when replenishing his drink on the last Saturday in August.

"Thanks Clarence. I better make this my last drink tonight because I can sure tell the difference when you fill up the shot glass."

"Just what the hell are you saying, Charlie?" demanded Clarence.

Even though Charles backtracked quickly, his comment rankled Clarence for the rest of the evening. He'd had about enough of his high and mighty neighbours keeping tabs on his pouring and then making their smart-aleck remarks.

When the band took their break, he signalled for the leader to come over to the bar. Stepping out of earshot of the attendees, he said, "This will be your last night to play at these barn dances, and I want you to give me a sign when you are ready to play the last piece. Before you do, I will make an announcement to our faithful patrons. Do I make myself clear?"

"Yes, Mr. Cardinal. I understand what you are saying, but you gave us no notice. This will give us little time to make a booking for next Saturday and for the rest of the summer."

"That's too bad. It cannot be helped, and if you want your money for tonight, you better do as I ask."

Striding back to the small improvised stage of four sheets of plywood resting on blocks of wood, Mr. Biggs thought, "and good riddance to you, too." If they would be given the boot tonight, he decided that they would play only another three selections before wrapping it up and making a quick exit. So, within twenty minutes, Mr. Biggs waved to Clarence to indicate that the band was about to finish playing for the evening.

Walking toward the stage, Clarence looked smugly around the hayloft with a perverse sense of power and pleasure. Waiting until the buzz of conversation died down and everyone was looking at him, Clarence announced loudly and clearly, "Grab your partners for the last dance of the evening and of the year. There will be no more."

~ 148 ~

Gustav and Amelia arrived that autumn to help with the harvesting, and the entire family pitched in to take off the crops. Robert and Justine were old enough now to help stook the sheaves of grain, and they worked alongside their father and grandfather, getting them ready for the threshing machine. Amelia and Ursula made and packed lunches to take out to the fields, and Ursula learned how to drive the car so she could deliver them while Elaine looked after her two younger sisters.

Perhaps being able to drive had the greatest impact on Ursula, but she was clearly the one to benefit most from their combined family efforts during the harvest. She realized that she could be much more independent, which was just what she needed to improve her frame of mind.

Furthermore, when the men were in the fields, she had to chop the wood, carry the water, and bring the cows in for milking. With all the physical activity, she soon noticed that she was feeling better about herself. She was again determined to lose weight and to take charge of her life. Ursula had never wanted so many children, but they were her offspring, and maybe it was time for her to try harder to raise them properly.

Actually, they were not bad kids, and now that they were getting older, they could take on many more chores and lessen the amount of work required of her. Already Robert and Justine were helpful with the outside tasks, and Sandra also liked to tag along to gather the eggs and to feed the chickens. Elaine, on the other hand, far preferred to stay indoors to help her look after the baby and to clean the house. At any rate, Ursula came to view her lot in life more favourably than she had for years.

Whereas she had essentially forgiven her mother for taking her to stay with Aunt Martha in Saskatoon, she continued to resent her father for having made the decision that had changed her life forever. Ursula could not forget that it was because she was sent to Martha Schweitzer's that she had lost her one true love, Hans Gerhart, and ended up marrying a man with whom she had little in common.

No, as much as Ursula would try to claim that she took after the Warner side of the family, she would never absolve Gustav for destroying her only chance for happiness.

⋙〜 149 〜⋘

"All three Cardinal girls into the school and straight up to my office this minute," sounded Mrs. Stone's strident voice across the school ground.

After slamming the office door shut and sitting behind her desk, Justine, Elaine, and Sandra stood quaking in their shoes.

"All right, which one of you said 'damn?'" I don't know what is allowed in the schoolyards in Saskatchewan, but swearing is absolutely not permitted anywhere near my school. So which one of you is the guilty party?"

In the deafening silence that followed, the three girls furtively looked at each other and then quickly back down at the floor. Even if they could remember what they'd said, none had the courage to speak.

"Hurry up and tell me or I will strap all three of you. I don't have all day; I have classes to teach."

At that moment Justine lifted her eyes and glanced toward Sandra, which was all that Mrs. Stone needed to make her decision. "Justine and Elaine, go back downstairs to your schoolroom. Sandra, stay right where you are."

As she anxiously awaited Sandra's return to the classroom, Justine vacillated between guilt and worry. Had she used the swear word? Had any of them said the word that Mrs. Stone claimed to have heard? Regardless of how hard she tried to remember, Justine could not recall if they had cursed. Then she began to wonder if the principal was just picking on them because they were new.

When Sandra came into the classroom, it was still obvious that she had been crying. As soon as the bell rang for recess, Justine followed her younger sister as she escaped to go outside. "I'm sorry, Sandra. I didn't mean for Mrs. Stone to strap you."

"Leave me alone. You left me in her office, so now don't bother trying to make it right."

"I never said it was you. I just looked up from the floor," Justine tried to explain, as she noticed the welts from the wooden strap on both of Sandra's palms.

"Yes, sure you did, and right at me. Well, see if I give a care," Sandra retorted, as she marched away.

Later when they arrived home, Sandra was subjected to another spanking, this time with a belt across her bottom. Her mother did not bother to inquire if she was the one who cursed.

⚜ 150 ⚜

Bertha Stone sat at her rickety wooden desk in the small alcove office on the second floor of Ross School long after the last bell tolled for the day. She was quite accustomed to meting out punishment whenever a student needed it. But something did not feel right about the strapping she had delivered at the beginning of the day.

Noticing that the overcast sky was becoming darker, she roused herself, thinking that she must hurry home to prepare Ralph's supper before he finished milking the cows. She could not, of course, alter her actions from the morning; but as she drove home, Bertha decided to go out of her way to help the Cardinal children.

Not since the day before the two oldest had started attending Ross School had any of them seen the inside of her office or been the recipient of her discipline. She could remember thinking that she'd never seen such serious-looking children; but as yet another one would begin grade one every year, they would again prove to be diligent pupils, working hard to learn their lessons.

Bertha had to admit that the negative opinion she'd formed about Ursula and Clarence Cardinal stemmed more from other parents' gossip than from what she had observed firsthand. The family rarely participated in the school's extracurricular activities, but she had a sense that the children were more familiar with toil than with fun and games.

Suddenly it occurred to Bertha how she could assist them. She would personally arrange for the three girls to join the 4-H club, and she would teach them how to sew and help them to make better-fitting dresses that were more like what the other girls wore to school.

~ 151 ~

It was not enough. Although he'd succeeded in restoring the Melville Pharmacy to its previous state as a successful business and recently built a comfortable home, the rueful reality was that Hans Gerhart had no one with whom to share his prosperity or his life.

More than a dozen years had passed since he graduated from the University of Saskatoon and attempted to become a pilot to join the fight against the Nazis in Europe. Recovering from his bitter disappointment, and at the end of his monetary resources, Hans returned to the University Hospital. He accepted the position he'd been offered upon graduation, but he soon tired of the daily grind of working with very ill and demanding patients.

After three months, when a classmate proposed that they buy City Pharmacy in Saskatoon, Hans leaped at the opportunity. Because Colin Bryce's father was prepared to help them secure a business loan, the two bright young men embarked upon the corporate venture of operating and eventually expanding the established drugstore.

At the forefront of his mind, Hans was intent on earning enough money to resume his search for Ursula. At the earliest opportunity, he had planned to return to

Neudorf and determine what had happened to the woman he loved and with whom he had vowed to spend his life. What he had not initially considered was the amount of energy and commitment required to operate a highly competitive business and the days becoming weeks before he could finally plan a trip back to the village in the German Lutheran township.

Finally in early October of 1943, Hans arranged with Colin to have four days off from the pharmacy. He borrowed his friend's newly purchased Ford roadster and headed to Neudorf, leaving before dawn to cover the more than 200 miles to his destination. As the warm late-autumn wind whipped his short blond hair and caressed his still-boyish face, Hans was optimistic that this time, come what may, he would track down his lovely Ursula. He was determined to not think about the unanswered letters he had written over the past two years but to focus instead on finding his one true love.

He would first drive to the General Store and speak with her Aunt Katherina before travelling to the homestead, where he fully intended to apprise Gustav Warner that he, too, was now a man of property.

Reaching Neudorf in early afternoon, Hans pulled up in front of the dress shop just as Katherina Werner was coming out the door. She was still a handsome woman with her fine head of brunette hair streaked with silver grey, the skin on her face revealing few wrinkles, and her soft blue eyes lively and bright. As he climbed out of the vehicle, Hans wondered if she would recognize him, but he had not even come around the front of his car before he heard her lilting voice.

"How lovely to see a face from the past, and I am thoroughly delighted that you have come to visit. Although I am running late today, it seems that you still know when to arrive for a meal, Hans, so won't you please come in and join me for a bite to eat."

"Thank you, Katherina. I would be honoured to join you. I suppose some things never change since I do recall invariably appearing just in time for dinner. And you don't seem to have changed either, still looking as lovely and vibrant as ever. As it happens, I have driven all day from Saskatoon this morning, and I have had little to eat, so I am starving."

Placing her hand snugly on Hans's forearm, she steered him in the direction of the house that she shared with Peter Mohr. Even as they walked, Katherina began to feel dread because she knew precisely why this handsome young man had come to call upon her.

She realized that the best way to postpone his inquiries was for her to ask her own questions. Guiding him to the kitchen table, Katherina launched in as she walked over to the icebox.

"Now tell me, Hans, have you graduated from university, and what are you doing now? Will you pursue your plan to become a pilot and go overseas?"

Between mouthfuls of baked ham, scalloped potatoes, and cucumber salad, Hans warmly responded to Katherina's numerous questions. But once satiated, he was ready to pursue the business at hand.

"That was delicious, and I usually am not so ill-mannered as to eat and run, but I can hardly contain myself any longer before I see my darling Ursula. I'm sure that you understand, Aunt Katherina?"

Standing up from the table and giving her an affectionate hug, he buoyantly quipped, "Soon I really will be your nephew by marriage."

"Hans, please sit back down. Although I do not relish the idea of being the bearer of bad news, I can't allow you to drive out to my brother's homestead in the hope of finding Ursula. I am very sorry to have to tell you that she is not there. In fact, she has not been home for over two years. And most disquieting of all, no one knows where she has gone."

Sinking into the high-backed kitchen chair and looking at Katherina with scepticism, he blurted, "What do you mean she is not there? Surely she is home by now. I guess you didn't hear that I came by train to see her at the beginning of May and I instantly had the misfortune of running into Gustav.

"He was irate, shouting at me and accusing me of having done something to her. I was frustrated so I went back into the train station and bought a ticket to Caron. But I know Ursula, and she would never worry her mother by not telling her where she is. Why are you telling me this? I always thought that you cared about me and Ursula," Hans beseeched of the woman who suddenly seemed a stranger to him.

Katherina was unbearably torn between her affection for this fine young man—who had strived against all odds to graduate from university and to be good enough to marry Gustav Warner's younger daughter—and her profound love for Amelia. She had solemnly vowed to keep Ursula's secret, and she could never betray her sister-in-law and closest friend. Still, Katherina was firmly convinced that it was the underlying reason for Ursula's unexplained disappearance, and she longed to say or do anything to help Hans in his obvious desolation.

Suddenly at the back of her mind, she had a niggling memory, which she considered might provide him with an answer; but the harder she tried to bring it into conscious recall, the more remote it became. Katherina could scarcely abide to look at Hans, but she had to speak—to offer him some measure of condolence as he continued to stare forlornly at his feet, immobilized by the news that she'd imparted.

In the end the meagre words would remain with him always; but instead of giving Hans any comfort, they would sear his soul for the rest of his life.

"My dear Hans, I am sorry to say this, but it seems that Ursula chose to leave, and it looks very much as though she does not want to be found."

Although Katherina managed to convince Hans to spend the night rather than to drive all the way back to Saskatoon, she could not get him to take another mouthful of food or drink, either during the evening or before he left the next morning. The journey home was a blur.

Throughout the trip he vacillated between abject despair and full-blown anger. He ranted as though she could hear him.

"Ursula, how could you leave? You did not have the right. We vowed to be together for life. We consummated our marriage even if we did not have the piece of paper. How could you find someone else and turn your back on me, your one true love, as you always whispered in my ear?"

When Hans arrived at his small one-bedroom apartment over the pharmacy, he was exhausted. Returning the car to Colin, he muttered something about not feeling well and then spent the next two days in bed, subsisting on water and what little food he had in the kitchen. Finally pulling himself together enough to resume working, Hans was withdrawn with the staff in the drugstore. When he was filling a prescription, he could barely muster a civil word to the patron.

Eventually Hans realized that he had to get a grip; although Colin had initially been circumspect, it was clear his patience was wearing thin, especially since Hans refused to disclose what had happened.

152

Time does have a way of healing all wounds, and he was a healthy young man with the rest of his life ahead of him. Since he was manifestly unlucky in love, Hans decided to prove that he could be successful in business, and he proceeded to pour himself into the operation of the pharmacy. When Colin married and started his family, Hans worked every weekend and most evenings. With his friend and business partner playing matchmaker, he did date other women, and over time he even asked one to be his wife. But three weeks before the wedding, he called it off, realizing that it would hardly be fair to Eloise when he still yearned for Ursula.

On those occasions when Hans took time off from working, he would be drawn to the German Lutheran townships and would drive around Neudorf and Lemberg, and then into Melville, always hoping to catch a glimpse of Ursula before returning to Saskatoon. Each time Colin queried him about his fixation 200 miles southeast of the city, he passed it off lightly until the day he drove through Melville and noticed that the old pharmacy on Main Street was for sale.

153

Hans had welcomed the challenge of putting his body and soul into restoring the building and the business until, before long, it turned a tidy profit. For the first five years, he'd been so busy that he rarely went roaming around the countryside; although whenever he was out and about town, he still searched for Ursula. And again as soon as the pharmacy was running smoothly, his restlessness returned.

Hans had hired a young, newly graduated pharmacist to assist him in the drugstore, so on his first Saturday morning off in years, he drove out of Melville. By the time he arrived in Duff, he felt peckish, so he stopped at the little café on the main street. Sitting down at a table next to four men whom he surmised were local farmers, Hans ordered the bacon and egg breakfast special.

As he was enjoying a second cup of coffee, he overheard one of the men telling the others that he might soon have to sell the other half-section of his land because his wife's illness was becoming progressively worse. Trying hard not to eavesdrop within the small room, Hans suddenly became all ears when he heard Gustav Warner's name mentioned. Apparently the farmer's land was adjacent to the Warner homestead in the township, and last autumn he had sold 320 acres to Gustav and his youngest son, Johann. They'd always been helpful enough as neighbours; but at the time of the purchase, he'd just experienced an uneasy feeling that the German farmers were planning to buy up as much land as they could in the English community.

Now he was afraid that he would need to accommodate their quest for property because he was not even certain that he could finish the spring seeding. As the elderly gentleman had been speaking, Hans was seized with a spur-of-the-moment inspiration; he would try his hand at farming. Why not, when every other of his undertakings had quickly turned successful? Perhaps he had the Midas touch.

Hans knew little about working the land, other than what he had learned during the two summers when he had accompanied Leonard home from university. But he did recall how invigorating and peaceful he had felt on the homestead, and he was eager for a new venture. Was he still hoping to encounter Ursula strolling about on her father's farm or bringing lunches out to her husband while he worked in the fields? Or was Hans Gerhart seeking an opportunity to upstage Gustav Warner?

"Excuse me, sir. I did not intend to listen to your conversation, but I am in the neighbourhood because I am very interested in purchasing some farmland. Please allow me to introduce myself. I am Hans Gerhart, and if I am not being too forward, I would like to talk to you about the possibility of buying your land," he said, quietly standing up, bowing his head slightly, and extending his right hand.

Taking an instant liking to the soft-spoken young man, Mr. Harold Brown shook Hans's hand and invited him to join them for a cup of coffee. Long before the day was over, Harold had taken Hans out to his farm, introduced him to Sally, his wife, and asked him to stay for a bite of supper.

Within the month, Hans was the legal proprietor of a half-section of prime farmland, the other half of which was owned by Gustav Warner. The south boundary of the adjoining property was directly across the creek from the comfortable farmhouse where Hans had spent the two most enjoyable summers of his life; although he still had not have the slightest notion why he had so completely fallen out of favour with his soon-to-be neighbours. Whereas he might in time accept that Ursula had chosen another man, he could not fathom why Leonard had stopped writing and ceased to be his friend.

At any rate, when the manager of the largest bank in Melville readily secured the loan using Hans's drugstore as the collateral, he gave Mr. Brown his complete asking price for the land, the farmhouse, and all of his farming equipment in one cash payment. Mr. Brown had fully expected to need to arrange an auction, so the benevolent farmer could hardly believe his good fortune when Hans Gerhart had agreed to buy his property in its entirety.

154

Alas, but for the demon rum, Clarence and Ursula Cardinal might have been able to stay on the straight and narrow. On one rare occasion that Clarence proved to be a man of his word, the dances in the big red barn on his farm were never started up again. But then he had a new problem. Where would he have ready access to alcohol? And how could he earn the money to purchase it?

While considering his dilemma, he received a telephone call from his father who said his grandmother was dying and wanted to see him one last time. When Clarence hesitated because Ursula would not want to take the children out of school, Henry pleaded with him to come alone then to honour her request. If James, his older brother, could travel all the way from Vancouver, surely he could muster a few hundred miles to say farewell to an old woman who had loved him dearly throughout his childhood.

During the week he spent in Amaranth, Clarence stumbled upon an idea that might just be the answer to his quandary. He had arisen early one morning to go ice fishing with his father, and over the next three hours, they had caught an abundance of pickerel. What if he froze the fish, took it home, and thawed and filleted it to sell it to his neighbours?

Even Clarence was surprised at how quickly the three-pound boxes of frozen pickerel sold, rather to Ursula's annoyance since she wanted to keep it to feed their family. When he proposed to return to Amaranth to bring home another catch, she nonetheless complained about the smell of the fish in the house when he was filleting it. At the end of another argument, he decided to build himself a small heated shed in which to store the smelly fish as he prepared it for sale.

Although women often told him that he had good hands, Clarence soon came to learn that he could put his practical skills to more functional purposes, and by the end of the winter he had developed a sizeable trade for his fresh fish business. Over the next decade he supplied multiple homes throughout the farming district in Miniota, and farther away in Virden, with tasty meals of frozen pickerel all winter long, an option they previously could not have considered.

If only Clarence would have chosen to spend any of his supplemental income on his wife and family, his children might not have had to depend on hand-me-down clothing and shoes from their cousins to wear to school. Or if Ursula could have insisted that her husband share the proceeds from his fishing business rather than so quickly accept the handouts from Otto's three daughters. Robert was the lucky one, since Ursula's brother had no son to provide him with clothing appropriate for a boy. Indeed, her girls might have been quite happy with Francis, Faye, and Darlene's dresses, which were more fashionable than what the other girls wore to school, if only they'd been the right size. The shoes were an entirely different problem; they did not properly fit Justine's, Elaine's, or Sandra's feet, and little could be done to modify them, even if Ursula had been so inclined.

However, since they were expected to wear them and be grateful that they had such generous cousins, Ursula's three oldest girls would reach adulthood with well-formed bunions from consistently squeezing their feet into improperly fitting shoes.

Instead of sharing the money for clothing and shoes, Clarence purchased a small truck on the grounds that he needed to haul the frozen fish from Amaranth and then drive around the district to sell his product once the boxes were prepared. It was remarkable how often he finished his last delivery of the day in either Miniota or Virden, just in time to join the local regulars in the beer parlour.

Clarence quickly discovered that the number of friends he acquired was directly proportional to the amount of drinks he would stand during the evening, and soon he became well liked in each of the town's hotels. It was not uncommon for him to have spent his entire proceeds from the day's delivery as he tried to think of some reasonable excuse to quell Ursula's expected ire.

Before long the arguments and fights between Ursula and Clarence reached an unprecedented peak. So Ursula eventually decided that since her husband intended to spend all of the money from his enterprise in the local bars, usually in Virden, she might as well join him. For years every Saturday evening, the five Cardinal offspring could be found huddled together in the backseat of the car under blankets, waiting for their parents to finish drinking and drive them home to their beds.

The years passed, and as the Cardinal children matured, they took over more and more of the heavier farm chores, and Robert and Justine learned how to drive the tractor under their grandfather's supervision. Gustav and Amelia always made sure to arrive in Manitoba during the spring seeding and fall harvesting to labour alongside their increasingly responsible grandchildren, neither trusting that they'd receive the help they required, especially from their father.

Clarence was absent for longer and longer periods of time, now in the summer as well as during the winter, and although Ursula often appreciated the peace and quiet, she resented that he was no doubt out having a good time. She acknowledged that her life was easier with her kids all being hard workers not only in school but with the myriad tasks necessary to keep the farm running.

During the summer months, the girls, including Jennifer, picked a variety of wild berries and helped with the canning to provide food for the winter while Robert assisted with the haying and summer fallowing under George Bailey's welcome tutelage.

The neighbours were mostly understanding and did what they could to take some of the burden off Ursula and her children. By now most of the men in the district knew that Clarence was a drinker and a womanizer; although they were all careful to keep that news from Ursula and their own wives while maintaining a watchful eye on his whereabouts.

One of the women, Mona Norton, started to invite each of the Cardinal girls to take turns spending a weekend with her to give them a little holiday. However, soon it became apparent that Mona was really only interested in Elaine, and after their token weekend, Justine and Sandra were no longer asked to stay with Charles and her.

Although Norma Bailey had always cherished little Jennifer, she thought Mona was being too selective, so she invited Ursula and all of her children to join them most Friday evenings to watch television. In addition, Mrs. Stone followed through with her undertaking to have the three oldest Cardinal girls enrolled in the local 4-H club, and she personally provided extra instruction to ensure that they all became adept with a needle and thread.

Heaven knows she had done her level best, but in all her years she had never come across three girls who would prove so inept. At least Elaine and Sandra tried, but Justine was about as interested in sewing as in flying to the moon. Bertha finally promised herself that this would be the last year she'd insist that the Cardinal girls learn to sew, and once their projects for the annual fair were finished, she would recommend to Ursula that they try their hand at some other activity.

Bertha long ago gave up the notion that she could teach them how to alter their hand-me-down dresses, having spent hours trying to assist each to finish what she considered a relatively simple task: sewing an apron. As it was, she had dedicated two full hours over each of the last three weeks, and she fully intended to have the three aprons sewn before their father arrived to pick them up at five-thirty on Friday evening.

Glancing at the clock on the mantel, she realized that it was almost six, but at last the job was done. Elaine and Sandra sewed most of their own aprons, but Justine did little more than thread her needle every day. But in the interest of completion, Bertha took the fabric from Justine's recalcitrant hands and used her sewing machine to quickly stitch it together. Then she handed it back and discussed the next steps.

"Well, girls, although we are running a little late, your projects are ready for the fair. Since your father has not yet arrived, you can help me make supper before Ralph comes in from doing the chores. Elaine, you can cut these boiled potatoes into this pan. Sandra, you can scrape these carrots. And you, Justine, can peel this onion and cut it into small pieces."

Supper was ready, Ralph had come in and washed for his meal, and still there was no sign of Clarence. He was now more than an hour late to pick up his daughters, and before her husband sat down, Bertha hastily placed three extra plates on the table. As Ralph was saying grace, there came a knock on the door, and without waiting for a response, Clarence let himself in and demanded with a slur, "Why aren't my girls ready to come home?"

"Since you are over an hour late, your daughters have helped me to make supper. Now they will sit at this table and eat with Ralph and me while you wait in that porch. And I don't want to hear another word from you," Bertha declared, as though talking to a group of unruly students. She knew the man was drunk, but she also suspected he was too much of a coward to disobey her.

As one can well imagine, the three Cardinal girls could hardly choke down any food, much less leftover dry roast beef, while their father was slouched up against the porch wall. Sensing their discomfort, Bertha turned to them.

"Take your time, girls. You will sit at my table until every one of us has finished the supper that you helped cook, and that is the end of that!"

~ 156 ~

In the spring does a young man's fancy turn to love? Or could he simply no longer resist the temptation to at least try to catch a glimpse of his beloved Ursula? There certainly was little doubt in Hans Gerhart's mind that unrequited love was the most lasting of all, because come what may he could not stop yearning for the only woman he had ever loved. He was into his second year as a farmer, and on the bright sunny morning after he finished sowing the crops, Hans vacillated between returning to Melville and paying his respects to his neighbour to the south of his property.

Last spring after purchasing Mr. Brown's farm, which was already mostly seeded, he continued to work in the pharmacy, driving out on Sundays to check how his grain was doing. It was thrilling to come every week and see his fields greening as the seeds germinated and burst forth rows of straight and even shoots. It was well into summer, and he was quite convinced that there was not much to being a farmer, until the afternoon when Harold came into the pharmacy and asked how his summer fallowing was coming along. Wondering what the elderly gentleman meant, Hans invited him to join him for a cup of coffee. As they sat down together in the café across the street, he said, "Mr. Brown, I have a confession to make."

"Ah, dear boy, how many times must I ask you to call me Harold? And as you very well know, I am not a priest; so I don't think I'm the right person to hear your confession."

Hans chuckled.

"Oh, it is not so serious, only that I have done nothing on the farm. I thought that once the grain was seeded, I just needed to wait until the harvest. Since there are no animals at the farm, I simply drive out on Sundays to look at my fields of growing grain."

"That's all good and well, but surely you know you must plow and harrow the fields that I did not sow with grain in the spring. I deliberately did not cultivate them so that the moisture and nutrient levels can recover. After fallowing them this summer, you seed them again next year."

"Ah, Mr.... Harold..., I think this is where my confession comes in. The day I met you in the café in Duff and asked about buying your land, I was acting on impulse. I was raised in a small town, in an orphanage as it happens, and I was lucky enough to be able to study to become a pharmacist. The only time I ever spent on a farm was when a friend of mine invited me to stay with his family during two summers of our years at the university. They were the best days of my life, so when I heard you say you were selling your farm, I decided to give farming a try. But I guess I don't know the first thing about it."

"Well, my boy, as soon as I make sure that Sally is doing okay tomorrow, I will come to get you and we will drive to the farm. I expect that you have someone to work in the pharmacy? Because in the morning your education as a farmer begins."

157

True to his word, Harold knocked on the door of his apartment on the second floor of the pharmacy at seven o'clock, and after a quick breakfast, they were on their way to the farm. They worked all day, stopping only when Hans made a hasty trip into Duff to buy sandwiches and juice at the café for their dinner while Harold meandered about in the farmhouse where he had lived for over thirty years. Aside from the old pieces of furniture that he and Sally could not move to their smaller residence in Melville, there was nothing in the house. Feeling forlorn that his old home was so empty, Harold decided that once they finished the summer fallowing he would help Hans turn his dejected-looking house into a home.

Whereas he might spend his winters in Melville to do a proper job of looking after his land, he would need to live on the farm for periods of time during the spring, summer, and fall months. As the men ate, Harold realized just how much he missed being on the farm and was struck with his own impulse. He would propose to Hans that as long as Sally felt well enough to manage a few hours alone in town he would accompany him every day until he had taught this fine young man all he knew about being a farmer.

With Harold as his mentor, Hans quickly acquired the skills he needed to farm his half-section of land and to turn the farmhouse into a comfortable home, a haven from his overcrowded apartment in Melville. Hans promoted Dennis Baron, his young assistant, to be the manager of the pharmacy so he could spend more and more time living in the country.

During the summer months when she felt up to it, Sally also came for the day. The men prepared the meals while she enjoyed the reprieve of nature. She knew in her soul that her disease, which the doctors could not diagnose, was killing her, and she was certain that God had sent Hans to her and Harold. How else could this gentle, caring man who'd been raised in an orphanage have found his way to them, a childless couple?

Now she could die in peace because daily she saw the closeness developing between the men, as though Hans was the son she'd never been able to give to her beloved husband. Sally had felt so guilty when Harold was forced to sell one half-section and then the other because of her illness, but now she envisioned him coming to the farm year after year once she was gone.

The harvest was bountiful, and Sally was still well enough to watch as the golden wheat fields succumbed to the new John Deere combine harvester.

During the winter Sally had more poor days than good, and before the arrival of spring she went into the hospital, not expecting to come home again. As much as Harold longed to accompany Hans to the farm to start the spring seeding, he would not leave his cherished wife for fear that she might die alone.

Subsequently, Hans told Dennis that he would be out of town until his crops were sown. And now lingering as he packed his soiled clothing to take home to wash, he wavered about paying his respects to his neighbour. All the while Hans had envisioned returning, taking Ursula into his arms, and then being enveloped in one of Amelia's endearing hugs. Amelia had been like a mother to him, giving him the gift of belonging to her family, and unequivocally sharing her feelings of warmth and love, which had been rekindled when fate blessed him with Harold and Sally Brown.

But Hans could not forget his grim encounter with Gustav those years ago in Neudorf. What if Ursula had never returned? Did Gustav still hold him responsible for his lost daughter?

Eventually it dawned on him, why not pay a visit to Aunt Katherina and get the lay of the land before calling on his neighbour? During the past year he'd been too busy to call on anyone in the community, and he'd not even driven to Neudorf to tell Aunt Katherina that he was now a landowner in the district.

Spurred into action on the way into Neudorf, Hans realized that he had been remiss in not taking the time last year to see Katherina, a woman like Amelia who had always treated him with kindness. Well, he would make up for it now. He vowed that he would become one of her most frequent visitors, a prospect that gave him considerable delight on the balmy spring morning.

On his arrival, Hans parked his car and headed into the dress shop when he spotted Fraya Roth strolling toward him.

"How wonderful to see you, Fraya. It has been years since we last saw one another."

"Yes, you certainly have been a stranger, Hans. What brings you into our humble village now?"

"I have come to see Katherina Werner and tell her that I have purchased a half-section of land adjacent to her brother's farm. I shall be honest and admit that for years I was like a lost soul wandering about in the wilderness, because the only woman I ever truly loved rejected me. But I am finally coming to terms with it. In fact, other than Katherina, the entire Warner family has turned their back on me for reasons I have never been able to determine."

"Petulance does not become you, Hans. Nor does self-pity. I understand that you lost Ursula, but you never even came for Leonard's memorial service, when I needed every caring friend I had for a shoulder to cry on."

Hans was struck speechless. A minute passed before he recovered his voice, and then he could only stammer. "Wh-wha-what do you mean? What are you saying? Memorial service?"

"You didn't hear that Leonard was killed overseas? His Lancaster Bomber was shot down over the English Channel. He was a war hero, and you knew nothing about it?" Fraya asked with stunned disbelief.

"I heard not a word from Leonard since the Christmas he withdrew from university. But before he left, he had received a letter from his father saying that I was no longer welcome on his farm. Then after he was gone, I wrote to Ursula almost every week, but I never got a reply. Oh, God, I am very sorry, Fraya. I had no idea." Tears welled up in his eyes.

"I am sorry that I am the bearer of the dreadful news about Leonard, but I think I should also tell you about Ursula. Eventually she did return to her father's farm with a husband, and within four years either my father or my aunt delivered four babies. Then just as suddenly as they came, they left, and the last I heard was that they were living on a farm somewhere in Manitoba. It looks like neither of us has been lucky in love, Hans, and right now I suggest that you come back with me to the office. I'll ask my father to fix you a drink of brandy, strictly for medicinal purposes, of course," said Fraya, gently placing her hand on Hans's arm.

The day passed with Hans remaining in Neudorf and eventually taking Fraya, Max and Rebecca Roth, and Aunt Katherina to Traders' Dining Room for supper. As the evening wore on, he accepted Katherina's offer to stay the night, and it was not until the next morning that he was on his way.

His indecision about calling on Gustav Warner was now replaced by a desire to convey his condolences, however long overdue. When Hans drove into the yard, he was out of the car and walking toward the house before he noticed a young man fuelling a tractor by the gas tank. He immediately realized that he was looking at the adult Johann, as Hans's recollection of his rescue of the eight-year-old boy from the charging bull flashed before his eyes.

But the recognition was not reciprocated. Before Hans could introduce himself, he was greeted with a brusque "I'm busy and not interested in purchasing anything from the Watkins salesman."

When he tried to clarify that he wished to speak with Gustav, he was told that he no longer farmed this land, which concluded Hans Gerhart's only attempt to call at the Warner homestead.

➤➤➤ 158 ➤➤➤

Ursula's emotions were spinning out of control. For periods that were becoming shorter, she would be fine, feeling euphoric rather than completely cheerless about her life. During those days she had an abundance of energy and could work rings around anyone. Whenever she was very excitable, she became even more insistent that her orders be obeyed. And if they were not, she became frustrated to the point of agitation. It was during these episodes that Justine would have been well-advised to do as her mother demanded.

Of course, if Justine did not agree with her mother, she always questioned her, even about minor concerns, and persisted until the inevitable happened. Ursula's beatings became more violent, and on one particular day, Robert chanced to come into the kitchen when she was kicking Justine repeatedly around the floor.

His eldest sister screamed, "Why don't you just go ahead and kill me and get it over with? I know you're not my real mother. Someday she will come and take me away from you."

Her threat only enraged Ursula and spurred her to strike out at Justine even harder, until soon the other girls came running from the bedroom to see what was causing the commotion. Finally her siblings could pull their mother away and help Justine to the safety of the backyard.

"When Mom is in that kind of mood, why don't you stay away from her? You know she'll fly off the handle at any little thing you say," Robert asked, as he gave Justine a piece of cloth to wipe her bloody nose.

"I was right. It is your turn to get the cows, Sandra, and she kept saying that I better get outside and do it if I knew what was good for me. Why does she think she can never be wrong?" Justine sniffled, as she wiped her face.

"What does it matter? Would you rather be dead just to prove that you are right? I will go find the cows," Robert exasperatedly replied before starting to walk toward the pasture.

Sitting on a chair, Ursula shouted to herself as she lit a cigarette, "What is the matter with that girl? Why can't she be like the other kids and just do what she is told? She always puts me in such a foul temper."

Then there were days that became weeks when Ursula could hardly get out of bed. At the last minute she dragged herself to the kitchen to cook the porridge. And once the kids had left for school, she often went back to bed where she remained for the better part of the day, especially if Clarence was not at home.

Finally one day when Norma let herself into the house and found Ursula lolling about, she dashed to the car to tell George that they should drive Ursula to Virden to see the doctor. The medication that he prescribed made her sleep even more, and when he changed it she became so agitated she could barely sit still. The physician again ordered a different drug, explaining that she was suffering from depression and that if she expected to recover she must take the pills according to the prescription.

With the third medication Ursula did begin to notice an improvement in her general well-being, and soon when she was having a bad day she was quick to reason that if one capsule made her feel better, why not take another?

Strangely at first, the doctor did not query how frequently she asked to have her prescription refilled. But then when he did, Ursula decided to attend the new physician in town.

159

Since her four eldest kids were old enough to stay at home and look after Jennifer, Ursula was now as free to go to Virden and have a good time as was her gay blade of a husband. If for yet another unexplained reason Clarence was not to be found, Ursula had become a skilled driver and was quite capable of going into town with the car.

One of the best decisions he'd ever made was to purchase that truck for his fish business, leaving the station wagon behind. If Clarence thought for a minute that his wife had no means to go out on the town, he had greatly underestimated her. Soon she developed a circle of male friends who were more than happy to see her and to stand her any number of drinks, especially when they learned that they might be rewarded later in the evening with sexual favours. Furthermore, it did not matter if Ursula encountered Clarence in the same establishment, because he usually was engaged in similar activities with certain ladies known to frequent that particular hotel.

Before long Ursula embarked upon a quest, a never-ending search, which she justified was the only motivation for her unseemly behaviour. As the number of men she was with increased, the more she yearned for Hans and the love they'd consummated in their youth. When she could not arouse the perfect feelings she'd experienced with Hans, she was compelled to try again.

Remarkably, one way or another the reality of their parents' promiscuous behaviour escaped the awareness of their young family, perhaps because of the sensibilities of their caring neighbours and grandparents. As they matured, the four oldest children became more curious about Clarence and Ursula's clandestine coming and goings, but they were much too busy with their schoolwork and farm chores to wonder for long.

However, when they were transferred to the Miniota School Division and Ursula became the school bus driver and spent the entire day in the small town with a man who often gave them chocolate bars, the suspicions of at least Robert and Justine were considerably heightened.

~ 160 ~

It was considerate of Rita and her mother to include Amelia in the preparations for the autumn nuptials. As the plans unfolded, she could barely believe the host of people invited to Johann's wedding, and soon she started to fret about the amount of food she needed to cook to feed them.

Still, Amelia hesitated to ask what she was expected to do, because from the moment her son introduced her to his bride-to-be she became more reticent than normal. Maybe if they had not laughed at her when she quietly asked when she should start preparing some of the food, saying that the bride's mother hardly had time to worry about the meal, Amelia might have felt more comfortable in their company.

Then Mrs. Weinberg used a word she'd never heard before, but she was not about to ask what it meant in case it gave rise to more mirth at her expense. Amelia didn't want to say anything to Johann, but she found it very confusing how Rita and her mother constantly switched back and forth between German and English. Amelia, surprised at how fluent Eva Weinberg was and how she spoke English with hardly an accent, she wondered why she could not speak nearly as well.

Luckily it was Justine's turn to spend her two-week summer holiday with them. Perhaps she could ask for her help. It was strange how in all the years Amelia had known Sarah Thompson she had never once felt embarrassed during their long conversations. Yes, she realized that she mixed up her words, turned numbers backwards, and often combined both languages in the same sentence; but Sarah always seemed to accept her and she certainly never would have laughed at her. If she used a word that Amelia did not know, she would tell her what it meant and then have her repeat it until she could pronounce it properly.

Perhaps Gustav had been right all along when he told her that she should try to speak more English; although it was easier for him because he could read in both languages, whereas she could barely read and write in German. Her mother had died in childbirth, and then Amelia had raised her two younger siblings, which precluded her from attending the German school. In fact, had it not been for her sister-in-law, Maria, who taught her three children around Gustav Werner's kitchen table on the original homestead, Amelia would have been illiterate.

When she went home, she quietly prepared supper. Even when Justine put away the book she was reading and came to peel the vegetables, Amelia did not feel like talking. And then as soon as the dishes were washed and dried, she went outside to her garden.

Deep in thought, Amelia did not realize that Justine had followed her.

"Grandma, is something bothering you? You have hardly said a word since you came home from helping with Uncle Johann's wedding."

"Shouldn't you be learning how to read your book, Justine? I am only a little tired, but I will feel better once I have worked in my garden."

"I know how to read that book, Grandma. Did someone say something to upset you? I can always tell when you are not yourself, and I want to find out what is wrong."

"Oh, I was just thinking that I should have listened to your grandpa and learned more English. Rita and her mother said a word today that I couldn't understand, but they had already been laughing at me, so I didn't want to ask them."

Justine threw her arms around her grandma's neck.

"Tell me what word they used, Grandma, and if I don't know it we will look it up in a dictionary."

"Well, there will be so many people at this wedding, and when I asked when I should start cooking, Mrs. Weinberg said that the meal was being catered. That's the word I didn't understand, Justine."

"The word 'cater' means that other people, usually a company, will bring all of the food and drinks, so none of the guests at Uncle Johann's wedding will need to prepare the meal.

"You know, Grandma, tomorrow when you go to help make the decorations, I am coming with you. I shall sit right beside you so we can talk, and then if anything is said that you don't understand, I shall quietly explain it."

When Justine first realized that she'd be visiting her grandparents before her uncle's wedding, she was so excited that she could hardly sleep. She had never been to a wedding, and she remembered that when she'd been introduced to Rita Weinberg, her beauty had intimidated her. She was not nearly as tall as her handsome Uncle Johann, but when she leaned on his shoulder with her beautiful blond tresses and sparkling blue eyes, they fit together like a glove. A delicate, silken glove. She could hardly wait to see her in a pure white bridal gown.

But once Justine heard that Rita and her mother had laughed at her beloved grandmother, her soon-to-be aunt lost some of her glitter. She did accompany Amelia for the rest of the week while the extensive nuptials were being completed, and as they worked beside each other, Justine encouraged her grandmother to share stories from her youth.

As the years passed and the size of the family grew, Amelia became more conscious of her broken English laced with a heavy German accent; during the social gatherings she tended to stay in the kitchen cooking and cleaning rather than mingling with the others. When she finally came into the living room, she always sat alone in a corner until Justine chanced upon her and soon had her telling tales about her father serving in the Czar's army and about how her parents had fled Russia with only the clothes on their backs.

During the last week of her stay, her grandparents took Justine to the farm for a visit. In three short days her parents and siblings would arrive for the wedding, and then she would have to return to Manitoba. It would be another two years before it was her turn again; until then, all she could look forward to was going back to school, and reading. Whenever she lapsed into the depths of self-pity, Justine considered that her only friends were books and nature, especially trees. She did not feel that she fit in any better at school than she did at home, and try as hard as she might, she could not get along with her mother.

Justine felt exactly the opposite with her grandparents. Whenever she visited them, she knew she was loved and accepted unconditionally. In their presence she was relaxed and confident, feeling as though she could achieve whatever she determined.

Subsequently, in the early afternoon, when her grandfather suggested that the two of them go for a stroll to the south wheat field to check if the grain was starting to ripen, Justine leapt at the opportunity. Autumn was her favourite season, and sauntering with Grandpa through his golden wheat fields was one of her preferred activities.

Justine especially loved walking with him, because as he strolled through his wheat fields, he would chew on a stalk of the ripening grain and reach out to hold her hand. His affectionate gesture was as meaningful to Justine as her Grandma's hugs, and whether he said it every time or not, she always remembered his sage words that she could go wherever she wanted, with confidence.

⤜ 162 ⤛

All morning Justine anticipated their customary amble. She had finally resolved to muster her courage and broach some questions with her grandfather about her mother, to perhaps improve her understanding of Ursula.

As soon as they reached the south field and her grandfather clasped her right hand, Justine took a deep breath.

"Grandpa, do you know why my mother never taught us German? I have always wanted to speak and understand your first language."

"That is a hard question, Justine, and I don't really know the answer. Whether she didn't teach you because she wanted to defy your grandma and me or because your father does not understand the language, I can't say. Maybe it had something to do with how she was treated in school during the war when the other students dipped her braids into the inkwells. I know she was called names like Kraut and Nazi. And then, of course, when your father and she get into one of their heated arguments, he always calls her a dirty German, not that she treats him any better."

Stopping several moments to reflect, Gustav then said, "But now I am glad that none of you can speak German because there are so many people, including your own father, who don't like the Germans and who believe we are all Nazis. One of my closest friends is a Jew; but still the entire German race will always be branded because of Adolf Hitler. No, Justine, for whatever reason that your mother did not teach you German, it is a good thing now, as the world learns more and more about the crimes committed by that barbarian. Keep reading and learning as many words as you can. Always remember to speak English very clearly. And above all else, never ever let anybody know that you come from a German family."

Unable to believe that her grandfather was advising her to deny her German heritage, Justine became silent. She had always taken pride in the fact that her grandparents, although coming to Canada from Russia, were born in Austria. Miss March had not taught them much about the horrific crimes to which Grandpa was referring. What did he mean? Surely war by its nature was always about fighting and killing people.

After all, Uncle Leonard, his own son, had been shot down flying over the English Channel, but there must be much more to it for Grandpa to order her to never tell anyone about being German. What could he feel so guilty about that he wanted to deny coming from the same country as his favourite composers, Beethoven and Mozart?

Lost in thought and resolving to read more about the Third Reich, Justine did not hear her grandfather the first time he asked, so he had to repeat his question: "How are you getting along with your mother lately?"

"Not very well, Grandpa, and I don't think I ever will. I don't know what is wrong with me. Many times I think I am doing something to gain her approval, but I always seem to end up making her mad. If I ever get invited to stay with one of our neighbours, and even after it is my turn to visit you, she always makes me pay for having any fun."

When she received no response from her grandfather, she began to think she'd expressed too much.

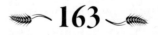

163

As it happened, Gustav had just noticed that the farmer on the adjacent field had stopped his tractor, climbed down, and started to walk toward them. His face was as white as a sheet, and Gustav returned the glare.

Gustav could not believe his eyes. Johann had mentioned that Mr. Brown sold the other half-section of his land, and he recalled how upset his son had been because the elderly farmer had clearly indicated that Johann would have first right of refusal.

Last year he had seen an outsider working the land with Mr. Brown, but he thought nothing was unusual until this spring when he saw the same man seeding the crops on his own.

Surmising that the stranger must be the new owner, Johann told his father how he had rebuffed him, not even bothering to find out his name when he later came to call. Although it had been years since Gustav had seen the younger man, who still had not batted an eye, he had no doubt that it was Hans Gerhart.

"Grandpa, are you all right?" Justine asked, as she began to tug on his hand.

"Come Justine, you don't need to worry about that man. Let's go home and see if Grandma is awake. And as far as your mother is concerned, she has had a lot of unhappiness in her life; so when she gets frustrated, I think she takes it out on you. Just try to stay out of her way, and always remember what I have repeatedly told you about believing in yourself."

When Gustav Warner abruptly turned from him, seized the hand of the young girl with him, and strode away without so much as a wave of recognition, Hans reached a decision. Shutting off the tractor, he stalked across the field and hurried back to the farmhouse.

Harold had been having a short nap after dinner, and was coming out the door when Hans arrived.

"Ah, you are awake. That's good because I have given a lot of thought to Eric Norman's inquiry about whether I'm interested in buying his farm. I initially thought that another section might be more land than I could successfully farm, but upon further deliberation, with all the new equipment being produced I think I could manage it. There is the matter of money, but I know that my manager at the pharmacy is anxious to become my business partner. If I sold Dennis half of the shares in the drugstore, I would probably have close to Mr. Norman's asking price for the land, since I don't need his implements. Shall we drive over now and see if he is at home?"

Looking fondly at the younger man, Harold replied, "Before we do that, Hans, there is something I want to tell you. You do not need to sell your shares in the pharmacy, because I still have all of the money you paid me for my farm. Now that Sally is gone, I have changed my will, and everything that I own will come to you when I die. I am quite prepared to give it to you today if you choose to purchase Eric's section of farmland.

Hans just listened.

"As you know, Sally and I were never blessed with children, and neither of us has any remaining family, other than a couple of distant cousins. When I met with my lawyer, he assured me that it is my legal right to bequeath my earthly goods to whomever I choose. It was actually Sally's idea, and before she passed on we agreed to leave everything to you, Hans. From the day we met you, we both felt as though God had sent you to us.

"You became the son we could not birth, and every single day you have more than proven how right we were to believe in His generous gift. There is no use in you protesting that you cannot accept my money, Hans, because it is only a matter of time before it is yours. If not for you, I would have no reason to live."

As Harold Brown grasped his shoulders in a fatherly hug, Hans wondered how two men who had farmed side by side for decades could be so drastically different.

164

The day of Johann's wedding dawned bright with sunshine and a breeze sufficient to cool the guests in their finery. His bride was radiant in a white satin gown with a long flowing train. The princess-style of the dress featured a close-fitting bodice of the finest floral lace and a flared skirt with a seamless waist. The deep scalloped hem matched the long lace sleeves, and the mandarin collar was edged with seed pearls. Iridescent dewdrop pearls adorned her tiara, with its attached veil so delicate that it scarcely concealed her blond locks.

The groom's fashionable suit of the deepest blue accentuated the snow-white purity of his bride's attire. Standing together in front of the altar, their appearance dazzled. In whispers, family and friends speculated that a man and woman could not perceptibly be more in love, and their radiance must surely emanate from within their souls, which were soon to become one.

As Reverend Lutz intoned the solemn oath, which in the sight of God and man gave Rita and Johann to each other "for as long as you both shall live," the congregation collectively had to refrain from standing and shouting a hurrah. Whereas tears of happiness overflowed the eyes of many of the women, especially

Rita's mother, Amelia, upon seeing the multitude of guests, said a prayer of relief that the dinner reception was being catered.

From the day Amelia understood that she would not be required to prepare the food, she had spent her time attending to other details, the first of which was to have Gustav drive her to Neudorf to visit Katherina. The two women, always delighted by seeing each other, set upon Amelia's plan to order four of the most beautiful dresses, four pairs of black patent-leather shoes, and the finest stockings available for young girls. Not forgetting her grandson, Amelia also ordered patent dress shoes, a powder-blue blazer, matching trousers, a white shirt, and a bow tie for Robert. On Johann Warner's wedding day, none of the Cardinal children would be dressed in hand-me-down clothing and shoes from their cousins.

Otto replied to his invitation, indicating that he would bring six guests. And although the family surmised that he would have his three daughters for the event, they could only speculate about the other two people. Surely he would not ask his former wife to come, the woman who only recently revealed that her actual name was Amelia Browning, and whom he was now divorcing. It was quite possible, of course, that he'd met another woman; but it was the first time that anyone in the Warner family had the slightest notion of it. At any rate, Amelia was determined that every one of the Cardinal children would be every bit as presentable as Otto's daughters.

Members of the congregation were distracted when a little black girl with dark frizzy hair entered the church in the presence of a Caucasian woman accompanied by three stylishly dressed females, strutting on ahead of them. Who could the child be? She was like a piece of charcoal surrounded by a sea of white faces, particularly to this flock of devout German Lutherans, most of whom had never before seen a coloured person.

Then their attention returned to the wedding party, and it was not until the bride and groom glided out of the church that they resumed their wondering. When the best man hastened over to the woman's side, several bystanders began to suspect that the black child must be one of Otto Warner's guests. They unabashedly stood and watched as Otto introduced Evelyn and her child, Natalie, to his parents before finally reining in Francis, Faye, and Darlene, and ordering them to greet their grandparents who had not recognized them.

Who was Natalie? And why had she come to Johann's wedding? Many of the adults couldn't conceal the surprise on their faces when Otto introduced mother and child, but the most pronounced look of incredulity was Gustav's.

The astute observer would have noticed that Amelia Warner was the only person who warmly greeted Natalie, wrapping her in the hug that had already been rejected by Francis, Faye, and Darlene. But then, to Amelia, all children were precious—particularly on a day when in her eyes her four Cardinal granddaughters were more beautiful than the blushing bride.

～ 165 ～

"There is no reason why we should worry about sending either Robert or Justine to that high school in Virden. They both have grade eight, which is more than I have, and the law says we can keep them out of school either when they have turned sixteen or have passed the eighth grade," Clarence grumbled, when Ursula told him that Mrs. Stone announced the closure of secondary classes at Ross School.

"No damn way are you keeping them out of school. You just want these kids to spend the whole day running this farm so you can go gallivanting around the countryside and sleep with any broad you can find," Ursula snapped, as she flung a hard crust of bread at Clarence's head.

"Every one of my kids will finish high school and beyond, if they want, rather than waste their lives on this useless farm. In fact, the last time they were here, I overheard Justine tell my father that she wanted to become a nurse. Come hell or high water, I intend to make damn sure she will have that chance.

"You are dumber than I thought if you think for one minute that I would let a lazy half-breed like you ruin my kids' future."

Recognizing the beginning of one of Ursula's rages, Clarence dropped the subject and left the kitchen. Every member of the Cardinal family had learned to make a quick exit when Ursula was ready to explode into a fit of fury—even Justine, of late, who diligently tried to take her grandfather's advice and stay out of her mother's way.

None could predict what would trigger her outbursts of wrath, but once Ursula got wound up there was no stopping her rampage; although she had even frightened herself the day she kicked Justine around the floor. Later it occurred to

Ursula that when she was in the throes of one of her uncontrollable storms, she might well do as the girl had asked and beat her eldest daughter to death.

Fortunately, both mother and daughter seemingly tried harder, if not to get along better then at least to minimize the amount of time in each other's presence. More significantly perhaps, for once in her life Justine had said something that met with Ursula's approval—even though it had been expressed to her father rather than to her, it pleased her mother that her eldest daughter might follow her dream.

⟫⟩～ 166 ～⟨⟪

When the school bus arrived at the end of the lane, the two oldest Cardinal children quickly climbed into it in order to begin their schooling at Virden Collegiate High School. Neither Robert nor Justine intended to spend the rest of their lives on this wretched farm with its rocky soil, grasshoppers, hailstorms, and whatever else nature could plague the harvest with so that they lived in perpetual poverty. They appreciated that their mother had defended their continuing education, and they did not even mind that they had to start the school year two days earlier than the town students in order to do a battery of psychological and intelligence quotient tests.

Although he knew his past academic performance was not nearly as strong as his sister's, Robert still found himself resenting that Justine was put in the A class of grade nine students while he was placed with the C pupils in grade ten. It was hard to be angry with her, though, because she agreed that it was not fair to label any student with an A, B, or C, especially once she learned that she was even more of a misfit in her classroom than she had been at Ross School.

The minute that Justine saw Linda Yates and Sarah Harris, she wished she could crawl into a corner and stay there for the entire school year. The two top students were tall, slender, attractive, and stylishly dressed, and she'd never felt so drab and dowdy in her life. The singular saving grace was that no one took notice of her—certainly not Linda and Sarah, who were completely unaware that she existed. The feelings of being excluded and isolated at Ross School paled in comparison to the loneliness and segregation she felt by the number of cliques within her new classroom, and she began to wonder if she would find one friend among the eighty-five students in grade nine.

A full month passed before a girl approached Justine and asked her if she could sit with her to eat lunch. Betsy Ogilvie, in the C class, noticed that Justine was always seated at the back of the cafeteria alone rather than with any of the other girls from the A class. At first Betsy hesitated, thinking that a stuck-up student from the top classroom would want nothing to do with her. But seeing her by herself day after day finally gave her the courage to speak.

Justine was so surprised that it took her several seconds to find her voice and affirm that the pleasant, short, plump girl could take the chair beside her. Before long Betsy and Justine became friends and often walked to the drugstore at lunchtime for a soda. At first Justine refused to go because she seldom had money. But Betsy would eagerly pay to be seen with an A student, although she kept her initial motive carefully concealed from her new friend.

By mid-October Justine had adjusted and was thoroughly enjoying high school. She had always been an avid student, and now there was so much to learn, an extensive array of books to read, and even a friendship. Justine often felt embarrassed that she rarely had any money to reciprocate Betsy's generosity at the soda fountain; but her friend quickly assured her that since she was an only child, her allowance was plenty for both of them.

Nonetheless, what Justine found most unexpected and astonishing was that her teacher, Mrs. Gill, seemed partial to her when seeking responses to her constant questions. However, this emerging pattern did little to improve Justine's acceptance by the popular students in the A class; now that they knew of her existence, she was subjected to their ridicule.

But Justine was not alone, since during recess she repeatedly overheard the most exclusive clique of students refer to their teacher as Mrs. Bird. She did rather resemble a bird with her small head, beak-like nose, closely spaced beady eyes, and short thick-set body that flared down from her unusually long neck. And the morning after the Christmas report cards were distributed and Mrs. Gill asked Justine to remain in the classroom at recess, she feared that she would be held responsible for the name-calling.

Instead, Mrs. Gill came straight to the point.

"Good work, Justine, but can you tell me what is holding you back from reaching your potential?"

"I'm sorry, Mrs. Gill, but I don't understand your question," Justine replied, glancing at her report card and thinking how pleased she was with her examination results and with placing sixteenth out of eighty-five students.

"According to the tests you took before coming into my class, you are capable of a much higher level of performance. Given your IQ and your responses to the battery of tests, I fully expect that by your next report card at Easter, you will be near the top of the class. Since I also grew up on a farm, I know about the chores. I suspect that if you had as much time to study as some of the other students, they could not come close to the marks you can achieve," Mrs. Gill predicted before beaming at Justine.

Over the years she came to realize that she was intelligent, thanks to affirmations from her grandfather and then from Mrs. Florence Gill. Those illuminating words would inspire Justine Cardinal to continually strive to reach her own unique potential and profoundly impact the balance of her academic life.

167

Within a year the Warner family gathered together for another wedding, albeit the antithesis of the one they attended the previous year. In total there were thirty-five people rather than the multitude invited to the reception for Johann and Rita's nuptials.

The bride wore a simple two-piece mauve ensemble of a light rayon fabric, and the groom was comfortably clothed in his best Sunday suit. The bridal party was small, consisting of Evelyn's friend, Clara, her maid of honour; the best man, Otto's brother Johann; and Natalie, the flower girl. There was little by way of decorations, as the minister performed the ceremony in the garden behind Otto's home, which was then followed by an informal reception in the living room of his farmhouse. This wedding supper was not catered, but rather prepared by Amelia and Ethel Kuss days in advance of the event. And instead of the music of a seven-piece orchestra, only a chorus of voices mingled throughout the rooms of the aging house on the bald Saskatchewan prairie.

Beautifully attired in a pure-white chiffon dress, the little black girl was conspicuous—a stunning ebony and ivory contrast—as she walked down the short garden path between the chairs toward the bride and groom. There had been no mention of Natalie's ancestry, nor would there ever be. As soon as the minister pronounced Otto and Evelyn man and wife, Otto proudly smiled at Natalie and announced that she was now Francis, Faye, and Darlene's little sister before asking his guests to welcome the two new members of the Warner family.

The ensuing silence lasted until Amelia quietly rose from her chair and bravely walked up to her son and daughter-in-law. Kneeling down in front of the child who stood frozen to the spot, she lovingly took Natalie into her arms. As far as Amelia Warner was concerned, Natalie was now her granddaughter, and her thirteenth grandchild deserved her love as equally as did the twelve who had preceded her.

Recognizing Amelia's courage, the other guests too began to welcome Natalie into the fold. The only three family members to ignore her were Francis, Faye, and Darlene; but then they totally disregarded everyone except Norman and Robert, their two cousins who they found interesting enough to engage in conversation.

 **168**

One year after making the daunting transition to Virden Collegiate High School, Robert and Justine learned that at the end of June 1960, Ross School would be closed completely and all students north of the road allowance would be transferred to the Miniota School Division.

From the beginning Robert was pleased with the move to a smaller high school in Miniota, with only one grade eleven class, since he never fully recovered from the stigma of being placed with the C pupils in Virden. However, by the end of the first month Robert realized that in the smaller class, he could seek extra instruction, and he steadily began to show improvement.

Recognizing that Robert's difficulty stemmed from his aversion to reading, and sensing that the youth liked to solve problems, Mr. Harry King, the English teacher and principal, disregarded the set curriculum and assigned mystery novels as his required reading. At first Robert could not believe that his teacher was asking him to read a book by Agatha Christie, a woman, but he complied and soon was drawn into *The Boomerang Clue* with its two amateur detectives.

Before long he could hardly wait until he finished his chores and homework every evening so he could get back to the book, and in record time he had finished it. Returning the book to Mr. King, he asked for another and then another. And just as Mr. King had anticipated, when Robert became more competent with reading, his comprehension in all subjects improved.

Most of the boys in his grade did not come from Miniota but from farms, and because they shared similar backgrounds, in little time Robert developed friendships with several of the other boys, becoming particularly close to Daryl Mitchell and Stephen Powell.

Then as an added bonus, a few girls seemed interested in him. Robert began to take more notice of his personal appearance, recognizing that he was as attractive as the rest of the young men in his class. And within months he unexpectedly gained access to the used station wagon. He had taken the test for his driver's licence in July, the day after he had turned sixteen, and in October when Ursula made a new male friend who came to pick her up on the evenings when Clarence was away, she usually allowed him to use her vehicle. Robert's status underwent an immediate boost now that he could drive to town to meet his buddies or invite a girl out for a date.

The change to Miniota Junior High School was equally positive for Elaine who as a grade nine student automatically joined the graduating class, which even in a small country school came with its attendant privileges. Sandra and Jennifer also made quick adjustments to their classes, liking their respective teachers and readily making friends.

Whether it was because of the small grade ten class or perhaps more because the information Mrs. Gill imparted had gone to her head, Justine began to question every teacher incessantly. It was not that her queries were irrelevant, but they had barely introduced the course material before she seemed to fully grasp the concepts. Still, it was disruptive to the lectures, and soon the teacher and the other students became frustrated by her constant interruptions.

Before long Justine's behaviour became the topic of practically every staff meeting, although unanimously the teachers could not find a solution that would not stifle her curiosity.

Once again it was Harry King's bold suggestion that solved the dilemma. As her history and English teacher, he had been similarly annoyed by her frequent questions.

"What if we tell Justine that she may quietly leave the room when she has completed the required assignments, provided that she remain silent as we present the material?"

"And where will she go?" asked Mrs. Tinker. As an Anglophone teaching French, she may have had the most difficulty with the new student.

"She loves to read and can go to the library. She wants to make the basketball team, so we could allow her free access to the gym to practise shooting baskets. Or she might improve her social skills if she could organize the school's extracurricular activities.

"When I am in the classroom, Justine could use my office telephone to arrange events, and lastly she could listen to the records in the staff lounge. She said that she enjoys classical music, but she never gets a chance to hear it except when she visits her grandparents."

The following day when Mr. King asked her to come to his office after she ate her lunch, Justine was certain she was in trouble. Ever since that morning at Ross School when the three Cardinal girls were summoned into Mrs. Stone's office, she gave any principal a very wide berth.

Hesitantly knocking on the closed door, she crept into the office when she heard Mr. King's request to enter. While seated in the chair to which he had pointed, he outlined his plan and her eyes grew larger and larger. She simply could not believe what she was hearing; she would essentially be given the run of the entire school to participate in all the activities she thoroughly enjoyed.

"Do you understand what I am telling you, Justine? You can choose to go the library, the gym, the staff room, or into my office to arrange social activities for the school as soon as you have finished the class assignments every day, rather than endlessly questioning the teachers."

Initially stunned by Mr. King's comments, Justine finally responded timidly.

"I am to leave the classroom when I am done my work, and I can go to any of the four places you mentioned?"

"Yes, you have understood correctly, but now I will caution you. If you ever make unnecessary noise, do any damage, or boast about your special privileges, you will lose them instantly and never be offered a second chance. In other words, Justine, you will need to be very accountable about your actions and the school property."

Over the last two and a half years of her secondary education, Justine floated about the school like an apparition. She devoured every book of interest to her. She listened to every classical record in the teacher's lounge until she nearly wore them out, and she proficiently organized the school's social activities using Mr. King's telephone. Justine even practised shooting baskets until she became the lead scorer on the school team, and when her mother said that she'd have to walk the eight miles to the farm if she stayed to play, Mr. King drove her home after every game.

Naturally, Ursula made her pay, if not with physical beatings then with constant verbal abuse and extra chores.

Not once did Justine complain, nor did she ever tell a soul where she went after she left the classroom. The other students were overwhelmingly curious, but nary a word crossed her lips. The teaching staff was only marginally reconciled to the special considerations, although eventually they grudgingly acknowledged that it did facilitate their instruction.

And his staff never did learn about his $100 bet that Justine could not score 100 per cent on the grade ten British history departmental examination. After she accepted Mr. King's wager, Justine memorized the textbook in its entirety because she knew she could not pay him if she lost. Upon her success, Justine surreptitiously concealed the proceeds.

⇛~ 169 ~⇚

At first the sound was so faint that it was barely audible. Then there it was again, only louder this time. Justine and Elaine huddled together in the double bed, which they shared, as did Sandra and Jennifer in their own room, which was further down and closer to the door. Too frightened to move or speak, the four girls waited in silence, And when five minutes passed, they breathed a collective sigh of relief that whoever it was had gone away.

Settling back down, they were abruptly aroused again from their repose by heavy pounding on the attic door, which caused each girl to practically jump out of her skin. Who could it be? They were alone at home. Their father was away in Amaranth, their mother was spending the evening with Graham Reed, who had brought them chocolate bars, and Robert was in Miniota, curling in a bonspiel. What if someone was trying to break into the house? Was there safety in numbers? But what could they use to defend themselves?

When the knocking started again, Justine decided that as the eldest she must climb out of bed and search in the darkness for the broom. Urging Elaine to come with her, she cautioned Sandra to stay in bed and guard Jennifer.

Quietly opening the closet door, Justine felt around the corner until she located their only possible weapon and then silently approached the entrance of the bedroom. Motioning Elaine to turn the knob and quickly pull open the door, she raised the broom, ready to push the interloper down the steep flight of stairs.

Justine was on the verge of action when a voice cried out, "Wait! Lower the broom. It's me, Robert."

"What did you think you were doing? You have scared the living daylights out of us," Justine snapped, as she placed the broom on the floor and turned on the light.

"I drove into the lane when the light went out and I thought I would play a practical joke on you. You don't have to get so mad about it," Robert replied, as Sandra and Jennifer ran to join them.

"Let me push you down the stairs with the broom handle as a joke, and you can decide how funny it is from the landing," Justine suggested, as she walked back to her bed in disgust.

"You won't tell Mom what I did, okay? Because she will have one of her fits. I won a set of dishes at the bonspiel, and I will give them to you girls if you promise not to say anything to her."

"We have already been bribed once tonight by that Graham guy, so why don't you just give them to Mom in the morning. Now let us try to get some sleep."

The next morning Robert gingerly came into the kitchen, expecting his sisters to squeal on him, but not even Jennifer mentioned the previous evening's incident.

When it became obvious that they said nothing to their mother, Robert said, "Our team won the curling last night and first prize was a complete set of dishes that I want to give to you, Mom. You can use them right away if you like."

"No, son. They look like really nice dishes, and you should put them away until you get married," Ursula replied, as she handed him his bowl of porridge.

"I will not live long enough to get married," Robert blurted, to the stunned surprise of his mother and sisters.

"Don't ever say things like that, Robert," Ursula scolded, as she cast a frightened glance at her only boy. But what she saw on his face was more foreboding than his words. His eyes had become dark and hollow and his own look of horror was almost more than a mother could bear.

Shuddering, he could not believe what he had exclaimed, and yet he immediately believed it was true. Had he said it to scare his sisters? That's what they thought too until they saw his morbid fear that shook his entire body. This was not one of Robert's practical jokes.

～ 170 ～

In the spring of 1962, Sarah quilted beside her dear friend in the basement of St. Paul's Lutheran Church.

"Oh, Amelia, this fall Gustav and you will have been married for fifty years. We must plan a big celebration for such an important occasion. I will bring it up at our next auxiliary meeting, and we will arrange a supper and dance reception right here in the church."

"You don't have to make such a big fuss over us, Sarah," said Amelia. She could not imagine anyone wanting to celebrate with them just because they had been married so long.

"Of course, we do. I remember you telling me how your parents arranged your marriage to Gustav before both of you were born and how, after meeting only twice, the next time you saw each other was on your wedding day. I don't think that many couples who choose each other make it to fifty years of marital bliss."

"Well, Sarah, he is my husband, and he has always taken good care of our children and me. What more can a woman ask? I don't know, though, if Gustav will want you to bother with getting people together for us," Amelia said.

"Don't be silly, Amelia. Other than buying a new suit for the occasion, all he will have to do is come. Oh, and drive us to Neudorf so we can get Katherina and Rebecca involved in making the arrangements. They would both be very annoyed if we did not let them help. When the Lutheran Women's Auxiliary selects an evening in September as close as possible to the actual date, we are off to Neudorf."

Sarah said, "It will be up to Katherina and Rebecca, since they know all your families and friends in the German and English townships, to invite everyone to your golden wedding anniversary. We will go through the catalogue with Katherina and have her order a suit for you, an elegant ensemble with matching hat and shoes. Naturally, you will wear a corsage of your favourite flowers, and Gustav will have a matching one in his lapel. We must choose a Sunday so Reverend Lutz can have a special service for you. We will decorate the altar and pews in the flowers that you are wearing. And the auxiliary ladies will cook the entire meal, starting well ahead, because there will be none of this catering for my dearest friend."

Once Sarah Thompson made up her mind, she was a force to be reckoned with, and soon there was no turning back—even if Amelia and Gustav decided they did not want an observance of their fiftieth anniversary. The more the group planned, the more ideas evolved, until Gustav and Amelia Warner's golden wedding celebration in mid-September 1962 would eclipse any similar milestone held in the St. Paul Lutheran Church in Melville.

The church overflowed for the Sunday morning service, with the steadfast members of the congregation and the more than 150 guests. Remarkably, all of Amelia's and Gustav's families and all of their invited friends attended, so the basement hall was filled to capacity for the evening dinner reception.

Coming down the stairs into the hall, Amelia and Gustav's eyes were much like those of a doe and her fawns caught in the beam of a car's headlights on a dark night. Neither realized so many people knew them, much less would come to celebrate their anniversary.

Now a grandmother of seventeen, Amelia's smooth facial skin turgor and white baby-soft hair belied her sixty-six years. She was demurely radiant in a two-piece royal-blue ensemble with a full-length navy satin jacket and a ribbon of the same fabric adorning her light pink hat. The vivid colour of Gustav's well-cut suit matched so closely that many were convinced that the tailor and dressmaker worked in the same shop. Naturally, Katherina would never disclose that she ordered Amelia's outfit from the Timothy Eaton's catalogue.

Once seated at the head table, they began to relax, and the evening proved to be an astounding success right up until the photographer was about to take pictures of them cutting the beautiful three-layered anniversary cake.

⇒ 171 ⇐

It started when someone offered Ludwig Schweitzer's, Amelia's older brother's, youngest daughter, Nancy, a cigarette. When her mother, Martha, saw the child accept it, she went berserk. She grabbed Nancy by her arm, and while yelling at her, started to kick her at her feet until she was nearly brought down to the floor.

Ursula pointed at her parents and shouted, "Finally you will see what it was like living with Aunt Martha when you threw me out and made me move to Saskatoon."

Nobody knew what Ursula was ranting about, and Sarah Thompson, for one, did not care. She would not let Amelia's daughter mar her parents' auspicious occasion—not when so many of them had spent six months organizing a hitherto perfect golden wedding celebration.

Motioning to Otto and Johann to pull Martha off her poor daughter and march her out the side door, she turned to Herbert and Norman Kuss seated at the next table and asked that they grab hold of Ursula and remove her from the hall by the back stairs. She acted with such quickness and authority that the four men responded instantly, before most guests were aware of any altercation.

Ursula's youngest daughter, Jennifer, who would always have an incredible memory, had heard every word, and she would wonder about her mother's accusation long after they were all dead and buried. It was the first reference Ursula had made regarding the interim years when she'd secretly disappeared from the Warner homestead. Had everyone not been so busy celebrating, many might have wanted to hear more of what she screeched at her parents.

⇜ 172 ⇝

"Just what do you think you are doing?" Justine demanded, when she noticed Mort Bailey digging holes for fence posts right across the centre of their field. She had returned home from her retreat to the Devil's Thumb on the edge of the Assiniboine River valley, which bordered their property.

It was the spring of 1963, and in three short months Justine would graduate from high school. She had applied to the Registered Nursing School at Brandon General Hospital, and once she left this wretched farm where she had known more than her share of oppression, she would never return.

"I'm building a fence. What does it look like I am doing?" Mort retorted to his teenaged neighbour. He was only two years older than Justine, but they had always been at odds. Whereas he quite liked her younger sisters, especially Elaine, he considered Justine arrogant and conceited.

"Since when do you go around fencing other people's property?"

"It just so happens this land belongs to us now. Maybe you should talk to your old man once in a while, and then you would know that he sold a quarter-section of your farm to my father and me last month."

Reluctant to allow Mort to spoil the feelings of peace and serenity she had achieved at Devil's Thumb, she abruptly left and hurried home. For once she might be able to deflect her mother's abuse by providing her with this critical piece of information. She knew the news would cause an argument, and sure enough, when she came into the kitchen where her parents sat at the table, she relayed what Mort Bailey had told her and Ursula turned her ire upon Clarence.

"What the hell do you think you are doing by selling half of my farm, and where is the money?"

"Can you ever simply ask a question without hollering?

"Yes, I did sell half the farm to George Bailey and that pimply faced son of his, but so what? It just so happens that it is not your land because the only name on the deed is mine. If you remember, your father took only me to Land Titles in Melville, and he signed the entire half-section over to me, so I will do with it what I damn well want."

"It doesn't surprise me one bloody bit. My father has never given me anything but grief in all the years I've been his daughter. Now how the hell are the kids and I supposed to make a living on only a quarter-section of this worthless godforsaken farm? If you had one bone of decency in your body, you would have sold the whole damn thing and bought a house in Virden. Don't think for a minute that you are doing us a favour," Ursula shouted, as Clarence calmly continued to drink his coffee.

"Well, I did just win a big, old two-storey house on a large corner lot in Virden in a poker game. But it has not been looked after and would probably need a bunch of work before you'd want to move into it. George Bailey was interested in buying the entire farm, and Will Reeves is desperate for a barn. Also Cecil Foster would really like to have the house, so if you want I can easily get rid of it all and you can live in town."

"How thoughtful of you to include me in your plans; but since you pretend to be such a good carpenter, you will help us fix up that house and make the move."

The five children could hardly believe their ears. For once in their lives every member of the Cardinal family was in accord. Robert had been offered employment as a teller at the Royal Bank in Virden as soon as he finished school; now he would not need to find a place to live.

When he first told his mother he was leaving the farm at the end of June, Robert worried about how they would manage, but he knew it was not his responsibility and that he had to get on with his life. He could not imagine Clarence winning a house in a poker game, and he wondered what would've happened if he'd lost, but Robert would eagerly help fix it up. Regardless of what condition it was in, at least his mother and sisters would not be stuck on the farm.

As their relocation to Virden started to become a reality, the entire family was more enthusiastic and energetic than any of them could remember being previously. Imagine living in a house with running water, a flush toilet, a bathtub, and a gas furnace with a thermostat to turn up when the house was cold. No more cows to milk, chickens and pigs to feed, wood and water to carry, and long summers slaving in the big garden so they could be stuck in the steaming kitchen canning food throughout the beautiful days of autumn.

The four Cardinal teenagers and ten-year-old Jennifer all agreed that it would be like staying at their grandparents' home every day of the year. They had no qualms about leaving the farm, although none considered how Clarence and Ursula would earn a living. But then it would no longer be their responsibility. Finally they could just be adolescents and do what other young people did rather than work and worry because of their irresponsible parents.

≫～173～≪

When the letter arrived, she was stunned. When she had applied to the nursing school, there had been no mention of a minimum age stipulation—only that she must have a passing grade in the five subjects that she required for her senior matriculation. Although she had only scored fifty-six per cent on the dreaded physics exam, it was a pass. And because she had performed so well in the other subjects, her average was still in the high seventies.

The letter informed her that she was accepted, but she had to wait a year until she was eighteen years old. Although the relocation to town had facilitated her obtaining employment at the Shell station on the highway, she had to find the way to start nursing training by this autumn.

Then it occurred to her to set up an appointment with the director of the nursing school to plead her case. She took the morning bus to Brandon, arrived early for her afternoon meeting with Miss Brenner, and decided to have lunch in the hospital cafeteria. As she ate, she looked around at all the young women in blue and white student uniforms and knew more than ever that she wanted to be one of them by the end of August.

Waiting to see the director, Justine was nervous. She must have used the lavatory ten times before her name was called and she was ushered into a large comfortable office. Seeing the stern woman sitting behind the desk, Justine briefly wondered what had possessed her to come, and she at last understood why people described her the way they had.

"Now, Miss Cardinal, how may I assist you? I had my secretary check, and she did send you a letter of acceptance for the program starting in 1964; thus I am at a loss about the reason for this appointment," Miss Brenner stated, peering over her half-moon glasses.

"I would please like you to reconsider and allow me to start training this fall, since I do have my senior matriculation," Justine responded with trepidation.

"As I outlined in the letter, your grades are not the problem, just your age. You are only seventeen, so you will not be old enough to write the Professional Nurse State Board examinations three years hence because they have a minimum age requirement of twenty-one years. Your only option, if I admit you this fall, would be to work as a graduate nurse for a year until you are able to take the examinations and meet the requirements of the Registered Nurses' Act."

"Thank you, Miss Brenner, I am prepared to accept that decision," Justine quickly replied.

Studying the young woman who maintained her steady gaze, Della Brenner was about to say that she had not given her the choice, when she suddenly changed her mind. "Very well, Miss Cardinal. We shall expect you to start on August 25 of this year in the class of 1966."

Life for the discordant Cardinal family was decidedly on the upswing. The aged house had been completely renovated, and modest furniture to augment what they brought from the farm was purchased with the proceeds from the other quarter-section of land. For all intents and purposes, the move to Virden seemed to be the solution to a host of the family's problems.

As soon as they settled in the large house on a double town lot, Clarence disclosed that he'd built a small bungalow two years ago on the outskirts of town and then told Ursula that he wanted a divorce. She had always wondered where he stayed all the time he was away from the farm; but she could not believe that the selfish bastard had been living in Virden while she and the kids struggled to eke out a living on *his* land.

Still, she unequivocally welcomed his news, because Graham Reed had promised for months to leave his wife and family to marry her.

Within weeks of arriving in town, Ursula found a full-time job at the Virden Creamery, which meant that her three youngest daughters took over the household chores, including meal preparation. Having a refrigerator and an electric stove rather than the old wood-burner certainly made cooking easier, and Sandra soon discovered that she had acquired her grandma's culinary skills. Elaine quite happily remained away from the kitchen, preferring to clean any day to slaving over a hot stove, while Jennifer was content to stay out of their way and watch the black and white television that provided hours of entertainment for all of them.

The truth was that any task paled against the chores and gardening they'd previously done on the farm. The girls happily adjusted to living in town and especially enjoyed the ample space in their large bedroom adjacent to a full bathroom.

With Clarence gone and Justine away in Brandon, the never-ending quarrelling ceased, and an uncharacteristic silence fell upon the Cardinal home. It was so quiet that Robert decided to stay, saving his money to eventually purchase his own house, and contributed by mowing the lawn. It was strange, though, how three months after her departure Ursula began to talk about Justine as if she could do no wrong.

Perhaps most importantly, for the first time in their lives the Cardinal offspring began to realize that they had a future. None were strangers to hard work; but when

Robert and Justine started to earn their own money, they quickly realized that they could be paid for their labour after not receiving any allowance on the farm.

In fact, after seven weeks of working as a waitress, Justine had made enough money to pay for her tuition, her books, and her uniforms, which came as a huge surprise to Ursula but not to Sandra. Every day she had seen her oldest sister come home from work with a bundle of bills, which she squirreled away in a small tin strongbox concealed under her bed. One evening when Justine caught Sandra watching her, she explained that she exchanged all the coins from her tips into dollar bills and was saving them for nursing school.

Sandra subsequently went out and got two jobs, one at the movie theatre on the weekends and the other at the Dairy Queen after school until it closed in late autumn. Instead of looking for work, Elaine agreed to care for Jennifer for remuneration from her mother and siblings because she was putting in extra hours of study, planning to apply to teachers' college after graduation.

The future was bright. Robert performed well at the bank, and within three months his manager proposed that if he rewrote and passed the matriculation exam in mathematics, he could start the bank's management training. Justine promised to take the bus home every weekend and help him study, and when she needed money for her ticket he would reimburse her. His parents had bought him a small Renault, on the condition that he drive his sisters to their jobs and school activities.

One evening when he'd gone bowling, Robert met the Mayor's daughter, and he and Sharon established an instant rapport. They had been dating now for six months and were becoming serious.

175

With a start, Amelia sat straight up in bed. "No. No, God. Please don't take him."

Gently shaking her shoulders, Gustav said, "Amelia, wake up. You are having another one of your bad dreams."

Slowly she became aware of her husband, and when she was able to focus on his face she began to tremble. "It was not a dream, Gustav. I could see what would happen, like I have so many times before. I know that it is coming."

Gustav readily recognized what was coming and whom she did not want God to take. Both of them realized that he was failing. The doctor had explained to him that he had emphysema, along with congestive heart failure. During the past two decades Gustav had progressively suffered from chronic bronchial asthma, which his friend Dr. Roth explained was aggravated by all his years of working with grain dust and, of course, smoking cigarettes.

The two conditions caused him to constantly feel tired and weak, and frequently he could hardly breathe, even when resting. It reached the point that the doctor ordered an oxygen tank for him to keep at home. Too often all Gustav could do was sit in his easy chair and look out the window. He didn't realize that the pain of trying to get his breath was etched on his drawn, anxious, and ashen face. There were many days when he questioned if the struggle to live was worth it, so it was little wonder Amelia was dreaming that his time was coming.

Pretending to fall back to sleep, Amelia lay beside her husband, knowing that he thought she had been dreaming about his demise; but she could not bring herself to tell him in the middle of the night whose death she had actually seen. She would only doze uneasily until dawn began to appear over the horizon, and then she had to get up and move about in her little bungalow to try and regain her composure. Amelia was so agitated all morning that she finally asked Gustav if he would drive the car the one block to the drugstore and pick up aspirin for her headache.

The minute Gustav was out the door, Amelia was on the telephone. But whoever had answered—she could not tell them apart over the line—repeatedly said that they were all fine. As soon as Amelia hung up the receiver, she prayed that her vision had been wrong. It was different from when Leonard had gone away to war. During those dreadful years every woman expected that her menfolk would be killed overseas and their bodies not returned for a proper burial. However, this time there was no reason for it. It was utterly senseless.

 **176**

At the last minute Justine decided to take the train home for the weekend instead of the bus. She did not have time to apprise either her mother or Robert of her change of plans, but she would call as soon as she arrived. It was a miserably cold Saturday in the middle of January 1964, but she was cozy and warm in the unoccupied dining car as the train crossed the frozen prairie that was blanketed in drifts of pure-white snow. The sun was shining, and other than the sound of the clickety-clack of the steel wheels on the track, it was as though she was the one and only being in the universe.

Although the weather was bitter, she resolved that after lunch she would bundle up in several layers of warm clothing and venture out for a walk. There was a park not far from the house, and even if she were outside for thirty minutes, it would feel like she was communing with nature, an activity she sorely missed and was about to confirm would be critical for her equanimity.

"How is your brother?" the ticket master wanted to know when she introduced herself and asked if she could borrow his telephone.

"He's fine. I want to use your telephone to tell him that I took the train rather than the bus home, so when could he pick me up?" Justine responded cheerfully.

"Haven't you heard? Jim Murray and he were in a terrible accident last night, and both are unconscious in the Virden Hospital."

177

Jim telephoned Robert an hour before they were to pick up the girls for their double date to the movies. His mother had finished her last bottle of whiskey and begged her only son to go to the liquor store to buy her another one. For the sake of his twelve-year-old sister who would otherwise spend a miserable night with Helen Murray ranting and raving about her useless children, Jim was eager to comply.

Since Robert was dressed and ready, he agreed that he could be over in a matter of minutes, and indeed the men accomplished the task in record time. It was such a blustery frigid night that scarcely anyone was out on the streets. And once they appeased the town's most notorious drunk, they decided to stop at the Virden Hotel for a cup of coffee before picking up Sharon and Rachel.

Had they not been so deeply engrossed in conversation, either one may have noticed Mickey Cowan's half-ton pickup truck parked across the road. There was no mistaking it because, for some strange reason, Mickey had had a heavy steel grille welded onto the front of it. Had they seen the vehicle, Robert and Jim would quickly have chosen another venue.

Waiting until they were comfortably seated in the coffee shop, Mickey belligerently approached the table.

"It's just like you sissies to order that horse piss instead of a real man's drink, which I've been stealing from my father's liquor cabinet since I was twelve. Let me buy you a beer and put some hair on your chests."

Neither Jim nor Robert wanted Mickey Cowan to purchase anything for them, much less alcohol before going out on a date, and certainly not on a wintry evening when Robert was driving his car.

What audacity that a poor farm boy would date the town mayor's daughter when everyone knew that it was Mickey's father's money that put her old man into office term after term. Mickey had gone out with Sharon twice, but she broke it off when it became apparent that he was only interested in sex. Although he had no genuine feelings for Sharon, he certainly would not allow some upstart who smelled of cow manure to steal his girl.

Realizing that Mickey intended to cause trouble, Robert and Jim decided to forego the coffee and leave. As they reached the door, two of Robert's colleagues from the bank, Allan Stone and Les Wagner, were about to enter. They knew their co-worker was seeing Sharon for the evening, and after quickly appraising that Mickey Cowan was being his usual obnoxious self, they attempted to distract him.

"Come on, Mickey. Let these courting men go pick up their dates, and we will join you for a drink," Les cajoled.

They were perhaps three or four miles out of town on a country road north of Virden when Robert noticed the lights of another vehicle shining in his rear-view mirror. Realizing that the downward slant of the headlights indicated a vehicle that was higher off the road than his small Renault, he went cold. Surely Mickey had not decided to follow them.

Knowing he should find a side road on which to turn around and get back to town as quickly as possible, he scanned along the ditch when, to his horror, his headlights went out. Immediately signalling, he pulled as far off the road as he dared and then braked, hoping that his tail lights were still operational.

With considerable relief, nineteen-year-old Robert Cardinal saw and heard the truck roar past them. And then when it appeared to be continuing on down the road, he flicked the switch on his dashboard in a futile attempt to get his lights to resume working.

 **178**

For the moment, the last supper order had been prepared. So when Sandra served the hamburger steak to her elderly customer, she joined her mother at the end table near the kitchen. Ursula had been hired as a short order cook at the Esso service station on the Trans-Canada Highway for the weekends. If not working at the theatre during the winter, Sandra was often one of the evening waitresses.

Sipping her coffee, she longed to ask Ursula for a cigarette. But since her mother did not know she started smoking, she'd have to wait until later.

"Oh, Mom, I forgot to tell you that Grandma telephoned just as I walked through the door from school this afternoon."

"How are they? Why did she call? I just talked to her a couple of days ago," Ursula said, exhaling a cloud of smoke directly into Sandra's face.

"No, she wanted to know how we all were. She did seem a little strange, though. She asked if Robert was home from work yet, and then if he was all right when I saw him this morning. Grandma must have asked me five times if Robert was okay, almost as though she expected something to be wrong with him," Sandra replied.

"Oh, you know your Grandma. She always worries that at least one of us is deathly ill. It's too late to call her tonight, so I'll give her a ring in the morning."

179

When the Renault's lights went out, Mickey went speeding by until he came to a back road about five miles down the highway. Throwing the truck into reverse, he turned around and gunned the engine to pick up speed. He must have reached fifty miles an hour before he rammed his half-ton truck with the heavy metal grille head on into the front of the stalled foreign car.

The deliberate crash happened so fast that neither Allan nor Les had any idea of Mickey's sinister intentions. Reeling from the sudden impact, Allan felt a rush of blood pouring from his forehead. Fortunately, he had the presence of mind to wrap his scarf tightly around it. Les, on the other hand, experienced a sudden sharp pain as the right side of his body was slammed against the door, severely fracturing the radius and ulna bones of his forearm.

When both men felt a blast of cold air, they turned and watched in amazement as the unscathed Mickey leaped down from the truck and scurried around like an oversized rat, hiding the box of beer in a snow bank.

⫸〜 180 〜⫷

Watching two RCMP officers jump out of the blaring and idling police cruiser with its red and blue lights flashing, Sandra was suddenly reminded of her strange conversation with her grandmother. And shivers ran up and down her spine. Initially they approached the manager at the cash register, and when he pointed one of the officers toward the kitchen, she broke out in a cold sweat. Then the other officer calmly approached her, saying that they were taking her mother to the hospital for a few minutes and that the manager would drive her home when her shift was over.

"Can you please take me to the hospital too? What is going on?" Sandra pleaded, as fear now permeated her body. Had something happened to Robert? Who else could it be? Justine was away in Brandon, and Elaine was at home watching television with Jennifer. Could her grandmother have known all along? Was that why she kept asking about Robert this afternoon?

As soon as the police car left, Sandra lit up a cigarette and proceeded to chain-smoke three in a row, lighting the next one before finishing the previous. Then before she left the service station, she purchased a carton of cigarettes and was well through them when the police finally brought her mother home after two o'clock in the morning.

When Sandra arrived home, Elaine and Jennifer, to her relief, were sound asleep in their beds. Closing the door, Sandra returned to the kitchen and telephoned the hospital. But she soon discovered during her repeated attempts to acquire information that it was like talking to a brick wall.

Sandra made a pot of coffee, but the minute she sat down she was back up on her feet and eventually she surrendered to her pressing need to pace. She was midway down the hall on her 100th return to the kitchen when she heard a vehicle pull through their semicircular driveway. As she butted her cigarette, Sandra grabbed the overflowing ashtray and carried it out to the back porch just as her mother opened the front door. She looked haggard and grey, and she barely made it into the living room before she slumped onto the sofa.

⚛~ 181 ~⚛

For years the two young RCMP officers agonized over what might have happened had they not followed their instincts and proceeded in the direction of the departing vehicles. In actuality, Constables Wainwright and Radcliff had been vigilant of Mickey since the incident last summer on the bridge to the cemetery on the south side of Virden.

Two days after Cowan had been heard fighting with seventeen-year-old Alvin Hamilton, the boy was found dead and his bicycle scattered in pieces several feet from his broken body. They were convinced that Mickey Cowan had paid retribution to the teenager for standing up to him, in front of his buddies yet; but there were no witnesses. They could not bring charges against the town's wealthiest punk, and they had to list it as a hit-and-run fatality before closing the file.

On the edge of Virden, Radcliff radioed for backup; but when they arrived and saw the horrific crash, he instantly called for the ambulance and the fire engine. He had only been on the force for five years, and although he'd been on the scene of several vehicle accidents, he'd never seen one that compared to the sight of the small car that had been squashed like a closed accordion.

Seeing the headlights, Mickey had run back to the truck. But Allan, still with his wits about him, grabbed the keys from the ignition and threw them under the seat. When the cruiser stopped, both men were out of it like a shot. While Wainwright raced to the crumpled car, Radcliff dashed to the truck and within minutes the inebriated Mickey Cowan was handcuffed to the backseat of the police car.

Then hurrying back to the truck and observing the blood-soaked scarf around the head of the man in the middle, Radcliff immediately signalled to the ambulance, which had just arrived. The paramedics instantly appraised that they had to get this critical casualty to the Virden District Hospital before he bled out, and they radioed for another rescue vehicle. Although the emergency medical assistants left the scene with the severely injured Allan Stone, they had ample time to return for the men in the demolished car. It would take the firemen and policemen well over an hour to pry apart the twisted metal enough to drag them from the decimated vehicle.

⤜ 182 ⤚

As Ursula waited at the hospital while the doctors provided emergency care to her son, she pressed to know the details of the accident. Neither Constable Wainwright nor Radcliff were inclined to gloss over the particulars, since they were both still reeling from the events of the night, unlike the physician who eventually asked them to take her home. Whether the doctor was deliberately trying to conceal the truth or it was far too early to provide more factual information, Ursula willingly came to accept his explanation that Robert only had two fractured legs. When she asked to see him, though, the doctor said her son was unconscious and quickly departed before providing a reason.

The next morning when Ursula arrived expecting to talk to Robert, he was still not awake. Looking aghast at his heavily bandaged head and the multitude of tubes running in and out of his body, Ursula feared that her son was suffering from more than broken legs. Noticing her, the head nurse quickly came to her side and explained that Robert was resting and that it would be better if she returned later in the afternoon.

But when Ursula drove to the train station to pick up Justine, there was no deterring her daughter from immediately going to the hospital. She was relieved when her mother had reported only fractured legs; but when she observed the bandages around his head and face, she knew he must have other injuries.

"Mom, if Robert only has two broken legs, why is his head bandaged? And why is he in a coma?" Justine asked. "And if he has a head injury, why is he still in this little thirty-bed district hospital? You need to ask the doctor to immediately transfer him to Winnipeg, or at the very least to Brandon."

Glaring at Justine, Ursula bellowed as though trying to wake the dead, "I don't want to hear another word out of you. Already you think you know more than the doctors. You just keep your big mouth shut for once because I don't want you causing any trouble. If you antagonize the doctors and nurses, then they won't give him the proper care."

Another sound reason to get him to a reputable hospital, Justine thought, but she was smart enough to not verbalize it.

Sunday dawned and neither Robert nor Jim had awakened. Whereas their respective mothers might have been alarmed, instead they were both eager to believe the doctors' reassurance that their sons' bodies needed the restorative sleep. Before Justine took the train to return to Brandon, she went to the hospital. Seeing her brother, she was again tempted to insist that he be transported to a larger facility, but Ursula's malevolent look was sufficient to stop her.

Justine struggled through Monday, which was hell on earth, as she tried to sit in class and absorb information. When her mother telephoned after supper to tell her that Jim Murray had died, Justine screamed at her to have Robert transferred to Brandon. Suddenly the line went dead, and as she persistently tried to reconnect, all she got was a busy signal. She knew that now she would live each day hour by hour, minute by minute in torment until she heard from Ursula again.

Finally the call came on Wednesday in the early evening, not to the residence but to Miss Brenner who happened to be working late. When the house mother knocked on her door and told her to hasten to the director's office, never in all her years could Justine recall a such a profound feeling of dread. The older woman was unusually solicitous as she explained that two of her mother's friends from Virden were at the Wheat Kings hockey game, and that they were coming to take her home.

Waiting on pins and needles for the men to arrive and then silently urging them to go faster as they drove the interminable miles to Virden, Justine walked through the door of her mother's house less than an hour before the telephone rang to advise the family that Robert Cardinal had passed away from his injuries without ever regaining consciousness.

～ 183 ～

Mickey Cowan was charged with vehicular homicide on two counts. Only this time, in addition to Constables Wainwright and Radcliffe arriving at the accident scene almost instantly and arresting Mickey Cowan in an inebriated state, the RCMP had two eyewitnesses. Perhaps justice would at last be served.

But they had not considered that the Cowan family would hire Aaron Sheps, the highest-paid criminal lawyer in Manitoba's history. In discovery, the Crown attorney disclosed that the defendant had premeditated his actions to murder Robert Cardinal and James Murray; whereas the defence counsel countered that both men were still alive when they were admitted to the Virden District Hospital.

Mr. Sheps then argued that his client could certainly not be held accountable for the negligence and incompetent treatment by the medical staff, and that the families of the plaintiffs should request the prosecution of the primary physicians for indictable offences on behalf of the Crown.

By the time Mickey Cowan's case was heard in the Winnipeg Law Courts, his lawyer had plea-bargained that his client be guilty of the lesser charge of two counts of vehicular manslaughter. Judge Friedman sentenced him to five years of incarceration at Headingly Penitentiary and suspended his driver's licence for ten years.

The guilty verdict and subsequent sentence were of no consolation to anyone. By now the only way to appease Helen Murray was to keep her plied with alcohol. Still, every time either Clarence or Ursula delivered the liquor, she accused them of killing her only son.

As it always had in the past, a common foe momentarily brought Clarence and Ursula together; but within months after Robert's death, the divorce proceedings were restarted. Several weeks passed before Ursula realized that she'd received no condolences from Graham Reed who, interestingly, disappeared off the face of the earth. She never heard from him again.

Not that it mattered. Nothing did. Nothing ever would. Ursula's sorrow over the loss of her only son overwhelmed her, and after years of animosity toward her father, they finally shared a commonality. Gustav's grief was as profound as hers, and if she thought that he would find any solace in hearing the man who had killed Robert was in jail, she was sadly mistaken.

Gustav's terse response was, "And what difference does that make? Just what good does it do Robert? The only thing that matters is that he is dead and gone. History has repeated itself, and now both of our firstborn children have been killed."

"No, Father. This time you are wrong," blurted Ursula before realizing that this was the second time in as many years that she'd nearly disclosed the secret she'd vowed to take to her grave. Was she starting to crack? Although she had made a solemn promise to keep silent, would the truth come out?

Suddenly feeling sorry for her father, a man who had become a shadow of his former self, Ursula longed to say that she loved and admired him more than anyone in her life, but years of bitterness tied her tongue. With a start, it dawned upon Ursula that Gustav Warner's influence over her was still as strong at forty years of age as when she had been a girl.

184

This time God sent two babies to bring Amelia back from the abyss. Almost four years to the day that Charlie was born, Rita was delivering her second child when the doctor realized there were two. Later, Johann and Rita went as far back into their ancestry as they could, but they found no evidence of previous twins in either family.

During their early months and years, these thriving children needed her helping hands and loving heart, and Amelia set aside her grief by providing unconditional love. Since Eva, Rita's mother, preferred older children, she gladly looked after Charlie, leaving Amelia to help her daughter-in-law with the needs of newborns.

Often when Amelia returned home to go to bed at night, she was so tired that she was asleep as soon as her head hit the pillow. And when Ben and Bill learned first to smile and then to laugh, she too began to remember the joys of living.

There was no salvation for Gustav. He had always worked out his grief by tilling the soil and walking about his land, but now he refused to go to the farm with Johann. His son had gone to the pharmacy to purchase a portable oxygen tank, but still Gustav would not leave the house. His car sat in the garage unattended while its owner perched at the dining room window and peered out into nothingness. Whether he had no energy or no will, Gustav barely spoke to anyone.

Amelia left his food warming in the oven for dinner, but most evenings when she returned home it had dried to a crisp without her husband bothering to touch it. He scarcely saw his new grandsons, and when Johann insisted that his father accompany him to his home for a meal, Gustav was more reticent than usual, if that was possible. Amelia was losing patience with him, and any other woman might have left him to drown in his sorrow.

There appeared to be no way to bring Gustav out of his despair, until one day a letter arrived from Justine. His granddaughter was making a request, which at last he could respond to. And by helping her to continue with her training, he could look forward to the day she graduated as a registered nurse.

⋙~ 185 ~⋘

When Justine returned to the nurses' residence, Miss Brenner and the instructional staff were solicitous to the point of being prepared to postpone her probationary examinations until she felt ready to write them. The seven exams scheduled to be written in two weeks—with a pass mark of seventy-five per cent in four of them and eighty-five in the other three—were crucial determiners of whether the student continued in the program.

To their surprise Justine welcomed the opportunity to take the exams; for her, studying was the consummate escape. She had always been able to completely immerse herself in learning, thus becoming oblivious to every other aspect of her life. But her classmates were not prepared to let Justine sink into the obscurity of books; many went out of their way to include her in their social activities to keep her mind off her grief.

For the first time in her life, she began to develop several close friendships and started to feel that her peers genuinely approved of her. At long last she recognized that she was affable, loyal, and trustworthy.

⋙~ 186 ~⋘

After eight young women failed the decisive exams, for the balance of the three-year training program they all committed to helping each other so that thirty-nine registered nurse graduates could walk across the platform. If a student experienced the slightest difficulty with any subject, it was her responsibility to seek tutoring from a classmate who comprehended the material, and no one had the right to refuse her the required assistance.

Before the end of the first year, Justine proved to be a natural teacher and began to appreciate how rewarding it was to help others learn. Instead of being shy and reserved around others, she realized she could be outgoing, energetic, exuberant, and even humorous, until none of her classmates believed she had ever been diffident. In actuality Justine was learning that she did not always need to be serious, but that she could relax and have fun without paying the price to her mother.

Furthermore, she was ready to engage in the pranks and high-jinks expected when over 100 young women lived in a residence with a particularly nosy house mother on the night shift.

Going back home was horrible—the estranged house held vivid memories of despair—and the minute she walked through the door she was reminded that her only brother was dead. She knew that she was cowardly; it must have been terrible for her younger sisters to be living under the same roof with a mother who'd recovered little since Robert's death.

And Clarence was still hanging around, and the constant conflict between the two of them could only have heightened the difficulty of being in the house. Sandra spent as much time away as she could, now working at three part-time jobs and essentially coming home to sleep. Elaine eagerly awaited the start of the fall semester at teachers' college, although she feared how Jennifer would fare after she left.

Still, Justine returned to Virden less and less often, until she only went when her grandparents planned to visit.

Perhaps the most rewarding aspect of Justine's newfound freedom and independence was being able to make her own choices. As she listened to stories about the upbringings of her closest friends, she began to realize just how controlling her mother had been during her childhood. Not once in all those years had she decided what to wear or how to do her hair or made any purchases, since she never had money of her own.

Then there were the undeniable facts that she could not drive a car and not even ride a bicycle or skate, because Robert had been the only one in the family permitted such privileges. But most significant of all, and a truth her classmates could scarcely fathom, Justine had never been out on a date. As is the wont of good friends, her classmates took great delight in rectifying these serious shortfalls of an overly dominated youth, and when they received their initial monthly stipend of six dollars for being a first-year nursing student, they took Justine shopping.

Socializing Justine soon became the pursuit of many of her friends, as they gradually grasped the magnitude of her never having been allowed to make a personal decision. The ventures were always undertaken empathetically, although not necessarily wisely.

One student from Brandon sought permission from Miss Brenner to leave her bicycle at the residence, and in short order Justine was riding around the hospital grounds before exiting for parts unknown for hours at a time until she was reined in by the bike's owner. On several occasions another of the local girls borrowed her mother's car with its standard transmission by promising to not disappear far from the premises, and attempted to teach Justine how to drive. With great hilarity, they jerked back and forth around a soccer field close to the residence, both soon realizing that there was little danger of Justine driving off into the sunset.

Naturally she had to be introduced to cigarettes and alcohol. She took to the former like a duck to water, but quickly discovered a lasting dislike of the latter. Her friends' primary endeavour, though, was to include Justine in social engagements for the sole objective of finding a young man with whom she could begin her romantic adventures.

⟫⟫〜 187 〜⟪⟪

How could her parents still believe in a loving God?

Long ago she had begun to question her faith, and Robert's death was the final straw. Ursula had lost every man she had ever deeply loved: Hans Gerhart, her one true love; Leonard, her favourite brother; and now her only son. If there was a God, he was one of hellfire and brimstone, not of kindness and benevolence, and He sure as hell did not care about her.

What difference did it make how she lived her life when all she encountered was frustration, despair, and grief? If punishment was to be her solitary fate, then why not commit the sins?

When she was not at work, she smoked, drank, and partied. At first her three youngest daughters could hardly believe the steadily increasing number of men, young and old, traipsing through the house at all hours of the day and night to come to their mother's escalating wild sorties, but they soon recognized it as their new reality.

Then it did not take long for the girls to realize the inherent dangers of being in a house with a mother who made the most rebellious and depraved teenager look pure as the driven snow. As the extent of Ursula's debauchery became apparent, it quickly occurred to them that they could be considered fair game.

Subsequently, at the slightest indication that more carousing was astir, they left. Sandra was off to one of her multiple jobs and then to a friend's, and Elaine to her boyfriend Dennis Clifford's home. In the event that Jennifer could not find a safe haven, Dennis's parents always invited the two sisters to share their guest bedroom. Mr. and Mrs. Frank Clifford had heard the rumours, as had most of the families in the immediate neighbourhood. And long after Elaine married their oldest son, they always kept the bedroom available for Jennifer if she needed it. The only time Ursula cleaned up her act was when her parents came to see them.

Whether from shame or the possible consequences, neither Elaine nor Sandra ever breathed a word about Ursula to their grandparents or oldest sister, all the while fervently hoping and praying that Jennifer did not understand what went on in their home.

～ 188 ～

"Why have we come to Virden?" Justine asked, unable to keep the anxiety from her voice.

"Since we were out for a drive on this beautiful Sunday afternoon, I thought it might be a good time to meet your mother," Kevin responded, not understanding why his confident and effervescent girlfriend suddenly became so apprehensive.

Justine became very silent. Did she dare introduce her boyfriend to her mother? What if Ursula was in one of her moods? Would she ruin their spontaneous spring outing?

Justine was still pinching herself that Kevin Hamilton chose her out of all her classmates that evening when an invitation came to attend a Christmas party at Brandon College. One of her friends loaned her a lovely turquoise soft-wool dress that accentuated the colour of her eyes, and she had never felt so smartly attired. Justine had little idea of what to expect before she arrived and was pleasantly surprised as she looked for a place to sit, when a young man approached her and asked for a dance. He was tall, slender, and handsome, with reddish-blond hair and brown eyes.

Coming out of her reverie, Justine heard Kevin, whose father was a judge, say, "At this rate, I shall have to subpoena your family if I am ever to meet them."

Justine's intuition told her not to take the risk, but Kevin could be pleasingly persuasive.

"If they are busy, we will only stay long enough to say hello and then we shall be on our way. Far be it from us to intrude upon their Sunday activities; but since we are in Virden, it would seem a waste not to at least be introduced, and I promise to be on my best behaviour."

Thinking that it was not Kevin's behaviour that concerned her, Justine chose to ignore her instinct and relented. But as soon as she walked through the veranda door, inhaled the lingering odour of alcohol and stale cigarettes butts, and spotted the aftermath of an obviously rip-roaring party, she should have grabbed Kevin by his hand and bolted out of the house.

But she was not quick enough. Ursula had seen them, and coming into the hallway with a cigarette hanging out of her mouth, she roared, "What the bloody hell are you doing here? Your precious grandparents are not around so there was no reason for you to come. And who the hell is this with you? You better not tell me that he is your boyfriend or I'll kick your ass right out the door. You're at Brandon to become a nurse, not a tramp. The last thing I need is for you to get knocked up and come back in disgrace."

Never having witnessed such a tirade in his entire life, Kevin stood rooted to the floor. At last he recovered enough to utter, "I'll wait for you in the car."

Glaring at her mother, Justine clenched her fists by her sides as she attempted to retain control over the level of her voice.

"Stop it right now. I will take no more of your abuse. I am finished with you unless you can treat me like a human being, with decency and respect. When you are ready to apologize for your humiliating behaviour and to ask for my forgiveness, you can telephone me, or you will never hear from me again."

Turning, and without a backward glance, Justine strode out of the house with Ursula yelling at the top of her lungs: "Oh, you'll be back. When you run out of money you'll come crawling back on your hands and knees and be as sweet as pie!"

It was a long and silent ride back to Brandon. Justine could imagine what a well-brought-up man like Kevin must be thinking about her ancestry. She had never been so embarrassed and she could barely raise her head to even glance at him.

Interminably arriving at the residence, Justine struggled to look at Kevin and said, "I am sorry."

"I am sorry, too," he replied.

As he drove away, Justine knew she would never see or hear from Kevin Hamilton again, nor would she have wanted to given the extent of her mortification with Ursula's behaviour. If Justine could have found a cache, she would have burrowed into it like a rabbit and then pulled it in behind her.

Her friends were surprised with her early return to the residence, but she had a more pressing issue to address. She went straight to her room and gathered up stationery and a pen before going to the library. She sat down and wrote a letter to her grandfather explaining what had taken place and that she'd given her mother an ultimatum. Justine then asked her cherished grandfather if it would be possible for her to borrow some money, because under no circumstance would she accept another penny from Ursula.

⁓ 189 ⁓

Finally someone needed him. It was one thing for Amelia to spend all her time helping Rita with the babies, but what could he do? He scarcely spent time with his own children in their infancy, and he certainly had neither the stamina nor the patience to begin now. There were days when Gustav barely had the energy to deal with the minimal tasks of daily living, and he often had to stop to use the new apparatus his doctor had prescribed.

But now Justine sought his assistance, and if there was one commodity he had more of than he'd need, it was money. Furthermore, there was no one he'd rather lend a hand to than his beloved granddaughter who wrote him regularly about what she was learning in her nurses' training.

It had been a long time since Gustav gave any money to either Ursula or Clarence, although Amelia always had cash for each Cardinal grandchild every time they came to visit. But his dear wife could not provide the funds Justine would need to sustain her for the last year and a half of her education, so a trip to the bank was in order.

With more energy than he'd felt in some time, Gustav rose from his chair. Grasping the telephone, he called Mr. Holger for an appointment. When the bank manager said he would see him right away, Gustav momentarily thought about driving his car and then decided to call for the taxi rather than risk anything untoward happening to either his vehicle or himself.

He was immediately ushered into Mr. Holger's office, and within the hour he had made a very satisfactory arrangement between the bank and Justine Cardinal at the nurses' residence in Brandon, Manitoba. Coming home, Gustav sat down at the kitchen table and penned this letter to his granddaughter.

April 20, 1965

Dear Justine,

I have returned home from meeting with my bank manager, Mr. Holger. I have arranged for him to send you a cheque for $100 from my account, and he assured me that you should receive it within the week. I have also signed another six postdated cheques, totalling $700, that the bank will send to your mailing address at three-month intervals.

Our existing arrangement will last until August 31, 1966, when you graduate as a registered nurse. If at any time you find that the funds are not sufficient to cover your needs, please write or telephone and I shall send whatever you require. There is one condition, and that is that you must accept the money as my gift to you and never try to reimburse any portion of the funds to your grandmother or to my estate.

Furthermore, I see no reason why your mother ever need know about my graduation present since, strictly speaking, it is between a grandfather and his much-loved granddaughter.

Thank you, Justine, for again helping an old man still feel useful.

Your loving grandfather,

Gustav Warner

190

The letter from Gustav and the cheque from the bank arrived on the same day. Justine was so touched by her grandpa's epistle that she had to compose herself before she could sit down and reply, thanking him for his generosity.

When three additional cheques, each for $100, arrived before the end of the year, she wrote three more thank-you letters, every time telling him how grateful she was for all the years that he had loved and encouraged her. She had never had so much money in her whole life, but she neither deposited nor spent a dime of it until she'd been to the school library to write her grandfather her letter of appreciation.

Before she reached her twentieth birthday, Justine believed beyond a doubt that had it not been for her esteemed grandparents, God knows what would have happened to her and her siblings.

When Gustav received Justine's fourth expression of gratitude, it occurred to him that of all the money he'd spent in his life, none had given him as much satisfaction as funding his granddaughter's educational endeavours.

191

It took more than seven months before her mother picked up the telephone to call Justine and say she was sorry. For the longest time Ursula had been confident that Justine would be compelled to come crawling back and beg for money; but as she'd done throughout her life, Ursula had drastically underestimated Justine's resourcefulness.

Then when Justine came on the telephone, she was not ready to accept her mother's apology until Ursula had unequivocally agreed to two conditions: that she never again presume to tell Justine what to do and that she never resume any form of abuse. The consequence of breaching either stipulation would be that Justine would disappear and Ursula could forget that she had ever birthed her eldest daughter.

192

Winter arrived early and by Christmas more snow than usual had fallen. The brutal cold along with strong easterly winds compounded life across the Canadian prairies.

For the first time since their move to Manitoba, Ursula questioned whether they should go to Melville. She was now the only one in the family who could operate an automobile, and although she had a newer car that had been fully serviced, she worried about driving on the icy roads.

Naturally, the girls could not imagine spending Christmas alone in Virden without their grandparents, but they would not make the trip because Gustav had not driven his vehicle since Robert's death. If the family did not go to Melville, Ursula was convinced that Justine would not bother to come home. After the incident in the spring, she had made it back to Virden only once, for her birthday, and Ursula knew that she had come more for her sisters than for her.

Then her mother telephoned to urge them to come because Gustav was becoming weaker and weaker, never leaving the house and scarcely moving beyond the bedroom and his chair by the dining room window. He sat there for hours, gazing outside while listening to a German singer named Elisabeth Schwarzkopf, until Amelia began to wonder if she might go mad.

Gustav told her that whenever he heard the woman's beautiful soprano voice, he thought about his grandmother, Elfrieda Reiner Wirth. Long ago he had told Amelia the tragic story that his mother had shared with him in confidence before she died. If Elfrieda had been allowed to decide what to do with her own life, he often wondered, could he have heard this recording of her singing with the Vienna State Opera?

Gustav realized that Amelia was setting the table for Christmas dinner, and she was losing patience with his music. He would turn it off and wait for their visitors. Perhaps after they arrived, Justine would sit with him. Since she too was enchanted with classical music, he would introduce her to the beautiful voice of Elisabeth Schwarzkopf while sharing with her the secret of his maternal grandmother's tragic death.

➤~ 193 ~◄

Trust her luck to be in the group of students scheduled for the three-month affiliation to the Brandon Hospital for Mental Illnesses from the beginning of December through to the end of February 1966. Having always considered their residence at the General Hospital antiquated, the building at the bottom of the steep hill, which housed the psychiatric nursing students, made it look like a veritable mansion.

The thirteen registered nursing students no sooner moved in than their counterparts jeered that they would never survive the miserable winter. Just wait until the first morning that they had to climb to the hospital, facing into the bitterly frigid north wind gusting up to thirty miles an hour.

Some of Justine's classmates placed wagers with their tormentors; but rather than waste her money, she made note of the information and the next morning was so thoroughly covered that only her eyes were visible. Nonetheless, there was not the slightest exaggeration in their depiction of the difficult ascent, and had it not been for their pact to have thirty-nine graduates within the year, many could have dropped out.

One positive was that their psychiatric nursing instructors did not work during the two-week period between Christmas and the New Year, and the hospital administration would not have the registered nursing students on the premises without proper supervision. Before she took the bus to Virden, Justine telephoned home to confirm that in spite of the inclement weather, they were still going to Melville; otherwise she would plan to return to the other residence.

There was no way she would spend two weeks in her mother's house, since she strongly suspected that her sisters escaped at every possible opportunity and she simply had no place of refuge. Justine knew that Ursula was wavering because she was worried about the roads, and she thought that only she could drive.

Sandra likely had not yet told Ursula that her boyfriend had taught her how to drive and that she had her licence; but if Sandra chose to keep Ursula in the dark, Justine certainly would not breathe a word about it. They needed to leave for Melville midday and telephone to alert Grandma and Grandpa about when to expect them while making sure they had packed the car with blankets, candles, matches, and extra warm clothing.

～ 194 ～

Once Gustav greeted Ursula and his granddaughters upon their safe arrival, he resumed his daydreaming by the window. Although he fully understood the perils of the harsh Canadian winter, he still considered that it was God's season.

In his mind, the white of winter's snow concealed the colours of mankind's destruction: the red for all the blood that had been spilled in endless wars and violence against its own, the brown of his decay, and the black of his death. Its arrival every year was as though God was purifying the countryside and giving humanity yet another chance for redemption to seek the eternal light of his Son. It was a time of beauty, with the tall conifers covered in snow and the barren branches of the deciduous trees hauntingly clad in hoarfrost, and a time for silence.

Gustav Warner knew that his time on earth was coming to an end, and now he seemed to spend most of his waking hours thinking about and thanking God for the restoration of his faith.

"Grandpa, are you alright? You look so sad." Justine had been standing beside him for some time, and he had been so lost in thought that he'd not realized she was there. "Mom will take Grandma and my sisters to the store, and I was wondering if I could stay to listen to music with you."

When the others left, Gustav asked Justine if she would like to hear one of the great German sopranos singing operetta arias. They always listened to orchestral music, but he intended to introduce Justine to Elisabeth Schwarzkopf before sharing the story of Elfrieda Reiner Wirth.

Seated in a comfortable chair beside her grandfather, Justine was soon enraptured by the singer's exquisite voice. For over an hour she did not move and she barely breathed, she was so mesmerized by the melodious music emanating from her grandfather's new stereo system. Justine could scarcely believe that a human voice was capable of producing such heavenly sounds. As she transcended beyond the confines of her grandparents' home, she did not want to return.

But when Gustav began to tell her about his maternal grandmother, Justine was jolted back to reality and felt anger surge through her body.

"How could her father do that? He ruined her life by exercising his control over her and making her choices."

Immediately Gustav found himself back at his mother's gravesite among the poplars. Justine had triggered the memory of his quarrel with his father, which was still so vivid and so painful that suddenly he gasped for air.

"Justine, please give me the mask for my respirator! I can't breathe!"

In mid-January, Justine started her six-week rotation on a men's ward at the Brandon Hospital for Mental Illnesses. Aside from the arduous climb each day, she had never found work so easy and enjoyable. This was the first year that the hospital administration had allowed the registered nursing students on the male wards; they were very circumspect about what level of care the students were permitted to provide.

Essentially the students were responsible for giving the patients their medications and helping in the dining room during meals. The balance of the day was spent in the games room, where Justine learned to play pool and became skilled at table tennis, competing with several of the attractive male attendants.

Then she had an evening assignment and was working with Nurse Gertrude Adolf. Initially thinking that her nickname stemmed from her unfortunate surname, she soon discovered why the middle-aged woman with the mousy brown hair and bulging eyes was called Nazi Bitch behind her back.

From the first morning she had taken the breakfast trays to two patients crouching at the dining room door, Justine was curious about them. She estimated that they were in their mid-fifties, although neither had greying hair, brown pigmentation on their skin, or wrinkles on their faces. When she placed the trays on the table, they used neither a fork nor a spoon; instead they bent over the plates and ate much like dogs woofing down their food. She could not believe what she was seeing. When they finished, she heard them grunting to each other. And when she tried to speak to them, they hurriedly departed with shuffling gaits.

Justine began to watch Michael Summers and John Taylor who maintained an almost crouch, never walking upright or raising their heads to look anyone in the eye. After days of observing the two patients, she'd heard not one intelligible word from them, and before long she was fascinated by their animalistic behaviour. What kind of mental illness could cause a person to seemingly lose all human traits?

But when Justine went into the nursing station to peruse their charts, they were nowhere to be found. As odd as that seemed, she had enough insight to not ask Nurse Adolf. She waited instead until one evening when Sally Banting was the nurse in charge; but all she could tell Justine was that the charts for Mr. Summers and Mr. Taylor were locked away in the small filing cabinet under the nurses' desk, and Miss

Adolf had the only key. Sally went on to disclose that when she'd begun working on the ward, she too had been very curious about their unusual disease; but in three years she had yet to learn its name.

Then one evening near the end of her rotation, Nurse Adolf told Justine that she was going to the cafeteria for supper and would be back in thirty minutes. As soon as she left, Justine noticed that she'd inadvertently left her file key in the cabinet. Here was her chance to open it and discover the bizarre ailment afflicting the two patients.

She found the charts easily enough, sat on the floor, and started to read while keeping one eye on the wall clock. As she flipped through first one chart and then the other, Justine's inquisitiveness continued to mount since she could find no nomenclature or classification of their illness. Although engrossed in her pursuit, she kept glancing at the time and would not have been caught had Nurse Adolf remembered to take her cigarettes with her.

"I don't know where my head is today. And just what the hell do you think you are doing? Why, you arrogant little brat, I must have also left my key. Finally I've got you right where I want you. I told the administration that they should not let you insolent registered nursing students on my ward. But they never listen to me."

Her voice became louder. So intent was she on punishing Justine that she was ready to forfeit her cigarette, and she did not hear the chief of psychiatry approach the nursing station.

"Pardon me, Nurse Adolf, can you explain what is happening here?"

Dr. Werner glanced at the recipient of her wrath. He had seen this student before, and at the time he thought she looked vaguely familiar. Observing her more closely, he was convinced that he remembered her from somewhere or that she looked very much like someone he'd known a long time ago.

"I caught this little bugger going through the charts in the locked cabinet, and I can tell you that she is now finished at this hospital. By tomorrow morning I will make damn sure that she is expelled from her training program. But why are you still here, Dr. Werner?"

"Please clean up your language and go about your patient care. I shall attend to this situation with Miss Cardinal," he quietly replied after glancing at Justine's nametag.

"Oh, don't worry, doctor. I am more than capable of handling this incorrigible student."

"You don't seem to have heard me, Nurse Adolf, and I wonder just how she came to have the key. Now do as I have asked.

"Miss Cardinal, could you please come with me?"

Fearing that her nursing career had come to a precipitous end, Justine walked beside the gentleman who appeared to be in his early sixties. He had a full head of silvery hair, handsome facial features, and a robust walk. She quickened her pace to stay beside him.

When they arrived at his office—made cozy with family pictures, plants, and throw rugs—Justine's attention became riveted to his nameplate on the desk. Of course she knew his name was Werner, but for whatever reason it hadn't yet registered.

"My grandfather's surname was Werner before he changed it to Warner almost forty years ago."

"I'm sorry, Miss Cardinal. What did you say? I didn't quite hear you."

Repeating her comment, Justine became aware that Dr. Werner was staring at her.

"And what is your grandfather's first name?"

"His first name is Gustav," Justine answered.

"And your grandmother's first name is Amelia, isn't it? From the first time I saw you on the wards, I thought you resembled someone I knew. She is my aunt and Gustav is my uncle, so that would make you and me second cousins. My first name is Mathias."

Now the elderly man and the young woman stared at each other, astonished.

"Oh, dear God. You are Mathias. My grandpa believes that you died years ago, and he has always blamed himself."

"No, that cannot be, Miss... what is your first name? I see Amelia often, sometimes twice a year. Surely your grandmother or his daughter Ursula has told Gustav that I am alive."

"My first name is Justine, Dr. Werner. Ursula is my mother, and neither of them could ever have told my grandfather. Not long ago he told me that you disappeared when he tried to explain that the original homestead was not your grandfather's and thus he could not bequeath it to you."

"Please Justine, could you start from the beginning? And please call me Mathias."

"I'm not sure why, but after my brother was killed in a car accident, Grandpa started to tell me some of the family secrets. One day he explained how when Friedrich Werner had gone to the Dominion Lands Office in Regina after your grandfather Christian and he proved the original homestead, he put only his name on the title deed. Then Friedrich was killed, and shortly after your mother moved to Melville, she telephoned Gustav and demanded that he meet with her in a lawyer's office.

"As it happens, your mother forced Grandpa to purchase the land, which he had farmed for years. Gustav never breathed a word about it to his father because he would have been broken-hearted to find out that he had never been a landowner. I can understand why Grandpa kept silent about Friedrich and Maria, but why would Grandma never tell him that you are alive and that you are a doctor? My grandfather's closest friends were a Dr. Spitznagel and now Dr. Roth. He would be so proud that his nephew became a psychiatrist."

"I can't imagine why Amelia has kept my existence a secret from Gustav. I just thought that I never heard from him because of his stubborn pride."

"It seems that I have a lifetime to catch up with you, Justine. What a fortunate turn of events that we have met. When will you come home with me for supper and meet my wife? Rebecca will be delighted to know that some of my family still acknowledges me."

"But, Dr.... Mathias, what about Nurse Adolf? She will have me expelled, and that will break my grandfather's heart."

"Oh, yes, Gertrude Adolf would like nothing better than to ruin your career. I shall ask you to sign a document that you will not disclose any information about what you have learned about the two patients. Then tomorrow I shall apprise her that the situation has been resolved. I shall make the consequences of her taking any action against you perfectly clear and also have her sign a written agreement."

"But Mathias, I still don't know what disease Michael Summers and John Taylor suffer from, and that was the only reason why I opened the filing cabinet. I am fascinated by their behaviour, and yet no one will tell me. Would you please give me the name of their psychiatric illness so I can study more about it?"

Taking several seconds to reflect, Mathias began.

"I believe it should be called the 'institutionalization syndrome.' And now what I will tell you neither gives me any professional gratification nor can you repeat a single word about it while this hospital is still standing, which I hope will not be for much longer. Those two patients were among my first admissions to the hospital when I began my career as a psychiatrist. It was during the Great Depression, winter was coming, and the two young men were starving. They came here and pretended to be mentally ill so they would have a warm place to sleep and food to eat. In fact, Dr. Spitznagel was here to have Franz admitted, and I consulted with him about what to do with them."

"Both Rolf and I suspected that they were of sound mind and body; but we decided to go along with their duplicity, agreeing that come spring they would be ready to leave and get on with their lives. But within months they developed an institutional mentality. That is, they became comfortable and willing to sit back and allow others to make their choices. And now thirty-six years later they have lost most of their recognizable human characteristics. They in fact represent the reverse process of what hospitalization and treatment are expected to do for mentally ill patients. Rest assured, Justine, had I a hint of knowledge then of what I know now about the potential success of applied psychiatry, I would have chased them as far away as possible from this godforsaken institution. I might very well have bolted with them."

As Mathias Werner drove Justine down the hill back to the residence, she had one last question.

"May I please write my grandfather tomorrow morning and tell him that I have met you? It would give him considerable peace of mind that you are alive and well, and he would be so happy to know you are a doctor. Education has always been very important to him."

"Yes, the protracted silences have sealed our family's secrets."

196

Getting up from his comfortable chair by the window, Gustav walked to the stereo and turned on the record. When he sat down again, he could not believe that it was such a struggle for him to catch his breath after so little exertion. Gazing out the window, however, he was soon wrapped in the silken embrace of Elisabeth Schwarzkopf's voice. As she was singing the serene *Nonnenchor* by Johann Strauss II, his mind carried him back to the secluded knoll in the poplar grove on that tranquil Indian summer afternoon when Katherina and he had taken their beloved mother on a picnic to meet his best friend, Andrew. Elizabetha had noticed every detail of her surroundings, and suddenly he could hear the sparrows singing and see the bright orange sun sinking over the horizon.

Sadly, though, the memory of his father yelling at him among the same stand of trees soon flooded his senses, and he recalled Christian's prediction: "You will be just like me, and you will decide what they do."

Then he recalled Justine's reaction when he told her Elfrieda Reiner Wirth's story. She had been so angered that her father had determined the course of her life. And Gustav at last understood the magnitude of his own error.

At the time he had been so certain that he made the right decision for his reckless younger daughter. It was his responsibility as her father. It had not occurred to him that it was not his choice to make. Now he realized that his strict control had probably cost Ursula her only chance for happiness. Her life had been so hard with Clarence. Had she married him out of spite? Yet not once had she talked about her secret or blamed him for determining her fate. After all these years, not one person in the Warner family had learned why they'd sent Ursula away—not even Johann who had still been at home but was far too young to understand.

The recording had finished, but Gustav was lost in his thoughts. Was it the essence of his German heritage, or did every father believe he had the right to choose for his children and control what they did with their lives? By making Ursula's decision, they had ruined her life as surely as had Elfrieda's father in another century, in another country. It took Gustav a long time to hear Amelia calling him to the table for supper. It occurred to him that instead of carrying this burden of guilt he must ask for Ursula's forgiveness.

An overwhelming sense of peace permeated his soul as Gustav reached his resolution. He had wronged Ursula; but perhaps now after all these years, she would pardon him for making the choice that had been rightfully hers.

Realizing that he was hungry, he slowly rose and walked into the kitchen and was greeted by the aroma of Amelia's delicious chicken and dumpling soup. It was the first time in days that Gustav had an appetite, and when he asked for another bowl, Amelia felt a ray of hope. He became unusually talkative, asking if Johann was winning his curling matches, how Charlie was liking school, and how the twins were doing, until she began to think that her dear husband of fifty-four years was showing some improvement. She was further heartened when he reached for a second piece of the smoked sausage that Johann continued to bring them every autumn.

"We have been silent for far too long, Amelia. We were wrong years ago when we decided to send Ursula away. It was not our choice to make, and we probably are the reason she has squandered her life. Tomorrow morning I will telephone Ursula and ask for her forgiveness.

"I will also tell her that Hans Gerhart, the only man I believe she ever loved, is farming a section and a half of land adjacent to our homestead.

"Do you remember the young man that Leonard brought home from university during those two summers before he went to war? Hans has become very successful, owning all that land as well as the Melville Pharmacy. Ursula and Hans might still be young enough to pick up the pieces of their future, which was denied by us thinking that we had the right to meddle. If Ursula could forgive us, I would be ready to go to Hans Gerhart and give him her telephone number. Then they can decide what they want to do with the rest of their lives."

Amelia was speechless. During the past twenty-five years, not one word had been breathed about Ursula's secret, and suddenly Gustav was ready to reveal it to their entire family. Is that what he'd thought about all those weeks he sat staring out the window and listening to that German singer?

No, it was too late. Why would they have sworn Ursula to secrecy and now, after all this time, betray her? Had he taken leave of his senses?

Glancing at Gustav, Amelia could not give him an answer until she realized that he was not seeking one. His mind was made up, and there appeared to be little she could do to change it. She was so upset that she rose from the table and began clearing away the dishes, silently praying that come tomorrow morning he would forget this foolishness.

By bedtime Amelia was still too angry to settle. Fearing that she would awaken Gustav, she quietly got out of bed and went into the guest bedroom, hoping to fall asleep there.

But silence would prevail. In his seventy-sixth year, Gustav Warner passed away peacefully in his sleep during the early hours of the next morning.

"Johann, can you come?! I cannot awaken your father. I think he is gone."

Amelia sobbed into the receiver. She had arisen at her usual time and gone into the kitchen to make breakfast. Finally falling into a restless sleep in the wee hours of the approaching dawn, her head felt groggy, and so she decided to drink a second cup of coffee before calling Gustav to the table. Immediately Amelia remembered why she had not slept, and she resolved to reason with Gustav before he telephoned Ursula. With luck she might have already left for her new job at the hospital, where she'd been hired as one of the cleaning staff.

Within minutes Johann arrived, followed shortly after by the doctor who pronounced his father dead. The lines of anxiety and pain that had become permanently etched on his face had softened, and Gustav looked like a man who had made peace with his Creator.

Gazing down at her deceased husband lying in their bed, the first thought that entered Amelia's mind was that God did work in mysterious ways; now Ursula's secret would be safe. Realizing what she was thinking, she blurted out, "Oh, dear God, please forgive me."

Assuming his mother was still in shock, Johann went to where she was standing and took her into his arms.

"Mama, you of all of people do not need to seek forgiveness. You have always taken good care of Dad. But he has been sick for a long time now, and these past few years have been so difficult, especially as he struggled more to breathe. I know how upsetting this is for you, but finally father can rest in peace.

"Come with me to the kitchen, Mom, and drink some coffee. The doctor will arrange to have Dad's body taken to the mortuary, and it is best for us to be out of his way. I will stay here with you, but first I must telephone Rita, and then I will call Otto and Ursula to tell them."

Soon Johann had taken over all of the arrangements for his father's funeral, knowing himself sufficiently well that, unless he kept busy, he would break down in front of his mother who was having a hard enough time as it was coming to grips with her new reality.

Thank God that he had come along later in her life and now could take care of her. Ursula was too far away, and Otto was busy with a second family and worrying about what his three oldest daughters were doing, as they frequently had brushes with the law. He and Rita lived five minutes from her house. He could visit her every day and, during the warm seasons, take her to the farm whenever she wanted to go.

198

During the three days before his funeral, Amelia walked around in a daze, wondering how she would carry on without Gustav by her side as he had been since she was sixteen years old. She had no idea how she would have made it if not for Johann and Rita, and as she had so many times before, she thanked God that he had sent her last son during her change of life, when everyone told her she was far too old to have another baby.

When they were ready to journey to Melville, Sandra told her mother that she had her licence and would drive the car because Ursula could not pull herself together. She vacillated between feelings of despair that her father was gone and bitterness that they never crossed the chasm between them. Ursula could find no comfort, and it seemed that his influence over her was as powerful in his death as it had been throughout his life.

When Justine received Ursula's telephone call, she sat immobilized in the cubicle, unable to believe that her revered grandfather was dead—and on the very morning she would break the silence regarding his long-lost nephew.

As soon as Justine recovered sufficiently, she telephoned Mathias and then accepted his surprising offer to drive her to Melville because he and Rebecca wanted to support Aunt Amelia. During the interminable trip, the thought that kept recurring was how tragic it was that Mathias Werner would only see Gustav in death. For the remainder of her days, she wondered what could have motivated her grandmother to keep a secret that would separate the two men for a lifetime.

199

It was a reconciliation of sorts. On a rare occasion Justine returned to Virden when she knew that her grandmother was not visiting. In the past two years, she only came back if she could see her grandparents, but she decided that since she was off for the last weekend in May, she would take a short break before beginning her final preparations for the State Board Professional Nurse Licensure Examinations.

At the end of January, the graduating class was ecstatic to hear about two significant changes regarding the sitting of the qualifying examinations. Students could write the exams in June instead of having to wait until they had received their nursing diploma. Furthermore, the Registered Nurses Act abolished the age stipulation, and Justine could write the exams with her class. The successful students would be registered nurses before they even graduated.

But for the weekend, she left her books behind and planned to relax by going for long walks and bicycle rides. In light of the fact she had not told her mother she was coming, and uncertain of the reception she might get, she stalled by eating a hamburger at the Virden Café and then strolling to the house by way of the park in the centre of town. Justine had scarcely walked through the front veranda when Ursula came out the door.

"Oh, you startled me. I was not expecting you. Where have you come from?" Ursula wondered if Justine had brought another young man home. This time, though, Ursula bit her tongue. Now that Elaine and Sandra were both dating, Ursula assumed that Justine had a boyfriend, even though she had not been confided in.

"I decided this morning to catch the bus to Virden since I have the weekend off. I plan to relax before starting to study in earnest for my examinations at the end of next month. Where are the other girls?"

"Elaine has plans with Dennis in Melita, Sandra is at work, and Jennifer is sleeping at a friend's. Since you are here, I don't suppose you would consider coming to Miniota with me for the day? They are having an annual fair, and I was just leaving."

"That sounds like it could be fun," said Justine, "and I might run into some old classmates. Let me just put my overnight bag in the house." This was definitely a first, Justine thought, her mother and her agreeing to go out and spend some time together.

⇝ 200 ⇜

During the forty-five minute drive to Miniota, both mother and daughter seemed lost in thought. Ursula noted how Justine never called Virden "home." Since their quarrel, her daughter was very distant, almost as though she barely tolerated her. And she did not ask for even a dollar.

Ursula was dying to know how Justine was buying her necessities. The eight-dollar stipend she now received for being in her third and final year of training, could not go very far, and with graduation coming, surely she would want a new dress and dress shoes.

Deciding to broach the subject, Ursula inquired, "How much money do you think you will need for your graduation?"

"Thanks for checking, Mom, but I don't need any money. I have already purchased a grad dress and a pair of heels."

She was genuinely surprised that her mother had asked. Her grandfather's cheques had continued after his death, and last week she received the last of the seven along with an extra $100 for any purchases she might need to make for her graduation. Nonetheless, Ursula's offer broke the tense silence between them, and perhaps for the first time, the two women conversed as one adult to another.

At one point that evening, Justine even sensed that her mother was about to confide in her; but then for whatever reason, she reverted to silence and it seemed as though a veil of secrecy was lowered, perhaps never to be lifted again.

During her training Justine had come to understand the overwhelming injustice that the medical profession had perpetrated when her mother was subjected to a total hysterectomy without subsequent hormone replacement therapy. While studying psychiatric nursing, Justine became convinced that Ursula suffered from manic-depressive psychosis. Although the students had been judiciously cautioned about presuming to diagnose, her mother's episodic and recurrent mood swings throughout Justine's childhood and adolescence were revealing, to say the least.

As the years passed Ursula's medicine cabinet became stocked with bottles of pills until she could have opened her own mini-pharmacy, and on many occasions Justine questioned whether she was receiving the proper medical treatment or simply financing the drug companies.

Still, Justine perceived that more drove her mother to engage in her promiscuous and destructive behaviour; the drinking and wild parties with men of all ages seemed to be an attempt to drown herself in a bottomless pit.

Ever since Justine had chanced upon the mystery of Mathias, she wondered what other secrets lay buried within her family. If her grandmother could conceal her nephew's existence from her husband for over fifty years, which continued to astound Justine, what other events were entombed in the past?

Little in Ursula's life seemed to satisfy her, and Justine thought she'd glimpsed the faintest flicker into her mother's mind and soul. But after that fleeting moment, Justine's gentle entreaties urging her mother to loosen her cloak of concealment fell on deaf ears. Later, they drove back to Virden in a constrained silence, ruefully ending the only day they would ever share a mother and daughter connection.

201

One by one, the names of the thirty-nine registered nurse graduates of Brandon General Hospital's class of 1966 were announced, and every woman proudly walked across the stage to receive her diploma. Dressed completely in white from the cap on her head to the smartly polished white shoes on her feet, each RN resembled the veritable angel of mercy. The twelve brilliant red roses in full bloom, gracefully carried in their arms, provided a radiant contrast. And each graduate beamed with pride and joy.

Before their training program, each student had been warned that their daily schedules would involve long hours of classroom instruction combined with rotation to the hospital wards for their practical work experience. Their three years had been filled with unbelievably early-morning starts, weird sleep hours before hours of classes that followed long night shifts, supervisory responsibilities during the busy evenings, and fear of being reprimanded by one of the intimidating supervisors. The three years also meant continuous study, endless examinations, constant procedures, stressful deadlines, and hard work. But they were also three of the most fun-filled years any of the women would likely experience again, with the camaraderie, the never-ending socialization, and the formation of new friendships that would last a lifetime. Before they went their separate ways, they were already planning reunions for their five-, ten-, and fifteen-year anniversaries of graduating.

For the first time in the school's history, not one student failed the final exams to complete the first, second, and third years of programming. In addition, the entire class of 1966 passed all five State Board Professional Nurse Licensure Examinations during the initial seating and achieved the highest average of any class of RNs at the Brandon General Hospital School of Nursing. The thirty-nine young women had every reason to celebrate, and the faculty, alumni, and hospital administration were eager to entertain them.

The last week of August was a whirlwind of excitement, lunches, afternoon teas, and dinners before the formal ceremony on the Friday afternoon, when families and friends were invited to join the graduates. As she waited for her grandmother, mother, and sisters to arrive, Justine was deeply saddened that her grandfather had not lived to come to her graduation and see her in her nurse's uniform.

When she saw her grandmother enter the large auditorium looking overwhelmed, Justine quickly made her way through the crowd and surprised her with a hug. During the entire ceremony Amelia listened with rapt attention, her eyes constantly searching for her granddaughter in the group of graduates. When Justine's name was called and she proceeded up the short flight of stairs onto the stage, Amelia was so intent upon following her every move that she scarcely remembered to breathe. Never before had Amelia Warner attended a ceremony that honoured one of her own family, and for the rest of her days she often spoke about Justine's beautiful graduation.

After each graduate received her diploma, they were asked to form a group on the stage for their class photograph, and for a woman who had loved flowers all of her life, the collective image of thirty-nine nurses in white, each holding a dozen red roses, was almost more than Amelia's eyes could behold. She was not alone in enjoying the flowers; as the celebrants posed for an extraordinary picture, the heavenly scent of their bouquets filled the front of the auditorium.

The graduates and their guests were then invited to proceed to the decorative dining room where they would partake in a dinner followed by the formal speeches and awards. When the dance was about to begin and her family preparing to depart, Ursula congratulated Justine and presented her with mother-of-pearl cufflinks engraved with the initials RN, one letter on either side of the medical insignia. Justine considered the gift the nicest Ursula had ever given her, and she proudly wore the cufflinks throughout her career.

As she was leaving, her grandmother remembered to dig in her purse and present Justine with a card of congratulations. Then Amelia gave her a goodbye hug and thanked her granddaughter over and over for inviting her to her nursing celebration. Much later, when Justine opened the card back at the residence, she was astonished to find five crisp $100 bills.

～ 202 ～

With Gustav gone, Amelia and Ursula became closer, but the slightly more than 100 miles between them still physically separated them. Both women lived in houses that seemed empty and forlorn, but neither was willing to relocate and live together.

By the spring of 1967 Amelia adjusted to being alone, although she often felt Gustav in the house with her. She could perceive his presence, usually behind her, watching what she was doing, but she was careful not to express her unusual feeling, especially to Johann, in case he would think she was losing her mind.

Still, it was comforting to her, and many times Amelia found herself talking to Gustav more than she had during the last few years when he was alive. She had always looked after her large garden and all the other activities of running their household, except for paying the bills, which Johann, as executor of her estate, now handled. Thankfully Gustav had never forgotten how his friend Andrew Thompson had made so little provision for his aging parents; when he signed his legal agreement with Johann, he stipulated that Amelia would receive one third of all profits from the farm upon his death so she would be very comfortable financially until the end of her life.

Although required to live with her mother, Jennifer spent as little time as she could at home. In fact, mother and daughter seemed to lead a revolving-door existence, and Jennifer made a rapid exit as soon as she sensed Ursula preparing another of her unruly parties. In the autumn of 1965, when Elaine obtained a teaching position in Hartney, it had dawned on Jennifer that she might soon be the only one left at home. And sure enough, early the next spring Sandra moved to Flin Flon and started working in the bank so she could be near Warren Davis, her boyfriend.

Before Jennifer was fourteen she found herself home alone with Ursula. She'd always dreaded her mother's parties, but that summer even stranger things occurred. Jennifer returned to the house late one day to find a party's aftermath, but her mother was nowhere in sight. Frantically searching without success, Jennifer finally went into the kitchen to make herself a sandwich. She debated about calling the police but decided it would be too embarrassing, so she anxiously sat up most of the night waiting for Ursula to return.

The next day when Jennifer came home from school, her mother still was not back, and while trying to decide what to do, she set about cleaning up the horrific mess. After three hours of gathering up beer bottles, emptying ashtrays, and washing dishes and floors, the front door opened and Ursula waltzed in, happy as a lark. When Jennifer asked her where she'd been for almost forty-eight hours, her mother said, "I was out having a good time for a change. I had the last two days off, so when I received an invite to get out of this dumpy little town, I accepted."

"The next time you decide to accept an invitation, could you leave me a note telling me when you are coming home?" Jennifer asked in disgust, as she threw the dishtowel on the counter and walked by her mother on the way to her bedroom.

"What's the matter? You don't like it when I just take off and go to a friend's, like you always do to me?"

Jennifer decided to bite her tongue and proceeded upstairs, where she remained for the rest of the evening. Fortunately, she had a stash of chocolate bars and peanuts hidden in her room; she would not go back downstairs to eat with her mother.

Thus began a new pattern of behaviour for Ursula. She would throw a party at the house and then leave for an indefinite period of time. Jennifer would return the day after the party after spending the night with an understanding friend. Soon Jennifer realized that if she telephoned the hospital and found out when Ursula was scheduled to return to work, she could at least guesstimate when she might arrive home.

But then another change occurred. One Thursday afternoon Jennifer came into the house. There was no evidence of an impending party, so she decided to stay home and cook dinner for her mother. The hours passed, the chicken and baked potatoes dried to a crisp, and by eleven o'clock when she locked the doors and went upstairs to bed, she assumed that Ursula had staged another disappearing act.

It was terrible. Each time her mother vanished Jennifer was beset with worry and fear. What if something had happened to Ursula and Jennifer didn't bother to report it. But she was also only fourteen, and she felt utterly confused and abandoned. She told no one about the latest disappearance, not even her closest friend, because she was already ashamed that Francine knew about the drinking parties. Jennifer often considered telling one of her sisters, possibly Justine, since her mother seemed to glorify her now, but she lived in Winnipeg and what could she do from there?

Jennifer had long ago realized that Ursula's erratic, irresponsible behaviour was abusive, and more times than she could remember, she would far have preferred Ursula's physical beatings to her sudden disappearances. The only time Jennifer found any comfort and normalcy in her home was when they drove to Melville and brought her grandmother back to Virden. Since Grandpa's death, Ursula seemed to be calmer around her mother, and Amelia invariably stayed with them for five or six days. During Amelia's visits Ursula was always on her best behaviour and showed no indication of a life of men, alcohol, and unexplained absences.

What if Jennifer asked her grandmother to come and live with them in Virden? It was heavenly having Grandma with them. She'd wake up in the morning to Grandma's delicious fried eggs and fresh toast. The only time she came home from school for lunch was when Grandma was there, and she'd have Grandma's chicken soup and dumplings along with some of the sausage she usually brought with her. Dinner was always a yummy surprise, whether stew and dumplings, cabbage rolls made with hamburger and bacon, or perogies. Jennifer not only delighted in her grandmother's meals but also the clean house and laundered clothes, which had kept her busy during the day.

Once her grandmother returned to Melville, any semblance of a healthy home life evaporated like the winter snow on the first warm day of spring. Jennifer alone attended to cleaning the house and washing the clothes, and she prepared meals when her mother decided to buy groceries. But Jennifer's dinner was often from a jar of olives that had been overlooked in the back of the refrigerator.

⇒⤳ 203 ⤳⇐

Jennifer could hardly wait until the next time they were in Melville. As soon as her grandmother went into the garden to dig out the last of her root vegetables, Jennifer offered to help her. In a secluded corner of the carrot patch, she asked, "Grandma, what would you think about coming to live with me and Mom? I know how much you miss Grandpa, and you must get very lonely being on your own all of the time. I promise that I would help you with everything just as soon as I came home from school."

"Oh, Jennifer, I could not leave my house and garden, and now that Johann and Rita have another baby, I must stay here to help with him. Also, I am busy every week with the Lutheran Women's Auxiliary, and Sarah would never let me move away. She has been my friend since we were very young, and when the weather is nice Sarah or Johann drive me to Neudorf to visit with Katherina and Rebecca Roth. Then there are my two sisters and still many of your Grandpa's family that I see often. If I moved to Virden, that's when I would be lonely, because soon you will be just like your sisters, ready to leave home. And then what would I do when your mother goes out with all her men friends?"

Jennifer was speechless. Could she possibly know about Ursula's ways? Grandma had never given the slightest impression that she knew about her daughter's behaviour, and she certainly could not have breathed a word to Ursula? Yet it seemed obvious that she'd recognized it all along. Her grandmother, however, could not know about Ursula's recent pattern of abandoning Jennifer for days at a time. The only thing Amelia would never abide was the neglect and abuse of one of her grandchildren.

But how could Jennifer tell her now? It had not occurred to her that her grandmother lived such a full life, and of course she would miss her home, family, and friends if she moved to Virden. As Jennifer grasped the bitter reality, an expression of profound unhappiness crossed her face. Amelia came over to hug her.

"I'm sorry, Jennifer. I just cannot move at my age. My whole life is here. Johann and Rita's baby will probably be my last grandchild, and with the four boys, she needs my help. When your Grandpa and I were first married, we waited so many years before we had a baby that I thought I would not be blessed with children. Looking after first my family and now my grandchildren has always been the best part of my life, and when August was born, Johann told me that Rita would have to make do without a daughter. As it is, August is such a sweet baby that even Ursula seems taken with him. I have not seen your mother make so much fuss over a baby since when Johann was born, and that was because the nurse let her stay with me."

Amelia continued to try to comfort her granddaughter. "You can come and stay with me again next summer, Jennifer, for as long as you like, since your sisters are now too busy to visit me. I know that your mother and I are getting along better than we have in years, but we could never live together in the same house."

Recognizing that Amelia's observation about Ursula's fondness for August was true, she admitted that she too was surprised. When Jennifer observed her mother holding and cooing to August, she would feel a ray of hope that Ursula could be a loving mother; but it was always short-lived. As soon as they were back in Virden, Ursula quickly resumed her dissipated life, and Jennifer had to cope as best she could along with all the turmoil of her adolescence. She lived for her summer vacations when she spent three or four weeks with her grandmother. And then at every opportunity, she convinced Ursula to drive to Melville to bring Grandma to Virden for a visit.

⠶ 204 ⠶

In just five days Sandra would return to Virden for her wedding to Warren Davis. It was the spring of 1968, and as Jennifer cleaned the big old house from top to bottom, she had yet to learn that this would be the first of three weddings within four months in the Cardinal family. Why the three oldest girls decided to marry during one summer remained a mystery; but by the end of August when Justine came back to Virden for her nuptials, Jennifer had had more than her fill of dusting, vacuuming, and washing floors. However, before the May long weekend she was so excited about seeing Sandra and Warren again that as she laboured away she was hardly aware she was working, and the house was immaculate when they walked arm in arm through the front door early Thursday afternoon.

Jennifer ran to welcome them with open arms, and as the sisters hugged she began to appreciate how much she missed Sandra's comforting presence. It was almost a year since she moved away, and although they'd had their share of sisterly quarrels, only after she was gone did Jennifer recognize how Sandra had buffered Ursula's erratic behaviour.

From the first time that Sandra brought Warren home, Jennifer had liked him. He was the tallest person she had ever met; but he was a gentle giant, and they soon established a rapport of teasing that would characterize their relationship. Within the hour, Ursula returned from work, and before they went out for a bite to eat, all of the last-minute wedding plans were finalized. Johann and Rita were arriving early tomorrow morning with their four boys and Amelia, who'd been busy in her kitchen preparing coffee cakes, apple strudels, and poppy-seed rolls for the rehearsal party at the house the next evening.

Sandra had telephoned to ask her mother to arrange for the women's auxiliary to cater a turkey buffet for the wedding supper on Saturday and to help set the tables and decorate the church hall for the celebration. Clarence and Ursula had divorced more than two years ago. Whether Sandra would have invited her father to her wedding was academic because they no longer knew where he was living. She had asked Uncle Johann to give her away, and he was more than happy to do so and then do so again with both of her older sisters later in the year.

The activity level in the too-oft-empty house began to heighten with the arrival of Rita and Johann's family, and although Amelia loved her grandsons dearly, she was relieved when Rita suggested that they take the boys to the park to burn off some of their pent-up energy before checking into the Virden Motel. Amelia was staying at the house, and as soon as they left, she went upstairs to settle into Ursula's bedroom. They'd scarcely finished lunch when Elaine and Dennis came over to visit. Because her sisters were both sleeping at home, they'd agreed to stay with his parents. Shortly after Justine and her boyfriend, Fred Forrester, knocked on the door, more guests poured in, until the large two-storey house was teeming with people.

Following a quick supper and the rehearsal at the church, more arrived—mostly Sandra and Warren's friends. Fortunately, it was a warm spring evening, so the young people spilled out into the large yard.

It was very late before the last guests departed, but Sandra and Warren were delighted that so many had come to their party. The next morning Amelia had everyone up bright and early for breakfast before they began the busy preparations for the day. If anyone was tired or suffering from the previous evening's consumption, she simply did not want to hear of it; she wanted only joy expressed around her granddaughter's wedding.

By early afternoon when Sandra walked down the aisle in her mid-length white bridal gown and short flowing veil, she brimmed with happiness. And Warren was as smug as a kitten with a saucer full of cream. After a turkey dinner with all the trimmings, the happy couple bade farewell before leaving for an abbreviated honeymoon, because they had to begin their return to Flin Flon early Monday afternoon to be at work for Tuesday morning. Still, they had enjoyed every minute of their convivial, albeit brief wedding celebration.

~≫ 205 ≪~

The next afternoon after most of the guests departed, Amelia, Ursula, and Sandra's three sisters washed and dried two days of accumulated dishes and glasses while Dennis and Fred relaxed in the living room. None of the women thought for a moment that the two men were eavesdropping until they heard them roar with laughter at the candid dialogue between Ursula and her mother.

Although they'd not heard the full conversation so missed the context, quite by chance they heard Amelia's response to Ursula's "I take after the Warner side of the family."

"I have never known a Warner to be anywhere near as loud as you are!" she said.

206

They had been high school sweethearts, and after arriving back at the house following Sandra and Warren's rehearsal on Friday evening, Elaine and Dennis happily announced that they were planning their wedding in July. Dennis had worked as a draftsman in Winnipeg for over a year, and when Elaine was offered a teaching contract at a small elementary school in Transcona for the beginning of September, they decided to marry before she moved to the city.

Upon hearing their exciting news, Justine could not believe that another younger sister had pre-empted her. While driving from Winnipeg she and Fred agreed to wait until the day after Sandra's wedding before telling her family that they'd set the date for their nuptials at the end of August. They'd dated for more than two years, and after finishing her certificate in public health nursing at the University of Manitoba, Justine had returned to her position with the St. Boniface Health Unit in Winnipeg; Fred had recently obtained an articling placement with a chartered accountancy firm.

Since giving Ursula her ultimatum about treating her with respect, Justine had refused to accept money from her mother. Justine had initially saved her grandmother's unexpected graduation gift to help pay the tuition for her first year at university, but then when she also received scholarships and bursaries, she left the $500 in the bank to collect interest.

With Fred's proposal of marriage, Justine immediately decided to cover the full cost of their wedding because she abhorred the idea of any enforced accountability to her mother. So the day after writing her last examination for her nursing certificate, she returned to work and began saving her pennies. Once Justine had acquired her financial independence, she determined to never again be beholden to Ursula, and certainly not when beginning her life as a married woman.

The fact was, throughout her adolescence Justine had vowed to never marry. After years trying to analyze why Ursula had lived a life of frustration and futility, the only conclusion Justine could reach was that a man had been responsible for ruining her happiness.

Then there'd been the spectre of her parents' life together, which was enough to make anyone flee as far from the institution as possible, although she did admit that her grandparents' arranged marriage had seemed much happier.

Since that fateful day when Kevin Hamilton and she had tacitly parted ways, Justine had courted several other eligible young men; but she did not allow herself to get close to any of them. She found it too painful. As a child she recognized that she preferred to be alone. Long before she'd completed her RN program, she realized the appeal of educational pursuits and happily determined to become an academic. But it was amazing how quickly that all changed once she met Fred Forrester.

~ 207 ~

By the third year of their training, Susan Beckham had been responsible for initiating the impending marriages of two of her other classmates, and most of the class of 1966 thought that if anyone could transform Justine's opposition to matrimony, it was Susan. To succeed, though, she would need to act quickly, as it was already the end of June. They had written their examinations, Justine had obtained a nursing position at City Hospital in Saskatoon, and she'd also been accepted for evening classes in the Bachelor of Science of Nursing program at the University of Saskatchewan.

Then one afternoon Susan's boyfriend called the residence to see if she could organize a date for a young man he'd met playing baseball. As though it were fated, Justine was available, and from the evening of their double date with Susan and Stephen, she became smitten with Fred, a third-year arts student from United College in Winnipeg.

Still, Justine was not about to change her plans and was convinced that if what they were experiencing was true love, it would surely endure a few miles. That is, until her closest friend Jacquelyn Janzen took her aside as they were coming off the hospital wards on the way to the residence.

"I've never been able to understand how you can be so smart when it comes to books, but with matters of love you don't have a clue. You know perfectly well that Fred is putting himself through university, and you have a five-year plan to study for a nursing degree, which you will have to pay for. So where will either of you get the money to travel the more than 400 miles between Saskatoon and Winnipeg?"

 **208**

Within two months, she completely altered the direction of her life and chose to move to Winnipeg, where she obtained a position as a public health nurse and could start her bachelor of nursing degree through an evening class at United College.

As it happened, she had applied to work in public health nursing in Saskatoon, but when no available positions were available she reluctantly accepted employment at the hospital. Justine did not find institutional nursing at all appealing, and now her only real obstacle was learning how to drive before the beginning of September. Perhaps a more pressing dilemma for many would have been finding a place to live, but if Justine was anything, she was resourceful.

During her initial interview with the director of public health nursing for the Province of Manitoba, she asked where she might reside. She was immediately referred to the assistant director, a matronly woman who was eager to assist. And placing a number of telephone calls, Miss Williams indeed located a private dwelling with an elderly French widow within a three-minute walk of the health unit. Then Fred taught Justine to drive his car, an aging Chevrolet that would earn the nickname "boat" because in the spring it took on water every time she drove through a puddle.

Following Justine's graduation in the spring of 1968, to Fred's considerable relief he finally convinced her to plan their wedding for that autumn.

209

As preparations for Elaine's wedding got underway, Ursula began to enjoy a certain kind of notoriety as the mother of a second daughter to marry in as many months. Realizing the attention she could garner from this rather unusual occurrence, Ursula could be heard loudly announcing her daughter's impending nuptials everywhere she went. Elaine had returned to Virden as soon as the summer holidays commenced at her school, and although she frequently asked her mother not to be so vocal about her wedding, it had little effect on her behaviour.

If not for Jennifer, Elaine would have far preferred to spend most of the three weeks prior with her future in-laws; but she quickly perceived how much her youngest sister appreciated her being at home. Of her three older sisters, Jennifer was closest to Elaine, never having forgotten that it was she who had chosen to stay at home with her rather than pursue a paying job after school. Jennifer had been so eager to convey her heartfelt gratitude that she'd willingly started cleaning the house in anticipation of Elaine's return and the other guests arriving for the middle of the month.

During the many years that Dennis had courted Elaine, his parents had also come to love her, recognizing that she was obsequious and quiet in nature, quite the opposite of her noisy mother. But they realized that Ursula was a lonely woman who craved attention, and as surprised as they were that she'd seek the limelight during her own daughter's wedding, they were still prepared to cover the full cost for the dinner and dance. Their concerns had more to do with how Ursula would behave during the festivities; but they were encouraged by Elaine's assurances that, lately in the presence of Grandma, her mother had become much calmer and appropriate around others.

Nonetheless, the four girls shared a collective sense of relief when Johann arrived with Amelia. And two days later, when her uncle gave Elaine away to Dennis in marriage, the bride was radiant as they came gliding out of the church under a hail of confetti. Dennis and Elaine knew from the first morning they collided in the hallway of Virden Collegiate High School that they were soul mates and at last they could begin their life together.

210

Five weeks later when Justine arrived in Virden to prepare for her wedding, Jennifer was less than eager to begin cleaning the large, aging house yet again. Not only was she weary of her expected role as the resident charwoman, but she also scarcely knew her eldest sister—except that her mother always put her on a pedestal. Jennifer was not yet ten years when Justine left home for nursing school, and once she departed she'd not exactly been a frequent visitor.

Perhaps Jennifer did not mind as much as Sandra did about Ursula's constant raving about Justine; Sandra especially took offence to being told often that she should be more interested in school and finishing her homework than in her part-time jobs, if she had any hope of succeeding. Still, why should she spend the whole week doing the housekeeping for Justine, who'd never offered to help her during all the difficult incidents with their mother? Although Jennifer had never asked for Justine's assistance, her older sister should have known. And considering how Justine had been physically beaten when growing up, how could she now be so oblivious to Ursula's abusive behaviours?

If she came home expecting to enjoy some camaraderie with her youngest sister, she was in for a rude awakening. When Justine arrived, she found Jennifer sullen and distant.

"Have I said or done anything to upset you?" asked Justine.

"Of course, it is always about you, isn't it? And how could you possibly annoy anyone? Just tell me what you want me to do, and let's get it over with so I can get on with my own life," Jennifer retorted.

Justine realized that Jennifer was no longer the small girl she had chided and even played tricks on along with her other siblings. Soon she would be fifteen years old, and it dawned on Justine that she knew very little if anything about her. How could she? During the past five years, she'd rarely come home to visit, so single-minded was she about her own life and career.

"It's a beautiful day. Instead of staying in this stuffy old house, why don't we walk to the soda fountain for a drink, Jen?"

"But what about all the cleaning I'm supposed to do before everyone arrives for your big day? You should hear how Ursula goes on about another daughter getting married this summer, as though she was the Queen of England and the three of you were the royal princesses!"

"We'll do it together when we get back," said Justine. "It's still five days away, and the two of us can finish it lickety-split." Justine's mind flashed back to all the posturing Ursula did during Elaine's wedding. She could certainly appreciate why that might be one reason for Jennifer's rancour.

The next several hours might have been the best time the two sisters had ever enjoyed together, as they walked through the park, drank orange floats, and then decided on the spur to go window-shopping. When Jennifer became concerned about preparing supper before Ursula returned from work, Justine assured her that she would lend a hand.

⁓ 211 ⁓

The A-line satin bridal gown and long flowing veil with matching brocade borders were elegant in their simplicity and accompanied by a unique story of creation. When Justine had finally agreed to set a date, Jacquelyn took her shopping to the best bridal boutiques Winnipeg had to offer. Clearly she rarely had insufficient funds, as she kept urging Justine to purchase one excessively expensive gown after another. Justine knew, though, that if she gave into her friend's suggestions, the wedding dinner would indeed be meagre.

Still, Justine was reticent to disclose to her friend that she was paying for her own wedding after the munificent celebration Jacquelyn's parents had obviously fully financed for her. Finally one morning during breakfast Justine shared her concerns with her much-loved landlady, Mrs. Lapierre.

"More and more it looks like I'll either have to choose between a nice bridal gown or dinner for my guests. I had no idea that it would cost a small fortune to buy a dress that I'll only wear for one day."

"Have you ever thought about getting your wedding dress made, Justine?" Mrs. Lapierre asked, as she placed the plate of eggs and toast in front of Justine.

"No," said Justine. "I have spent precious little time thinking about a bridal gown, and now it is a bit late even if I did know someone who could sew."

Justine dejectedly stared at the eggs she did not want, but that she'd eat so as to not hurt Mrs. Lapierre's feelings.

"The other day I was telling the Sisters at the Basilica about you getting married, and one said it might be interesting to sew a wedding gown. The others agreed, and they asked if you needed any help."

Over the past two years the elderly woman had become very fond of Justine. And if she had to lose her favourite boarder to a man, she was happy that it was to Fred, whom she had included along with her son, a priest, for Sunday dinner practically every week since Justine had come to live with her. Since she reciprocated Mrs.

Lapierre's feelings, Justine consented to accompany her and meet the Catholic Sisters after breakfast.

During her growing years Justine had often vowed to become a nun, and later when her nursing classmates teased her about not wanting to get married, she countered by saying she would join a convent. Now Justine was curious about the group of women who graciously offered to make her wedding gown, and she was exceedingly humbled when they refused to accept a penny more than the forty dollars they'd spent to purchase the fabric.

Although the week before the wedding, Mrs. Lapierre decided it was too far for her to travel, Justine affectionately smiled inwardly with every compliment she received during the day about her stylish bridal gown. Some remarked on its ingenious simplicity and refined grace, but none would ever learn about its origin, not even Jacquelyn who was bent out of shape that Justine could afford such a luxurious dress when all she'd done was complain about the high costs at the bridal boutiques.

Still, the morning of her special day, Justine awoke with fleeting questions about whether she was making the right choice. Not about Fred, but about the lifelong union of marriage. She knew that once she said "until death do you part," she would honour her commitment to the religious rite. Furthermore, she knew that she wanted children, and she would never consider raising them without a father.

212

In the spring of the year she turned seventy, Amelia Warner would become her own person, no longer overshadowed by her husband of more than five decades. It was not that Gustav had not allowed her to make any decisions during their married life; he'd always expected her to make most choices about the running of the household and the care of their offspring.

Rather, it had been the little aspects of living, like the ordering of her day around the meals and the hour that she was to return from her activities at the church with the women's auxiliary or even when she was out with Sarah. Now when busy working in the garden she could continue until she felt like stopping—rather than stopping when it was time to prepare dinner—and if crocheting, she could come to the end of a certain section before going to bed, and if she did not feel like getting up at the crack of dawn to make breakfast, she could arise when she was ready.

Little by little as Amelia began to overcome her grief at losing Gustav and to adjust to being alone, she realized that she now only needed to meet her own expectations. Once she'd become accustomed to the originally daunting feeling of freedom, she rather liked making her own decisions about how she would spend her days and what time she came and went. Still, it was hardly conceivable that Amelia would ever become selfish; she continued to dote upon her grandchildren and to help her offspring when they sought her assistance. She was healthy, energetic, and strong; in spite of her advancing years, Amelia could keep pace with Rita while gardening or canning the produce for the long winter months.

When Ursula came to visit and to take Amelia back to Virden with her for several days, they were beginning to enjoy a camaraderie they'd not experienced since before she took her daughter to Saskatoon. They were likely bridging the schism in their relationship because of their shared affection for August, the youngest son of Amelia's youngest son.

Even Rita was surprised by how fond Ursula seemed to be of August, and to Amelia it was little short of remarkable. During all the years she was raising her own children, Ursula had never been as demonstrative with any of them as she presently was with August, nor had she taken the same time or interest in playing with them. Was it because August reminded her of Gustav, or was she remembering how close she'd been to Johann from his birth until his eighth year, before her abrupt departure from the farm? At any rate, both aunt and nephew benefitted from the mutual bond between them, and perhaps for August it was particularly fortuitous since he was already slow in his development compared to his three older brothers.

Of course, as far as Amelia was concerned, he was a child deserving of her affection, and she loved August beyond measure, as she did her other nineteen grandchildren. Conversely, Ursula, who was recently blessed with her own first grandchild, seldom seemed to talk about Sandra and Warren's baby daughter, Monique. Whatever the reason for her unusual attachment to August, it appeared that she'd be no closer to her grandchildren than she'd been to her own offspring.

How any woman could not love a child, and especially one she'd brought into the world, was beyond Amelia's comprehension. When Ursula had returned to the homestead and birthed four babies in as many years, Amelia initially experienced overwhelming feelings of guilt, convinced it was either something that she had done or perhaps not done while mothering that caused Ursula to be so disinterested in her children. But then she'd think about Otto's first wife, Millie, recalling how little attention she'd given to her three daughters, and remember that Ursula had always looked up to her. Although Amelia would never have expressed her beliefs to anyone at that time, now when she conversed with Sarah about women like Millie and her own daughter, she agreed with her friend that they were simply too selfish to think about others.

➤~214~➤

In the years since Gustav's death, her only grandchild who came to stay with Amelia now was Jennifer, and on occasion one of Johann's boys, usually August, would come for a night or two at a time. When her great-grandchildren visited, as they often did, it was with their parents and sometimes with their grandparents; but Amelia was insightful enough to recognize that she could no longer care for a young child even if one of her great-grandchildren asked to stay. So when the telephone rang on a beautiful morning in early autumn, Amelia was surprised to hear Justine on the line asking if she could come to visit with her for a week.

"Fred is busy studying for his uniform final examinations to become a chartered accountant, and I think that the best way I can help him is by going away to give him peace and quiet. I have one week of holidays left before I return to university for the last year of my nursing degree. I am planning to leave Winnipeg tomorrow morning, and I will stop in Virden to see Mom and Jennifer. If you will be home, I would like to come to Melville from Sunday until next Friday. Will that be alright with you, Grandma?"

"You want to come and stay with me and leave Fred at home alone?" Amelia inquired, wondering if her ears were beginning to fail her.

"Yes, Grandma, you did hear me correctly. Fred is grumpier than an old man, and I certainly can't help him to study. He didn't help me when I was finishing my summer course in organic chemistry, nor will he next year when I am back at university. Will you be in Melville, or do you have plans to go visit Aunt Katherina and the Roth family in Neudorf?"

"I will be at home except for Wednesday afternoon when Sarah and I have our women's auxiliary at the church. It has been many years since you have stayed with me, Justine, and it will be nice to have you come."

It was the last week of August in 1970, and although Justine had been married for nearly two years she still loved to spend time with her grandmother. Seven years had passed since she'd stayed with her, and although she knew it would be different without her grandfather, Justine realized that this opportunity to visit with her might well be her last. Fred kept pressing her to start a family, and she'd managed to postpone the inevitable until after she had completed her bachelor of nursing degree, but she knew his patience would not continue for long.

Furthermore, from comments her mother had made, Justine suspected that her grandmother had changed since Grandpa's death. Justine believed her grandmother was as near a perfect human being as one could meet, displaying a childlike innocence that she'd rarely seen in any other adult.

Still, she appreciated that her grandmother must have faults too. For one, she'd never revealed her long-time relationship with Mathias to Gustav. From the time that Justine chanced upon her grandmother's secret, it had mystified her that she'd not told her grandfather, who had virtually raised him during the early years of his life. It was totally out of character, particularly because she would have known that no one would've been prouder than Gustav about his nephew becoming a doctor and the hospital's chief psychiatrist.

One breezy morning they weeded side by side in the large garden that Amelia continued to plant every spring and harvest in the fall so she could give most of the produce away.

"Grandma, from the time I met my second cousin Mathias at the Brandon Hospital for Mental Diseases, I have wondered why neither you nor Mom ever told Grandpa that he was living in Brandon. Grandpa always feared that Mathias died after their quarrel that caused him to vanish from the homestead; Grandpa would have been so relieved and happy to find out that he was alive and had become a doctor. Yet, as far as I know, neither of you said a word about visiting with him and Rebecca every time you went to Brandon to see Uncle Franz. Why didn't you tell Grandpa?"

"A wife does not need to tell her husband everything, and your grandfather always kept secrets from me—like why he and Dr. Spitznagel put Franz in that big hospital to begin with. It is more like a prison with all those locked doors. Instead of it helping Franz get better, he only seems to get worse. He will never get out of there and have a chance for a life like the rest of us, but your grandfather always stubbornly refused to say why he had to go to such a dreadful place. I guess one secret just leads to another and we chose to keep silent all these years."

Noticing the uncharacteristic terseness in her tone of voice, Justine knew she should stop before she angered her grandmother. But since she'd broached the subject of family confidences, this might be her only chance to ask some candid questions about her mother.

"I think you are right, Grandma, that one secret begets another. I happen to think that Ursula has hidden something all these years and that it might be why she's never found happiness or peace in her life. During the only day we ever spent together on a mother and daughter outing, she was about to tell me something. But she stopped, as though someone or something suddenly appeared to her and forced her to resist revealing it. I suspect you know her secret, Grandma, and if you would tell me, then I could understand Ursula better."

Becoming cross, Amelia snapped, "No, it is not up to me to say anything to you. If your mother wants you to know, which I doubt, she would tell you herself. Now we better go in and make some dinner."

The swiftness with which her grandmother arose from her hunched position surprised Justine, and she continued to kneel in the garden long after Grandma made her hasty retreat into the house. It dawned on Justine that if they would enjoy a harmonious visit, she should forget about delving deeper into the Warner family secrets.

By the time she tentatively entered the kitchen, her grandmother was serene, and Justine resolved to not upset her again. Instead, for the balance of the week they enjoyed the rapport that they'd grown accustomed to during her childhood years. Justine often encouraged Amelia to recall events from her past—in particular, stories about her parents and how her father had served in the Czar's army before fleeing Russia. At other times, they sat side by side in blissful silence, Amelia crocheting and Justine reading a novel, content simply to be together.

～215～

It would be one of the most tranquil weeks of her life, as Justine savoured sleeping alone in the comfortable double bed with its cozy eiderdown quilt and waking to the sounds of her grandmother preparing breakfast. Justine would never meet another woman who could make the most ordinary meal—even a fried egg on toast—taste so delectable.

Nonetheless, on Wednesday afternoon Justine arrived at the church just as Sarah and her grandmother were finishing their activities with the women's auxiliary, so she convinced the two elderly friends to allow her to treat them to supper.

The week passed much too quickly, and before long she had to hug her grandmother goodbye. During the drive back to Virden, Justine fondly reflected that her childhood memories flavoured everything about staying with her grandmother in her homey two-bedroom bungalow, and she fervently yearned for some miraculous way to keep her from growing any older.

～216～

As the years passed, Jennifer spent even less time at home. Ursula's wild drinking parties came to an end and she stopped disappearing for days at a time, but Jennifer ceased to care about her mother's activities. She met the love of her life, graduated from high school, and got a full-time job managing the Virden Dry Cleaners, hardly satisfying, but she was putting in time until her wedding day.

Rick Coyne had repeatedly asked her if she would become his wife as soon as he completed his apprenticeship to become an electrician; when he had his papers, they planned to marry and move to Alberta where his parents lived. They spent every weekend together in Brandon, and during the balance of the week Jennifer frequented her mother's house as though it were a hotel.

For years she'd been making her own meals, following hours of cooking lessons with her grandmother, doing her laundry, and keeping the house reasonably presentable. Jennifer and Ursula had long ago perfected passing each other like ships at sea. It was not that her mother did anything now to upset her; she had adjusted years before to her mother's emotional abuse by finding consolation with her many friends and, more importantly, by becoming increasingly self-reliant, until Jennifer Cardinal became so independent that she scarcely had expectations of anyone, particularly her three older siblings.

When she was younger, Jennifer had felt that her sisters, when they left home one by one, had abandoned her with their mother. With each departure she experienced a sense of betrayal. But soon it would be her turn, and in less than three months she would marry Rick before they left for the west, where his parents, Bill and Martha Coyne, owned a construction company. As soon as she had finished high school and started working, she'd begun saving her earnings to fully cover the cost of her wedding, fervently wanting to be free from any obligation to Ursula.

For the past several years Jennifer had purchased all of her own food, and once when Ursula broached the subject of her contributing more to the finances of the household, she looked at her mother with such disdain that she quickly changed the topic. Jennifer was counting the days, hours, and minutes until she would be gone forever from the aging, cheerless house. Although she'd spent hours scrubbing for her sisters' weddings, she knew that not one would arrive in time to lift a finger to assist her.

As the day she was to marry Rick steadily approached, Jennifer sensed that her mother was feeling sad that she would soon be alone. However, in her mind she believed that her mother was about to reap what she had sown. Other than her grandmother, she very much doubted that Ursula would have many visitors during the years to come. Of course, Elaine would drop in whenever they were in Virden visiting Dennis's parents, but Jennifer intended to be even more elusive than Justine had been since leaving more than ten years ago.

When she told Rick that she would not be returning to Virden for a very long time, he could not understand Jennifer's hard-heartedness; but she was not going to enlighten him about her mother's abusive past. At any rate, it certainly eased his guilt about expecting her to move so far away from her home, and he too was counting the days before they would marry and begin their life together. As Jennifer warily anticipated, none of her sisters considered arriving early enough to help with her preparations, but they did all come with their children. And when Uncle Johann gave her away to Rick in marriage, she experienced profound feelings of joy and happiness, which were strangely mingled with relief.

It was quite amazing, given their parents' awful marriage, that all four Cardinal girls did marry, and even more remarkable was that all four marriages would endure the test of time.

Nevertheless, although she considered that all four of her daughters had married compatibly enough, Ursula believed that none had come close to experiencing the love she'd felt for Hans Gerhart. Ursula had given her heart and soul to her one true love. She would have leapt off a cliff with the man she loved to pursue their perfect passion. She had loved with utter abandon; but alas, when they lost each other Ursula's life became as barren as her father's precious wheat fields at the end of every harvest, heralding the bleak mid-winter on the bald Saskatchewan prairie.

➤~ 218 ~➤

Reality is relentless, and desperate times call for desperate measures. Whereas Ursula might have come to terms with the loneliness of being on her own in the large house, she would soon be forced to sell it to pay her mounting bills. Last October when she'd injured her back cleaning at the hospital, she realized that her small pension was seriously inadequate. Then even though two of the doctors assisted by certifying that she could be eligible for a disability pension, her combined income was still below the poverty level. Nor had she saved any money for her retirement, choosing to live from one payday until the next, usually spending surplus on her endless parties.

Ursula couldn't even lament the cost of her daughters' weddings, since none had asked her for help. Although she'd not offered them any financial assistance, she repeatedly gave people the impression of being snowed under by having funded four sizeable marriage ceremonies. Aside from the $200 that Ursula consistently saved from Grandmama Margareta's bequeath and concealed in a secret compartment of her purse, she had essentially no savings from which to pay her impending property tax bill.

As she racked her brain for a possible solution to her money problems, more and more it seemed that she should accept Ned Clemens's offer of marriage. She had met the elderly bachelor at a social function at the Virden Legion, and he had latched onto her as soon as they were asked to take a seat at a table for supper. As it turned out, he was only five years her senior, but he appeared older with his slow deliberate movements and speech, not that he ever had much to say.

Since that evening, Ned had stuck like glue, and Ursula eventually found herself accepting his presence by her side every Friday evening. Clarence had been a gay blade with quick charm. And Ned was certainly not the sharpest knife in the drawer; but, so far, at least he was steady. He owned a half-section of land near Oak Lake that had been in his family for generations—so long, in fact, that he was one of the few remaining farmers around Virden, the oil capital of Manitoba, who had retained the mineral rights on his land. In time, Ursula learned that should oil be drilled on his farm—not farfetched given its proximity to Virden—Ned Clemens would become a very rich man.

Beyond a doubt, Ursula did not love Ned nor was she ever likely to, but she had long ago reconciled herself to the reality that she would never rediscover the passion she'd shared with Hans Gerhart. If all four of her daughters could marry for love, not that she had breathed a word to them about the seeming lack in their relationships, perhaps she should learn from their example and settle for security. It was certainly a viable resolution to her existing financial inadequacies, and when Ned promised to move to Virden, sell her old house with its oversized yard, and build a modern bungalow on the vacant lot down the street, Ursula accepted his marriage proposal.

It would be a new beginning in a different house, and at least she would have companionship instead of spending day after day by herself, since it had become painfully apparent that her offspring, except for Elaine, were far too busy to come to Virden. Now that they were starting their families, Ursula realized, it was easier for her to go visit them. But coming up with the money to travel was far beyond her budget, and not one had offered to contribute to the cost of her driving her old blue Nova the hundreds of miles.

⤞ 219 ⤝

A year after Jennifer married Rick Coyne, another wedding was to happen in the Cardinal family. Since their new house was not completed and Ursula was still living in the big old house on the corner of the street, it became the scene of the fifth wedding celebration within six years.

On this occasion Ursula would have to do her own cleaning, and since she'd not bothered much after Jennifer's departure, she nearly drove to Melville to bring Amelia back early to help her. But Johann pre-empted her by immediately telephoning Amelia and offering to bring her with them. Ursula wondered if he knew she'd have put their mother to work. Regardless, in the end she had to prevail upon Ned for assistance.

The man lived for routine. He'd agreed readily enough to come and help Ursula, and two weeks before their wedding when they began making the unkempt house presentable for their expected guests, Ned arrived every morning at precisely ten o'clock. He did whatever Ursula asked, whether washing the walls or vacuuming; but minutes before the clock struck twelve he stopped whatever he was doing and told Ursula that it was time to drive to the Esso outside Virden for lunch.

At exactly one they'd return, and after an hour nap on the sofa, Ned resumed his assigned tasks, doing his best until the big hand on the clock reached four. Regardless of whether he was midway through washing the floor, he ceased for the day, preferring starting again the following morning over finishing. Ursula considered his strict adherence to the clock somewhat unusual, but she was just happy that Ned was helping her.

By the end of the week the house was cleaner than it had been since Jennifer's departure, and Ursula forgot about Ned's obsession with his wristwatch. It was timely to have it scrubbed from top to bottom, because when they returned from their honeymoon to the west coast, their new home was ready and they could put the old one on the market. Neither Ursula nor Ned had ever seen the majestic Rocky Mountains or been to Vancouver, and although obviously not world travellers they looked forward to crossing the Saskatchewan border. And they promised Jennifer and Rick that they would visit with them in Alberta on the way back.

On the Sunday morning of their departure, Ned was up at precisely eight o'clock, waiting somewhat impatiently for Ursula so they could have their slice of toast and share a grapefruit. When they were on the road, they had to find a restaurant shortly before noon so they were seated at the table as the clock struck twelve. Fortunately, Ursula could drive after lunch to facilitate Ned's hour-long nap. Of course, where they spent the night was strictly determined by the town they were nearest to as four o'clock approached.

By the end of the two weeks, Ursula had Ned's routine down pat. Not only were their activities precisely regulated by the time of day, but his preference was to eat the same meals from one day to the next. Once they arrived back in Virden and moved into their new home, Ursula did eventually convince Ned to try different foods. She was still a good cook, and she could eventually vary the menu for supper. But breakfast for their entire marriage was one slice of toast and half a grapefruit, and lunch was at the Esso until she convinced him to change venues from where she had been a short-order cook.

Long before their marriage was a year old, Ursula began to ponder how anyone could not be bored with the new routines, and she began to rue that she'd decided to marry Ned. Yes, the bills were always paid on the last day of the month, but soon Ursula realized that she preferred the uncertainty and mayhem of her turbulent years with the alcoholic and womanizing Clarence Cardinal to her long tedious days with Ned.

 **220**

For the four young married couples, life unfolded as it should, with Ursula's three oldest daughters presenting her with three grandsons within one and a half years. Shortly after the birth of Sandra and Warren's second child, a beautiful baby boy with carrot-red hair and green eyes, whom they named Craig, Ursula made a trip to Flin Flon, presumably to help care for Monique while her mother tended to her newborn. Only hours after Ursula arrived, she knew that her almost three-year-old granddaughter was not impressed by Grandma's notion that small children should be in bed by seven sharp every evening.

During the week of her grandmother's visit, the seeds of dissension were planted between Ursula and her eldest grandchild. Try as hard as she might, Ursula could not fathom why her mother always fussed over the birth of yet another grandchild, and she returned to Virden wondering why she bothered to spend the time and money to make the long trip.

Although Ursula doubted she could learn what her mother meant when she said each grandchild added another dimension to her life, she initially drove to Melville to arrange for Amelia to accompany her.

The following afternoon when they arrived at the new bungalow Justine and Fred had constructed, Amelia was instantly taken with Aaron, marvelling at how closely he resembled the Warner side of the family. His fair colouring was remarkable, considering that Fred was dark-skinned with dark brown hair and eyes, obviously from his mother's Métis genes.

Aaron had a surprising aversion to sleep, and whereas Amelia delighted in cuddling and rocking him, Ursula was more than content to maintain her distance.

Whenever Justine was providing Aaron's care, she spoke in a soft soothing tone of voice. Finally one morning while bathing him in a small tub on the kitchen table, Amelia said, "Listen to how she talks to her baby, as if he could understand what she is saying to him."

Her daughter interpreted her comment as sarcastic. To concur with her, Ursula answered, "At last there is something we can agree on about grandchildren. What a ridiculous notion, and trust Justine to come up with it to spend more time with her kid. She should get the bath over with as soon as possible and put him back in his bed. Maybe then that baby would sleep for a change."

Justine chose to ignore Ursula's spiteful remark.

"I know you are right, Grandma, about Aaron not understanding a word. But he can hear the sound of my voice. I will constantly talk to him to tell him that I love him. I will repeat that he is my best baby boy until he comes to know that I am his mother and how much I love him."

If Ursula had not been there, Justine would have confided to her grandmother that she was scared stiff about being a mother. Other than during her nurses' training, she'd scarcely held a baby—let alone been solely responsible for it.

As soon as she found out she was pregnant, Justine devoured every book and article that she could find on becoming a mother. No amount of studying, however, prepared her for the moment when Fred collected her and Aaron from the hospital to bring them home.

When the front door closed, it struck Justine like a bolt of lightning. She was now completely alone and accountable for whatever happened to their newborn son. During her stay in the hospital everyone had been very helpful. When they commented on how exceptionally beautiful Aaron was with his perfect features, blond hair, and bright blue eyes, she glowed with pride; but as the reality of the commitment hit her, Justine was suddenly overwhelmed.

The only thing Justine knew at that point was that she would breast-feed her babies. During her obstetrical rotations, she had frequently observed young mothers nursing their newborn infants, and that beatific image became her most lasting and endearing memory. Fortunately, Aaron took to the breast immediately, but in short order he refused to feed from a bottle or suck on a soother.

Almost three years later when her daughter was born, Kiri was exactly like her older brother, and Justine never purchased a baby bottle, a can of formula, or a soother. During those contented years, whenever Justine put her babies to her breast, she experienced such serenity that the whole world could have crashed down around her; neither mother nor babe would have noticed.

As her love for her offspring continued to grow, it gave her increasing cause to wonder why her mother had never been able to love her and her siblings, consistently choosing instead to be distant and uncaring. In all her years Justine had no recollection of Ursula ever hugging, kissing, or calling her any term of endearment. For as long as she could remember she had been eager to gain her mother's approval, trying to please her to the point of striving for perfection, but repeatedly falling short.

As far as possible, Justine emulated her grandmother when raising Aaron and Kiri. Throughout their growing years she reminded them that whenever any were at odds, Aaron, Kiri, or she could stop, ask for a time out, and say, "I need a hug."

Her friends began to say that she was smothering her children—as though by doting on them she could compensate for the lack of love from her own mother—and that she should go back to nursing. But Justine was so committed to her children that she did not consider returning to work. She knew she could always resume her career but she could never regain Aaron's and Kiri's childhood.

221

In the autumn of 1974 immediately following Ursula's wedding, Fred and Justine expressed their farewells and embarked on a camping trip through the Rocky Mountains. Although they intended to travel as far as Vancouver, they did not dare mention their plans to Ursula and Ned for fear that the newly married couple would expect them to link up with them somewhere on their respective journeys.

Fred and Justine had recently purchased a tent trailer and were anticipating spending as much family time together as they could in the remaining two weeks of Fred's vacation, enjoying the beauty of nature and the majesty of the mountains.

Justine found Ned dreary at best, and after three days of observing his strict routines, she suspected there was more to his habitual behaviour than met the eye.

They did, however, stop to visit Justine's grandmother in Melville on their return trip to Winnipeg. When they arrived just before supper, they tried to take her to a restaurant, but she would not hear of it. Within an hour the seventy-eight-year Amelia asked them to sit down at her table, where she served a complete meal that started with her chicken and homemade noodle soup.

222

Although Ursula felt locked into Ned's routines, Ned seemingly adjusted to being married and living in the new bungalow in Virden, surprising since he'd spent his adult life living alone.

During one of their rare visits to Virden so their daughter Kiri could meet her great-grandmother, Ursula complained to her daughter while the men went for a drive in the country.

"I just don't understand why Ned has to do exactly the same thing at the same time every day. It's driving me crazy, but when I try to make any changes he becomes as silent as a stone and goes ahead with his rigid schedule as if I did not exist."

"I have seen how firm he is about his routines," said Justine, "and he also tends to say the same things to everyone. I have also learned to never ask him how he is, because he invariably tells me that he is dying."

"Well, you sure in hell don't have to tell me that. I have been living with the man now for almost a year. What I want to know is what I can do about it?" Ursula lamented.

"After our last visit, I decided to do some research," continued Justine. "I think Ned might have a mild form of an unusual syndrome called Asperger's, which would explain some of his behaviours. There is no definitive diagnostic test for it, and doctors have little to offer in the way of treatment. As difficult as it might be for you, your best course of action is to accept his routines while being flexible when making your own choices. Otherwise you will just end up putting pressure on yourself until *you* become ill."

For a while, Ursula attempted to heed Justine's advice, but eventually she forgot and became increasingly aggravated until her daughter's prediction rang true and her protracted depression deepened. Regardless of what her doctors prescribed, the drugs seemed to do little, and it was with considerable relief that Ursula discovered a young female doctor who'd recently opened her practice in Virden. After little satisfaction with the three male physicians in town, she was more than willing to give Dr. Audrey Burke a chance to treat her.

Soon she was on new anti-depressant and anti-anxiety medication, which added two new vials to her collection. Ursula had forgotten when she decided to save all of the medications she would not use and store them in an old tote bag under her bed. Soon the bag was overflowing, so she decided to empty all of the bottles and vials, tossing their contents together in the old piece of luggage.

She hadn't the heart to throw them out, with all their bright colours, sizes, and shapes, and it was of little consequence to Ursula that she could no longer remember why each medication had been prescribed in the first place.

When the tote bag was completely filled, she found a small carry-on case that she had not used and began to store her extra drugs in it. Ursula was always careful to add to her collection only when Ned was napping, and even then she locked the door to her bedroom to ensure no interruptions. As soon as she was finished, she locked it and stashed the luggage far under the centre of the bed until it reached the wall.

Then it dawned on her that if she refilled her prescriptions at all three drugstores in town, she could quickly augment her assortment. Ursula recognized that her medication stockpiling was rather bizarre, for she had no intention of doing much with her collection of analgesics, anti-depressants, sedatives, anti-anxieties, anti-emetics, mood elevators, and at least a dozen types of sleeping pills. But when she started to return to Dr. Burke's office regularly requesting another prescription long before it should have been required, the young physician became suspicious.

A follow-up meeting with the three pharmacists in Virden quickly revealed that Ursula Clemens had been refilling her medications at each of their drugstores and then insisting that the copy be returned to her for submission to the Canada Pension Plan. Dr. Burke subsequently made a referral to the health unit, asking that a public health nurse visit the Clemens's home on whatever trumped-up pretense and subtly confirm that Ursula was hoarding medication.

Miss Barrett was a clever and experienced community nurse; but she chose to bring a health inspector with her, claiming that there'd been a problem with the water in the area. While Mr. Williams took a sample from the kitchen tap, Miss Barrett asked if she could use the lavatory. With the faucet turned up as high as possible, she did a quick perusal of the medicine cabinet. It appeared to be in order, with only Ursula's and Ned's current prescriptions on alternate sides of the cupboard. When Miss Barrett reported her findings, Dr. Burke thanked her before noting on her chart to diligently monitor Ursula's appointments.

When Dr. Burke stopped giving her early refills on her prescriptions, Ursula changed her approach and convinced Ned to start going to Brandon so she could see physicians specializing in her illnesses. She soon discovered that it was considerably easier to shop for doctors in the city within an hour's drive. Although she continued to keep her appointments with Dr. Burke because she preferred her bedside manner, Ursula asked for her specialist referrals from the male practitioners in Virden.

Had a Canada Pension Plan medical underwriter tracked Ursula Clemens's appointments with members of the medical profession, the findings would have been astounding. It was not uncommon for her to visit five or six different doctors at any given time. And with the number of physicians ordering medication for her, Ursula's pill collection began to increase by leaps and bounds.

 **225**

"Who is telephoning at quarter to twelve? Surely everyone who knows us must realize that Ned will be getting anxious about leaving for lunch," Ursula thought, as she vacillated about whether to pick up the receiver. Finally grabbing it as though it was a hot potato she answered, "Hello?"

"Hi, Mom. You sound upset. Is this a bad time?" Justine thought she had yet to find an appropriate hour to telephone Ursula and Ned.

"Of course, just before noon is one of the worst times to telephone. Ned is already in the car waiting for me to go for lunch, and you should know that Justine."

"Okay, I'll let you go, but when should I call back?"

"Phone after Ned's nap and before our soap opera, so between two and three." The line went dead before Justine could say goodbye.

It was the last request in the world that Justine wanted to make, but she could put it off no longer, with Fred becoming increasingly insistent about her going to San Francisco with him next month. Two years ago he'd been promoted to vice president of finance with the moving company, and now they were offering to send him and his accountant and their wives for a one-week conference to the famed seaside city. Fred persistently argued that neither of them had ever been to California and, furthermore, they'd not been away as a couple since before their children came along.

Justine had little inclination to be separated from Aaron and Kiri, but her friends encouraged her to take advantage of a wonderful opportunity. They just assumed they could leave them with her mother; but little did they know about Ursula's lack of interest in her grandchildren, much less about her shortcomings as a mother. On the other hand, Fred's parents were too elderly to care for her two energetic offspring, and his father would never consider leaving the house on the farm for a week when Fred's sisters could scarcely get him to come to Winnipeg for a day.

 **226**

At precisely two in the afternoon, Justine rang Ursula's number again, praying that Ned did not answer the phone. She was in no mood to again hear that he was dying.

As much as Justine dreaded asking her mother to care for her children, it was inconsequential compared to how she dreaded telling the children that their parents were leaving them for a week with Ursula and Ned. Long before she and Fred were ready to depart, Justine knew they were staging a fiasco, but there was no changing Fred's mind. For once, luck was on her side and Ursula picked it up on the first ring.

"How was your lunch, Mom, and where did you go?" Justine asked, hoping Ursula was in a better frame of mind.

"It was the same as usual, but I must say I was surprised to hear from you. You must want something for you to phone me on a Wednesday," Ursula baited.

"As a matter of fact, I do need to ask if you and Ned will come to Winnipeg and look after Aaron and Kiri during the second week of September." Justine had bristled at her mother's tone and choice of words, but realizing that she had no choice, she decided to be open and direct in response.

"What? You want us to stay with your rambunctious kids for a whole week when neither you nor Fred will be at home?"

"Yes, Mother. Fred is adamant that I go to San Francisco with him for a conference; he absolutely refuses to let me stay home. And, as you well know, his parents are too old to come to Winnipeg to care for the kids."

"Why in God's name do you think I would agree to that? We didn't even go to Winnipeg when Elaine had either one of her boys, and other than when Grandma is here with me, she is the only one of you girls we ever see."

"Come on, Mother. Since Dennis's parents came to stay when both Nicholas and Scott were born, Elaine hardly needed your help. With both sets of grandparents in the same town, of course they will visit more often, and then when they do go home, they can stay with the Cliffords in their large house. Every time we come to Virden, we need to rent a motel. And let me assure you that none of them are great. As far as the two other girls are concerned, now that Sandra and Warren have moved with their family to near Jennifer and Rick, it would be considerably easier for you and Ned to plan a trip to visit with them. Anyway, do you think that you can keep the kids?"

"You have to give me some time to think about it and then to convince Ned. I'm not even sure we have the energy to look after your uncontrollable kids."

It was beyond Justine's comprehension that by fifty-three her mother already viewed herself as old, and she vowed to not call herself a senior until she was in her eighties. She had never heard Grandma refer to herself as old, and she was much livelier around children than her daughter was.

"Can you get back to me in a couple of days because Fred needs to let his boss know. Remember that Aaron now goes to kindergarten, and I shall arrange for one of my friends to take him and pick him up at eleven thirty. Then he will be home in time for all of you to go out for lunch, and the kids can tell you where the restaurants are. Aaron usually spends every afternoon playing with the two little boys next door, and I often take Kiri for a walk or to play in the park across the street. If you decide to come, I would suggest that you plan to arrive two or three days before we leave so Aaron and Kiri can become used to your routines."

How strange that it would be necessary for her children to adapt to their grandparents' needs. Three days later when at last Ursula telephoned to say they would come to Winnipeg to take care of Aaron and Kiri, Justine was more anxious than relieved with their decision. She had steadfastly hoped and prayed that their response would be negative. Then Fred would have had to accept that she could not go.

In some ways Justine suspected that Fred tacitly endorsed their friends' notion that she was too involved with their children, seemingly forgetting that he'd pressured her to start a family. During the nine years of their marriage, Justine felt that by now Fred should know that when she committed, she honoured it. After first Aaron's and then Kiri's birth, she'd been overwhelmed by the miracle of creation, and from the moment of their arrival, Justine loved her children more than life itself. Considering that she fully intended to live until well over 100, Justine's devotion was definitive.

➤➤➤ ~ 227 ~ ◄◄◄

The disaster began an hour after Ursula and Ned arrived and unpacked their suitcases. When both went into the bathroom carrying a small valise, Justine thought it odd but busied herself to start supper. However, when Kiri ran up to her and said, "Mommy, I need to pee, and Grandma and Grandpa are in the bathroom," she nearly knocked, just as the door opened.

Justine was stunned. Along the full length of the bathroom counter stretched two rows of medication vials and bottles, not unlike the shelf of a pharmacy.

"I'm sorry, Mother, but with a five-year old son who's curious about everything and a toddler who gets into anything within reach, you must remove every one of your medications and keep them under lock and key in the bedroom while you're here."

"What a ridiculous notion! Do you have any idea what a nuisance it would be to unlock our suitcases and find our pills every hour when we need to take them?" Ursula snapped at her unbelieving daughter.

Wondering how a woman who had birthed five offspring could have such limited awareness of the safety needs of children, Justine knew she must quickly placate Ursula if Aaron and Kiri were to survive her care for seven days. Although she firmly believed that the Cardinal siblings had been graced with guardian angels while growing up, she was not prepared to depend upon divine intervention with her own son and daughter.

"As soon as we finish supper, I shall drive to Woolworths and buy a filing cabinet that comes with two keys. Then you can put your pill bottles on one level and Ned can store his on the other. But you must lock it when you finish getting what you need. And remember to always keep the key on you instead of in the cabinet. Are you perfectly clear on this, Mother?"

"Oh, all right," said Ursula, "if you will be such a pain about it. What I have never understood is why you just can't teach your kids to leave things alone instead of getting into everything in the house!"

228

On the first evening when Justine telephoned home to talk to her children, Aaron answered the phone breathless. Although it was only seven o'clock, he'd jumped out of bed and raced to reach the telephone before his grandparents could answer it.

But Aaron could not say much more before the telephone was wrestled away and Ursula came on the line. For the balance of the week, although Justine telephoned every day to speak with Aaron and Kiri, her mother refused to let them come on the line, using one excuse after another: "it's too expensive" or "it'll only upset them." Beside herself with worry, Justine counted the hours until the conference would be over and she could be back home to know all was okay with Ursula and her children.

By the time the airplane touched down at the Winnipeg International Airport, Justine was sick with worry. Though Ursula repeatedly said that Aaron and Kiri were fine, her most telling comment to Justine was that all Kiri had done since they'd left is sleep.

The minute Aaron spotted his parents, he dashed in front of everyone and flew into Justine's arms. But when she reached for Kiri, her daughter turned away. Kiri eventually allowed Fred to cuddle her, but she wanted nothing to do with her mother until much later, after Fred gave her a bath and Justine went into her bedroom with her favourite storybook.

Kiri started to cry and scream, demanding to know why her mother had abandoned them. She didn't settle until Justine lay down on her daughter's bed and promised to not leave her side during the night and that it would never happen again. Not until the next morning, when Ursula and Ned left, did the truth come to light.

229

As soon as Justine and Fred had departed for the airport, Aaron and Kiri were put into their bedrooms and told to not come out until Grandma or Grandpa opened the door. Their parents did not close the doors to their rooms, so Kiri sobbed and yelled until eventually she fell asleep and slept through to the next morning. When Aaron asked to check on his baby sister, he was ordered to stay out of her bedroom and not wake her.

The Forrester children were forced to take an afternoon nap, something neither had done regularly, and then were put to bed as soon as they ate supper.

In due course Justine deduced that Kiri had chosen sleep as her escape from Ursula's regime, and it would be months before she no longer had nightmares and again became her happy, loving daughter. Aaron had coped better by playing with his toys and reading his books; nonetheless, during the first weeks of her return he also asked his mother repeatedly to never leave them alone with their grandparents again.

230

The large manila envelope arrived in the morning mail. When Amelia opened it, she was delighted with the picture of a beautiful baby boy with dark brown hair and hazel eyes.

However, now she must wait until Johann stopped by on his way back from the farm to read the letter so she could find out the names of his happy parents. Amelia had long ago lost track of how many great-grandchildren she was now blessed with, and she began to wonder, given the baby's darker complexion, if Fred and Justine had had another baby.

This baby finally had Fred's Métis colouring, instead of the fair skin and blue eyes of their first two children; but she could not remember Justine telephoning her with the news. To the best of her recall, her granddaughter had not appeared to be with child when she visited with the Forrester family in Virden during the summer.

During the years after Leonard was killed in the war, if not for Otto's three daughters she would not have returned from her despair. Although Amelia had been totally estranged from Francis, Faye, and Darlene for many years now, she could not forget that she owed them a tremendous debt of gratitude. Similarly, when Robert had been struck down so young by that dreadful boy driving his truck, if not for the birth of Johann and Rita's twin babies, Amelia might have willed herself to die.

And August, who needed her more than any of her other grandchildren had because he was slower in school, had arrived shortly after Gustav's death. The birth of every new baby heralded God's wondrous gift of life and invariably delivered Amelia from the very brink of despondency.

But this awareness was also the source of Amelia's most profound regret. More than ever before, she could not escape from the guilt of the decision she'd forced Ursula to make so many years ago. At the time, she had convinced her daughter that it was Gustav who had prevented her from making her own choice; but in her heart Amelia knew it had been her doing and, furthermore, that it had ruined Ursula's life. Amelia had fervently prayed for absolution, and although she firmly believed that God had forgiven her, she had never been able to forgive herself.

Remorse would shadow her until the end of her days unless she asked for Ursula's forgiveness. But even though mother and daughter had achieved a measure of reconciliation since Gustav's death, Amelia's intuition warned her not to trust that Ursula would pardon her. If only she had listened to Gustav that fateful day before he died and then chose to tell Hans Gerhart where Ursula was living, he could have sought her out and they might still have made a life together. But no. Her guilt and shame had stopped her, just as it had decades before, and then Ursula married Ned.

Amelia now realized that Hans was a far better man than either Clarence or Ned, and that he would have given Ursula the kind of life that she'd had with Gustav. Fortunately, her painful reverie was interrupted by Johann knocking on the door before entering. He was later than usual, although as she often did these days, she had lost track of the hour. Amelia could tell he was hungry and in a hurry to get home for supper, but she could not let him leave until he told her the identity of the baby boy.

"I'm sorry to bother you when you are tired, Johann, but could you please read me this letter and tell me his parents' name. Look at this beautiful picture."

"It has been a very tiring day, Mother, and I don't feel like sitting down to read through this long letter. Give me the envelope and I can tell you whose baby he is, but can you wait until some other time for me to read you the letter?

"This is from Jennifer and Rick Coyne. They have called him Thomas Michael. And it seems that they are planning to stop and see you next week."

⇝ 231 ⇜

Amelia was delighted that Jennifer and Rick were coming to visit and bringing Thomas. She thought fondly of all those summers when Jennifer had stayed with her, but she realized she did not know what day to expect them.

So the following morning she arose early, stripped the sheets on the bed in the spare bedroom, and by lunch had cleaned the rest of the house. Johann then stopped by to read Jennifer's letter, and Amelia now knew that they were coming during the late afternoon of the day after tomorrow. She took a chicken out of the freezer and had it boiling in a large pot on the stove to start the soup with egg dumplings, one of Jennifer's favourite meals. Since she did not move as quickly as she used to, Amelia wanted her preparations to be well under way to ensure she was ready when her houseguests arrived.

During the past several years, Ursula's daughters and families had been her only overnight company, and by supper time on the day of their arrival Amelia contentedly sat Jennifer and Rick at her table.

When Johann came to the door just as they were finishing grace, the delectable scent of his mother's cooking and the sight of her table laden with food made him wonder why he was thinking of suggesting that she move into an old folks' home. He also realized that if he breathed a word about his intentions in front of Jennifer, she would set him straight in a minute. As soon as he had made the acquaintance of Tommy who sat happily on Rick's knee, Johann departed for home.

Jennifer tended to Tommy's bath and supper while Rick dried the dishes, then they retired to their bedroom, fatigued from the full day of driving. They'd talked about staying with Grandma for only one day before continuing on—perhaps as far as Virden since Ursula and Ned had yet to see Tommy. But the following morning they awakened to the smell of coffee and the sound of Grandma bustling around in the kitchen. She had prepared bacon and fried eggs with toast made from her fresh bread, and homemade raspberry jam. And she asked Jennifer if once she put Tommy down for a nap she would help her dig up the last of the root crop in her garden.

Before they were aware the day had passed, it was far too late to consider leaving. So Jennifer suggested that they take her out for supper.

"I have lots of food in the house," said Amelia. "When Johann read your letter that said you'd be here for a week, I had him take me to the grocery store. I bought bags and bags of food. Maybe before you leave we can go to a restaurant, but right now I want to cook your favourite meals from those summers when you stayed with me."

Realizing that Grandma had misunderstood her letter, Jennifer asked, "Grandma are you sure we won't tire you out if we stay here for a week? We can drive on to Virden if we are too much of a bother for you."

"How could you ever be a bother to me Jennifer?" said Amelia. "When Johann stops by tonight I was thinking of asking him if Rick can spend a day with him at the farm, if he wants to, so he has something to do while you are helping me in the garden."

Thus it came to be that Jennifer, Rick, and Tommy spent their entire vacation with Amelia. It was their most relaxing and enjoyable since Rick had started working with his parents in their extremely busy construction company. Fortunately, they had not told Ursula they might journey to Virden, where Jennifer knew they would have inconvenienced her and Ned.

During the day, Jennifer and Amelia cared for Tommy, cooked meals together, and worked side by side in the garden. In the evenings, Rick and Jennifer read while Grandma finished crocheting the round tablecloth she'd promised to make for Justine. Rick, after enjoying the day with Johann, decided to accompany him again.

 **232**

The house was so empty. Not until after Jennifer, Rick, and Tommy left did Amelia realize how truly lonely she was. Most of her family and friends had passed on: her elder sister Wilhelmina and husband Peter, Gustav's sister Hanna and brothers Johann and Rolf, and their respective wives, Rebecca and Dr. Max Roth.

Although Gustav's sister and her younger sister, Katherina and Katie, were still alive, they lived in Neudorf; if Amelia saw them once a year she was fortunate.

Several years ago when Katherina started to have difficulty with her vision, Vera Roth had purchased her dress shop and, shortly after, the General Store. Neither Vera nor her elder sister, Dr. Fraya Roth, had ever married, and when Katherina became totally blind, Vera changed residences with her. Now Fraya cared for her Aunt Trudi and Katherina in her parents' home, which also served as the office for her medical practice.

But the worst had come last spring when her dear friend Sarah Thompson succumbed to the cancer that reduced her to skin and bones. Until two years before her illness, she and Amelia had continued with the Lutheran Women's Auxiliary; but when Sarah could no longer go with her, Amelia had lost all interest, choosing instead to spend her time at Sarah's bedside.

Still, Amelia was not complaining. She had lived a long and satisfying life and was in reasonably good health considering her advancing age. Other than arthritis, primarily in her hips, which was most painful when trying to fall asleep at night, she continued to walk unaided and even to work in her garden.

Some time ago Amelia had limited her vegetable garden to half of the backyard, consenting to allow Johann to seed the balance in grass, which one of his sons came to mow every week. Ursula and Ned still came to visit twice a year, usually in the spring for her birthday on the first of April and in the autumn. Each time Amelia would return to Virden with them for a week or two and then enjoy seeing Elaine and Justine with their families. It had been more than two years now since Sandra, Warren, Monique, and Craig had come to stay with her on their way to Alberta where they were moving, but Elaine and Dennis usually arrived once a year and visited her for several days at a time.

Strangely, only Justine and Fred had not come to Melville to stay with her, at least not since they had had Kiri. Amelia enjoyed seeing them in Virden, and she loved Aaron and Kiri as much as all her other great-grandchildren. But since Fred, Justine, and Aaron had stopped overnight on their way back from Vancouver that autumn before Kiri had been born, they had not been to her home. The last time she saw them, Amelia asked when they were coming; but Justine said that Fred was so busy and worked such long hours that they rarely had time to travel anywhere as a family.

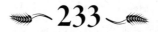

Johann arrived one afternoon and asked her to accompany him to the St. Paul Lutheran Old Folks Home. It was a bitterly cold day at the beginning of November, and already Amelia dreaded the long, harsh winter of the Saskatchewan prairie. Still, she put on her heavy coat, hat, warm mitts, and boots, and eagerly went, since Johann always had the heater in his car going full blast.

As they entered the front foyer of the home, she saw people sitting in a large comfortable room enjoying drinks and cake. Removing her outerwear and glancing around, Amelia was pleasantly surprised by how many people she recognized from church. Before long she too was seated at a table with a cup of hot coffee and apple strudel and visiting with Mrs. Marks, who used to live one block from her street.

At least an hour passed before Johann returned to her side and asked her to come and look at one of the rooms down the hall. It was a nice bedroom, although it was completely empty, and it was then that Amelia wondered why her youngest son took time from his busy day to bring her to the Old Folks Home outside of Melville.

But Johann waited until they were back in the car before asking, "Wasn't it nice for you to see so many of your friends from the women's auxiliary and to visit with them in that bright and sunny living room? And what did you think of the bedroom, Mother? It is probably large enough for your three-quarter bed and your dresser."

"Yes, the room looked pretty big. But I am not moving my furniture in there when I am perfectly comfortable in the house. I might be an old woman, Johann, but don't think you will pull the wool over my eyes. I like living in my own home. Until I can no longer get around and look after myself, I am staying right where I am, so you can forget any notion you have of putting me in that place."

"Mother, you always say how lonely you are because hardly anyone comes to see you anymore. If you moved into St. Paul's, you could visit with people you have known for years: friends, neighbours, and members of the church. You would always have someone to talk to instead of sitting all alone day after day in that house hoping someone will visit. Besides, I am planning to curl a lot more this winter, and Rita and I want to go to several bonspiels in other parts of the country. Who do you think will come and see you every day when we are away?"

"Now that your oldest son is old enough to drive a car, I'm sure I could telephone Charlie." Amelia was surprised by her youngest son's persistence.

After dropping Amelia off, Johann realized it would be more difficult than he'd anticipated; he wondered what else he might say to convince his mother to move into St. Paul's. He had pinched himself when the director, a long-time curling friend, had phoned to say that a private room had finally come available at the home. Johann and Rita agreed that his mother should no longer live on her own way across town, so he was not prepared to let this opportunity slip by, particularly when Carl Reiner was prepared to ignore the long waiting list.

Over the next three days, both Johann and Rita visited Amelia to try every which way to convince her that she would enjoy living at St. Paul's; but they failed. Because Carl said he needed a definitive answer by the end of the week, Johann would have to tell a lie. What choice did he have? He and Rita were leaving for Halifax in just ten days, and the room would be given to the elderly Lutheran man next in line. Only God knew when another bed would be vacated.

⟫⟫~ 234 ~⟪⟪

When Johann promised that it would only be for the winter and that she could return to her own house in the spring to attend to her flowers and garden, his mother agreed to give St. Paul's Old Folks Home a six-month trial.

That first week, Amelia was quite happy visiting with friends and distant relatives she had not seen for years. For the first time in her life, she felt like she was on a holiday, with no meals to prepare or dishes to wash.

But by the beginning of the second week, Amelia became restless wondering when she could get into the kitchen and cook. Furthermore, she was tired of sitting around all day with little to do other than talk and crochet. She had energy to work instead of just watching the women in blue uniforms rush about performing their chores.

Amelia offered to help them, but she was repeatedly told that her assistance was not required and that she could sit in the lounge and watch television. Amelia Warner never said that she could barely understand the language spoken on the screen; nor would she say that she'd done more sitting in the last month than ever before in her life.

235

Every time Johann came to visit, she said she wanted to go home. Amelia fully understood what Justine meant when she said that a person needs something to do. For as long as she could recall, Amelia had believed that work was its own reward, and now with the first signs of spring she was as eager as a foal in the pasture to break out of the old folks home and do an honest day's toil.

She had suspected her son was not being honest, but when Johann arrived on the first of April and said he wanted to take her to an auction, she'd had enough.

"I want to go home for my birthday, not to some sale. I need to start putting in my bulbs if my flowers are to bloom this year."

Johann sighed. "Mother, it's time I told you that I had a buyer for the house last month, but he asked us to clear out all the old furniture and stuff that you and Father kept for years. There is no point in getting all upset about this. Both Otto and Ursula agreed that since you have a place to live, we should accept the offer. It is very reasonable for that little house."

"In fact, Ursula and Ned have come from Virden and they've been helping us get ready for the auction. Otto, too busy to be here, of course, insisted that I bring you to the house first to see if you want to keep anything."

Amelia at first thought it was an April Fool's joke. But when she saw her kitchen and dining room tables laden with her prize possessions, she realized that Johann was not jesting, and she was instantly devastated by her children's duplicity.

Encountering Ursula in the kitchen, Amelia demanded, "What is the meaning of this? And where are your four daughters? Not one of them would allow you to do this to me, and if they can't stop my own offspring from selling my home from under my feet, at least they would be here to pick out what they want of mine."

"That's where you are wrong, Mother," said Ursula. "I telephoned your granddaughters to tell them about the sale today, but not one took the trouble to come. So Johann is right when he says we will get rid of everything that we can."

Fortunately, Amelia had left Justine's tablecloth at the nursing home, but still she went into every room in her little house picking out as much as she could to give to the Cardinal girls. After the way Johann had lied to her, she didn't trust Ursula's story about telephoning her daughters. Even if she had, how could they have come when their children were in school?

She still could not believe her own children had sold her home behind her back. Gustav had asked Johann to look after her, but he never would have expected his youngest son to be capable of this.

Amelia soon had to accept that her own offspring were more interested in what was good for them than for her; furthermore, she was powerless against all three. And within four months of her obligatory return to St. Paul Lutheran Old Folks Home, Amelia Warner lost all that remained of her memory and no longer recognized anyone.

～ 236 ～

When she drove Fred to the airport, Justine knew he would be offered employment with the firm in Alberta. But neither she nor her children wanted to leave Winnipeg where they were happily settled in a new subdivision in St. Vital.

During the fourteen years that Justine had lived in Winnipeg she had made many friends. And Aaron loved his school and Kiri could hardly wait to begin school in September with her closest friend from down the street. They lived in a new home with a large, well-treed backyard and were close to beautiful parks along the river, right across the street from the community centre. They were a mile from well-maintained tennis courts and three blocks from the school. The shopping centre, which was readily accessible by car, could even be considered a safe excursion now that Kiri had graduated to a larger bicycle. Justine, Aaron, and Kiri had little if any incentive to leave their comfortable neighbourhood, except that Fred was unhappy in his job. In recent years, the moving company had been sold and his new boss with his excessive demands was making work a nightmare.

The look on Fred's face when they arrived to pick him up instantly told Justine that her premonition was right. Later when Aaron and Kiri were tucked into bed, he related how Ed Stanski, the young president of the thriving construction-trailer leasing company, had offered him the position of VP Finance. It came as such a shock that even Fred was ambivalent about what to do and the entire Forrester family subsequently lived in a state of vacillation for the better part of a week.

When Ed phoned to get an answer, Fred was unable to respond. Detecting his hesitation, his prospective employer offered to send the lear jet to Winnipeg to bring his family to Edmonton to enjoy the Canada Day long weekend.

When they touched down at the Municipal Airport, the Stanski family greeted them, presented them with a rental car, directed them to the Mayfield Inn, and then encouraged them to enjoy their four days in Edmonton. Although pressure was not blatantly applied, Fred and Justine fully understood that they would be expected to reach a decision before being flown home on Tuesday morning.

⋙∼ 237 ∼⋘

It was as though the forces of fate were conspiring to shift the Forrester family home from one capital city on the Canadian prairies to another. Still, neither Justine nor Fred wanted to subject their children to relocation, and they began to believe that if they persisted with unreasonable prerequisites the decision would be made for them.

So Justine chose a house, a large four-level split that was well beyond their price range even though their offer was $15,000 less than the asking price. And Fred presented Ed Stanski with what he considered an inordinate list of demands, including an interest-free house loan, a top-of-the-line move, and a return flight for the family back to Winnipeg for the Christmas vacation. To their stunned disbelief, every request was met and they were faced with an offer they could not refuse.

An additional stipulation of Fred's employment contract was that the company would cover all expenses that Justine incurred while driving Aaron and Kiri across the prairies to their new home in St. Albert. For all intents and purposes, the sky was the limit for the anticipated move. Their beloved dog would be kennelled and all of Justine's houseplants stored in a greenhouse until she and the children arrived and they could be delivered to their new residence.

Nonetheless, Aaron and Kiri were reluctant to leave the only home they'd ever known and all of their young friends. After heart-rending preparations and multiple promises that they would drive back to Winnipeg the following summer, Justine was ready to begin the journey across the prairies with Aaron and Kiri. Although none looked forward to seeing them, they did make the obligatory stop in Virden to take Ursula and Ned out for supper before departing the next morning.

The relationship between Ursula and her daughter had become even more strained once Justine learned that her mother and brothers had conspired to place Grandma in the home and had auctioned off all of her belongings without informing the Cardinal sisters. Although they likely could not have prevented Amelia's move to the three-storey brick building, Justine would have made every effort to be with her beloved grandmother throughout the ordeal.

For the rest of her days Justine would also feel that she'd been robbed of the opportunity to walk through every room of the cozy bungalow on Third Avenue in Melville and to commune with her grandmother. They would have surely reminisced about the fondest memories of her life.

238

"I don't know why you're in such a hurry to leave. If you're thinking of stopping in Melville to visit your grandmother, you may as well not waste your time. During our last two or three visits, she didn't have a clue who we were or where she was. She just sits in the chair staring at the four walls," said Ursula in her usual strident tone of voice, which seemed only to heighten when she spoke of her mother.

At last Justine understood why she'd been told repeatedly that her grandmother could not come to the phone. When told she was indisposed, she'd never thought to take it literally. Justine was again furious that critical information about her grandmother had been withheld.

The atmosphere in Ursula and Ned's stifling house became so oppressive as a result that she wanted nothing more than to be as far from it as possible. Justine hurriedly asked Aaron and Kiri to gather their books, use the bathroom, and say goodbye while she expressed her terse farewell. And not until they were several miles on the other side of Virden did Aaron quietly inquire.

"Mommy, are we going to stop and visit your Grandma? Why did your mother say she did not know her?"

"Yes, Aaron, we shall be in Melville by lunch time, and after we eat, we will visit Grandma in the nursing home where she now lives. Please listen carefully, Aaron and Kiri. Sometimes when people become very old—and Grandma turned eighty-four on her last birthday—they can start to forget many things about their lives and sometimes even the people who are most important to them. But we will stop and see Grandma, and although she may not remember who we are, we can still visit and love her with our words and hugs. Just think back to all those warm hugs she always used to give us, and soon you will feel that she is still your loving great-grandmother."

～ 239 ～

For once in her life Justine wished she'd taken her mother's unsolicited advice. It was heart-rending to see her grandmother staring vacantly without a flicker of recognition. She looked exactly the same as Justine could always remember; she wore a colourful print dress and dark-rimmed glasses, she had a demure smile upon her soft face, and her skin was nearly devoid of wrinkles, belying that she was an octogenarian. She was still her grandma, the woman she'd loved beyond all measure from her earliest recollection.

Nonetheless, the only factor that could have caused a chasm between them, senile dementia was very much in evidence. Immobilized in her despair, it took a long time before Justine registered that Aaron and Kiri were tugging on her arms and pleading, "Mommy, can we please give Grandma our big hugs so we can leave?"

Once they returned to their car, Justine felt drained. With a heavy heart, she drove to the nearest Esso station to buy a cup of coffee for herself and soft drinks for Aaron and Kiri. Realizing that she no longer wanted to drive, she decided to take the highway to Yorkton to stay the night. Her children seemed to sense how upset she was, so they were on their best behaviour, and after a long play in a park in the middle of the city in central Saskatchewan and then a relaxing supper, they were ready for bed unusually early.

As much as Justine wanted to explain more about her grandmother's memory loss to her children, she knew she would have to wait until she had vented her own sorrow. She'd thought she could break through the clouds of senility and reach her grandmother, which now seemed ridiculous. Justine read the children's bedtime stories and lovingly tucked them into bed and then sobbed her heart out at the dramatic decline of her beloved grandmother.

The year sped by in a blur and soon it was the summer of 1981. Aaron and Kiri had adjusted without a hitch to the move and their school, forming new friendships, many of which would last their lifetimes. Justine was busy purchasing furniture and decorating her large home, and if she thought Fred had worked long hours in Winnipeg, his position in Edmonton redefined the possible number of hours of employment in a workweek.

Since it was unlikely there'd be much time for a family vacation in the summer, Fred agreed that Justine should keep her promise to drive back to Manitoba with the kids to visit their friends. Happily, the three planned their trip. The first leg would take them to Saskatoon where they would spend two fun-filled days with Justine's Australian friend, her husband, and their three energetic children. There would be yet another activity to pursue or another conversation to have, as was the case whenever the two families got together. So it was much later in the afternoon before Justine, Aaron, and Kiri embarked upon the second leg of their exciting return to Winnipeg via Yorkton.

241

When they mapped out their route, Justine had given considerable thought to stopping in Melville to visit Grandma again. She'd been so distressed after seeing her in the home that she wondered if it was wise to subject them to the experience a second time in as many years. Subsequently, Justine decided to continue on the Yellowhead and bypass Highway Ten, which would have taken them into Melville.

Never in a 100 years would Justine have thought they would not find a single motel room in Yorkton on a Monday night. As one after another "no vacancy" signs flashed before their eyes, Justine decided they should decide what to do over dinner.

Obtaining a table in a restaurant proved equally challenging. Sensing that Aaron and Kiri were becoming anxious, Justine reassured them that as soon as they placed their order she would telephone Uncle Johann to ask him to book accommodation for them at a motel in Melville, only sixty kilometres away.

Fortunately, they got into a quaint motel on Ninth Avenue, and since they were all worn out upon arrival, they were soon sound asleep in the two double beds with eiderdown quilts, which were blissfully reminiscent of Grandma's cozy bedcovers. Waking before her children, Justine was faced with a dilemma. Since St. Paul Old Folks Home was located mere blocks west of the number ten, she decided to take a few moments to visit with her grandmother.

Still, she did not like to renege, having repeatedly taught her children that their word was "golden." Waiting until Aaron and Kiri had consumed a hearty breakfast of French toast and bacon, one of their favourites, Justine spoke.

"I would like to suggest a minor change to our travel plans. Since we're in Melville, I want to spend a little time with my grandma. I realize we had all agreed we would not see her this year, but I don't feel right driving by without stopping to give her a hug."

"But Mommy, it was so hard to visit Grandma last summer when she didn't remember any of us. Later I heard you weeping when you thought I was asleep, and you know I don't like it when you cry," Aaron protested.

"Me, either," echoed Kiri. Justine had seldom cried in front of her children, so she didn't want to upset them. Still, she knew she had to see her grandma at least once more.

242

It was love, pure love that lifted the veil of senility that had enshrouded Amelia Warner for the past three years. It was a miraculous seven or eight moments of time that she saw them with crystal clear recognition.

"Oh, Justine. You have come all the way from Edmonton with Aaron and Kiri just to see me!" Justine stood rooted to the spot as tears of joy slid down her cheeks. Not so with her children, though, as they flew into their great-grandmother's outstretched arms for one of her much-sought-after hugs. Recovering from her wonder, Justine too joined in her grandmother's warm embrace.

None was willing to release her, until soon Amelia said, "Come with me, Aaron and Kiri. I want to give you all something to remember me by, although I don't have much left since my own children sold everything in an auction. Look here. I have found two dimes for each of you. Let's put them in this little container along with these buttons from my old dresses, some of which had been your Mommy's favourites."

Immediately after she presented Justine, Aaron, and Kiri with her final gifts, the fog of senile dementia again separated Amelia from those she so dearly loved.

 **243**

In death as in life, Amelia Warner put the needs of others before her own. In her eighty-sixth year, she slipped from this world into the next in mid-November of 1981, having waited until after the birthdays of two of her grandchildren, Justine and Elaine Cardinal, who were fifty-one weeks apart to the day. Amelia would not have wanted anyone to suffer on her behalf, and even though her time to meet her Maker came in the midst of a bleak winter on the Canadian prairie, there was a most unusual moderation in the weather.

After a lengthy spell of bitter cold, the morning of Amelia's funeral dawned bright and clear, with brilliant sunshine warming the atmosphere. By the afternoon when the bereaved journeyed to the Redeemer Lutheran Cemetery outside Melville for the interment, they had removed their heavy outerwear and wore shirt sleeves.

Throughout the day of her grandmother's funeral, and for years and even decades later, Justine quivered when she realized how close she'd come to missing those miraculous moments when Amelia recognized her, Aaron, and Kiri. Thirty years later, whenever Justine sat and held the small oval Yardley tin in the palm of her hand with the picture of a mother and her two children on the lid, she could still hear her grandmother's words and feel the warmth of her hugs.

As she gazed at the decorative tin, she wondered where, why, and when her grandmother had received the container, which might have at one time held a bar of soap or a candle made from lavender. Whereas its origin and contents would remain an enigma, it still occupied a spot of prominence in Justine's living room and contained the four dimes and the assortment of colourful buttons from her grandma's dresses.

When Amelia had presented them to Justine, Aaron, and Kiri, she deemed them her parting gifts to her granddaughter and her great-grandchildren who had viewed her more as their grandmother than they ever would Ursula. However, Amelia Warner's final gift would be far more precious, as never again would Justine Forrester doubt the presence of God and the wonder of His love.

Finally, in the summer of 1984, Ursula and Ned decided that if they would ever see her daughters in Alberta, they would have to make the journey west, since none could be bothered to come back to Manitoba.

Ursula had listened the Sunday afternoon when Justine telephoned and perfunctorily expressed that she had returned to the paying workforce. Alberta apparently was not the "land of milk and honey" that they'd originally anticipated and the company that had been exceedingly extravagant when enticing them into relocating was in serious financial difficulty. As Fred had announced one evening when he arrived home from work unusually early, "This company has one foot on a skateboard, and the other on a banana peel!"

Now, since all three of her daughters were employed outside of their homes, Ursula realized that they'd like never return to Virden. Justine especially would never leave the majesty of the mountains, thought Ursula, which is where they always loved to camp.

After taking weeks to convince Ned that they could make the trip, Ned decided that he wanted to venture out to Oak Lake and check on the tenant farming his land before leaving the next day. Knowing that he'd be driving most of the first leg, he let Ursula drive.

By the time they were headed west back to Virden, the setting sun reflected off the windshield, blinding Ursula who, for the balance of her days, would never recall seeing a cyclist on the side of the road. Indeed, it took her several minutes after she'd struck him to realize that her vehicle had made contact. Glancing in his rear-view mirror, Ned was the first to know that something bad had happened, and he finally convinced Ursula to stop the car and turn around. Arriving back on the scene, she was appalled to see the twisted frame of a bicycle in the ditch and an elderly man sprawled several feet in the tall grass.

As two bystanders attempted to resuscitate him, another person raced ahead to town to alert the ambulance, but the aged Caucasian male was pronounced dead upon arrival at the Emergency department of Virden District Hospital. With four eyewitnesses testifying that she had initially fled the scene, Ursula Clemens, at sixty years of age, was charged with vehicular manslaughter. Ned, incensed with the indictment, threw his full financial support behind his wife.

Ursula contacted the Criminal Law Office of Sheps & Sheps in Winnipeg, very aware of their auspicious history of successfully reducing an indictable crime to a less serious summary conviction. Once again, Mr. Sheps proved why he was extolled as the best criminal lawyer in the province of Manitoba; in due process of the law, Ursula's charge was reduced to criminal negligence. By pleading guilty and agreeing to the suspension of her driver's licence for five years, the actual settlement occurred outside the law courts.

245

When her mother lost her memory, Ursula was convinced that little remained that could make her life bleaker. Even when Johann had telephoned to tell her that Amelia had been diagnosed with cancer of the cervix and the doctor was recommending, in view of the senile dementia, no active course of treatment, Ursula had not been as distressed as when her own mother ceased to recognize her.

On the fateful day of the auction, Amelia had been so angry with her children that Ursula had neither the chance to express her birthday wishes nor to say goodbye. When it had become abundantly clear why Johann had picked her up at the Old Folks Home and that there was no changing his mind, Amelia had demanded he drive her back and then refused to speak to them for the balance of their stay. Subsequently, Ursula and Ned returned to Virden without taking her with them as they had anticipated and, by their next trip, Amelia had already become senile. Never again would Ursula visit her mother when she had not the slightest awareness of her identity.

However, when forced to sign the legal agreement that her driver's licence would be revoked, Ursula was devastated. She instantly envisioned herself reverting back to that appalling level of dependency that she'd been subjected to when initially married to Clarence Cardinal. Obviously the anticipated trip to Alberta had to be cancelled, because Ned refused to drive the full distance. Neither Ursula nor Ned would consider any other mode of transportation, and when Justine suggested that they take a bus, the train, or an airplane, her idea was absolutely rejected.

Hence, five years passed with Ursula and Ned not venturing beyond a fifty-mile radius of Virden. And then when Ursula learned that she would be required to repeat her driving test, she stubbornly refused. Soon in the midst of all her other cares and woe, Ursula could not fall asleep at night. Regardless of how tired she was, she tossed and turned night after night until the wee hours of the morning. She'd soak in a nice warm bath, read a boring book, or have a nightcap; still, she simply could not drift off into the repose that she needed in order to feel energized the next day.

One particularly frustrating night, she got up, closed the door so Ned could not hear her from his bedroom, and reached under the bed for the tote bag full of pills. Lifting up handfuls of her little gems and letting them run through her fingers, Ursula wondered what harm could happen if she swallowed two or three. Even though she no longer knew which drug was which, or what any of them was meant to do, they'd likely all relax her enough to make her drop off to sleep. Eventually selecting a bright pink and yellow capsule along with a sky-blue tablet—or perhaps two because they were so tiny—Ursula quietly got a glass of cold water from the kitchen, and swallowed four—or was it five?—of her unique collectibles.

The next morning, Ned was just about at the end of his patience when he decided to see why Ursula was not preparing breakfast. When he called to her several times and heard no reply, he ventured into her bedroom. She was curled up, sound asleep, so he reached over and forcibly shook her shoulder. But she remained unresponsive.

Ursula seldom slept so deeply. He was about to panic when she turned over and snapped, "What do you want? Can't you see I am sleeping for a change?"

If Ned had not been concerned, he might have let her stay in bed; but her eyes were glassy and her speech was slurred. What if she had taken the wrong medicine? Oh, God, what should he do? Then he remembered Dr. Burke and how kind she always was with Ursula. After telephoning her office, the doctor's nurse told Ned to take his wife to Emergency while she contacted Dr. Burke.

It was no easy task trying to get Ursula out of bed and dressed. She kept flopping over and pushing him away, saying that she wanted to go back to her dream. At last, Ned managed to get her into the backseat of the car where she promptly fell over as though drunk. They were soon met at the entrance of the Emergency department, where two orderlies helped Ned to place her on the stretcher.

Soon Dr. Burke arrived. Once she'd thoroughly examined Ursula, whose vital signs started to stabilize, she turned to Ned and asked what medications his wife had taken within the past twelve hours. Before he could respond, Ursula began to come around.

"What am I doing at the hospital, Ned? For once I was having a good sleep, and you drag me here. What is the matter with your head?"

Dr. Burke didn't wait for Ned's answer and she began to drill Ursula with questions. When her patient refused to provide information, the doctor's usual pleasant bedside manner vanished. Ursula was now furious with the doctor as well her husband, who'd hauled her off to the hospital and interrupted her most wonderful dream of being in Hans's arms.

"I need to know more about your drug usage, Ursula, thus I intend to make a referral to the health unit. By early afternoon, a community nurse will come around to visit, so please plan to be at home."

246

Once again, Miss Barrett followed up on Dr. Burke's request. Ursula sat in her rocker in the living room and smugly watched as Miss Barrett painstakingly went through every cabinet, dresser drawer, cupboard, and closet in the two-bedroom bungalow.

Ursula felt better rested than she had in months, and she was thoroughly enjoying what she knew would amount to nothing other than a futile and unproductive quest. There was no way that Miss Barrett could find her stash. Even with the light on in her room, the area under the bed that hid her two small pieces of luggage was completely in the dark, and the nurse had not come equipped with a flashlight.

When she was ready to acknowledge that Ursula was not concealing drugs, Miss Barrett thanked them for being cooperative and left. From that day onward, Ursula made certain to take her pills, and never more than two, as soon as she went to bed, ensuring that she would readily fall asleep and then awaken the next morning at a timely hour without causing anyone to become unnecessarily alarmed.

247

Everyone concurred that it had been the four Mann brothers who originated the trend of family reunions in the German Lutheran townships. Then when the Lutz family promptly followed suit the subsequent year, Albert began to talk about planning the first Warner/Werner Reunion. Instantly Katherina was in full agreement, and the minute the dynamic duo, as they were affectionately called by their coffee clique, put their heads together, the wheels of organization were set in motion. They decided on a date of July 1988, long before any other member of the family knew of its emergence.

Emulating her Aunt Margareta who was long since dead, Katherina continued to stroll about town for twenty or thirty minutes every day during the warmer seasons on the prairie. She carried a walking stick, which had been presented to her years ago by an infatuated wood carver, but she only used it as a means to portend any potential hazard that might be invisible to her. Holding her head erect and her back straight, Katherina still gave the impression of being sturdy on her feet, and her trim figure graced every street corner in Neudorf.

Katherina was always impeccably dressed and attractively groomed. Many of her devout friends still considered her to be the most comely woman in their community, with her soft, smooth skin and manicured fingernails, interesting considering her limited sight. Katherina's other senses had obviously heightened and, combined with her prodigious memory and razor sharp mind, she was still a force with which to be reckoned.

Perhaps Katherina's most enthusiastic supporter was her nephew Albert, who, having been pampered and adored by his seven older sisters from the moment of his long-awaited birth, far preferred the company of women than to men.

Albert eventually took over farming his father's section of land when Rolf and Maria decided to move into Neudorf. And then when they passed on, his sisters thought it only proper for him to inherit their house in town. Albert, who'd always led a charmed life, unlike his father found mixed farming tedious, so he promptly sold off the livestock. Grain farming still had its seasons of intense activity; but once the crops were sown in the spring and harvested in the autumn and the fields were fallowed, the rest of the time was his own.

No one could recall who'd started the coffee clique, but it had long since become a significant part of the seven members' day. When Katherina had sold both of her businesses to Vera Roth, she missed the daily interaction of other people. So after being urged by Albert, she finally decided to join them, on one condition.

The infamous Silent Critics of Neudorf were still indelibly etched in her memory, and under no circumstance would Katherina tolerate the slightest hint of rumour mongering. To her way of thinking, nothing was as ill-mannerly as gossiping about another person; so if she heard even a whisper of a scandal, she'd leave and never return to their group.

With Katherina as a member, the activities of the coffee clique took a decided upturn; they'd sooner discuss current events and books they'd read than complain about the weather. Of course, the friends of seven also initiated practically every fowl supper, cribbage tournament, and whist drive to be organized in their close-knit community.

248

It had to have been over twenty years now since Dr. Fraya Roth had first walked into the Neudorf Café with a gentleman unknown to most of them. Katherina had not heard his voice for more than two decades, and she could only see a dim outline of his still-handsome face, but she knew instantly that he was Hans Gerhart.

"Welcome back to our small community, Hans. I have been awaiting your return for many years. Unless you are the busiest farmer in the English township, I wonder why it has taken you so long."

Not surprisingly, she was accurate in her recollection, and Hans was at a loss for words. After expressing his condolences to Gustav Warner on the death of his son and being subjected to the most ill-mannered rebuff of his life, Hans had vowed that he wanted nothing further to do with any member of the Warner family.

Katherina, though, had treated him with kindness and respect during their every encounter, and it occurred to him now to claim that he'd been exceedingly busy over the past years. He *had* been, as he had thrown himself into farming during the day and working in the pharmacy in the evenings. However, the sad truth was that Hans Gerhart did not have the heart to interact with anyone who would remind him of the past and of all he had lost.

Soon Albert Werner, a man he'd never met, came to his rescue.

"I'd heard it rumoured that someone had purchased Mr. Brown's farm in the English township; but far be it from me to risk your invaluable membership in our coffee group, Katherina, by spreading the slightest inkling of gossip. Now would you please introduce us to this gentleman? We are anxious to meet anyone known to both Dr. Roth and yourself."

In actuality, Albert had been thoroughly apprised of the stranger to whom Harold Brown had sold the other half-section of his farm. His cousin had gone to great lengths to complain about how the elderly English farmer had reneged on his promise to give Johann the right of first refusal, and then suddenly an outsider tilled his fields year after year.

Albert remembered how pleased he was that Mr. Brown had not sold to Johann. He secretly disliked his cousin for many reasons, not the least of which was his greed for prime farmland and the fact that he shunned everyone in Neudorf, including Aunt Katherina. Johann was also morose and ill-humoured, perhaps to a greater degree than his father had been. But his lack of deference for Aunt Katherina was unbelievably rude.

From that day onward, Hans was accepted as a member of their coffee clique; but he could not meet with the group on a regular basis. He still maintained half ownership in the Melville Pharmacy and, being solely responsible for farming a section and a half of land required a great deal of his time and energy. Unlike Albert, Hans did not have two adolescent sons to whom he could delegate a portion of the work.

But after years of being on his own, other than with his staff and the patrons at the pharmacy, Hans realized just how lonely he was, and soon he found himself longing to drive into town for a refreshing cup of coffee.

He was especially drawn to Fraya and on occasion he wondered whether they could become more than friends. But Hans recognized that Ursula had been his one true love and Leonard Warner had been Fraya's, so whenever he was tempted to pursue a courtship, the image of his dead friend loomed before his eyes.

Still, Hans was happy to be included in the coffee clique and welcomed the chance to re-establish his friendship with Katherina. He marvelled at how capably she was managing, and he hoped that he could maintain a comparable level of competence if he reached her advanced age. He also was thoroughly enjoying Albert, who he hardly believed was a male descendant of Werner ancestry.

Leonard had never been sullen and ill-mannered like his youngest brother, but during the years he had been Hans's friend, he was a serious and deeply dedicated young man. Albert, on the other hand, was a convivial individual with a warm sense of humour and a spontaneous amicability. He viewed life with the bright and clear vision of innocence and youth and could buoy the spirits of the grumpiest person. At last Hans asked, "Are you sure that you really are a Werner, Albert?"

Bursting into laughter, Albert needed several seconds to recover.

"When my parents persisted in trying for a son after the birth of seven daughters," he explained, "it was with absolute certainty that they would dote upon me. I quite simply do not have the right to be anything but jovial!"

~ 249 ~

Once Katherina and Albert selected the date of the Warner/Werner Family Reunion, the next issue was its locale. Hans had stopped in at the café for his coffee that afternoon, but up until this point he had refrained from giving his opinion.

Now, however, he was quick to contribute.

"You surely would want to host your reunion in the new community hall that you've just built. It appears to be plenty large enough, and then the children can play in the surrounding park on a warm summer evening. It is a beautiful site and, as far as I can figure, most of the older members of your community still live in Neudorf or on their farms and the young people who have left can travel with far greater ease than can their parents."

"That's very thoughtful of you, Hans, but I don't imagine many of the younger family members will come back to our small village, especially out of convenience and respect for us old relics," Katherina responded sagely.

But Albert supported Hans's recommendation.

"Should the young folks not come, it will only be their loss, because I assure you that we will have the time of our lives. Hans, can I count on you to be my right hand man when it comes to getting the hall ready for our memorable event?"

At that juncture in the conversation, Dr. Fraya Roth, who still saw patients but now set aside an hour every afternoon to join her friends at the Neudorf Café, promptly replied, "I too will help in any way that I can. My only regret is that I am neither a Warner nor a Werner, and subsequently I shall not be included. I guess we shall have to arrange our own outing for that weekend away from town, won't we Hans, so we don't feel left out of the festivities?"

"Absolutely not! If fate had not intervened, Fraya and Hans, both of you would have married into our family, and I expect you to be right, front, and centre at our reunion. Other than Albert and his dear wife, I consider you two more like family than any of my blood relatives," Katherina proclaimed.

~ 250 ~

When the invitations were printed, Hans Gerhart and Dr. Fraya Roth received them first, by hand delivery. As pleased as he was to be included in the Warner/Werner Family Reunion, Hans could not decide whether to attend. What if Ursula were to suddenly appear in front of him? He was still haunted by her, and he had laboured like a slave for most of his life in part to attempt to erase her image from his mind.

Nonetheless, being addicted to work had never proved successful, and now the mere possibility of meeting Ursula face to face overwhelmed him. Hans was torn between the conflicting feelings of delight and despair. He yearned to take her into his arms and to be buried in her embrace. But then he became filled with fury that they had lost one another and wasted their true love. Never before had Hans Gerhart experienced such a roller coaster of emotions, until he fervently wished he'd not heard about the Warner/Werner Family Reunion.

~ 251 ~

When Ursula opened her invitation, she scarcely took the time to read the details before tossing it into the garbage. What would they think of next? Who could she possibly want to see at a family reunion? And even if she did want to go, how would she get there, since Neudorf was well beyond Ned's circumscribed fifty-mile radius?

They had not travelled anywhere except to Brandon for years, and other than the occasional trips Johann and Rita made to Virden, Ursula was even deprived from the opportunity to spend time with her favourite nephew, August. His three older brothers could not be bothered to come with their parents, and she could not remember when she last saw them.

On the other hand, Otto and his new wife along with their four children were much more diligent about visiting Ursula and Ned, usually making the journey once or twice every year. Otto was a completely changed man since he married Evelyn, and he'd been surprisingly supportive during Ursula's trials when she'd struck and killed the elderly cyclist. To this day, Ursula had never understood what such an old man was doing on a bicycle, much less riding on the Trans-Canada Highway.

But when Otto and Evelyn offered to journey to Virden and drive Ursula and Ned to the Warner/Werner Family Reunion in Neudorf, Ursula was overwhelmed with trepidation and adamantly refused to go.

252

Should he attend out of spite for Johann? Or would he go to satisfy his burning desire to see Ursula, if but for one last time? In the end, Hans skipped the afternoon activities, waiting until the evening banquet was about to begin in the Neudorf Community Hall on July 17, 1988, and then appeared only because of his profound admiration and respect for Katherina Werner.

When the family's matriarch entered the building that had been constructed on the site of her late Uncle Peter's lumberyard, Katherina was gently and unobtrusively guided to the head table at the front of the beautifully adorned room by Albert and his cheerful, plump wife, Diane.

The expectant guests surfaced from their seats like a wave in a standing ovation. She was elegant in a long black gown with her soft silvery hair piled high on her head, as she took her place at the decorative table.

253

The meal, which consisted of all the traditional German fare, had been prepared by the women of the two townships. And it was delectable. Seated beside Fraya at a round table with four younger people, the two longstanding friends enjoyed each other's company without providing any explanation about their inclusion in the family celebration. As the sumptuous dinner was being served, Hans scanned the room for Ursula after observing that she was not one of the guests of honour seated at the head table.

Long before Katherina's entrance, Hans had noticed Johann and presumably his wife on the left side. And although he had not seen him in decades, his older brother and another woman were to the right. But Ursula was nowhere in sight. When Hans finally came to accept that she was not in attendance, he was embarrassed by his tears of bitter disappointment and he was forced to turn away.

Then Hans saw her. Her resemblance to Ursula Warner was striking, but she was far too young to be his true love. Knowing that he was staring, Hans tried to avert his eyes; still he kept returning to gaze at the woman who was helping to move the centre tables along the walls to make room for a dance floor.

Planning to pay his regards to Katherina and then leave the festivities with Fraya as she prepared to depart, Hans now sat frozen in his chair. Noticing that he'd become remarkably still, Fraya followed Hans's line of vision.

"Oh, my God, Hans. She looks just like Ursula Warner. But Ursula would be of our vintage, and I'd say that woman is in her early or mid-forties."

Who was she? And was that her husband who had entered the hall by her side? The overhead lights, which had been dimmed during dinner, were now turned up high as the volunteers and guests began to clear the dishes in anticipation of a presentation to honour Katherina and then a dance.

Katherina, ironically, was the only individual in the township who may have discovered her identity. And the weight of the secret that had been revealed to her was still a burden, years after Amelia was gone, since Katherina could no more betray her dearest friend and sister-in-law in death than she could have in life.

254

"I told you that we should not have come, Richard. Every time I go to a table to meet one of your relatives, the conversation comes to an embarrassed halt, and I just know that they're talking about me behind my back."

Richard quietly assured her.

"Please, don't let them upset you, Barbara. We have every right to be here. Even if we had to find out about the reunion from Carl, I am tired of being the Werner family secret. I did not receive an invitation since I only just found out that Carl was my cousin."

Pausing to drink his wine, he continued.

"I am much more fortunate than my father was. He died without knowing that his father was Friedrich, Gustav's eldest son, and that Mathias, Julianna, and Elisabetha were his half-siblings, even though he lived his entire life three blocks down the street from them. But just because we chose to come to the reunion does not mean I will tell them who I am. And if they won't talk to you, then stay at our table and visit with Carl and Donna."

Taking her husband's advice, she was perhaps relieved that Richard did not intend to disclose his ancestry. Barbara decided to leave them to their gossiping and enjoy Donna's company. She'd ignore the stares and whispers she'd felt since first stepping into the hall. But now she was not altogether sure that she wanted to be a Werner, even if only by marriage.

Sometime later, when Barbara was returning to the table after using the lavatory, an elderly gentleman subtly motioned to her.

As she approached him, he arose from his chair and greeted her courteously.

"Good evening, please allow me to introduce myself. My name is Hans Gerhart, and I was wondering if I might ask you for a few moments of your time.

"I could not help but notice that a number of the guests, including myself, have been staring at you to the point of rudeness. And please let me explain that I am neither a Warner nor a Werner; I am only here at the express invitation of Katherina and her nephew Albert, very dear friends of mine. I don't suppose that you might humour an old man and join me for a cup of coffee?"

"I think that I would enjoy having coffee with you," said Barbara, "but I must let my cousin know I have not become lost in the festivities. I shall return in a minute. By the way, my name is Barbara Schmidt and, like you, I am not a family member."

Once they were seated at his table, Hans began.

"I cannot speak for everyone, but you are the spitting image of a young woman from Neudorf I once knew and loved more than life itself. And now that I am much closer, I am even more fascinated because your mannerisms are so similar to hers."

"How long has it been since you last saw her?" asked Barbara. "I once read that we all have a twin in the world, so maybe I am hers. What was her name?

"I'm sorry," she continued, "I'm bombarding you with questions and not giving you a chance to answer any of them." Barbara laughed and Hans thought it sounded like the Hallelujah Chorus.

"That is quite all right. I cannot believe how much you remind me of Ursula. She too was invariably full of questions. She was an inquisitive, bright, vibrant, young woman with more than ample energy for two people. I also have heard that everyone has a lookalike, but my true love was closer to my age than yours. Ursula Warner would be in her mid-sixties by now, so she would be old enough to be your mother, not your twin."

Suddenly it was Barbara's turn to stare.

"Why did you say that? And I did not know that she was a Warner."

"I am dreadfully sorry," Hans replied. "Please do not take any offence. It is a very long story, and I'm certain that you would rather be dancing with your husband than listening to a lonely old man bring up the past."

"Neither Richard nor I are fond of dancing," she said, deciding she'd rather hear more from Hans.

Thus, Hans began his synopsis of every detail that he could remember about Ursula Warner. And Barbara never once interrupted.

Stopping in his discourse, Hans was lost in reverie. From across the room, Albert had glanced again in the direction of the table where Hans and Barbara Schmidt, a woman to whom he had been introduced earlier in the evening, were seated side by side. They both leaned forward, Barbara listening intently while Hans spoke. At that moment, the lights in the hall came on, and Albert froze as he viewed the two of them in profile.

Albert Werner was a convivial man, he was nobody's fool; he instantly struck up an earnest conversation with Otto regarding the whereabouts and current name of his younger sister. He now knew what had been intriguing every adult present at the Warner/Werner Family Reunion Banquet.

255

Wiping away tears, Barbara was uncertain how to respond. She was overcome with empathy for the kindly elderly gentleman. Even then she sensed that more, much more than his tragically sad story, was causing her feelings of distress.

From the first moment she'd looked into Hans's eyes, Barbara had felt a connection that she could not explain. At last, she uttered, "I am so sorry. I think that I always realized how fortunate I was that Hilda and Josef Wendel adopted me as an infant.

"They were wonderful with me throughout my growing years, but since they've both passed on, I've wondered about my biological parents and whether I should search for my mother. Now hearing about you spending your childhood in an orphanage, I'm appalled by my selfishness. I've so often wallowed in self-pity simply because I did not know who my real parents were."

Barbara reached across and wrapped her arms around Hans. And it had been longer than he cared to remember since he'd received such warm spontaneity.

256

The telephone call came on a scorching summer afternoon on the third Sunday in June 1989. Ned and Ursula had only just returned from lunch at the Shell on the highway, and he had yet to lie down on the sofa for his nap. Fortunately, though, he was in the washroom, and she was the first to pick up the receiver.

As soon as she heard the man's voice on the line responding to her curt salutation, "Hello, this is Hans Gerhart, and I would please like to speak with Ursula," she dropped the phone as though it was a burning piece of wood. Dare she bring it back up to her ear? Ursula could hear the urgency in his tone.

"Hello, hello. Is anyone there? Please answer me. I want to talk to Ursula. This is Hans Gerhart calling."

Just then Ned trudged into the living room.

"Did I hear the telephone?" he asked. "Who would call during my nap?"

Ignoring Ned and quickly gripping the telephone to her ear, Ursula listened for several seconds to the voice she'd spent her lifetime craving to hear.

"No, it is too late! It is far, far too late!" she cried, before hanging up the receiver.

257

The day seemed endless. While Ned napped, Ursula sat immobilized in her brown La-Z-Boy chair, casting her eyes back and forth between the hastily disconnected telephone and Ned snoring on the couch. Then, fifteen minutes before he was due to awaken, she arose, still in a daze, and went into the kitchen to brew his tea.

After he'd emptied the cup, she asked, "Why don't we go for a drive now that you are rested? I feel like going for a walk around my old farm, and maybe we could stop in and visit with Will and Shirley Beaver. We haven't seen them for a long time, and they might even want to come with us to check on their crops."

The instant Ursula had hung up on Hans Gerhart, she knew what she must do. The sound of his voice had rung her death knell. How could she bear to tell him what she had done so many years ago? Then, on what she'd abruptly decided was to be her last day on earth, she got the compelling urge to reconnect with her roots.

Since there was not enough time for her to return to her father's homestead, and because it was well beyond Ned's circumscribed driving distance, she would commune with nature on the land that she and Clarence had farmed in Manitoba. She neither knew whence Hans telephoned nor how he tracked her down after decades of her yearning for him, but if he was determined to find her, she did not have much time.

Aside from her unforgivable act of giving away their love child, Ursula had no desire to let Hans see her as a stout old woman, far preferring to die knowing that he would retain the image of her as his pretty young love. Fortunately for her, Ursula Clemens had the means for her demise ready at her disposal.

258

Seated at the large kitchen table, Ursula began to wonder if she had made a mistake choosing to stop and see her friends. Not only did Shirley and Will accompany them to the farm and walk for what seemed like miles, but they also insisted that Ursula and Ned stay for supper. Ursula had little appetite and furthermore did not want food in her stomach to slow down the action of her pills.

Once, though, when lagging behind the others near the willow trees, Ursula surprisingly experienced the serenity and restoration of nature; for fleeting moments, she felt like the vibrant young woman who'd been so in love with Hans.

Unexpectedly, she began to doubt her precipitous decision. Was she making the right choice? Could she not allow herself to wait and at least see Hans, and find out why he called? Or should she go to her grave with the memory of their love forever untouched?

On the other hand, what if she divorced Ned Clemens? Could she and Hans finally be together for their twilight years? What would her daughters say about their mother running off with another man when she was sixty-five years old? Would it matter since, other than Elaine, the others rarely visited?

Still, she could not deny her secret. And although no longer bound by the oath to her late father, if Hans were ever to learn the truth, Ursula knew she could never endure his wrath.

259

Arriving back in Virden just as they were starting up their street, Ursula suddenly had a dreadful feeling. What if Hans was sitting at the door of the house?

"Ned, would you mind driving around the block? I would like to see our big old home on the corner."

"What has come over you? You have been acting strange all day," Ned said grumpily before complying with Ursula's request.

After confirming that her long-lost love was not lingering around her home, Ursula hastily entered, eager to execute her plan as soon as Ned went to bed. Deep in thought, she was startled when Ned spoke.

"Look, you left the phone off the hook. Where is your head today, Ursula? What if someone was trying to call us?"

The last thing Ursula wanted was to become embroiled in an argument with Ned, so she quickly apologized before going into her bedroom to prepare for a long hot soak in the tub. She wanted to relax and reminisce about the two summers when she and Hans had been so captivated with each other that no one else in the world existed. During those ecstatic days, their lives had been full of promise, with the two young lovers committing their hearts and souls to their glorious future together.

Ursula did not want to dwell on their love lost to the calamities of life, on the years she'd spent in frustration and drudgery, yearning for the one and only man who'd ever fulfilled her. Rather, she chose to relive every enraptured moment that Hans Gerhart and she had shared, rejoicing in the passion of a love so profound that she was now ready to die to spare him from learning about the consequences of their actions.

Much later, as though in a trance, Ursula Warner returned to her room, snugly closed the door, and brought the tote bag with her first collection of pills onto her bed. Ursula ravenously swallowed pill after pill until the small pouch was empty and then crawled blissfully under the covers.

⤜⤙ 260 ⤚⤛

Justine heard the telephone ringing as she was opening the front door. Reaching it just in time, she was surprised by the distress in Elaine's voice.

"I can't understand what you are saying. Please speak into the receiver."

When Justine eventually deciphered what Elaine was telling her, she sank down into a chair in the kitchen. Her mother had had a stroke and had been rushed to Brandon General Hospital. Justine hadn't known that her mother suffered from hypertension, which seemed unusual since she'd heard about every other of her ailments. Surely if Ursula's blood pressure had been so high, Dr. Burke would have prescribed antihypertensive agents and monitored whether they were controlling her condition.

She first tried to telephone Ned and, when she could not reach him, she called the hospital to speak to the nursing supervisor. After identifying herself, she asked, "Can you please tell me how my mother is doing? Have the doctors been able to bring her blood pressure under control? Which side of her body has been affected by the stroke?"

In short order, Mrs. Powell questioned Justine's information and then clarified that Ursula had not been admitted with a cerebrovascular accident, but rather because of a massive overdose of drugs.

Ursula's vital signs had stabilized and, although she was in a coma, she would not be alive had her husband not heard her collapse on the floor of the bathroom adjoining his bedroom. Obviously she'd needed to empty her bladder, but the fact that she'd been able to get up and walk in her heavily stuporous state was amazing, as was the rapid response of the Virden paramedics who immediately began to pump her stomach.

By the time the ambulance reached Brandon, the emergency medical workers had removed what they identified as "the most colourful and assorted mass of semi-digested medication they'd ever seen in a human being's stomach."

～261～

After being unconscious for six days, Ursula awoke from her coma, furious. Her heart was sound and she was physically strong given her age, which is why the team of physicians had been confident that she could be saved.

Poor Ned was there to bear the brunt of her ire.

"Where am I? That's not you, Ned? Don't tell me you brought me to the bloody hospital again? What the hell is the matter with your stupid head? Why can't you figure out that I am sick to death of you? I just want to die, and you keep rushing me to the damn hospital to save my worthless life."

Ned sat stunned, mutely staring at the woman he'd married late in life. Surely Ursula could not mean what she was saying? It must be all those pills that she'd swallowed. He could not be the problem, especially after everything he'd done for her these past few days.

Every morning after making his own breakfast, he'd made the long drive back to Brandon where he sat patiently waiting for her to awaken. He had even eaten his lunch in the cafeteria, had his afternoon nap in the uncomfortable hospital chair, and then driven back to Virden in the evening, where he had to find his own supper and eat alone.

And what about the endless questions he'd answered until he felt like it was his fault that she'd hoarded her pills? Imagine being forbidden to touch anything in her bedroom in the house that he had built and paid for.

At least Miss Barrett's visit was short this time. As soon as she'd found the remnants of medication in the tote bag still beside the bed, she had drilled Ned, repeatedly asking why he knew nothing about Ursula's stash before grabbing the nearly empty pouch and storming out.

262

Once Ursula made a full recovery, she was transferred to the new psychiatric unit at the General Hospital. She was alert enough to appreciate that she did not have to be sent to the mausoleum on the outskirts of Brandon. She had spent sufficient time in the Hospital for Mental Illnesses, and was happy it had finally been closed and torn down.

Still, Ursula had the presence of mind to wonder what became of Uncle Franz and all of the other inmates. But more importantly, she knew that long-term hospitalization was not in her future. A young female psychiatrist had interviewed and diagnosed her with acute depression with suicidal intentions and recommended a minimum of eight treatments of electroshock therapy.

Appalled by the number of medication vials that Ned produced, Dr. Ainsley stopped all of Ursula's medicine. Only once she ascertained how her patient was responding to the shock therapy would she consider prescribing additional meds.

263

As soon as her last class of students graduated from the college program she administered and her children were out of school, Justine planned a trip back to Manitoba. She suspected that Aaron would not come since he'd found a summer job, and she was only able to convince Kiri to accompany her by promising to bring her best friend, Susan, with them.

After enjoying the anticipated visit with their friends in Saskatoon, Justine drove to Regina to link up with the Trans-Canada Highway and, bypassing Virden, drove straight into Brandon. When they arrived, however, Kiri refused to go into the hospital with Justine to visit with her grandmother. No amount of persuasion could entice the two teenage girls to enter. After buying them a coke and telling them to wait for her in the adjacent park, Justine proceeded into Ursula's room on the fifth floor of her first post-secondary alma mater.

Justine was not prepared for Ursula's decrepit condition, and could barely believe that the shrunken, frail, and broken-spirited woman was her mother. Perhaps for the first time, Justine experienced an unusual disquietude, stemming from her compassion and sorrow for the woman who had given her life. But it was too late.

Ursula was beyond Justine's reach. And the irony that her mother was now choosing to ignore her was not lost on Justine.

～ 264 ～

Determined to return home as soon as possible and anxious to make sure that her other pill collection had not been discovered, Ursula complied with every requirement of the medical and nursing staff. They were optimistic, given her favourable response to the prescribed therapy. And Dr. Ainsley was confident that, with continued supervision by Dr. Burke and the community health nurses, Ursula could soon be discharged.

Over the past two months, Ned had become unusually distant, only making the journey to visit her in the hospital every Sunday afternoon after his nap; but Ursula hardly seemed to care and never commented on his long absences. Although he had yet to reproach her, Ned was still annoyed by her cruel remarks to him—delivered in front of the nurses yet—when she'd come out of the coma. He patiently awaited her apology.

Then there was the business of that strange man who continued to telephone at all hours of the day and night. After disturbing his nap, Ned finally ordered him to stop his incessant attempts to reach Ursula. The tiresome man had still not heeded his warning, and since it had never occurred to Ned to inquire about changing his number, he became increasingly annoyed and continued to slam the receiver down on its cradle.

Neither Ursula nor Ned spoke a word on the ride back to Virden on the morning she was discharged. He wondered when Ursula would say she was sorry and thank him for all of his efforts. But day after day tediously passed as she vacantly went about their routines in a suffocating silence; he began to think that the doctors had sent her home far too early.

～ 265 ～

Again it was the third Sunday of the month when Ursula answered the ringing telephone. She said "Hello" and the male voice on the other end pleaded with her.

"Please, do not hang up the telephone. I only want to speak with you, my dearest Ursula. This is Hans Gerhart, and after so many years, I still long to hear the sound of your lovely voice. As well, I have a very special individual standing beside me. She too would dearly like to express her love for you."

The telephone went dead when Ursula pulled the cord out of its wall connection. This time she did not wait until nightfall. Without a glance at her husband who was still sleeping on the living room sofa, she marched into her bedroom, securely locked the door, and yanked the small suitcase from under the bed. Sitting down on the floor, she stuffed handful after handful of pills into her mouth, ceasing only to stop gagging, and she eventually collapsed into a heap against the wall.

Unknown hours elapsed before her body was discovered. On September 17, 1989, Ursula Warner Cardinal Clemens did not fail this time, and she was confident that she was taking her secret to the grave.

Epilogue

1998

The old farmhouse was still standing. It had been ten years since August had opened the invitation to the first Warner/Werner Family Reunion. A decade had come and gone, and August Warner was standing still. He had made no changes in his life, and like the wallpaper and the paint in the house, he was becoming older and fading.

In an era when the landscape of the Saskatchewan prairie was dotted with abandoned farmyards and the exodus of farmers with their small families to the nearest town was never-ending, Hans Gerhart had constructed a huge four-bedroom, two-storey home in the grove of willows, although still visible to the Warner homestead, on the opposite side of the creek. If he had to build such a monstrosity, why there, where August had to stare at it every time he drove into his own yard?

And, who was that woman and the four young adults? Where had they all come from? And what made them think they could just move into the farming community with Hans Gerhart?

It had scarcely been a year since the reunion, and suddenly they'd surfaced like mushrooms sprouting through the damp soil in the spring. August had anticipated meeting a healthy, young German woman with whom he could share his life, and to rear a houseful of sons. But instead his neighbour, an old man, had obviously found a ready-made family with a mother, her three sons, and a daughter.

Now as August opened the envelope inviting him to the second Warner/Werner Family Reunion, he wondered if he should even bother. He was not confident that his chances of being introduced to someone were better—quite likely they were worse—than they'd been ten years ago. At least then he had looked forward to seeing his favourite Aunt Ursula, but she had not come.

Then August recalled how he had searched every face as the guests entered the hall for the banquet, eagerly anticipating her arrival. He was still astounded by how he had almost rushed up and hugged a woman to whom he would be introduced later in the evening. August had stared at Barbara Schmidt until he thought he might go cross-eyed. She looked, walked, and talked just like her; he was sure his eyes deceived him as he beheld a younger version of Aunt Ursula. Even now when August caught glimpses of Barbara walking along by the creek on the other side of the barbed wire fence, he would stop and stare until he remembered that Aunt Ursula was dead.

Before long he would be too old to raise a family, and he would always be alone on his vast tracts of land without children to reap the fruits of his labours, to appreciate the joy of tilling the soil in the spring, and to stroll among the ripening golden stalks of wheat as they readied for their harvest.

As year after year flew by, August was steadily forced to face the harsh reality that he would not be able to preserve his grandfather's legacy. There would be no progeny to inherit all of the prime farmland that Gustav Warner had struggled and strived to procure over his lifetime solely to bequeath to his descendants.

On the Thursday morning after the reunion, Hans drove up to his farmhouse to find Albert Werner sitting on the stoop with a large thermos perched beside him.

"Good morning, Hans. I see that I have arrived just in time. Come and sit for a few minutes and have a cup of coffee with me."

"It sounds like my preferred way to start a day. I see that you've recovered from your busy weekend," Hans warmly replied, accepting the mug of coffee.

Sitting beside his friend, Albert wondered how to begin.

"First of all, I am to tell you that Diane does not agree with me telling you this and she wants no part of it."

"My goodness, Albert. What's on your mind? Spit it out, man, before I die of curiosity."

"And Hans, you also need to understand that I am not saying this lightly—I have been wrestling with it since I became aware of it, and I've scarcely been able to sleep at night. But, I shall get on with it.

"My enlightenment occurred during the banquet when you and Barbara Schmidt were sitting side by side at a table at the back of the hall. I discerned that you were father and daughter. The longer that I looked, the more convinced I became. And now, as I have already said, I cannot stop thinking about the two of you."

"What have you laced your coffee with this morning, Albert? I think you have taken leave of your senses. As you well know, I don't have a daughter, however much I longed to have children," Hans responded.

"Please hear me out, Hans, since the only reason I'm saying this is because I believe that you have a right to know. After seeing Barbara, I recalled the rumours about Ursula Warner's abrupt departure from the township. Please remember that I have seven older sisters, and it was impossible for me not to overhear all the gossip."

Desperate to lighten his solemn declaration, Albert continued. "Why do you think I drove all the way out here this morning rather than wait until you came into town this afternoon? I could not have Katherina think I was spreading rumours!"

Staring at Albert as though he had two heads, Hans was dumbfounded.

"I am sorry, Hans. Perhaps Diane was right that I should say nothing. Of course, I have no way of proving my suspicion. I was much too young to remember what my cousin looked like, but every adult at the reunion kept commenting on the striking resemblance between Barbara Schmidt and Ursula Warner."

"Oh my God!" said Hans. "No wonder Gustav told Leonard I was never to set foot on the Warner farm again. The whole family must have been mortified, and Ursula would have felt so ashamed and abandoned. Oh, my poor darling Ursula. Of course, her father would have given her no choice but to put the baby up for adoption—to force her to give our child away!"

Hans imagined the anguish to which Ursula would have been subjected. And then he imagined the torment she would have carried with her throughout her life.

Weeks elapsed before Hans Gerhart decided what to do with Albert's staggering information. All of the scattered pieces of his life-long puzzle had finally come together. As soon as Hans thanked his friend for having the courage to share his suspicion, Albert provided Barbara's telephone number and address from the reunion guestbook. Albert also gave him Ursula's contact information, which he'd assiduously sought from Otto. But now it was up to Hans.

Driving back to Melville after a long meditative walk through his wheat fields on a hot autumn afternoon, Hans decided to phone Barbara and ask if she and Richard would meet him for coffee in North Battleford on Saturday morning. She seemed pleased to hear from him, and after consulting with her husband, they agreed to join Hans at the Husky restaurant on the outskirts of town.

Arriving early, Hans was nervous and not sure how to broach the subject of his paternity with a woman he barely knew. Still, he remembered Barbara expressing interest in searching for her birth mother. Now with her biological father's assistance, surely the process could be expedited. He had had little interaction with Richard, but Hans had every reason to hope that her husband would support her quest.

Spotting Hans the moment she entered the coffee shop, Barbara warmly greeted him.

"How nice to see you again, Hans. Do you remember my husband, Richard? I have said so much about our lengthy conversation that he was happy to come along this morning."

After their coffee had been served, Hans was anxious to deal with the matter at hand.

"I am uncertain how to tell you my purpose in asking you to meet with me, so I will just say it. I wonder if you recall Albert Werner, the master of ceremonies at the reunion, since I am here because of his conjecture."

Pausing in vain to settle the butterflies swarming in his stomach, Hans continued.

"I have since learned that Ursula abruptly left her father's farm in the fall of 1941, and many speculated that she was pregnant. If indeed it were true, then I am the father of the baby that she would have birthed in the late spring of 1942."

From the moment Barbara told him about the telephone call, Richard had been suspicious. Now he was incensed with the man's implication.

"What are you saying? Are you suggesting that you are Barbara's father? And if so, can you prove it?"

"Richard, what has come over you? You are being exceedingly rude to a man who has driven a long way to see us," said Barbara.

"Good God, Barbara, just think about it. If Ursula Warner was your mother, than you and I are cousins. All the time I had thought that I was the Werner family secret, but if what this man says is true, then we're both the lost children of an uncle and his niece's concealed liaisons. What a bloody good thing I decided not to say anything to anyone at that damn reunion about Friedrich Werner being my grandfather! If this is true, all of our children could have been born freaks."

"Well, they are all perfectly normal, so calm down, Richard. If what Hans says is true, then we are only second cousins. I've wanted to search for my mother, so if Hans is my father, together we can try to find Ursula."

"No damn way! I forbid you from looking for Ursula Warner. What has been said today will not leave these four walls. Now let's go!"

❧ ❧ ❧

Hans sometimes wished that Albert had not told him about Ursula possibly being the mother of his only child. Still, he could not stop thinking about Barbara being his daughter. Not only was he a father, but he was also grandfather to four young people he had yet to meet. As the cold months of a prolonged winter slowly passed, he found himself dreaming about how he'd felt during those two wonderful summers he spent on the Warner farm. Amelia had come to view him as one of her own children, and Ursula had been the light of his otherwise solitary and sombre life.

From his earliest memory, Hans had longed to be part of a family, and now when it was highly likely that he had his own offspring, the old man was denied the chance to know and love them.

Inevitably the sun began to warm the earth, the snow began to melt, and spring began to return to the frozen Saskatchewan prairie. And one early morning Hans drove out to check on his farm and to seek the companionship of his coffee clique. He returned to his apartment in Melville in a pensive mood, took a quick shower, and prepared a bite to eat before leaving to manage the pharmacy. But the telephone disrupted his deepening melancholy.

Although he'd not heard her voice for months, Hans immediately recognized Barbara Schmidt. Steeling for yet another rebuke, Hans listened.

"Hans, this is Barbara. Taking a page from your book, I shall come straight to the point. I want to apologize first for Richard's brusque behaviour last autumn, but also tell you that he is no longer with us. During the harvest he had a massive heart attack, and although we tried to revive him, he was gone by the time the ambulance arrived."

"I am very sorry for your loss, Barbara. You and your children must miss him terribly," Hans said.

"We just never expected to be alone so soon," said Barbara. "However, even as I say that, I cannot help thinking about you, Hans, and wondering if that's how you have felt for most of your life. I realize I probably have no right to ask, but I'd like to ask whether you'd help me to find out if Ursula Warner is indeed my birth mother and to also help me to find her."

"I desire nothing more, Barbara, than to confirm that you are my daughter and to bring my family together at last."

Within the week, Hans returned to North Battleford to have lunch with Barbara at the Husky before they drove eagerly to City Hospital in Saskatoon. After explaining their intent, they were directed to the records department, where a kindly clerk, seated them comfortably in the archives.

Once they'd located the birth records for 1942, it was amazing how quickly they found Ursula Warner's name. She had delivered an eight-pound, seven-ounce baby girl at three in the afternoon on May 29th of that year. She then signed the form to give up her infant daughter for adoption, before holding or even seeing her baby.

On July 2nd of that year, the infant was signed over to Mr. Josef and Mrs. Hilda Wendel of North Battleford. Neither Hans Gerhart nor Barbara Schmidt required further information to prove that they were father and daughter.

Leaving the hospital, Barbara insisted that Hans return with her to the farm because she could hardly wait to introduce him to her children. They were waiting in the yard when the school bus arrived at the end of the road, and Barbara's four energetic teenagers bounded down the steps. Even though Hans was nervous about his reception, he could not stop from marvelling that they were his grandchildren.

Barbara ushered them into the farmhouse to serve the peanut butter cookies and Kool-Aid she'd prepared before meeting Hans that morning. As it happened, since all of their other grandparents were deceased, the four Schmidt children were enthusiastic about meeting a grandfather they'd never known existed.

Within the hour, Hans was regaling his new family with humorous stories about his upbringing in the North Battleford orphanage that was managed by the Catholic Sisters, and they were sorry when their mother reminded them about the afternoon chores.

On a hot summer day on the third Sunday of June, Barbara and her family stood anxiously beside him as Hans placed a telephone call to Ursula. He recognized her voice immediately, but he was amazed when first she did not acknowledge him and then the line went dead.

Although he rang again and again and continued for the rest of the afternoon and well into the evening, the line remained engaged. Thoroughly frustrated by his lack of success, Hans left for Melville after assuring Barbara that he would continue to call Ursula every morning, noon, and night until he reached her. And Hans persisted for more than a week before a man finally picked up the telephone to tell him that Ursula was not there.

Summer had proven exceedingly busy with Barbara accepting Hans's offer to relocate with her family to his farmstead. Over the past decade, her neighbour on the adjoining farm had hoped to acquire more land. Now with his daughter wanting to live close by, he had readily purchased Barbara's entire property at her asking price. As soon as the end of the school year arrived, the Schmidt family packed their personal belongings and moved, and Hans already started constructing a large new farmhouse.

Following the dozens of unsuccessful telephone calls to Ursula, Hans was preparing to travel to Virden when he decided to try yet again. This time, Ursula answered the telephone and Hans had been able to say more than during all of the other aborted calls.

But soon the line went dead again, this time with even more finality than before; when he rang again, there was not even a busy signal. And when preparing to drive to Virden with Barbara on Saturday, he placed his last call. The man on the other end did not even say hello before saying, "You can stop phoning here. Ursula is dead."

In the midst of a blustery November 1997 storm in the city of St. Albert, Justine Forrester received a call from her sister Elaine. No sooner had she hung up the receiver than Dr. Mathias Werner's exclamation, years earlier, about how the Werner secrets had been safeguarded flashed through her mind. He had been absolutely right; the family's austerity had led to secrets passed down through the generations until the ensuing silence became deafening and dulled their sensibilities.

Justine realized that it would never have occurred to her mother to reveal and rejoice in the result of her liaison with the only man she'd loved. The singular recourse in her mind was death by her own hands to ensure that her secret went to the grave with her.

Nonetheless, Justine believed Ursula's secret was ordinary. There could be little doubt that it had happened to many other young women of her day, and it continued with heightened regularity into the present. The fact that Ursula Warner had listened to and been so profoundly influenced by her father whom she both loved and hated, though, had made her secret extraordinary.

In July 1998, at seventy-eight years of age, Hans Gerhart walked proudly with his daughter Barbara, his four grandchildren, and his two great-grandchildren to the second Warner/Werner Family Reunion at Neudorf Community Hall.

Other than to see his cherished long-time friend Katherina who had serenely slipped into the next world to join her beloved David in the hereafter, Hans wished for nothing. During the festivities Barbara Schmidt met Elaine, the only one of her four half-sisters whom she would ever meet.

Still, the wellspring of her profound contentment was knowing that, at long last, Ursula Warner's daughter, Barbara, was home.

Book Club Questions

Arriving: 1909–1919

1 What drew you into and kept you reading *Arriving: 1909–1919*, a relatively long novel?

2 What might be the significance of the frequent detailed descriptions of Mother Nature and the changing seasons throughout the books?

3 With which character(s) could you most identify? Did any surprise you as you began to discover their true characteristics?

4 What might the author be conveying through the Silent Critics? Why might these seven characters play such a significant role in the story?

5 Rolf is typically described as a "follower" to his younger brother, Gustav. Do you think this is accurate and, if so, why do you think he is like that?

6 How do you feel about Gustav's actions towards his father and his opinions about "becoming a Canadian"? Do you agree more with Gustav or with Christian?

7 When Elisabetha dies, the Werner family is left feeling lost and depressed. How did each character deal with the loss, and how do you think it will change their relationships?

8 The author, Corinne Jeffery, had breast cancer while writing this novel but didn't discover it until after Elisabetha died from that very disease. Do you think the character's outcome may have been different had the author known while writing that part of *Arriving*?

9 In dealing with her mother's death, Katherina experiences extreme bouts of depression. Do you think Katherina is overemotional, or were you compelled to sympathize with her?

10 When Amelia leaves her family behind to marry Gustav, we learn that her father becomes abusive towards Katie and Franz. Why do you think that this is? Were they right in hiding it from Amelia?

11 How do Gustav's feelings for Amelia change over time? Do you believe he is genuine and do you agree with his actions?

Thriving: 1920–1939

1 What themes have you seen threaded throughout the trilogy? Why do you think the author included them?

2 There are a number of scandalous events in the books that relate to different characters. What, to you, was the most surprising turn of events, and why did you find it so?

3 There are many strong female characters in the trilogy. Which did you find to be the most prominent and why?

4 Contrast the young Amelia to whom you are introduced in *Arriving* with the emerging woman in *Thriving*. How is she influenced by Margareta, Katherina, and Sarah?

5 Which of the male and female characters were you most drawn to as you came to know and trust them in *Arriving*? Did your preferences continue as you delved deeper into their personalities in *Thriving*?

6 Reflect upon the dynamics of Gustav and Amelia's relationship: how they communicate, their specific contradictions, etc. Which one really "wears the pants in the family?"

7 As you begin to know Amelia's daughters, Elisabeth and Ursula, comment on their attributes, similarities, and differences. Did you consider either or both of them manipulative?

8 In both *Arriving* and *Thriving*, Dr. Spitznagel and Reverend Ulmer, beyond their respective responsibilities as doctor and minister of the townships, are consistently called upon to be voices of authority in the community. How realistic was this expectation, and why?

9 If you were the author of these books, what characters, plot, dialogue, or scenes might you have written differently, and why?

10 What lasting impression or learning have you gained from this story?

11 Do you think *Thriving* is an appropriate title for a Depression-era story? Why do you think the author chose to call it this?

Choosing: 1940–1989

1 Was it plausible to you that a family could harbour so many secrets?

2 What do you think spurred the author, Corinne Jeffery, to title her trilogy *Understanding Ursula*?

3 As you reached the conclusion of the trilogy, to which characters could you most readily relate?

4 Did your thoughts and feelings about any of the family members change over time?

5 Were you able to attribute any specific characteristics to either of the two dominant nationalities in this series? If so, what were they?

6 In your opinion, did Ursula present as a villain or a tragic character? Why?

7 What did you find most appealing about the story and the family?

8   Do you believe *Choosing* is a suitable title for the concluding book about this controversial family?

9   What impact does the lack of independent decision-making have on the outcome of so many of the characters?

10 What changes did you notice in the writing style, dialogue, and the influence of God and nature on the characters as the trilogy progressed through eighty years?

11 How did the intrigue and the often-surprising behaviours of many of the characters influence your perceptions and feelings about this story?

About the Author

Corinne Jeffery was born in Saskatchewan in 1945 and raised in Manitoba from the age of five. A graduate of the Brandon General Hospital School of Nursing with a Bachelor of Nursing from the University of Manitoba, she is a former educator with Grant McEwan College in Edmonton. After many years in Winnipeg, she moved to St. Albert, Alberta, where she has been a long-time resident with her husband and family. *Choosing: 1940–1989* is her third novel.

Book a Reading at Your Seniors' Lodge

When I wrote my books, I did not anticipate one amazing outcome at a seniors'/ retirement lodge in Stony Plain, Alberta. Thanks to Kim Abraham-Schutz, Meridian Foundation, for sharing this with me:

In the last year at Whispering Waters Manor in Stony Plain, we started our "fireside reading" of the *Understanding Ursula* trilogy every Friday morning. We began the program to read to residents that no longer have the ability to read, find it more difficult to read, are illiterate, or just want to participate in the group discussion. I had wanted to do readings with my residents for years, but it was difficult to find books that 80- and 90-year-olds would find of interest. It was clear to me, after Corinne did a reading and inspired interest and excitement in the residents, that this was the book.

The conversations with our residents after the readings have been incredible. They have become excited to share their own stories, and those with early stages of dementia and Alzheimer's are recalling their own early memories and feeling a great sense of accomplishment. Residents that normally do not participate in activities are coming out of their rooms to take part every Friday morning. Residents who've found it difficult to fit in or are loners have made new friends, because through the discussions they find commonalities with other residents.

Our reading program has created excitement among our residents, a sense that at 80- or 90-plus they still have something to contribute in conversation (because they lived a life similar to that described in Corinne's books), or at 60 or 70 (because they recall their parents' struggles and accomplishments). This program has added a bounce in their step, increased their social interaction, and increased their participation in other activities. It has been well worth the time spent.

Because of this incredible letter, I would like to offer a complimentary "fireside reading" to any lodge in Alberta. Contact me at corinne@corinnejeffery.ca to book my visit, and then invite your friends and families to join in. Of course, I'll also have books available for purchase.

Thanks again, Kim!

Corinne Jeffery